"To the extent that we ... ... true peace with freedom, peace based on individual and sovereign rights and on the principle of resolution of disputes through negotiation, we must acknowledge and follow our interests in creating conditions in which democratic forces can gain and thrive in this world. A world not of our making, but a world in which we must fight to maintain our peace and our strength. And a world in which the very best way to maintain peace is to be militarily strong and thus deter war."

—Secretary of Defense Caspar Weinberger

CREATED BY J.E. POURNELLE

WARRIOR

THERE WILL BE WAR

VOLUME V

Associate Editor, John F. Carr

A TOM DOHERTY ASSOCIATES BOOK

Dedication

For the *mujahadeen* of Afghanistan, who know
the value and are paying the price of liberty.

WARRIOR!

Copyright © 1986 by J. E. Pournelle

First printing: July 1986

A TOR Book

Published by Tom Doherty Associates
49 West 24 Street
New York, N.Y. 10010

ISBN: 0-812-54959-7
CAN. ED.: 0-812-54960-0

Printed in the United States

0 9 8 7 6 5 4 3 2

ACKNOWLEDGMENTS

The editors gratefully acknowledge that research for non-fiction essays in this book, including "Defense in A N-Dimensional World" by Stefan T. Possony, was supported in part by grants from the Vaughn Foundation. Responsibility for opinions expressed in this work remains solely with the authors.

Contents

INTRODUCTION
WARRIORS AND STATESMEN
Jerry Pournelle

Western myth and legend stress the importance of the warrior in society. From the *marryanu*, chariot warriors of the battle-ax people, to Cuchulain of Ireland, to George Patton and Douglas MacArthur, the West has looked to its warriors for safety.

There is another tradition equally as ancient and as important. Military leadership and authority is indispensible, but it is vital that it submit to another sovereign. The French scholar Georges Dumezil, drawing on a passage in Tacitus, divides authority into the *dux* or war leader, and the *rex* or fountain of justice; and *dux* must serve *rex*.

This is the glory of the warrior: to serve justice, to do so with courage, and protect the weak; just as the three sins of the warrior are rebellion, cowardice, and rapine and wanton destruction. We have known all this and more for a very long time; it is only in our modern age that we have forgotten.

We forget it to our peril. Dr. Richard Garwin, IBM Fellow and supporter of the Union of Concerned Scientists, has said recently: "Even though we feel a moral repugnance for ensuring survival by threatening to kill tens of millions of men, women, and children—as President Reagan put it when he first proposed Star Wars—that is no reason to reach out recklessly for something new." All of which shows a profound misunderstanding.

It is the glory of the warrior to protect the weak and spare the helpless. It is no less sin to slaughter the innocent than to run from battle or slaughter the sovereign. These precepts are buried deep in the western soul; within every myth and legend, from the Rig Veda to Livy's History of Rome, from the Eddas to the songs of the '45. Loyalty to sovereign; courage in battle; and mercy to the helpless. They all spring

9

from the same sources. Weaken one and you weaken them all.

Now true: it has always been the destiny of the warrior that he is, in battle, released from the common bonds of the law; that he may and must fight and kill and destroy. Because the warrior has been released from the bounds of law, it is all the more important that he return to them after battle. Again every culture has stressed this. Cuchulain must be cooled in three magic cauldrons to remove the heat of battle; only then can he return to his people. The Romans stressed the example of Cincinatus, and before our schoolbooks were written by positivists and others ignorant of the importance of myth and tradition, the United States ceaselessly told of George Washington. Today our textbooks seem more concerned with Washington's teeth, and whether he drank brandy, than with the simple fact that he held all the military power on the continent—and laid it down. The French had Bonaparte; we, more fortunate, had Washington.

The knowledge lies deep in the myths, legends, and history of the west: the warrior in his wrath may destroy his own people; let him be cured of it, and submit to his king, before he comes again among us. We know this, but we try to forget. We want our warrior to be—to be something other than a warrior. And that is dangerous and uncharted territory.

As the warrior has special virtues, so is he prone to characteristic sins. Few warriors escape them. The stories of every hero of every land are stories not only of virtue, but of the fall from grace. As there are three special virtues, there are three sins of the warrior: disloyalty, cowardice, and wanton violence.

Heracles rebels against his king; by stealth kills a guest, rather than facing him in battle; and in madness slaughters his own children. Similar destinies await other great warriors, Starcatherus of Scandinavia, Indra of the Rig Veda. They are heroes who have fallen; and as their lives are heroic, so are their punishments. Perhaps punishment is the wrong word. The heroes ask for judgment, and undertake great tasks in atonement.

We know the characteristic sins of the warrior. There are also sins of the sovereign. One is to take to himself the duties of the warrior.

Now true: some societies have been led by soldier kings.

Most have not been glad of it. The virtues of the soldier are not those of the sovereign. The warrior focuses all energies on a single goal. The *rex* must see to the good of all, balance a thousand goals of justice and order. The duties conflict. It is best that *dux* and *rex* be separate. Each has authority, each has power, but their roles are different.

Once again myth and legend abound with examples. The greatest warriors are those who serve their king. Those who do not are villains. The most despicable warrior villains are those who murder their king by stealth and go from there to wanton slaughter. Macbeth comes instantly to mind. The most despicable kings are those who waste the courage of their warriors, and dishonor their returning heroes. So says western tradition; so says western experience.

Is all this more than sentimental twaddle? After all, we live in an age of reason; who cares for myth and legend and tradition? Away with them. We will build our army on rational principles.

Perhaps. But recall Montaigne: "A rational army *would* run away." Societies defended by armies that run away do not endure. Rational principles are of little use to young men about to die ten thousand miles from home. Recall also Machiavelli. "Gold cannot get you good soldiers, but good soldiers can always get you gold." Building an army on rational principles has its problems.

Indeed, more problems than appear on the surface: for if you build a rational army, why does it submit to *you*? Why should those who have a monopoly of force and violence take orders from those who hire them?

Perhaps there is more to the ancient traditions than this age supposes.

I recently had a letter from a veteran of Khesanh and Quangtri. He says, "They stole our war, and they threw our heroism to the winds."

Indeed. And now no one remembers, and if there are heroes of the Vietnam War they are, supposedly, those who fled to Canada, or rampaged through Chicago in their days of rage; even those who smashed windows of university book stores, trashed offices, disrupted classes, engaged in acts of terrorism. I recently met one such who invited all and sundry to admire his courageous action in opposing the war, and seemed to think he deserved medals no less than any soldier. After all, he had been arrested five times and had spent *weeks* in American jails. "We ended the war," he cried.

Which is nonsense. The Vietnam War was ended because it was won. In 1972 the United States pretty well withdrew and left the defense of South Vietnam to ARVN, the Army of the Republic of Vietnam; and from '72 to '75 ARVN was successful. With the help of a rather small number of US Air Cavalrymen, ARVN even stopped the 1973 invasion in which the North sent down 150,000 men (and got fewer than 100,000 back).

It wasn't until 1975 that South Vietnam fell to an invasion of more armor than the Wehrmacht ever possessed, more trucks than Patton even commanded. Even then ARVN might have won, but the Congress of the United States was more interested in Watergate. The Soviets supplied North Vietnam; no one supplied our allies in the South. Saigon accordingly became Ho Chi Minh City, and most of the South Vietnamese middle class departed for what were euphemistically called re-education camps.

Our warriors were sent halfway around the world to defend a little-known people. They accomplished their task in the face of the contempt of the media and the intellectuals. Then they were brought home and told to be ashamed.

The West has not honored its warriors.

Then there came others, who would do worse.

They said that we lived in the nuclear era: a time of pushbutton death, a time when battle was impersonal, and if warriors could not find courage, computers could instill it in weapons; or so thought some of the scholars turned strategist.

We need not honor warriors: we can, they said, dispense with them. Politicians, neither warriors nor sovereigns, can control power directly; they need no warriors, only someone to build and maintain weapons. From this sprang ludicrous attempts to turn the officer corps into managers, the sergeants and chiefs into technicians, and the private soldiers into artisans. Alas, some of those efforts met success. We are fortunate that most of them failed.

We are more fortunate that there are signs of returning sanity within the government.

We can hope that sanity returns in other places.

"The leaders of the West have too often failed to set forth vigorously the crucial differences that separate our system from the Soviet system," writes Secretary of Defense Caspar Weinberger. "Indeed, our intellectual elites have developed the notion that there is a 'moral equivalence' between the United States and the Soviet Union. This was clearly evident in the numerous attempts to equate the Soviet invasion and occupation of Afghanistan with the American rescue in Grenada."

Precisely. In most of our universities, learned professors who ought to know better speak of "the superpowers," and act as if the global protracted conflict were one between moral equals, rather than a contest between freedom and totalitarian principles.

It was not always that way. A few years ago eminent scholars said:

"It is quite evident that the possibility for peaceful coexistence of the nations peopling this world presupposes the disappearance of the totalitarian dictatorships. Since, according to their own loudly proclaimed professions, their systems must be made world-wide, those who reject the system have no alternative but to strive for its destruction. Any relaxation of the vigilance required to face such ideological imperialists as the totalitarians is likely to result in disasters such as the Second World War, or worse." (Carl J. Friedrich and Zbigniew Brzezinski, *Totalitarian Dictatorship and Autocracy*.)

That remains true today. The Soviet regime *must* proclaim that its destiny is to sweep the world; what else could justify the wide discrepancy in incomes, the grey lives of the masses and the immense privileges of the ruling elite? Arthur Koestler said in 1946 that the only hope for the world was opening up Soviet society to the free flow of information. That has not happened yet.

There is hope. The computer revolution makes information easier to get, harder to suppress. Technology impacts everyone; even totalitarian regimes. Our grandchildren may live in a world in which information flows so freely that not even the KGB can suppress it. That would be the end for totalitarianism.

Meanwhile, though, the way is long and hard; for the warriors must ever stand on guard, be ever vigilant: not in war, but to preserve the peace.

EDITOR'S INTRODUCTION TO:

HE FELL INTO A DARK HOLE
Jerry Pournelle

In 1970 Stefan Possony and I published *The Strategy of Technology*. In the introductory chapter (reprinted with revisions in *Men Of War*, Volume II of this series, Tor Books) we argued that technology can be thought of as an impersonal force much like a stream. Those who doubt that will probably find illuminating a close reading of James Burke's wonderful book *Connections*. What one tinkerer does not invent, another will.

At the same time, the analogy can be carried too far. Technology is created by people, and the technological stream can be directed—or diverted. Possibly it can be dammed.

Given the present international situation, suppression of technological development is highly unlikely. Neither the US nor the Soviet Union would trust the other without the most stringent verification measures: measures that I doubt even the US would submit to, while Soviet resistance to any inspection amounts almost to an obsession. Moreover, even if bilateral agreements were implemented and worked smoothly, even if NATO and the Warsaw Pact nations were brought under the agreement, there remains the rest of the world. China, Japan, Israel, South Africa, India, Pakistan—the list goes on and on. All these nations are capable of developing, implementing, and deploying high technology weapons; and as Possony and I argued (I hope persuasively) in *The Strategy of Technology*, the Technological War could be bloodlessly decisive.

Suppose, though, that the United States and the Soviet Union formed a CoDominium, and through that structure brought the entire world under their joint control. The two super powers need not care for each other. It is only needful that they be dedicated to the notion that it is better that they rule jointly than for anyone else to rule at all.

Under those circumstances technology might be suppressed by sufficiently ruthless action by the FBI, KGB, and the CoDominium intelligence services. It would require a massive intelligence effort, and a great deal of cooperation among US and USSR security services; nothing less would do the job. Given that cooperation, though, science and technology could be slowed if not halted so long as the alliance held.

It seems arguable, anyway; and this was the premise of my first science fiction stories. The CoDominium series takes us from about the turn of the century to the far future, and includes *The Mercenary*, *The Mote in God's Eye*, and *King David's Spaceship*.

After I wrote this story I got a call from Dr. Robert Forward of Hughes Research. Bob Forward was even then preparing a scientific article on black holes and gravity waves, and the danger of getting too near them; and he was calling to congratulate me on publishing first. I'm rather proud of that.

HE FELL INTO A DARK HOLE
Jerry Pournelle

CDSN Captain Bartholomew Ramsey watched his men check out, each man leaving the oval entry port under the satanic gaze of the master-at-arms. After nearly two years in space the men deserved something more exciting than twenty hours dirtside at Ceres Base, but they were eager for even that much. CDSS *Daniel Webster* got all the long patrols and dirty outsystem jobs in the Navy because her captain didn't protest. Now, when these men got to Luna Base and Navy Town, Lord help the local girls. . . .

Well, they'd be all right here, Ramsey thought. The really expensive pleasures were reserved for Belt prospectors and the crews of Westinghouse mining ships. Bart glanced at the screens displaying ships docked at Ceres. None of the big ore-processing ships were in Thorstown. Things should be pretty quiet. Nothing Base Marines couldn't handle, even if *Daniel Webster*'s crew hadn't been on a good drunk for twenty months. Ramsey turned away from the entry port to go back to his cabin.

It was difficult to walk in the low gravity of Ceres. Very inconvenient place, he thought. But of course low gravity was a main reason for putting a Navy yard there. That and the asteroid mines. . . .

He walked carefully through gray steel bulkheads to the central corridor. Just outside the bridge entrance he met Dave Trevor, the first lieutenant.

"Not going ashore?" Ramsey asked.

"No, sir." Trevor's boyish grin was infectious. Ramsey had once described it as the best crew morale booster in the Navy. And at age twenty-four Dave Trevor had been in space eleven years, as ship's boy, midshipman, and officer. He would know every pub in the Solar System and a lot outside.

16

. . . "Never cared much for the girls on Ceres," he said. "Too businesslike."

Captain Ramsey nodded sagely. With Trevor's looks he wouldn't have to shell out money for an evening's fun anywhere near civilization. Ceres was another matter. "I'd appreciate it if you'd make a call on the provost's office, Mr. Trevor. We might need a friend there by morning."

The lieutenant grinned again. "Aye, aye, Captain."

Bart nodded and climbed down the ladder to his cabin. Trevor's merry whistling followed him until he closed the door. Once Ramsey was inside he punched a four-digit code on the intercom console.

"Surgeon's office, Surgeon's Mate Hartley, sir."

"Captain here. Make sure we have access to a good dental repair unit in the morning, Hartley. Even if we have to use Base facilities."

"Aye, aye, sir."

Ramsey switched the unit off and permitted himself a thin smile. The regeneration stimulators aboard *Daniel Webster* worked but there was something wrong with the coding information in the dental unit. It produced buck teeth, not enormous but quite noticeable, and when his men were out drinking and some dirtpounder made a few funny remarks . . .

The smile faded as Ramsey sat carefully in the regulation chair. He glanced around the sterile cabin. There were none of the comforts other captains provided themselves. Screens, charts, built-in cabinets and tables, his desk, everything needed to run his ship, but no photographs and solidos, no paintings and rugs. Just Ramsey and his ship, his wife with the masculine name. He took a glass of whisky from the arm of the chair. It was Scotch and the taste of burnt malt was very strong. Bart tossed it off and replaced it to be refilled. The intercom buzzed.

"Captain here."

"Bridge, sir. Call from Base Commandant Torrin."

"Put him on."

"Aye, aye, sir." The watch midshipman's face vanished and Rap Torrin's broad features filled the screen. The rear admiral looked at the bare cabin, grimaced, then smiled at Ramsey.

"I'm going to pull rank on you, Bart," Torrin said. "Expect that courtesy call in an hour. You can plan on having dinner with me, too."

Ramsey forced a smile. "Very good, sir. My pleasure. In an hour, then."

"Right." The screen went blank and Ramsey cursed. He drank the second whisky and cursed again, this time at himself.

What's wrong with you? he thought. *Rap Torrin is as good a friend as you have in the Navy. Shipmate way back in Ajax under Sergei Lermontov. Now Rap has a star, well, that was expected. And Lermontov is Vice Admiral Commanding, the number two man in the whole CoDominium Space Navy.*

And so what? I could have had stars. As many as I wanted. I'm that good, or I was. And with Martin Grant's influence in the Grand Senate and Martin's brother John in charge of United States security, Senator Martin Grant's son-in-law could have had any post no matter how good. . . .

Ramsey took another whisky from the chair and looked at it for a long time. He'd once had his star, polished and waiting, nothing but formalities to go, while Rap and Sergei grinned at his good luck. Sergei Lermontov had just made junior vice admiral then. Five years ago.

Five years. Five years ago Barbara Jean Ramsey and their son Harold were due back from Meiji. Superstitiously, Bart had waited for them before accepting his promotion. When he took it he'd have to leave *Daniel Webster* for something dirtside and wait until a spacing admiral was needed. That wouldn't have been long. The Danube situation was heating up back then. Ramsey could have commanded the first punitive expedition, but it had gone out under an admiral who botched the job. Barbara Jean had never come home from Meiji.

Her ship had taken a new direct route along an Alderson path just discovered. It never came out into normal space. A scoutcraft was sent to search for the liner, and Senator Grant had enough influence to send a frigate after that. Both vanished, and there weren't any more ships to send. Bartholomew Ramsey stayed a captain. He couldn't leave his ship because he couldn't face the empty house in Luna Base compound.

He sighed, then laughed cynically at himself. Time to get dressed. Rap wanted to show off his star, and it would be cruel to keep him waiting.

The reunion was neither more nor less than he'd expected, but Admiral Torrin cut short the time in his office. "Got to get you home, Bart. Surprise for you there. Come along, man, come along."

Bart followed woodenly. *Something really wrong with me,* he thought. *Man doesn't go on like this for five years. I'm all right aboard Old Danny Boy. It's only when I leave my ship; now why should that be?* But a man can marry a ship, even a slim steel whisky bottle four hundred meters long and sixty across; he wouldn't be the first captain married to a cruiser.

Most of Ceres Base was underground, and Bart was lost in the endless rock corridors. Finally they reached a guarded area. They returned the Marines' salutes and went through to broader hallways lined with carpets. There were battle paintings on the walls. Some reached back to wet navy days and every CD base, insystem or out, had them. There were scenes from all the great navies of the world. Russian, Soviet, U.S., British, Japanese . . . there weren't any of Togo at Tshushima, though. Or Pearl Harbor. Or Bengal Bay.

Rap kept up his hearty chatter until they got inside his apartment. The admiral's quarters were what Bart had visualized before he entered; richly furnished, filled with the gifts and mementos that a successful independent command captain could collect on a dozen worlds after more than twenty years in service. Shells and stuffed exotic fauna, a cabinet made of the delicately veined snakewood of Tanith, a table of priceless Spartan roseteak. There was a house on Luna Base that had been furnished like this. . . .

Bart caught sight of the man who entered the room and snapped to attention in surprise. Automatically he saluted.

Vice Admiral Lermontov returned the salute. The admiral was a tall, slim man who wore rimless spectacles which made his gray eyes look large and round as they bored through his subordinates. Men who served under Lermontov either loved him or hated him. Now his thin features distorted in genuine pleasure. "Bartholomew, I am sorry to surprise you like this."

Lermontov inspected Ramsey critically. The smile faded slightly. "You have not taken proper care of yourself, my friend. Not enough exercise."

"I can still beat you. Arm wrestling, anything you name—uh, sir."

Lermontov's smile broadened again. "That is better. But you need not call me 'sir.' You would say 'sir' only to Vice Admiral Lermontov, and it is quite obvious that the Vice Admiral Commanding cannot possibly be on Ceres. So, since you have not seen me . . . ."

"I see," Ramsey said.

Lermontov nodded. "It is rather important. You will know why in a few moments. Rap, can you bring us something to drink?"

Torrin nodded and fussed with drinks from the snakewood cabinet. The ringing tone of a crystal glass was very loud in the quiet apartment. Ramsey was vaguely amused as he took a seat at the roseteak table in the center of the lush room. A rear admiral waiting on a captain, and no enlisted spacers to serve the Vice Admiral Commanding, who, after all, wasn't really there in the first place . . . the whisky was from Inveraray and was very good.

"You have been in space nearly two years," Lermontov said. "You have not seen your father-in-law in that time?"

"More like three since Martin and I really talked about anything," Ramsey said. "We—we remind each other too much of Barbara Jean and Harold."

The pain in Ramsey's face was reflected as a pale shadow in Lermontov's eyes. "But you knew he had become chairman of the appropriations committee."

"Yes."

"The Navy's friend, Grand Senator Grant. Without him these last years would have been disaster for us all. For the Navy, and for Earth as well if those politicians could only see it." Lermontov cut himself off with an angry snap. The big eyes matching his steel gray hair focused on Bart. "The new appropriations are worse," the admiral growled. "While you have been away, everything has become worse. Millington, Harmon, Bertram, they all squeeze President Lipscomb's Unity Party in your country, and Kaslov gains influence every day in mine. I think it will not be long before one or the other of the CoDominium sponsors withdraws from the treaties, Bart. And after that, war."

"War." Ramsey said it slowly, not believing. After a hundred and fifty years of uneasy peace between the United States and the Soviets, war again, and with the weapons they had . . .

"Any spark might set it off," Lermontov was saying. "We must be ready to step in. The fleet must be strong, strong enough to cope with the national forces and do whatever we must do."

Ramsey felt as if the admiral had struck him. War? Fleet intervention? "What about the Commanding Admiral? The Grand Senate?"

Lermontov shrugged. "You know who are the good men, who are not. But so long as the fleet is strong, something perhaps can be done to save Earth from the idiocy of the politicians. Not that the masses are better, screaming for a war they can never understand." Lermontov drank quietly, obviously searching for words, before he turned back to Ramsey. "I have to tell you something painful, my friend. Your father-in-law is missing."

"Missing—where? I told Martin to be careful, that Millington's Liberation Army people . . ."

"No. Not on Earth. Outsystem. Senator Grant went to Meiji to visit relatives there . . ."

"Yes." Ramsey felt the memory like a knife in his vitals. "His nephew, Barbara Jean's cousin, an officer in the Diplomatic Corps on Meiji. Grew up in the senator's home. Barbara Jean was visiting him when . . ."

"Yes." Lermontov leaned closer to Ramsey so that he could touch his shoulder for a moment. Then he took his hand away. "I do not remind you of these things because I am cruel, my friend. I must know—would the senator have tried to find his daughter? After all these years?"

Bart nodded. "She was his only child. As Harold was mine. If I thought there was any chance I'd look myself. You think he tried it?"

"We do." Lermontov signaled Torrin to bring him another drink. "Senator Grant went to Meiji with the visit to his relatives as cover. With the Japanese representation question to come up soon, and the budget after that, Meiji is important. The Navy provided a frigate for transportation. It took the usual route through Colby and around, and was supposed to return the same way. But we have confirmed reports that Senator Grant's ship went instead to the jumpoff point for the direct route."

"What captain in his right mind would let him get away with that?"

"His name was Commander John Grant, Jr. The senator's nephew."

"Oh." Bart nodded again, exaggerating the gesture as he realized the full situation. "Yeah. Johnny would do it if the old man asked. So you came all the way out here for my opinion, Sergei? I can give it quick. Senator Grant was looking for Barbara Jean. So you can write him off and whatever other plans you've got for the goddam Navy you can write off too. Learn to live without him, Sergei. The goddam jinx has another good ship and another good man. Now if you'll excuse me I want to get back to my ship and get drunk."

Captain Ramsey strode angrily toward the door. Before he reached it the vice admiral's voice crackled through the room. "Captain, you are not excused."

"Sir." Ramsey whirled automatically. "Very well, sir. Your orders?"

"My orders are for you to sit down and finish your drink, Captain." There was a long silence as they faced each other. Finally Ramsey sat at the expensive table.

"Do you think so badly of me, Bart, that you believe I would come all the way out here, meet you secretly, for as little as this?"

Bart looked up in surprise. Emotions welled up inside him, emotions he hadn't felt in years, and he fought desperately to force them back. *No, God, don't let me hope again. Not that agony. Not hope . . .* But Lermontov was still speaking.

"I will let Professor Stirner explain it to you, since I am not sure any of us understand him. But he has a theory, Bart. He believes that the senator may be alive, and that there may be a chance to bring him home before the Senate knows he is missing. For years the Navy has preserved the peace, now a strong fleet is needed more than ever. We have no choice, Bart. If there is any chance at all, we must take it."

Professor Hermann Stirner was a short Viennese with thinning red hair, improbable red freckles, and a neat round belly. Ramsey thought him about fifty, but the man's age was indeterminate. It was unlikely that he was younger, but with regeneration therapy he could be half that again. Rap Torrin brought the professor in through a back entrance.

"Dr. Stirner is an intelligence adviser to the fleet," Lermontov said. "He is not a physicist."

"No, no physicist," Stirner agreed quickly. "Who would want to live under the restrictions of a licensed physicist? CoDominium intelligence officers watching every move, suppressing most of your discoveries . . ." He spoke intently giving the impression of great emotion no matter what he said. "And most physicists I have met are not seeing beyond the end of their long noses. Me, I worry mostly about politics, Captain. But when the Navy loses ships, I want to know what happened to them. I have a theory about those ships, for years."

Ramsey gripped the arms of his chair until his knuckles were white, but his voice was deadly calm. "Why didn't you bring up your theory before now?"

Stirner eyed him critically. Then he shrugged. "As I said, I am no physicist. Who would listen to me? But now, with the senator gone . . ."

"We need your father-in-law badly," Lermontov interrupted. "I do not really believe Professor Stirner's theories, but the fleet needs Senator Grant so desperately we will try anything. Let Dr. Stirner explain."

"Ja. You are a bright young CoDominium Navy captain, I am going to tell you things you know already, maybe. But I do not myself understand everything I should know, so you let me explain my own way, ja?" Stirner paced briskly for a moment, then sat restlessly at the table. He gave no chance to answer his question, but spoke rapidly, so that he gave the impression of interrupting himself.

"You got five forces in this universe we know about, ja? Only one of them maybe really isn't in this universe; we do not quibble about that, let the cosmologists worry. Now we look at two of those forces, we can forget the atomics and electromagnetics. Gravity and the Alderson force, these we look at. Now you think about the universe as flat like this table, eh?" He swept a pudgy hand across the roseteak surface. "And wherever you got a star, you got a hill that rises slowly, gets all the time steeper until you get near the star when it's so steep you got a cliff. And you think of your ships like roller coasters. You get up on the hill, aim where you want to go, and pop on the hyperspace drivers. Bang, you are in a universe where the Alderson effect acts like gravity. You are rolling downhill, across the table, and up the side of the next hill, not using up much potential energy, so you are ready to go again somewhere else if you can get lined up right, O.K.?"

Ramsey frowned. "It's not quite what we learned as middies—you've got ships repelled from a star rather than—"

"Ja, ja, plenty of quibble we can make if we want to. Now, Captain, how is it you get out of hyperspace when you want to?"

"We don't," Ramsey said. "When we get close enough to

a gravity source, the ship comes out into normal space whether we want it to or not.''

Stirner nodded. ''Ja. And you use your photon drivers to run around in normal space where the stars are like wells, not hills, at least thinking about gravities. Now, suppose you try to shoot past one star to another, all in one jump?''

''It doesn't work,'' Ramsey said. ''You'd get caught in the gravity field of the in-between star. Besides, the Alderson paths don't cross each other. They're generated by stellar nuclear activities, and you can only travel along lines of equal flux. In practice that means almost line of sight with range limits, but they aren't really straight lines. . . .''

''Ja. O.K. That's what I think is happening to them. I think there is a star between A-7820 and 82 Eridani, which is the improbable name Meiji's sun is stuck with.''

''Now wait a minute,'' Admiral Torrin protested. ''There can't be a star there, Professor. There's no question of missing it, not with our observations. Man, do you think the Navy didn't look for it? A liner and an explorer class frigate vanished on that route. We looked, first thing we thought of.''

''Suppose there is a star there but you are not seeing it?''

''How could that be?'' Torrin asked.

''A Black Hole, Admiral. Ja,'' Stirner continued triumphantly. ''I think Senator Grant fell into a Black Hole.''

Ramsey looked puzzled. ''I seem to remember something about Black Holes, but I don't remember what.''

''Theoretical concept,'' Stirner said. ''Hundred, hundred and fifty years ago, before the CoDominium Treaty puts a stop to so much scientific research. Lots of people talk about Black Holes then, but nobody ever finds any, so now there's no appropriations for licensed physicists to work on them.

''But way back we have a man named Schwartzchild, Viennese chap, he thinks of them.'' Stirner puffed with evident pride. ''Then another chap, Oppenheimer, and some more, all make the calculations. A Black Hole is like a neutron star that goes all the way. Collapsed down so far, a whole star collapsed to maybe two, three kilometers diameter. Gravity is so tough nothing gets out. Not light; not anything gets out of the gravity well. Infinite red shift. Some ways a Black Hole isn't even theoretically inside this universe.''

The others looked incredulous and Stirner laughed. ''You think that is strange? There was even talk once about whole galaxies, a hundred billion stars, whole thing collapsed to smaller than the orbit of Venus. They wouldn't be in the universe for real either.''

"Then how would Black Holes interact with—oh," Rap Torrin said, "gravity. It still has that.''

Stirner's round face bobbed in agreement. "Ja, ja, which is how we know is no black galaxy out there. Would be too much gravity. But there is plenty of room for a star. Now one thing I do not understand though, why the survey ship gets through, others do not. Maybe gravity changes for one of those things, ja?''

"No, look, the Alderson path really isn't a line of sight, it can shift slightly—maybe just enough!" Torrin spoke rapidly. "If the geometry were just right, then sometimes the Hole wouldn't be in the way . . .''

"O.K.," Stirner said. "I leave that up to you Navy boys. But you see what happens, the ship is taking sights or whatever you do when you are making a jump, the captain pushes the button, and maybe you come out in normal space near this Black Hole. Nothing to see anywhere around you. *And no way to get back home.*''

"Of course." Ramsey stood, twisted his fingers excitedly. "The Alderson effect is generated by nuclear reactions. And the dark holes—''

"Either got none of those, or the Alderson force stuff is caught inside the Black Hole like light and everything else. So you are coming home in normal space or you don't come home at all.''

"Which is light-years. You'd never make it." Ramsey found himself near the bar. Absently he poured a drink. "But in that case—the ships can sustain themselves a long time on their fuel!''

"Yes." Lermontov said it carefully. "It is at least possible that Senator Grant is alive. If his frigate dropped into normal space at a sufficient distance from the Black Hole so that it did not vanish down.''

"Not only Martin," Bart Ramsey said wonderingly. His heart pounded. "Barbara Jean. And Harold. They were on a Norden Lines luxury cruiser, only half the passenger berths taken. There should have been enough supplies and hydrogen to keep them going five years, Sergei. More than enough!''

Vice Admiral Lermontov nodded slowly. "That is why we thought you should go. But you realize that . . .''

"I haven't dared hope. I've wanted to die for five years, Sergei. Found that out about myself, had to be careful. Not fair to my crew to be so reckless. I'll go after Martin and— I'll go. But what does that do for us? If I do find them, I'll be as trapped as they are."

"Maybe. Maybe not." Stirner snorted. "Why you think we came out here, just to shake up a captain and maybe lose the Navy a cruiser? What made me think about this Black Hole business, I am questioning a transportee. Sentenced to the labor market on Tanith, the charge is unauthorized scientific research. I look into all those crazies, might be something the Navy can use, ja? This one was fooling around with gravity waves, theories about Black Holes. Hard to see how the Navy could use it. I was for letting them take this one to Tanith when I start to think, we are losing those ships coming from Meiji, and click! So I pulled the prisoner off the colony ship."

"And he says he can get us home from a dark hole in blank space?" Ramsey asked. He tried to suppress the wave of excitement that began in his bowels and crept upward until he could hardly speak. Not hope! Hope was an agony, something to be dreaded. It was much easier to live with resignation . . .

"Ja. Only is not a him. Is a her. Not very attractive her. She *says* she can do this." Stirner paused significantly.

"Miss Ward hates the CoDominium, Bart," Lermontov said carefully. "With what she thinks is good reason. She won't tell us how she plans to get the ship home."

"By God, she'll tell me!" *Why can't anything be simple? To know Barbara Jean is dead, or to know what mountain to climb to save her.* . . .

"If I can't think of something we can borrow a State Security man from the—"

"No." Lermontov's voice was a flat refusal. "Leave aside the ethics of the situation, we need this girl's creative energies. You can't get that with brainscrubs."

"Maybe." *And maybe I'll try it anyway if nothing else works. Barbara Jean, Barbara Jean* . . . "Where is this uncooperative scientist?"

"On Ceres." Vice Admiral Lermontov stretched a long arm toward the bar and poured for everyone. Stirner swished his brandy appreciatively in a crystal snifter. "Understand something, Bart," the admiral said. "Miss Ward may not know a thing. She may hate us enough to destroy a CD ship even at the cost of her life. You're gambling on a theory we don't know exists and could be wrong even if she has one.''

"So I'm gambling. My God, Sergei, do you know what I've been through these last years? It isn't normal for a man to brood like I do, you think I don't know that? That I don't know you whisper about it when I'm not around? Now you say there's a chance but it might cost my life. *You're* gambling a cruiser you can't spare, my ship is worth more to the Navy than I am.''

Lermontov ignored Ramsey's evaluation, and Bart wished it had been challenged. But it was probably true, although the old Bart Ramsey was something else again, a man headed for the job Sergei held now. . . .

"I am gambling a ship because if we do not get Martin Grant back in time for the appropriations hearings, I will lose more than a ship. We might lose half the fleet.''

"Ja, ja," Stirner sighed. He shook his round head sadly, slowly, a big gesture. "It is not usual that one man may be so important, I do not believe in the indispensable-man theory myself. Yet, without Senator Grant I do not see how we are getting the ships in time or even keeping what we have, and without those ships . . . but maybe it is too late anyway, maybe even with the senator we cannot get the ships, or with the ships we can still do nothing when a planet full of people are determined to kill themselves.''

"That's as it may be," Lermontov said. "But for now we need Senator Grant. I'll have the prisoner aboard *Daniel Webster* in four hours, Bart. You'll want to fill the tanks. Trim the crew down to minimum also. We must try this, but I do not really give very good odds on your coming home.''

"STAND BY FOR JUMPOFF. Jump stations, man your jump stations.'' The unemotional voice of the officer of the watch monotoned through steel corridors, showing no more excitement than he would have used to announce an off-watch solido show. It took years to train that voice into Navy officers, but it made them easier to understand in battle. "Man your jump stations.''

Bart Ramsey looked up from his screens as First Lieutenant Trevor ushered Marie Ward onto the bridge. She was a round, dumpy woman, her skin a faint red color. Shoulder length hair fell almost straight down to frame her face, but dark brown wisps poked out at improbable angles despite combings and hair ribbons. Her hands were big, as powerful as a man's, and the nails, chewed to the quick, were colorless. When he met her Ramsey had estimated her age in the mid-thirties and was surprised to learn she was only twenty-six.

"You may take the assistant helmsman's acceleration chair," Ramsey told her. He forced a smile. "We're about to make the jump to Meiji." In his lonely ship. She'd been stripped down, empty stations all through her.

"Thank you, Captain." Marie sat and allowed Trevor to strap her in. The routine for jumpoff went on. As he listened to the reports, Ramsey realized Marie Ward was humming.

"What is that?" he asked. "Catchy tune. . . ."

"Sorry. It's an old nursery thing. 'The bear went over the mountain, the bear went over the mountain, the bear went over the mountain, to see what he could see.' "

"Oh. Well, we haven't seen anything yet."

" 'The other side of the mountain, was all that he could see.' But it's the third verse that's interesting. 'He fell into a dark hole, and covered himself over with charcoal—' "

"Warning, warning, take your posts for jumpoff."

Ramsey examined his screens. His chair was surrounded by them. "All right, Trevor, make your search."

"Aye, aye, sir."

Lieutenant Trevor would be busy for a while. He had been assigned the job of looking after Marie Ward, but for the moment Ramsey would have to be polite to her. "You haven't told us much about what we're going to see on the other side of the mountain. Why?"

"Captain, if you knew everything I did, you wouldn't need to take me along," she said. "I wish they'd hurry up. I *don't like* starjumps."

"It won't be long now—" Just what do you say to a convict genius? The whole trip out she'd been in everybody's hair, seldom talking about anything but physics. She'd asked the ship's officers about the drive, astrogation, instruments, the guns, nearly everything. Sometimes she was humorous, but more often scathingly sarcastic. And she wouldn't say a word about Black Holes, except to smile knowingly. More and more Ramsey wished he'd borrowed a KGB man from the Soviets. . . .

"WARNING, WARNING. Jumpoff in one minute," the

watch officer announced. Alarm bells sounded through the ship.

"Lined up, Captain," Trevor said. "For all I can tell, we're going straight through to 81 Eridani. If there's anything out there, I can't see it."

"Humph," Marie Ward snorted. "Why should you?"

"Yes, but if the Alderson path's intact, the Hole won't have any effect on us," Trevor protested. "And to the best we can measure, the path is there."

"No, no," Marie insisted. "You don't measure the Alderson path at all! You only measure the force, Lieutenant. Then your computer deduces the existence of the path from the stellar geometry. I'd have thought they'd teach you that much anyway. And that you could remember it."

"FINAL WARNING. Ten seconds to jump." A series of chimes, descending in pitch. Marie grimaced. Her mannish hands clutched the chair arms as she braced herself. At the tenth tone everything blurred for an instant that stretched to a million years.

There is no way to record the time a jump takes. The best chronological instruments record nothing whatever. Ships vanish into the state of nonbeing conveniently called "hyperspace" and reappear somewhere else. Yet it always *seems* to take forever, and while it happens everything in the universe is wrong, *wrong*, WRONG . . .

Ramsey shook his head. The screens around his command seat remained blurred. "Jump completed. Check ship," he ordered.

Crewmen moved fuzzily to obey despite the protests of tortured nerves. Electronic equipment, computers, nearly everything complex suffers from jump induced transients although there is no known permanent effect.

"Captain, we're nowhere near Meiji!" the astrogator exclaimed. "I don't know *where* we are. . . ."

"Stand by to make orbit," Ramsey ordered.

"Around *what*?" Lieutenant Trevor asked. "There's no star out there, Captain. There's nothing!"

"Then we'll orbit nothing." Ramsey turned to Marie Ward. "Well, we've found the damn thing. You got any suggestions about locating it? I'd as soon not fall into it."

"Why not?" she asked. Ramsey was about to smile politely when he realized she was speaking seriously. "According to some theories, a Black Hole is a time/space gate. You could go into it and come out—somewhere else. In another century. Or another universe."

"Is that why the hell you brought us out here? To kill yourself testing some theory about Black Holes and space/time?"

"I am here because the CoDominium Marines put me aboard," she said. Her voice was carefully controlled. "And I have no desire to test any theory. Yet." She turned to Lieutenant Trevor. "Dave, is it really true? There's no star out there at all?"

"It's true enough."

She smiled. A broad, face-cracking smile that, with the thousand meter stare in her eyes, made her look strangely happy. Insanely happy, in fact. "My god, it worked! There really is a Black Hole. . . ."

"Which we haven't found yet," Trevor reminded her.

"Oh. Yes. Let's see—it should have started as about five stellar masses in size. That's my favorite theory, anyway. When it began to collapse it would have radiated over eighty percent of its mass away. X rays, mostly. Lots of them. And if it had planets, they might still be here . . . Anyway, it should be about as massive as Sol. There won't be any radiation coming out. X rays, light, nothing can climb out of that gravity well. . . . Just think of it, infinite red shift! It really happens!"

"Infinite red shift," Ramsey repeated carefully. "Yes, ma'm. Now, just how do we find this source of tired light?"

"It isn't tired light! That's a very obsolete theory. Next I suppose you'll tell me you think photons slow down when they lose energy."

"No, I—"

"Because they don't. They wouldn't *be* photons if they *could* slow down. They just lose energy until they vanish."

"Fine, but *how do we find it?*"

"It can't reach out and grab you, Captain," she said. The grin wasn't as wide as before, but still she smiled softly to herself. It made her look much better, although the mocking tones didn't help Ramsey's appreciation. "It's just a star, Captain. A very small star, very dense, as heavy as most other stars, but it doesn't have any more gravity than Sol. You could get quite close and still pull away—"

"If we knew which direction was away."

"Yes. Hm-m-m. It will bend light rays, but you'd have to be pretty close to see any effect at all from that. . . ."

"Astrogation!" Ramsey ordered crisply. "How do we find a star we can't see?"

"We're about dead in space relative to whatever stopped us," the astrogator told him. "We can wait until we accelerate toward it and get a vector from observation of other stars. That will take a while. Or we can see if it's left any planets, but with nothing to illuminate them they'll be hard to find—"

"Yeah. Do the best you can, Mister." Marie Ward was still looking happily at the screens. They showed absolutely nothing. Ramsey punched another button in the arm of his command chair.

"Comm room, sir."

"Eyes, there are ships out there somewhere." *God I hope there are. Or one ship.* "Find them and get me communications."

"Aye, aye, sir. I'll use the distress frequencies. They might be monitoring those."

"Right. And yes, see if your bright electronics and physics boys can think of a way to detect gravity. So far as I can make out that's the only effect that a Black Hole has on the real universe."

"On *our* real universe. Imagine a universe in which there are particles with non-zero rest masses able to move faster than light. Where you get rid of energy to go faster. Sentient beings in that universe would think of it as real. It might even be where our ships go when they make an Alderson jump. And the Black Hole could be gates to get you there."

"Yes, Miss Ward," Ramsey said carefully. Two enlisted spacers on the other side of the bridge grinned knowingly at each other and waited for the explosion. They'd been waiting ever since Marie Ward came aboard, and it ought to be pretty interesting. But Ramsey's voice became even softer and more controlled. "Meanwhile, have you any useful suggestions on what we should do now?"

"Find the Hole, of course. Your astrogator seems quite competent. His approach is very reasonable. Yes, quite competent. For a Navy man."

Carefully, his hands moving very slowly, Captain Bartholomew Ramsey unstrapped himself from his command chair and launched himself across the bridge to the exit port. "Take the con, Mr. Trevor," he said. And left.

*   *   *

For fifty hours *Daniel Webster* searched for the other ships. Then, with no warning at all, Ramsey was caught in the grip of a giant vise.

For long seconds he felt as if titanic hands were squeezing him. They relaxed, ending the agony for a brief moment. And tried to pull him apart. The screens blurred, and he heard the sound of rending metal as the hands alternately crushed, then pulled.

Somehow the watch officer sounded General Quarters. Klaxons blared through the ship as she struggled with her invisible enemy. Ramsey screamed, as much in rage and frustration as pain, hardly knowing he had made a sound. He had to take control of his ship before she died, but there were no orders to give. This was no attack by an enemy, but what, what?

The battle damage screen flared red. Ramsey was barely able to see as it showed a whole section of the ship's outer corridors evacuated to space. How many men were in there? Most wouldn't be in armor. *My God! Daniel Webster too? My wife and now my ship?*

Slowly it faded away. Ramsey pulled himself erect. Around him on the bridge the watch crew slumped at their stations. The klaxons continued, adding their confusion, until Ramsey shut them off.

"What—what was it?" Lieutenant Trevor gasped. His usually handsome features were contorted with remembered pain, and he looked afraid.

"All stations report damage," Ramsey ordered. "I don't know what it was, Lieutenant."

"I do!" Marie Ward gasped excitedly. Her eyes darted about in wonder. "I know! Gravity waves from the Black Hole! A tensor field! And these were tensor, not scalar—"

"Gravity waves?" Ramsey asked stupidly. "But gravity waves are weak things, only barely detectable."

Marie Ward snorted. "In your experience, Captain. And in mine. But according to one Twentieth Century theory—they had lots of theories then, when intellectuals were free, Captain—according to one theory, if a Black Hole is rotating and a mass enters the Schwartzchild Limit, part of the mass will be converted to gravity waves. *They* can escape from the Hole and affect objects outside it. So can Alderson forces, I think. But they didn't know about the Alderson force then. . . ."

"But—is that going to happen again?" Ramsey demanded.

Battle damage reports appeared on his screens. "We can't live through much of that."

"I really don't know how often it will happen," Marie answered. She chewed nervously on her right thumbnail. "I do know one thing. We have a chance to get home again."

"Home?" Ramsey took a deep breath. That depended on what had been done to Danny Boy. A runner brought him another report. Much of the ship's internal communications were out, but the chief engineer was working with a damage-control party. Another screen came on, and Ramsey heard the bridge speaker squawk.

"Repairable damage to normal space drive in main engine room," the toneless voice said. "Alderson drive appears unaffected."

"Gunnery reports damage to laser lenses in number one battery. No estimate of time to repair."

Big rigid objects had broken. Ramsey later calculated the actual displacement at less than a millimeter/meter; not very much, but enough to damage the ship and kill half a dozen crewmen unable to get into battle armor. Explosive decompression wasn't a pretty death, but it was quick.

With all her damage, *Daniel Webster* was only hurt. She could sail, his ship wasn't dead. Not yet. Ramsey gave orders to the damage control parties. When he was sure they were doing everything they could he turned back to the dumpy girl in the assistant helmsman's seat.

"How do we get home?"

She had been scribbling on a pad of paper, but her pencil got away from her when she tried to set it down without using the clips set into the arm of the seat. Now she stared absently at her notes, a thin smile on her lips. "I'm sorry, Captain. What did you say?"

"I asked, how do we get home?"

"Oh." She tried to look serious but only succeeded in appearing sly. "I was hasty in saying that. I don't know."

"Sure. Don't you want to get home?"

"Of course, Captain. I'd just love to get back on a colony ship. I understand Tanith has such a wonderful climate."

"Come off it. The Navy doesn't forget people who've helped us. You aren't going to Tanith." He took a deep breath. "We have a rescue mission, Miss Ward. Some of those people have been out here for five years." Five years of that? Nobody could live through five years of that. *O God, where is she? Crushed, torn apart, again and again, her body drifting out there in black space without even a star? Rest eternal grant them, O Lord, and let light perpetual shine upon them. . . .*

"How do we get home?"

"I told you, I don't know."

But you do. And come to think of it, so do I. "Miss Ward, you implied that if we knew when a mass would enter the Black Hole, we could use the resulting Alderson forces to get us out of here."

"I'll be damned." She looked at Ramsey as if seeing him for the first time. "The man can actually—yes, of course." She smiled faintly. "I *thought* so before we left Ceres. Theory said that would work. . . ."

"But we'd have to know the timing rather precisely, wouldn't we?"

"Yes. Depending on the size of the mass. The larger it is, the longer the effect would last. I think. Maybe not, though."

Ramsey nodded to himself. There was only one possible mass whose entry into the Hole they could predict. "Trevor."

"Sir?"

"One way you might amuse yourself is in thinking of ways to make a ship impact a solar mass not much more than two kilometers in diameter; a star you can't see and whose location you can't know precisely."

"Aye, aye, skipper." Dave Trevor frowned. He didn't often do that and it distorted his features. "Impact, Captain? But unless you were making corrections all the way in, you'd probably miss—as it is, the ship would pick up so much velocity that it's more likely to whip right around—"

"Exactly, Lieutenant. But it's the only way home."

One hundred and eight hours after breakout Chief Yeoman Karabian located the other ships. *Daniel Webster*'s call was answered by the first frigate sent out to find the Norton liner:

DANIEL WEBSTER THIS IS HENRY HUDSON BREAK BREAK
WE ARE IN ORBIT ELEVEN ASTRONOMICAL UNITS FROM
WHATEVER THAT THING DOWN THERE IS STOP WE WILL
SEND A CW SIGNAL TO GIVE YOU A BEARING STOP

THE NORTON LINER LORELEI AND CDSN CONSTELLATION
ARE WITH US STOP YOUR SIGNAL INDICATES THAT YOU

ARE LESS THAN ONE AU FROM THE DARK STAR STOP YOU
ARE IN EXTREME DANGER REPEAT EXTREME DANGER STOP
ADVISE YOU MOVE AWAY FROM DARK STAR IMMEDIATELY
STOP THERE ARE STRONG GRAVITY FLUXES NEAR THE DARK
STAR STOP THEY CAN TEAR YOU APART STOP ONE SCOUTSHIP
ALREADY DESTROYED BY GRAVITY WAVES STOP REPEAT
ADVISE YOU MOVE AWAY FROM DARK STAR IMMEDIATELY
AND HOME ON OUR CW SIGNAL STOP.

REQUEST FOLLOWING INFORMATION COLON WHO IS MAS-
TER ABOARD DANIEL WEBSTER INTERROGATIVE BREAK
BREAK MESSAGE ENDS.

Ramsey read the message on his central display screen,
then punched the intercom buttons. "Chief, get this out:

"HENRY HUDSON THIS IS DANIEL WEBSTER BREAK BREAK
CAPTAIN BARTHOLOMEW RAMSEY COMMANDING STOP WE
WILL HOME ON YOUR BEACON STOP HAVE EXPERIENCED
GRAVITY STORM ALREADY STOP SHIP DAMAGED BUT SPACE-
WORTHY STOP

"IS SENATOR MARTIN GRANT ABOARD CONSTELLATION IN-
TERROGATIVE IS MRS RAMSEY THERE INTERROGATIVE
BREAK MESSAGE ENDS."

The hundred-and-sixty-minute round trip for message and
reply would be a lifetime.

"Trevor, get us moving when you've got that beacon,"
Ramsey ordered. "Pity he couldn't tell us about the gravity
waves before we found out the hard way."

"Yes, sir." The acceleration alarm rang through the ship
as Trevor prepared the new course. "We can only make
about a half G, Captain. We're lucky to get that. We took
more damage from that gravity storm than Danny Boy's ever
got from an enemy."

"Yeah." *Pity indeed. But communications did all they
could. Space is just too big for omni signals, and we had
maser damage to boot. Had to send in narrow cones, lucky
we made contact this soon even sweeping messages. And no
ecliptic here either. Or none we know of.*

"Communications here," Ramsey's speaker announced.

"Yes, Eyes."

"We're getting that homing signal. Shouldn't be any problem."

"Good." Ramsey studied the figures that flowed across his screen. "Take the con, Mr. Trevor. And call me when there's an answer from *Henry Hudson.* I'll wait in my patrol cabin." *And a damn long wait that's going to be. Barbara Jean, Barbara Jean, are you out there?*

The hundred and sixty minutes went past. Then another hour, and another. It was nearly six hours before there was a message from the derelicts; and it was in code the Navy used for the eyes of commanding officers only.

Captain Ramsey sat in his bare room and stared at the message flimsy. In spite of the block letters from the coding printer his eyes wouldn't focus on the words.

DANIEL WEBSTER THIS IS HENRY HUDSON BREAK FOLLOW-
ING IS PERSONAL MESSAGE FOR CAPTAIN BARTHOLOMEW
RAMSEY FROM GRAND SENATOR MARTIN GRANT BREAK
BREAK PERSONAL MESSAGE BEGINS

BART WE ARE HERE AND ALIVE STOP THE SCOUTSHIP WAS
LOST TO GRAVITY WAVES STOP THE LINER LORELEI THE
FRIGATE HENRY HUDSON AND THE FRIGATE CONSTELLA-
TION ARE DAMAGED STOP LORELEI IN SPACEWORTHY CON-
DITION WITH MOST OF CREW SURVIVING DUE TO HEROIC
EFFORTS OF MASTER OF HENRY HUDSON STOP

BOTH BARBARA JEAN AND HAROLD ARE WELL STOP RE-
GRET TO INFORM YOU THAT BARBARA JEAN MARRIED COM-
MANDER JAMES HARRIMAN OF HENRY HUDSON THREE
YEARS AGO STOP BREAK END PERSONAL MESSAGE BREAK
BREAK MESSAGE ENDS.

Ramsey automatically reached for a drink, then angrily tossed the glass against the bare steel wall. It wouldn't be fair to the crew. Or to his ship. And *Daniel Webster* was still the only wife he had.

The intercom buzzed. "Bridge, Captain."

"Go ahead, Trevor."

"Two hundred eighty plus hours to rendezvous, Captain. We're on course."

"Thank you." *Damn long hours those are going to be. How could she—but that's simple. For all Barbara Jean could know she and the boy were trapped out here forever. I can bet there were plenty of suicides on those ships. And the boy would be growing up without a father.*

Not that I was so much of one. Half the time I was out on patrol anyway. But I was home when he caught pneumonia from going with us to Ogden Base. Harold just had to play in that snow. . . .

He smiled in remembrance. They'd built a snowman together. But Harold wasn't used to Earth gravity, and that more than the cold weakened him. The boy never did put in enough time in the centrifuge on Luna Base. Navy kids grew up on the Moon because the Navy was safe only among its own. . . .

Ramsey made a wry face. Hundreds of Navy kids crowding into the big centrifuge . . . they were hard to control, and Barbara Jean like most mothers hated to take her turn minding them. She needed a hairdo. Or had to go shopping. Or something. . . .

She should have remarried. Of course she should. He pictured Barbara Jean with another man. *What did she say to him when they made love? Did she use the same words? Like our first time, when we—oh, damn.*

He fought against the black mood. *Harriman. James Harriman. Fleet spatball champ seven years ago. A good man. Tough. Younger than Barbara Jean. Harriman used to be a real comer before he vanished. Never married and the girls at Luna Base forever trying to get—never married until now.*

Stop it! Would you rather she was dead? The thought crept through unwanted. *If you would, you'll goddammit not admit it, you swine. Not now and not ever.*

She's alive! Bart Ramsey, you remember that and forget the rest of it. Barbara Jean is alive!

Savagely he punched the intercom buttons.

"Bridge. Aye, aye, Captain."

"We on course, Mister?"

"Yes, sir."

"Damage control parties working?"

"Yes. sir." Trevor's voice was puzzled. He was a good first lieutenant, and it wasn't like Ramsey to ride him . . .

"Excellent." Ramsey slapped the off button, waited a moment, and reached for another whisky. This time he drank it. And waited.

*   *   *

There was little communication as *Daniel Webster* accelerated, turned over, and slowed again to approach the derelicts. Messages took energy, and they'd need it all. To get out, or to survive if Marie Ward proved wrong with her theories. Someday there'd be a better theory. Lermontov might come up with something, and even now old Stirner would be examining ancient records at Stanford and Harvard. If Ward was wrong, they still had to survive . . .

"Getting them on visual now," the comm officer reported. The unemotional voice broke. "Good God, Captain!"

Ramsey stared at the screens. The derelicts were worse than he could have imagined. *Lorelei* was battered, although she seemed intact, but the other ships seemed *bent*. The frigate *Constellation* was a wreck, with gaping holes in her hull structure. *Henry Hudson* was crumpled, almost unrecognizable. The survivors must all be on the Norton liner.

Ramsey watched in horror as the images grew on the screens. *Five years, with all hope going, gone. Harriman must be one hell of a man to keep anyone alive through that.*

When they were alongside, Navy routine carried Ramsey through hours that were lifetimes. Like one long continuous jump. Everything *wrong*.

Spacers took *Daniel Webster*'s cutter across to *Lorelei* and docked. After another eternity she lifted away with passengers. CDSN officers, one of the merchant service survivors from *Lorelei*—and the others. Senator Grant. Johnny Grant. Commander Harriman. Barbara Jean, Harold—and Jeanette Harriman, age three.

"I'll be in my cabin, Trevor."

"Yes, sir."

"And get some spin on the ship as soon as that boat's fast aboard."

"Aye, aye, sir."

Ramsey waited. Who would come? It was his ship, he could send for anyone he liked. Instead he waited. Let Barbara Jean make up her own mind. Would she come? And would Harriman be with her?

Five years. Too long, he's had her for five years. But we had ten years together before that. Damned if I don't feel like a Middie on his first prom.

He was almost able to laugh at that.

The door opened and she came in. There was no one with her, but he heard voices in the corridor outside. She stood nervously at the bulkhead, staring around the bare cabin at the empty desk and blank steel walls.

Her hair's gone. The lovely black hair that she never cut, whacked off short and tangled—God, you're beautiful. Why can't I say that? Why can't I say anything?

She wore shapeless coveralls, once white, but now grimy, and her hands showed ground-in dirt and grease. They'd had to conserve water, and there was little soap. Five years is a long time to maintain a closed ecology.

"No pictures, Bart? Not even one of me?"

"I—I thought you were dead." He stood, and in the small cabin they were very close. "There wasn't anybody else to keep a picture of."

Her tightly kept smile faded. "I—I would have waited, Bart. But we were dead. I don't even know why we tried to stay alive. Jim drove everybody, he kept us going, and then—he needed help."

Ramsey nodded, it was going to be all right. Wasn't it? He moved closer and put his hands on her shoulders, pulling her to him. She responded woodenly, then broke away. "Give me—give me a little time to get used to it, Bart."

He backed away from her. "Yeah. The rest of you can come in now," he called.

"Bart, I didn't mean—"

"It's all right, Barbara Jean. We'll work it out." Somehow.

The boy came in first. He was very hesitant. Harold didn't look so very different. He still had a round face, a bit too plump. But he was *big*. And he was leading a little girl, a girl with dark hair and big round eyes, her mother's eyes.

Harold stood for a long moment. "Sir—ah," he began formally, but then he let go of the girl and rushed to his father. "Daddy! I knew you'd come to get us, I told them you'd come!" He was tall enough that his head reached Bart's shoulder, and his arms went all the way around him.

Finally he broke away. "Dad, this is my little sister." He said it defiantly, searchingly, watching his father's face. Finally he smiled. "She's a nuisance sometimes, but she grows on you."

"I'm sure she does," Ramsey said. It was very still in the bare cabin. Ramsey wanted to say something else, but he had trouble with his voice.

*   *   *

Daniel Webster's wardroom was crowded. There was barely room at the long steel table for all the surviving astrogation officers to sit with Ramsey, Senator Grant, and Marie Ward. They waited tensely.

The senator was thinner than Ramsey had ever seen him despite the short time he'd been marooned. *Constellation* had been hit hard by a gravity storm—it was easier to think of them that way, although the term was a little silly. Now the senator's hands rested lightly on the wardroom table, the tips of the fingers just interlocked, motionless. Like everyone else Senator Grant watched Commander Harriman.

Harriman paced nervously. He had grown a neatly trimmed beard, brown, with both silver and red hairs woven through it. His uniform had been patched a dozen times, but it was still the uniform of the Service, and Harriman wore it proudly. There was no doubt of who had been in command.

"The only ship spaceworthy is *Lorelei*," Harriman reported. "*Henry Hudson* was gutted to keep *Lorelei* livable, and Johnny Grant's *Constellation* took it hard in the gravity storms before we could get him out far enough from that thing."

Senator Grant sighed loudly. "I hope never to have to live through anything like that again. Even out this far you can feel the gravity waves, although it's not dangerous. But in close, before we knew where to go . . ."

"But *Lorelei* can space?" Ramsey asked. Harriman nodded. "Then *Lorelei* it'll have to be. Miss Ward, explain what it takes to get home again."

"Well, I'm not *sure*, Captain. I think we should wait."

"We can't wait. I realize you want to stay out here and look at the Black Hole until doomsday, but these people want to go home. Not to mention my orders from Lermontov."

Reluctantly she explained her theory, protesting all the while that they really ought to make a better study. "And the timing will have to be perfect," she finished. "The ship must be at the jumpoff point and turn on the drive at just the right time."

"Throw a big mass down the Hole," Harriman said. "Well, there's only the one mass to throw. *Lorelei*." He stopped pacing for a moment and looked thoughtful. "And that means somebody has to ride her in."

"Gentlemen?" Ramsey looked around the table. One by one the astrogation officers nodded mutely. Trevor, seeing his

captain's face, paused for a long second before he also nodded agreement.

"There's no way to be sure of a hit if we send her in on
automatic," Trevor said. "We can't locate the thing close
enough from out here. We can't send *Lorelei* on remote,
either. The time lag's too long."

"Couldn't you build some kind of homing device?" Senator Grant asked. His voice was carefully controlled, and it
compelled attention. In the Grand Senate, Martin Grant's
speeches were worth listening to, although senators usually
voted from politics anyway.

"What would you home on?" Marie asked caustically.
"There's nothing to detect. In close enough you should see
bending light rays, but I'm not sure. I'm just not sure of
anything, but I know we couldn't build a homing device."

"Could we wait for a gravity storm and fly out of that?"
Trevor asked. "If we were ready for it, we could make the
jump. . . ."

"Nonsense," Harriman snapped. "Give me credit for a
little sense, Lieutenant. We tried that. I didn't know what we
were up against, but I figured those were gravity waves after
they'd nearly wrecked my ships. Where there's gravity there
may be Alderson forces. But you can't predict the damn
gravity storms. We get one every thousand hours, sometimes
close together, sometimes a long time apart, but about a
thousand-hour average. How can you be in a position for a
jump when you don't know it's coming? And the damn
gravity waves do things to the drives."

"Every thousand hours!" Marie demanded excitedly. "But
that's impossible! What could cause that—so much matter!
Commander Harriman, you have observed asteroids in this
system?"

"Yeah. There's a whole beehive of them, all in close to the
dark star. Thousands and thousands of them, it looks like.
But they're *really* close, it's a swarm in a thick plane, a ring
about ten kilometers thick. It's hard to observe anything,
though. They move so fast, and if you get in close the gravity
storms kill you. From out here we don't see much."

"A ring—are they large bodies?" Marie asked. Her eyes
shone.

Harriman shrugged. "We've bounced radar off them and
we deduce they're anywhere from a few millimeters to maybe

a full kilometer in diameter, but it's hard to tell. There's nothing stable about the system, either.''

Marie chewed both thumbnails. "There wouldn't be," she said. She began so softly that it was difficult to hear her. "There wouldn't be if chunks keep falling into the Hole. Ha! We won't be able to use the asteroids to give a position on the Black Hole. Even if you had better observations, the Hole is rotating. There must be enormous gravitational anomalies.''

Harriman shrugged again, this time helplessly. "You understand, all we ever really observed was some bending light and a fuzzy occultation of stars. We deduced there was a dark star, but there was nothing in our data banks about them. Even if we'd known what a Black Hole was, I don't know how much good it would have done. I burned out the last of the Alderson drives three years ago trying to ride out. We were never in the right position. . . . I was going to patch up *Constellation* and have another stab at it.''

Just like that, Ramsey thought. *Just go out and patch up that wreck of a ship.* How many people would even try, much less be sure they could . . . so three years ago they'd lost their last hope of getting out of there. And after that, Barbara Jean had . . .

"Did you ever try throwing something down the Hole yourself?" Trevor asked.

"No. Until today we had no idea what we were up against. I still don't, but I'll take your word for it.'' Harriman drew in a deep breath and stopped pacing. "I'll take *Lorelei* down.''

Bart looked past Harriman to a painting on the wardroom bulkhead. Trevor had liked it and hung it there long ago. John Paul Jones strode across the blazing decks of his flagship. Tattered banners blew through sagging rigging, blood ran in the scuppers, but Jones held his old cutlass aloft.

Well, why not? Somebody's got to do it, why not Harriman? But—but what will Barbara Jean think?

"I want to go too." Marie Ward spoke softly, but everyone turned to look at her. "I'll come with you, Commander Harriman.''

"Don't be ridiculous,'' Harriman snapped.

"Ridiculous? What's ridiculous about it? This is an irreplaceable opportunity. We can't leave the only chance we'll ever have to study Black Holes for an amateur. There is certainly nothing ridiculous about a trained observer going.''

Her voice softened. "Besides, you'll be too busy with the ship to take decent observations."

"Miss Ward," Harriman compelled attention although it was difficult to say exactly why. Even though Ramsey was senior officer present, Harriman seemed to dominate the meeting. "Miss Ward, we practically rebuilt *Lorelei* over the past five years. I doubt if anyone else could handle her, so I've *got* to go. But just why do you want to?"

"Oh—" the arrogant tone left her voice. "Because this is my one chance to do something important. Just what am I? I'm not pretty." She paused, as if she hoped someone would disagree, but there was only silence.

"And no one ever took me seriously as an intellectual. I've no accomplishments at all. No publications. Nothing. But as the only person ever to study a Black Hole, I'll be recognized!"

"You've missed a point." Ramsey spoke quickly before anyone else could jump in. His voice was sympathetic and concerned. "We take you seriously. Admiral Lermontov took you so seriously he sent this cruiser out here. And you're our only expert on Black Holes. If Commander Harriman's attempt fails or for any other reason we don't get out of this system on this try, you'll have to think of something else for us."

"But—"

Harriman clucked his tongue impatiently. "Will *Lorelei* be mass enough, Miss Ward?"

"I don't know." She answered softly, but when they all stared at her she pouted defensively. "Well, I don't! How could I! There should be more than enough energy but I don't *know*!" Her voice rose higher. "If you people hadn't suppressed everything we'd have more information. But I've had to work all by myself, and I—"

Dave Trevor put his hand gently on her arm. "It'll be all right. You haven't been wrong yet."

"Haven't I?"

Senator Grant cleared his throat. "This isn't getting us anywhere at all. We have only one ship capable of sailing down to that Hole and only one theory of how to get away from here. We'll just have to try it."

There was a long silence before Bart spoke. "You sure you want to do this, Commander?" Ramsey cursed himself for the relief he felt, knowing what Harriman's answer would be.

"I'll do it, Captain. Who else could? Let's get started."

Ramsey nodded. *If 'twere done, 'twere best done quickly
. . . what was that from? Shakespeare?* "Mr. Trevor, take an
engineering crew over to *Lorelei* and start making her ready.
Get all the ship's logs too."

"Logs!" Marie smiled excitedly. "Dave, I want to see
those as soon as possible."

As Trevor nodded agreement, Ramsey waved dismissal to
the officers. "Commander Harriman, if you'd stay just a
moment . . ."

The wardroom emptied. There was a burst of chatter as the
others left. Their talk was too spirited, betraying their relief.
They didn't have to take *Lorelei* into a Black Hole. Ramsey
and Harriman sat for what seemed like a long time.

"Is there something I can say?" Ramsey asked.

"No. I'd fight you for her if there wasn't a way home. But
if there's any chance at all—you'll take care of Jeanette, of
course." Harriman looked at the battered mug on the table,
then reached for the coffee pot. After years in space he didn't
notice the strange angle the liquid made as it flowed into the
cup under spin gravity. "That's fine coffee, Captain. We ran
out, must be three, four years ago. You get to miss coffee
after a while."

"Yeah." *What the Hell can I say to him? Do I thank him
for not making me order him to take that ship in? He really is
the only one who could do it, and we both knew that.* Unwanted, the image of Barbara Jean in this man's arms came to
him. Ramsey grimaced savagely. "Look, Harriman; there's
got to be some way we can—"

"There isn't and we both know it. Sir. Even if there were,
what good would it do? We can't both go back with her."

And I'm glad it's me who's going home, Ramsey thought.
*Hah. The first time in five years I've cared about staying
alive. But will she ever really be mine again?*

Was that all that was wrong with me?

"Your inertial navigation gear working all right?" Harriman asked. "Got an intact telescope?"

"Eh? Yeah, sure."

"You shouldn't have too much trouble finding the jumpoff
point, then."

"I don't expect any." Marie Ward's ridiculous song came
back to him. "He fell into a dark hole, and covered himself
over with charcoal, he went back over the mountain—" But
Harriman wouldn't be back over the mountain. Or would he?

What was a Black Hole, anyway? Could it really be a time tunnel?

Harriman poured more coffee. "I better get over to *Lorelei* myself. Can you spare a pound of coffee?"

"Sure."

Harriman stood. He drained the mug. "Don't see much point in coming back to *Daniel Webster* in that case. Your people can plot me a course and send it aboard *Lorelei*." He flexed his fingers as if seeing them for the first time, then brushed imaginary lint from his patched uniform. "Yeah. I'll go with the cutter. Now."

"Now? But don't you want to—"

"No, I think not. What would I say?" Harriman very carefully put the coffee mug into the table rack. "Tell her I loved her, will you? And be sure to send that coffee over. Funny the things you can get to miss in five years."

DANIEL WEBSTER THIS IS LORELEI BREAK BREAK TELL TREVOR HIS COURSE WAS FINE STOP I APPEAR TO BE ONE HALF MILLION KILOMETERS FROM THE BLACK HOLE WITH NO OBSERVABLE ORBITAL VELOCITY STOP WILL PROCEED AT POINT 1G FROM HERE STOP STILL CANNOT SEE THAT BEEHIVE AT ALL WELL STOP NOTHING TO OBSERVE IN BEST CALCULATED POSITION OF BLACK HOLE STOP TELL MARIE WARD SHE IS NOT MISSING A THING STOP BREAK MESSAGE ENDS.

Barbara Jean and her father sat in Captain Ramsey's cabin. Despite the luxury of a shower she didn't feel clean. She read the message flimsy her father handed her.

"I ought to say something to him, hadn't I? Shouldn't I? Dad, I can't just let him die like this."

"Leave him alone, kitten," Senator Grant told her. "He's got enough to do, working that half-dead ship by himself. And he has to work fast. One of those gravity storms while he's this close and—" Grant shuddered involuntarily.

"But—God, I've made a mess of things, haven't I?"

"How? Would you rather it was Bart taking that ship in there?"

"No. No, no, no! But I still—wasn't there any other way, Daddy? Did somebody *really* have to do it?"

"As far as I can tell, Barbara Jean. I was there when Jim volunteered. Bart tried to talk him out of it, you know."

She didn't say anything.

"You're right, of course," Grant sighed. "He didn't try very hard. There wasn't any point in it anyway. Commander Harriman was the obvious man to do it. You didn't enter the decision at all."

"I wish I could believe that."

"Yes. So does your husband. But it's still true. Are you coming down to the bridge? I don't think it's a good idea but you can."

"No. You go on, though. I have to take care of Jeanette. Bill Hartley has her in the sick bay. Daddy, what am I going to do?"

"You're going to go home with your husband and be an admiral's lady. For a while, anyway. And when there aren't any admirals because there isn't any fleet, God knows what you'll do. Make the best of it like all the rest of us, I guess."

The bridge was a blur of activity as they waited for *Lorelei* to approach the Black Hole. As the minutes ticked off, tension grew. A gravity storm just now would wipe out their only chance.

Finally Ramsey spoke. "You can get the spin off the ship, Mr. Trevor. Put the crew to jump stations."

"Aye, aye, sir."

"Can we talk to Harriman still?" Senator Grant asked.

Ramsey's eyes flicked to the screens, past the predicted time of impact to the others, taking in every detail. "No." He continued to look at the data pouring across the screens. Their position had to be right. Everything had to be right, they'd get only the one chance at best. . . . "Not to get an answer. You could get a message to *Lorelei* but before we'd hear a reply it'll be all over."

Grant looked relieved. "I guess not, then."

"Damnedest thing." Harriman's voice was loud over the bridge speaker. "Star was occulted by the Hole. Made a bright ring in space. Real bright. Just hanging there, never saw anything like it."

"Nobody else ever will," Marie Ward said quietly. "Or will they? Can the Navy send more ships out here to study it? Oh, I wish I could *see*!"

They waited forever until Harriman spoke again. "Got a

good position fix,'' they heard. ''Looks good, Ramsey, damn good.''

''Stand by for jumpoff,'' Bart ordered. Alarm bells rang through *Daniel Webster*.

''Another bright ring. Must be getting close.''

''What's happening to his voice?'' Senator Grant demanded.

''Time differential,'' Marie Ward answered. ''His ship is accelerating to a significant fraction of light velocity. Time is slowing down for him relative to us.''

''Looks good for jump here, skipper,'' Trevor announced.

''Right.'' Bart inspected his screens again. The predicted time to impact ticked off inexorably, but it was only a prediction. Without a more exact location of the Hole it couldn't be perfect. As Ramsey watched, the ship's computers updated the prediction from Harriman's signals.

Ramsey fingered the keys on his console. The Alderson drive generators could be kept on for less than a minute in normal space, but if they weren't on when *Lorelei* hit . . . he pressed the key. *Daniel Webster* shuddered as the ship's fusion engines went to full power, consuming hydrogen and thorium catalyst at a prodigal rate, pouring out energy into the drive where it—vanished.

Into hyperspace, if that was a real place. Or on the other side of the Lepton Barrier. Maybe to where you went when you fell through a Black Hole if there was anything to that theory. Marie Ward had been fascinated by it and had seen nothing to make her give it up.

Wherever the energy went, it left the measurable universe. But not all of it. The efficiency wasn't that good. The drive generators screamed. . . .

''There's another bright ring. Quite a sight. Best damn view in the universe.'' The time distortion was quite noticeable now. Time to impact loomed big on Ramsey's screens, seconds to go.

Marie Ward hummed her nursery rhyme. Unwanted, the words rang through Ramsey's head. ''He fell into a dark hole—'' The time to impact clicked off to zero. Nothing happened.

''Ramsey, you lucky bastard,'' the speaker said. ''Did you know she kept your damned picture the whole time? The whole bloody time, Ramsey. Tell her—''

The bridge blurred. There was a twisted, intolerable, eternal instant of agony. And confusion. Ramsey shook his head. The screens remained blurred.

"We—we're in the 81 Eridani system, skipper!" Trevor shouted. "We—hot damn, we made it!"

Ramsey cut him off. "Jump completed. Check ship."

"It worked," Marie Ward said. Her voice was low, quiet, almost dazed. "It really worked." She grinned at Dave Trevor, who grinned back. "Dave, it worked! There *are* Black Holes, and they *do* bend light, and they *can* generate Alderson forces, and I'm the first person to ever study one! Oh!" Her face fell.

"What's wrong?" Trevor asked quickly.

"I can't publish." She pouted. That was what had got her in trouble in the first place. The CoDominium couldn't keep people from thinking. *Die Gedanken, Sie sind frei.* But CDI could ruthlessly suppress books and letters and arrest everyone who tried to tell others about their unlicensed speculations.

"I can arrange something," Senator Grant told her. "After all, you're *the* expert on Black Holes. We'll see that you get a chance to study them for the fleet." He sighed and tapped the arm of his acceleration chair, then whacked it hard with his open palm. "I don't know. Maybe the CoDominium Treaty wasn't such a good idea. We got peace, but—you know, all we ever wanted to do was keep national forces from getting new weapons. Just suppress *military* technology. But that turned out to be nearly everything. And did we really get peace?"

"We'll need a course, Mr. Trevor," Ramsey growled. "This is still a Navy ship. I want the fastest route home."

Home. Sol System, and the house in Luna Base compound. It's still there. And I'll leave you, Daniel Webster, *but I'll miss you, old girl, old boy, whatever you are. I'll miss you, but I can leave you.*

Or can I? Barbara Jean, are you mine now? Some of you will always belong to Jim Harriman. Five goddam years that man kept his crew and passengers alive, five years when there wasn't a shred of hope they'd get home again. She'll never forget him.

And that's unworthy, Bart Ramsey. Neither one of us ought to forget him.

"But I still wonder," Marie Ward said. Her voice was very low and quiet, plaintive in tone. "I don't suppose I'll ever know."

"Know what?" Ramsey asked. It wasn't hard to be polite to her now.

"It's the song." She hummed her nursery rhyme. "What did he really see on the other side of the mountain?"

EDITOR'S INTRODUCTION TO:

COUP
by Mack Reynolds

I first met Mack Reynolds at the 1972 World Science Fiction Convention in Los Angeles. He had long been one of my favorite authors.

We had what at first would seem to be insurmountable political differences. Mack had grown up in an American Socialist Labor Party family—his father was twice the party's candidate for president—and although he had abandoned party allegiance, he considered himself a militant radical. By the time I met him he was a rather tired radical, but there were still flashes of militancy. On the other hand, Mack was never doctrinaire; and unlike many radicals, never lost his commitment to individualism.

Needless to say, we had many arguments; but they were quite civil, and usually ended when we'd both drunk too much and sung the old songs of rebellion. In music the snake has all the lines. . . .

For many years before his death in 1983 Mack lived in San Miguel de Allende, Mexico. To say that is not to say enough. San Miguel has become home to a number of American writers, and while he lived, Mack was a sort of Mexican national treasure, and certainly the unofficial dean of the writers' colony there; while Mrs. Jeanette Reynolds was well known as the proper person to turn to for assistance of any kind, from difficulties with the local police to finding a reliable housekeeper.

In his younger days Mack traveled extensively through the world as a sometime news correspondent and permanent researcher and observer. He was, I think, the best amateur anthropologist I ever knew, and his powers of observation rivalled those of any professional. One trip through the Soviet Union convinced him that the present system was despicable, and that even at its best institutional communism would be distasteful and unpleasant. He also spent much time in both Arab and Black Africa, and his stories of the possible futures of that unhappy continent are among his best. Eventually he retired from travel (but not from writing) and settled in San Miguel de Allende.

It is arguable that Mack lived there too long, and that his last stories reflect his stint in lotus land. He certainly didn't think so. I recall when he proudly sent me a copy of *Looking Backward From the Year 2000*. The inscription reads: "Here's my utopian novel. Where's yours?" And certainly there are interesting ideas in Mack's last works. I only wish he were around so that I could argue with him about them. If there's any justice in the universe, one day I will.

"Coup" is a story from the time when Mack Reynolds was arguably the best story teller actively writing science fiction. Caledonia is a lost colony; one which has built its culture from Sacred Books. The culture has learned to live with war and warriors and combat.

"Coup" tells of a warrior who is so inferior in weapons and technology that he ought to gibber with fear; but it is the nature of the warrior to emphasize one's own strengths, not those of the enemy. . . .

COUP
Mack Reynolds

I

John of the Hawks brought his steed to a sudden halt just short of the top of the hill they had been ascending. Some instinctive alarm had sounded. Something there is in the warrior born that warns of danger and if the warrior would live, he heeds it ever. Were this not so there would be scarce a clansman from Dumbarton to Stonehaven, for the ambush is a way of life on the planet Caledonia.

He slid from his animal and snaked his carbine from its scabbard. He tethered the animal lightly, so that no time would be wasted were it necessary to beat a quick retreat, and made his way quietly to the hill's crest. The last few yards he went on hands and knees, the last few inches he squirmed on his belly.

There were several bushes on the crest. He wiggled up behind one and peered through its branches and leaves. John of the Hawks sucked in air.

Below was a stream, flanked by trees and other vegetation. By the stream were standing four saddled horses and three draft animals. The latter were burdened down with what were obviously butchered cattle, and, since this was Hawk preserve, obviously raided beef cattle.

Now he could make them out. Three of them, and from their kilts, they were of the Clan Thompson. The kilts they were in the process of removing. The situation was obvious. They had butchered the animals and were now about to take a swim to clean up. Being deep in Aberdeen territory, they had not wanted to be slowed down by herding the beef back to their town, but had butchered them on the spot and packed the choice portions of the carcasses on their extra animals.

Moving slowly, quietly, John flicked three cartridges from his bandolier. He threw the breech of his carbine and inserted one of the shells. The other two he stuck, point first, into the ground near his right hand, instantly available for a quick reloading.

The others had left their saddle guns in their scabbards, but John had no illusions about the fighting qualities of the Clan Thompson. Thieves they might notoriously be, but also competent fighters. Once he opened fire, the bets would all be down and there were three adult clansmen down there, and he was but a lad, not yet raised up to full Phyletic level.

Three of them?

He hesitated at squeezing the trigger, though he already had the sights trained on one who was just about to enter the water. There were four saddle horses.

He let his eyes go over the scene again, and immediately received his answer.

Slightly up the stream, in a thicker clump of trees, was the other member of the party. She had drawn away from the men for privacy. John of the Hawks made a wry mouth. He had heard that the women of the Thompsons were shameless, but it was unseemly and not meet that one should accompany a raiding party.

He watched for a long moment. All were in the water now. The girl's body gleamed white in the clearness of the stream. She was young, probably having no more years than John's own seventeen.

He grunted his irritation. One does not fire upon men in the presence of their feminine kin, although in this particular case there was little, if any, danger of his bullets going so far off aim that she would be endangered. There was no stronger ban than that against injuring a woman, even though vendetta was involved. The male of a species does not destroy the female, not even man. At least, not on the planet Caledonia.

He thought about it. It was too far back to Aberdeen to expect to be able to ride for assistance, enough assistance that the raiders, girl and all, might be captured without bloodshed.

But even as he thought about it, he knew the answer. It was foolhardy, without doubt, but it was the only thing he could do, given the situation.

He took up the two extra cartridges and returned them to his bandolier and began squirming backward. Once off the rise, he came to his feet and hurried to his animal. He put the carbine back into its scabbard and then unbuckled his belt with its claidheammor and skean and attached them to the saddle. He took his coup stick from its sheath and tucked it temporarily in his belt and then ascended the hill again.

They were all swimming and even at this distance he could hear their shouts and jests as they made at their horseplay. He grinned wryly as he began squirming his way down the hill toward them. They would sing a different song, if he was successful in his scheme.

He took what advantage he could of trees, shrubs and bushes, and finally achieved his immediate goal, a place in the shrubbery along the river, between where the girl and the men bathed. Now, he had a slight advantage. If the clansmen heard him stirring in the brush, they would think it the girl; if she heard a stirring, she would think it part of the noise the men were making as they splashed, dove and swam.

On hands and knees he crawled in the direction of the animals. This, now, was the crucial point. It was all a matter of how soon they spotted him.

And there was a matter of sheer luck, too. There were four saddle horses. If he made the mistake of attempting one which was so trained that it would only seat its master, he was destroyed.

The answer to that, or so he hoped, came to him as he crept nearer. One of the beasts had no carbine scabbard. The girl's of course! And a girl's horse was less apt to be clansman trained to accept no stranger on its back. At least, so was his prayer to the Holy.

There was a shout from the river bank.

He was on his feet and dashing.

The shouts trebled.

He flung himself on the back of the animal he had chosen, even as he mounted tearing free the tether that had tied the horse to a small bush. He sunk heels into the beast's side, screaming the battle halloo of the Clan Hawk. He pulled the coup stick from his belt and slashed at the other three mounts. He gripped their tethers, one by one, and pulled them free. He slashed their haunches, driving them before him. From the river's edge, the Thompson clansmen were coming at the run, shouting their anger and threats.

He pulled hard on the reins of his mount, turning it, and headed back for the raiders. Only now, they saw what he held

in his hand and tried to take last minute measures to avoid
him.

The coup stick came up and down, so fast as to be a blur.

He slashed them, one-two-three, calling in repetition so
quickly that the words came out all a jumble, *"I-count-coup-I-
count-coup-I-count-coup!"*

Then he was around again and away, dashing after the
horses he had just stampeded. He looked over his shoulder in
triumph and just in time, even as he was shouting his halloo.

Two of the three were seated on the ground, heads in
hands, wailing their disgrace and frustration. But the other
had turned and sped back to the river's edge. And only now
did John see the carbine leaning there against a tree trunk.

He cut short his battle cry in mid-syllable and flung down
on the far side of the horse, clinging to the saddle by but one
heel, his left hand grasping a handful of mane.

And just in time. The carbine barked its command. One of
the horses screamed. John came back full into the saddle
now. The wounded horse ran another twenty yards then stumbled and pitched suddenly, and fell.

John considered, only momentarily, halting long enough to
strip it of its trappings but gave up the possibility. For all he
knew, the rifleman had additional rounds of ammunition, and
John was still within range. He scrambled up the hill, kicking
his heels ever into the frightened animal he rode, herding the
remaining two beasts before him.

There was another element. Undoubtedly, already, behind
him the Thompsons were stripping the beef carcasses from
the remaining animals and would soon be in pursuit. John
doubted that the draft animals were as fast as those he now
possessed but one never knew. They had the carbine and,
give the Clan Thompson its due, they were as good marks-
men as ever participated at the annual shoots at the assembly
of the Dail of the Loch Confederation.

Up the hill, shouting again the halloo of the Clan Hawk, up
and over the crest. He galloped to his own steed and flung
himself from the saddle of the girl's horse into the one to
which he was more accustomed, without descending to the
ground.

He took up the reins of the three remaining captured beasts
and started off, making a beeline for Aberdeen and the security of the town of his birth. He was chuckling happily now.
He had taken his risk and all had come off as though rehearsed.

He had counted coup on three of the redoubtable Clan Thompson raiders and had stolen their horses and most of their weapons. How the town would respond! How the criers would shout his name. Though but of seventeen years, none would dare speak against his being raised up to full participation in the Phylum. The sachem himself would acclaim him, the caciques and sagamores. He would be a man among men and free to participate in the muster.

He pushed hard, not sparing the horses.

When he had ridden out of Aberdeen, a single lad on a horse, though warned by his uncles to take care, if he went beyond the lands of the clan there were none to say him nay. A clan does not remain strong by preventing the young men from learning to scout, to raid, to defend themselves from the foe. But he had been in comparatively little danger then. Had he run into a raiding party of Bruces, Davidsons, or Thompsons for that matter, he could honorably run for it, being one against many. And it would have been unlikely the others would have taken after him, there being small profit in chasing lads still not of full Phyletic age.

But he was now in possession of worthy booty and fair game for any clansman, save the Hawks and the sister clans, of course, did any spot him returning to Aberdeen.

He rode through the night, the pace being awkward since he continued to hold onto the reins of the captured beasts, rather than try to herd them. They were unused to him and nervous, after all the excitement, and he was afraid of losing one or more in the night.

He entered Aberdeen in the early afternoon of the following day, both he and the animals exhausted. He had paused along the way only for water. His luck had held and he had seen no clansmen, not even his own kin.

At the gate, the warder goggled at him. The other was a Fielding, not a Hawk, but he knew John well, having stolen a Hawk girl as his bride.

"Where in the name of the Holy did you find those animals, John of the Hawks?" he called.

"It was nothing," John grinned down at him. "I came out from ambush upon three, nay four, if one counts women, of the Clan Thompson. I confounded them and seized these, their horses, as well as two carbines and these other trappings you see."

The other was still staring. "Did you kill any?" he demanded, unbelievingly. He was fully aware of the fact that John was under no compulsion to tell the truth to him, a Fielding and hence not a clansman of John's even though of the same Phylum.

"*Kill* any?" John said loftily, still grinning. "I counted coup on all three!"

The other snorted. "As to that, I will wait to hear your declamation before the muster." He snorted again. "No one exaggerates before the assembly of the muster. That is the ban."

But John was a man now, before men, and he said coldly, "Do you suggest that I would break a ban, before the muster or anywhere else, warder of the gate?"

The other grunted, but backtracked, being in the wrong and knowing it, and also being conscious that whether or not John was exaggerating, that somehow he had acquired three priceless battle steeds, the proof being there before him.

"No, I make no such suggestion, John of the Hawks. Enter, and congratulations."

John was grinning again, even as he herded the loot before him. "There will be shouting of my name by the criers tonight," he boasted.

The other had his petty revenge. "I doubt it," he said.

John halted his horses and scowled puzzlement. "How do you mean?" he demanded. "How long has it been since either a Hawk or a Fielding counted coup on three raiders in a single day and seized their possessions as well?"

"A long time indeed, John of the Hawks, and your feat is praiseworthy, but, unfortunately, for your moment of honor, the muster is to go into session shortly."

It was John's turn to stare. "The muster! But this is only Apriltime."

"Yes, and ordinarily the sachems and caciques would not join in the muster for three months, but they are gathering to discuss the travelers from Beyond."

"Beyond? Beyond what?"

"You do not read the Holy books sufficiently, lad," the warder said condescendingly. "Surely you have heard of Beyond."

"But that's legend! Myth!"

"You'd better not let any Keeper of the Faith hear you say that. Besides, the proof is there before you. Two days before this, the ship from the sky arrived, landing between Aberdeen and Dumbarton. The travelers from Beyond sent out a group and now accept the hospitality of town ''

John gaped.

II

But for the moment the sensational news could wait. John was weary and hungered beyond the point where anything else mattered. He rode in the direction of his clan's longhouse, somewhat miffed at the timing of his moment of glory. Travelers from Beyond, indeed!

At the entrance to the longhouse, two of his closest friends duplicated the goggling of the warder of the gate.

John of the Hawks dismounted with considerable dignity, and tossed his reins to one of the others.

"Don of the Clarks," he said loftily, "be a good lad and take my animals to the pastures." He looked at the other young man, who wore kilts similar to his own, those of the Clan Hawk. "And Dewey, would you mind, first, stripping the animals of the weapons and harness and taking them to the council hall, until I need them in my declamation before the muster, upon being raised up to the Phylum?"

The one addressed as Dewey stuttered, "Where . . . where . . . ''

But John raised a hand, exaggerating his weariness. "Later, lads, later. You'll hear it all when each clansman recites his victories to the assembly."

He turned and entered the community house and headed for his family's quarters.

They called after him, something urgent, but he was too tired now to chatter with them, no matter the glory. He wanted food, to bathe, and fresh clothing. The aftereffects of the excitement and hard riding were upon him.

In the small room that was his own, he began to strip, but then paused, scowling. He could hear voices in the next room, the family living quarters, but they were not the voices he recognized, those of his mother, younger brother and two sisters. They were adult male voices, and now he could even realize there was a strange accent.

He went to the door and pressed an ear against it, frowning still in puzzlement. The voices were clearer now.

One was saying, "Well, you're the nearest thing to an ethnologist we've got. What do you think?"

There was a pause before another voice said hesitantly and dourly, "I'm no ethnologist and your guess is probably as good as mine. I'd say they're the result of a crash of some pioneer group, Skipper. A very bad crash, since they lost communication."

"Why pioneers? Why not some passenger ship?"

"For one thing, they've got horses and cattle. Even trees of Earth-side type, now adapted, of course, to this world's ecology. Besides, what would a passenger ship be doing this far in?"

A third voice broke in. "What was a pioneer ship doing this far in, for that matter? From what we've seen so far, they've been here a long time. They're obviously originally an Earth culture, but they don't seem to have much more than legends about their origins."

The first voice, heavier than the others and with a note of command in it, said, "Well, it goes both ways. I've never heard of them, either. They must go so far back that you'd have to go deep into the archives to even check on the possibilities."

The third voice said, "I just thought of something. They must go so far back that they might have had trouble with the warp. One of the very earliest colonizing ships. Before the bugs were all ironed out. They must have had trouble with the ship's warp and it was thrown all the way in here."

"Maybe," somebody else growled in disgust. "They're certainly primitive. Look at this. Look at these plumbing fixtures, over here."

A fourth voice spoke up for the first time. "What're you complaining about? We're lucky they've got plumbing at all. Did you notice those overgrown stickers all the men carry? Good grief, swords, in this day and age."

"They also carry rifles," the second voice said. "We're lucky we weren't assassinated before we ever got the chance to tell them who we were."

"Single shot rifles," the second voice said. "Krishna! Look at these plumbing fixtures."

"What about them?"

John of the Hawks drew back from the door and stared at it. He was tired to the point where his mind was half blank or the reality of the situation would have come home to him quicker. He scowled his puzzlement and put his ear back to the door.

A voice was saying, "They're *platinum*."

"Platinum? Don't be ridiculous."

"I think Harmon's right. Look at this, Skipper."

"Who'd ever use platinum for faucets?"

Another voice, the second one John had heard, broke in. "A people who have so much of it that it's comparatively worthless, that's who." There was an element of awe in the tone.

"Here, let me scratch it with this knife blade."

John had removed his belt with its skean and claidheammor, but now he went over to his bed and picked the harness up again and belted it about his waist, still scowling. He went back to the door and pressed his ear against it once more.

The voice which had disclaimed knowledge of ethnology, whatever that was, was saying, "A really primitive culture. They must have an unbelievable system of rituals and taboos."

He, who was addressed as Skipper, said, "Why do you say that?"

"Because their language has changed, over a period that must amount to centuries, so little from Earth Basic. And they still retain so many customs of the original Earth. Only very strict adherence to taboos and rituals would maintain such institutions so well. It's too bad we're not a larger expedition with a few anthropologists and such along."

"Oh, no it isn't."

The Skipper's voice said, "What do you mean, Harmon?"

"I mean platinum. Probably mountains of it. There are only eight of us. Four back on the ship, and us. Good. Only that number to split it with."

There was a long pause.

John could stand it no longer. He opened the door and walked through, staring.

There were four of them and he'd never seen such dress in his life. It was evidently some sort of uniform and all were garbed almost identically, so undoubtedly they were fellow clansmen. The dress was colorless, drab by any kilt standards, and each leg was completely sheathed. Above everything in strangeness was the fact that though all were obviously adult, none wore claidheammor nor even a skean.

It came to him then that these, of course, were the travelers from Beyond, in short, men from another world. Until this very moment, John had never really believed in such, in spite of the Holy books and the preachings of the bedels and the Keepers of the Faith.

And it came to him also that, although the others wore no swords nor daggers, the holstered devices on each hip were undoubtedly weapons—weapons that would have come under the ban in any Phylum John of the Hawks had ever heard of.

Two were seated in the most comfortable chairs the room provided, and two were leaning against the fireplace. All eyes turned to John when he entered.

He blurted, "What are you doing in this home?"

The youngest of the four, one of those leaning against the fireplace, let his hand drop nonchalantly to the holstered object on his hip. It was, John decided, probably some sort of gun. He had never seen a gun smaller than a carbine.

The eldest, who was seated, scowled at the intruder. "Who, in the name of Krishna, are you?"

Although their voices were heavily accented to John's ear, the words were almost all understandable, although he didn't know what Krishna meant.

He said, "I am John of the Hawks, and these are my assigned quarters."

The other seated man said, "Oh. Of course, sorry, John, uh, of the Hawks. The . . . what did they call him? The head man."

One of those at the fireplace said, "The sachem."

"That's right. The sachem offered us this apartment. Your family has been moved in with one of your cousins, I think he said. You were away. We're very grateful, of course."

John of the Hawks flushed. "I am shamed.. My home has been honored by being chosen to provide hospitality for travelers."

The oldest, a heavy-set, heavy-faced man, said, "I am Skipper William Fowler of the exploration Spaceship *Golden Hind*. And these are three of my officers." He indicated them. "First Officer DeRudder; Perez, First Engineer; and Mr. Harmon, my Second."

Harmon, who was the one who had put his hand on his weapon when John had entered, was seemingly not too much older than John himself, possibly twenty-five and notable largely for a somewhat twisted, sardonic mouth.

Perez was a little man, and nervous of movement. DeRudder,

next in age to the one they called Skipper, was the largest of
the four, which wasn't saying much. None were more than
six feet tall, so that even John, who hadn't reached his full
growth, towered above them.

John said, still flushing embarrassment, "May the bards
sing your exploits. My family is honored. My excuses for
bothering you. Undoubtedly, you rest before the council of
the muster. My claidheammor is at your command." He
turned to leave.

The one named DeRudder said, "Just a moment, son."

Son? This was a term that could be used only to a fellow
clansman, and from an elder. Certainly the otherworlder
couldn't claim to be kin of the Hawks. John was taken aback.
However, he turned politely.

The other said, "In there. I suppose it's a bathroom. That
metal the faucet's made of. What is it?"

John looked at him blankly, but now the conversation he
had eavesdropped upon came back to him. It wasn't quite
clear just what the excitement had been about.

"Why, it's called platinum, I believe. The Hawks are
herdsmen, not scrabblers in the dirt, nor metalworkers. However, it is called platinum."

There seemed to be a narrow-eyed quality in all four of the
strangers now.

DeRudder said carefully, "And it is in good supply on this
planet, uh, Caledonia?"

John said, blankly, "Why, honored guest, it is certainly
the most common of metals, is it not?"

The other licked his lower lip, unconsciously. "Your sword,
there, is steel, isn't it?"

John nodded, still puzzled.

"Ah, is platinum more common than iron? Cheaper?"

"Cheaper?" John said, blankly.

The Skipper was leaning forward and John again got the
impression of narrowed eyes, though he didn't know why.

The older man said, "We don't know anything about your
means of exchange, but this platinum is so abundant that you
use it instead of iron for such things as household fixtures?"

"Why, yes, honored guest. I suppose so. As I say, we
Hawks are herdsmen, not metalworkers. I know little about
it."

DeRudder cleared his throat. "All right," he said. "Thank
you."

John shrugged inwardly and turned again to leave.

He heard their voices, in excited conversation when he had emerged into the long hall beyond. He made a face, accentuating his youth. The travelers from Beyond were certainly an incomprehensible group.

Robert, Sachem of the Clan Hawk, came hurrying up, his face anxious. As was usual, he was a clan elder and deserved the respect granted him by his clansmen. Past the age of raiding, he devoted full time to participating in the government of the clan and of the Phylum, and younger Hawks took over the burdens of herding the flocks and otherwise participating in the economies of the clan.

John saluted him respectfully.

The sachem said, "John! I left messages for you, but evidently you have failed to receive them. Your home has been given to travelers."

"Yes," John said unhappily. "I am ashamed. I intruded upon them."

The sachem looked at him. "There was no intended discourtesy, and hence it was not unseemly." He beamed suddenly. "Don of the Clarks has informed me of your triumph. If all wasn't confusion, with the coming of the travelers from Beyond, I would insist we adjourn to my quarters and, over your first glass of *uisgebeatha* of manhood, you tell me in detail. As it is, I must summon the visitors for the muster. But quickly, did you kill or wound any of the raiders?"

John smiled his satisfaction at the compliment of his clan sachem. "Robert of the Hawks, I counted coup on three of them."

He was again awarded the goggling of the warder of the gate and his two younger friends.

"You counted coup! On *three!*"

John nodded.

Robert stood suddenly straighter. "It will be until Junetime before the next regular meeting of the muster, but on my own responsibility as Sachem of the Hawks, I grant you permission to sit with the clansmen at this assembly."

John was stricken speechless.

The sachem turned to hurry on, but as he went he muttered, "Three! In all my life I have counted coup but twice. *Three!*"

John, in a daze of glory, made his way to the apartment of the cousin with whom he suspected his family was quartered.

He was correct, for although no one else was present he recognized various possessions of his mother, sisters and brother. He found a container of his own things as well, and after stripping and bathing, put on fresh clothing.

He then went to the community kitchen and found food. There was no one else here, either, and he realized that all must be in the town square for the unusual muster of the sachems, caciques and sagamores.

Tired as he was, he made his way in the same direction, unable to resist the opportunity of joining the clansmen as a fellow. Ordinarily, he could have expected at least another five years of acting as a herdsman and scout before being raised up to full clansman.

The muster was in progress.

The four strangers were seated together in positions of honor in the circle of the eight sachems of the Aberdeen Phylum. Behind them were seated the second circle of the Phylum caciques, sagamores and noted raiders. Behind them were seated circles of clansmen, each clan together. Beyond, a respectful distance, were standing the women, young men and children of the Phylum and beyond them crowded against the walls of the council building, the great kirk, the Phylum arsenal and the structure that held the archives, were the clanless ones.

Trying not to be ostentatious, but miserably failing, John made his way through the ranks of the women, children and younger men to where the Clan Hawk sat, passing his mother, brother and sisters as he went. They stared at him, uncomprehending, as he joined the full clansmen and took a place.

There were a few raised eyebrows from his adult kinsmen, but none spoke. He knew they would hold him to account, later, probably not having heard of the sachem's permission for him to join them.

The eldest of the Phylum sachems, Thomas of the Clarks, was speaking, he alone of the inner circles on his feet. The speech was predictable. He was welcoming the outworlders, tendering them the hospitality of Aberdeen as travelers in a strange land. Evidently, a bedel, or possibly one of the Keepers of the Faith, had already completed the praise.

When Thomas of the Clarks was finished—and he was a garrulous speaker—he resumed his place among the other clan sachems and all eyes went to the newcomers.

The one who had announced himself as Skipper William Fowler came to his feet and cleared his throat. He looked about at the assembled muster and bobbed his head in a sort of greeting, in all directions.

"You must forgive us, if we are unacquainted with some of your customs," he said. "As you know, we come from a great distance."

Which was a strange thing to say, John thought. Surely customs were the same everywhere. The bans laid down by the Holy were as necessary on one world as another, and surely the Holy presided over all creation.

The commander of the strangers was saying, "Briefly, we are part of the crew of the exploration Spaceship *Golden Hind* and our assigned task is to map out this sector. We represent the League, a confederation of planets settled by the human race, originally from Earth. You will, of course, be invited to join the League. Frankly, we had been of the opinion that the *Golden Hind* was the first craft ever to penetrate this far into the galaxy. But here you are."

Robert, Sachem of the Clan Hawk, came to his feet. His face duplicated the expression of puzzlement of all the sachems and caciques.

He said, "But, honored guest, this League of which you speak. Surely you must realize that this muster represents only the Phylum of Aberdeen and we can speak only for ourselves. The meeting of the Dail, of all the Phyla of the Loch Confederation, would still only represent this immediate region. And even the Dail could speak only for *our* confederation. We know of twenty-three other confederations to the north, south, east and west, and how many more lie beyond, what man can say? Save for our two sister confederations, with whom we are at perpetual peace, of course, how could we possibly hold council with the others to decide whether or not to join this League?"

It was the Skipper's turn to frown lack of understanding. "You mean you are at war with all other, uh, confederations?"

"War?" Robert of the Hawks said in puzzlement.

"War. Conflict between nations, uh, that is, confederations."

One of the caciques said, "Ah, he means raids."

The Skipper looked at him. "More than that. A conflict in which the full, uh, confederation would throw its united power against another confederation."

A bedel came to his feet, his face in horror. "But that would be against the ban."

The otherworld officer, who had been introduced to John as DeRudder, said hurriedly, "A taboo. Easy, Skipper."

The leader of the strangers said smoothly to the bedel, "I was not advocating war, simply requesting information about the way of things on Caledonia."

Thomas of the Clarks came to his feet. "Assuming that by some means it was possible to unite all the confederations of Caledonia into a gigantic Dail and all agreed to join this League, of what advantage would it be to us?" He sat again.

The Skipper held out his hands in a gesture to indicate that the answer was obvious. "Why, for trade, for one thing."

One of the caciques spoke up. "Trade of what?"

The Skipper said, "Why, that would have to be decided. Trade for the things you have in abundance, for goods, ideas and so forth of which you have need."

A sagamore said, "But I can think of nothing which we need from the stars. Those items for which we must trade are easily available from other Phyla and we need go no further than the yearly Dail."

DeRudder stood and said, "Do you mind, Skipper?"

The Skipper muttered, a frustrated element in his voice: "You're the nearest thing we have to an ethnologist. Go on."

DeRudder said, "Perhaps we can start this trade right here and now. Evidently, somewhere near Aberdeen there is at least one mine from which platinum is extracted. Very good. We will draw up a paper giving all right to exploitation of these mines to we eight crewmen of the *Golden Hind*. In return, we will immediately have shipped to Caledonia, and to your town of Aberdeen, enough repeating rifles and sub-machine guns to arm each of your clansmen."

Thomas of the Clarks stood once more. "I do not understand. Some of your words are confusing. What is a repeating rifle and what is a submachine gun?"

DeRudder said, "You have single-shot rifles, and use cartridges in them. These guns fire the same type of cartridges at great speed, five hundred a minute and more."

The bedel was on his feet again, his eyes popping. "But that is against the ban!"

Thomas of the Clarks motioned him to his seat. He turned to the strangers, coldly. "You are travelers and hence eligible to remain in Aberdeen for the three traditional days of hospitality. But as to granting you the exclusive rights to the mines of platinum, obviously that is against the ban. The products of the earth belong to all. Even should we wish to grant them to you, the other Phyla would hardly agree. And, above all, we would not trade them for what you call repeating rifles which are most surely against the ban. Furthermore . . .''

But he was interrupted by the sounding of the conch.

Clansmen leaped to their feet, dashing for their individual longhouses. The caciques and sagamores were shouting orders. Women ran to the arsenal for extra bandoliers of cartridges.

A voice shouted from a housetop, "Raid! Raid! The Thompsons! Raid!''

III

John of the Hawks, with the speed of youth, got back to the longhouse where he had left his carbine as quickly as did any of the clansmen. He tore into the room he was sharing with his brother, ripped his rifle from the wall, grabbed up a bandolier, made a snap decision and sped to the roof, deciding he had no time to await the orders of the raid cacique of the Hawks.

The longhouse of the Hawks served on one side as part of the defensive wall of the town of Aberdeen. The wall was windowless on the side looking out over the fields and the roof flat, save for a parapet.

John sat down behind the parapet, slipped a cartridge from the bandolier, threw the breech and inserted the bullet. He breathed deeply, getting his breath after his run.

They were after the horses, that was obvious. There was shooting and shouting over in the direction of the pastures, and a great deal of dust.

Undoubtedly, the raid caciques would shortly launch a counter blow, but meanwhile John's position was an advantageous one, just in case the aggressive Thompsons attempted to force the town.

He heard someone come up behind him, but didn't turn. He had his elbows resting on his knees, the muzzle of the gun resting on the parapet.

The newcomer sat down next to him. It was one of the men from Beyond, the one called DeRudder. He was puffing.

He said, "What's happening?"

John said, "The Thompsons. They're raiding our horses."

"Oh. Members of one of the other confederations, eh?"

"No. The Thompsons are part of our confederation."

The other stared at him. "And they're attacking you?"

John put off answering for the moment. Through the swirl of dust a double score and more of mounted men came dashing at full tilt, shouting the battle halloo of the Clan Thompson. In the fore, at breakneck speed, rode two who held only coup sticks in their hands.

John's lips thinned back over his teeth in a grimace of excitement. They were not quite in range. He held his fire. At the pace they were coming, they would be to the wall, and directly below him, before he could get off more than two or three rounds from his carbine. He pulled two more shells from the bandolier and placed them on the low parapet.

DeRudder said, "Mari, mother of Krishna, look at them come! What are those small weapons the first two are carrying?"

"They aren't weapons," John said. "They're coup sticks." He darted the other a look of surprise.

"Sticks? You mean the only weapon they have is a stick of wood and they're riding into rifle fire?"

John had no time to argue the niceties of the glory of an unarmed man counting coup upon an armed enemy. His eyes narrowed and he drew a bead on the first of the fast approaching Thompsons. He thought he recognized the man, and wondered at the speed at which the other had been able to organize this raid, after his disgrace at the stream.

He squeezed the trigger gently, but at that split second the two leading raiders flung themselves to the sides of their horses, even as he, John, had done in the affair at the stream, clinging by foot and hand to the far side of the beasts they rode.

DeRudder said excitedly, "The horse! Get the horse and the man'll break his neck when he falls."

John was so startled at the idea that he took his eyes from the carbine's sights and looked at the space explorer.

"But one doesn't shoot a good animal, deliberately." He shook his head and returned to his gun. His eyes narrowed, and he began the squeeze again. The carbine barked.

DeRudder blurted, "You hit him. You hit his foot! Krishna, what a shot!"

John grunted in satisfaction, threw the carbine's breech, extracted the spent cartridge with a flick and inserted a new one. He upped the gun again for another shot.

The leading Thompson, wounded, had fallen from his beast but one of the others who trailed behind caught him up with a sweep and turned his own beast around to head back.

Others of the Clan Hawk were streaming up from below now, and joining in the fire. The raiders were firing back, while at full tilt. John kept his head as low as was compatible with staying in the action, being fully aware of the famed marksmanship of the Clan Thompson.

DeRudder, in high excitement, pulled his hand weapon from its holster. "Here," he blurted, "let me train this on them. I'll show 'em what a *real* gun can do."

Shocked, John of the Hawks dropped his own gun and knocked the barrel of the other's weapon up, just in time. A livid beam reached far into the sky, seemingly into infinity.

DeRudder stared at the Hawk clansman. He said, "I can wipe them all out with one sweep of this."

"And break the ban by using such a weapon! Do you wish a blood feud with the Clan Thompson when there are but eight of you?"

"But they're firing at us!"

"It's only a raid. In revengement for my stealing four horses from them."

DeRudder crouched down behind the parapet. "I give up," he muttered.

The charge had been broken, the oncoming raiders realizing that their attempt had come a cropper, that too many of the Aberdeen clansmen had come on the scene to make the surprise successful. Besides, John suspected that all this was but a diversion, while other Thompsons rounded up as many of the Aberdeen animals as they could before the main body of the defenders came up.

There was no further value in remaining here. John joined his fellow clansmen in dropping to the ground on the farther side of the wall and dog-trotting toward the pastures where the main body of the raiders was making its play. He left the spaceman behind, not bothering to speak to him further. John was still feeling his shock at the other's words and actions. The man conducted himself like a clanless one.

He thought he understood what must have happened. The group of four, counting the girl, had been a small unit of a larger group of the Clan Thompson, a major raiding party rounding up Clan Hawk cattle. After he, John, had stolen their horses they had re-contacted the other Thompsons and followed him to take their revengement at the disgrace of three of their clansmen being counted coup upon.

Their luck had been better than they could have hoped. When they arrived at the Hawk pastures it was to find that there were but a handful of guards. Almost the entire population of Aberdeen had been at the muster to gape at the visitors from Beyond.

Somehow, in the heat of combat, John had shaken off the better part of his fatigue and was among the first of the defending clansmen to arrive on the scene of action.

It was a debacle.

The Aberdeen clansmen and young men who had been guarding the herds had been cut down or driven off and the Thompson raiders, ever top men in this sort of thing, had decided upon an offbeat strategy. All had dismounted from their own tired horses and thrown their saddles upon fresh mounts. Each was now busily rounding up a half dozen or more captured steeds and were driving them off, leaving their own jaded mounts behind.

Here and there, hand-to-hand combat was taking place, claidheammors flashing, as the Thompson clansmen attempted to break off the action and make their escape. They knew themselves outnumbered, representing but one clan, while in Aberdeen there were a full eight. Those that were escaping were heading in a dozen different directions, rather than remaining in a single, easy to pursue, group. They were scattering.

John of the Hawks gritted his teeth even as he dashed into the fray. On wearied horses, the Aberdeen clansmen would have their work cut out catching up with all the raiders. And those who they did successfully trail, would, when caught up with by revenging clansmen, simply desert their booty and ride for it back to the safety of their own town of Caithness.

Aiii! He came up upon one of them who was having trouble with a Clan Clark steed he had captured. John knew the animal well, a highly trained stallion which fought against having any other on his back save his master.

Shouting the battle halloo of the Hawks, John brought up his carbine to fire. The other rode toward him, swinging his claidheammor, desperately fighting the animal, tearing its mouth with the heavy raiding bit, deliberately designed for use on captured steeds. He shouted the halloo of the Clan Thompson and slashed at the man on foot.

John caught the blade on the barrel of the carbine which he only now found was empty. He dropped the gun, tore his own claidheammor from its scabbard.

The horse reared up, shrilling its fear and anger at being dominated by a stranger.

John darted under its belly, coming up on the other side of the desperate enemy clansman. He slashed upward, cutting deep into the other's side. Slashed again, before the man could turn to defend himself.

The other's sword dropped from his hand. For the briefest of moments, he tried to keep his seat on the plunging animal. Then he fell, crashing to the ground.

John of the Hawks was up and onto the steed, taking over the position of stranger in the saddle. But at least he knew the animal's name and had, in his time, petted it in admiration.

Now, even as he battled, he spoke soothingly, calmly. Called it by name. Resorted to knees, rather than overly heavy use of the bit. Around him, as he fought to dominate the horse, the battle faded off.

Most of the Clan Thompson were escaping, heading in all directions as the Aberdeen clansmen attempted to catch horses, saddle them, get on with the pursuit. Unhappily, little harness was available, most of it being back in the town. The Hawks, Clarks, Fieldings and other defenders of Aberdeen, scrambled up bareback in an excited attempt to pursue the thieves.

John was one of the few with a saddled mount and a fresh one at that. He darted his eyes over the ground, looking for his carbine. He couldn't see it. He and the horse had moved over a considerable area in the past few minutes.

No matter. He had claidheammor and skean, weapons enough for any clansman. He headed after the foe, at full gallop, blade in hand.

But then his eyes narrowed. This was what the enemy had in mind. At best, with such tactics, he would catch one, or at the very most, two of the raiders. And even then, he might be fought off by a Thompson who still retained his firearm.

His mind raced. There must be something more effective than chasing off after a retreating enemy and vainly shouting his battle halloo. In fact, there was a ludicrous quality to it all and without doubt at the next meeting of the Dail, when the clansmen of all the confederation's Phyla recited their victories, there would be great laughter on the part of the Clan Thompson at the expense of the men of Aberdeen.

And it suddenly came to him that much of the laughter would be directed at him, John of the Hawks, who, although he had stolen three horses, had not been able to retain them for more than a few hours, so quick had come the revengement.

There must be something more effective.

And, yes, there was. The raiders were scattering, but in order to return to their own town, they must sooner or later, head in that direction, after eluding pursuit.

As a Hawk scout, and as a young herder of the cattle, John knew this countryside as well as he knew the longhouse of his birth. He cast his eyes around quickly, trying to spot one or more fellow clansmen that he could bring into his plan.

But there simply were none. His fellows who had also acquired mounts were taking off after the enemy, in all directions. He must go it alone.

John shrugged and dug heels into flanks and headed out over the countryside. Any of the Aberdeen clansmen who saw him must have thought him either daft or a slink, for there were no enemies, herding their booty, going in this direction. He grimaced, knowing the dishonor that would be his, did his plan fail.

He rode hard, pushing his newly acquired and dominated animal—over field, over heath, through clumps of trees, up and over the hills. *Aiii.* He knew this land well, but never had he ridden it at such breakneck speed.

The hills grew higher as the horse began to weary, and shortly he was in a narrow valley—narrower and narrower.

Until at last he reached his destination. Reached it and passed through the narrow way.

On the far side of the pass, he leaped from the horse's back, took its reins and hurried it into the shelter of the patch of trees to one side. Tethered it. He considered momentarily binding its mouth so that it could not whinny at the sound of other horses approaching. But no, the animal was too weary from its hard gallop to be interested in the company of its fellows.

John took in hand the scabbard of his claidheammor, to keep it from tripping him up, and began his ascent of the steep hill at a trot.

At the top, at the spot he'd had in mind from the first, he looked back over the way he had come. And doubts hit him. There was nothing in sight—not so much as a flurry of dust. He had, perhaps, miscalculated.

But no, how could he have? Given scores of Thompsons scattering, and then converging again on their home town of Caithness, surely at least one enemy clansman and his stolen horses must come through here. Simply must.

He settled himself down to wait, sitting on a rock. At this stage he would not be spotted. He considered his plan of action, when and if the raider, or raiders, did appear. He cursed himself, now, for not having taken the few more moments of time it might have needed for him to have located his carbine.

A more beautiful ambush than this could hardly be asked. The fleeing raiders would not be thinking in terms of Hawk clansmen *before* them, but would, undoubtedly, be constantly looking over their shoulders. Given a carbine and John could knock at least two off their horses before they could take defensive measures. But there was little profit in dwelling upon that. The fact remained that all the weapons he had were his heavy claidheammor and his skean.

He thoughtfully picked up a large rock and hefted it. But no. The foe would pass directly below, and it was possible he might hit one in the head—possible, but hardly probable. He was no great marksman with a thrown stone. There was no occasion for him to be. The youth of Aberdeen played with wooden weapons, not balls.

And now, at a distance, he could spot a cloud of quickly rising dust.

Aiii! He had won!

At least, to this point he had won.

Just in case, he gathered half a dozen suitable heavy stones and put them ready to hand. Then he crouched behind his boulder. It would hardly do for the other, or others, to be keen enough of eye to spot his movement up here.

The newcomers were approaching at a rapid pace and he could make out individual forms. Four horses and but one rider. As a now full-fledged clansman, or, at least, one suffered to sit among the clansmen until being formally raised up at the next regular muster, he couldn't admit relief that there was only one foe with whom to deal, but deep within the relief was there. In spite of his efforts of the past two days, he was a young man still with neither the physical capacity nor the experience of a Thompson clansman.

He ducked lower and peered from behind his defense. And now he scowled. There was something he couldn't quite put his finger upon.

And then it came to him. The lead horse, scurrying along before the others, herded by the raider, was his own personal steed, stolen with the other Hawk animals in the pastures. And, added wonder, now that they came closer, the rest were the three he had stolen himself, at the stream, precipitating this whole affair. He was taken aback. It was an unexpected coincidence.

He tried to measure the enemy clansman who was pounding along hard behind the rapidly tiring beasts. And again there was relief. Unless he was mistaken, at this distance, the other could be little older and larger than John himself. Possibly not even a full clansman, but simply a youth brought along to help with the stolen herds.

John gathered himself. His plan of action was now clear. He put his claidheammor down beside him and took up two of the stones.

The fleeing group had entered the narrow way, slowed slightly by the rocky character of the pass. And on they came.

Suddenly, he heaved the rock in his right hand at the first, riderless, horse, even as it passed beneath him. He quickly shifted his second stone to his right hand and threw it as well.

The lead animal screamed terror and reared, slowing all those behind, who also took fright.

He jumped to his feet, grabbed his skean from his belt, and leaped. Luck was ever with him. He launched himself full onto the back of the Clan Thompson raider, who, completely startled by the unexpected attack, toppled from the horse, John still atop.

While they were atumble on the ground, John raised the knife, preparatory to the stab. But it was uncalled for. The enemy was unconscious, a cut on the side of the head that had been taken in the fall.

But there was another reason for the stay of John of the Hawks' blow.

There was no stronger ban than that against injuring a woman.

IV

And as he came to his feet and stared down at her, he realized that she was not even a woman but merely a lass. Certainly no older than himself.

She wore the kilts of the Clan Thompson and her hair was cut short in the style of young men. And at her side was a skean. He gaped at her. In all his life, he had never heard of a lass so de-sexing herself. Shameless, Thompson women might be rumored to be, but most certainly he had never seen one at the yearly Dail, dressed as a man and carrying a weapon.

The horses, all trained battle steeds, had come to a halt at the far end of the pass. John, deciding she would be out for a time, at least, or, if she recovered, would still be of little danger, went and secured them and tied them where he had left his own animal. Then he went to the hill crest and regained his claidheammor and returned it to its scabbard.

He strode down then to where he had left her.

She was beginning to regain consciousness.

He had no water, or he might have bathed her head a bit. As it was, he sat on a boulder and waited, still scowling disbelief. So far as he knew, in all the history of his Phylum, never had a woman, armed or otherwise, participated in a raid. There was even a puzzling aspect about it. How did one defend himself against a lass? Suppose she came at you with carbine, claidheammor or skean. What did a clansman do, turn and run? What else was there to do?

But now she was stirring. Stirring and moaning. John of the Hawks squatted down beside her, lifting her head to his knee and stroking the forehead, awkwardly.

By the Holy, she was a pretty thing! High forehead, reddish hair, cut short though it was, a generous mouth, perhaps just a shade overly wide. Teeth that were white, white; a firm chin.

And, suddenly, blue eyes staring, unbelievingly, up into his own.

She snatched quickly for her skean.

John took it from her as gently as the situation warranted and threw the dagger down the pass.

He said awkwardly, "I would not harm you, lass. We of the Clan Hawk do not harm women."

She sat up now, and John came to his feet. He scowled at

her, not knowing what to say. What did a clansman say, upon capturing a raider who turned out to be a woman—a lass?

She stood up, too, and looked at him scornfully, but then began to sway. She put a hand to the cut at the side of her head, brought it back and looked at it and seemed about to swoon at the sight of the blood. There was not much, but it was blood.

John stepped forward and put a hand about her waist.

She began to react in fear but he said gently, "Easy, I wouldn't harm you. Come over here and sit on the heather a bit. You'll get over your dizzy spell."

She suffered him to take her over to a softer area and to seat her more comfortably than would have been possible in the stony pass.

He waited patiently, for long minutes, and finally realized she was peering at him from between the fingers she had been holding over her eyes.

Seventeen, perhaps only sixteen, he decided. What in the name of the Holy did the Thompson clansmen have in mind, bringing such a child on a raid? He was conveniently forgetting that he himself was not yet eighteen, and, except in an emergency, at the time of a raid, confined to such activities as holding the horses for full clansmen while they fought on foot, or bringing up ammunition or water, perhaps assisting the wounded.

He said, trying to force gruffness into his voice and failing miserably, "Now tell me all about this."

"About what?" she said defiantly.

"Come on, the proof is there before us. You are armed. You are on a raid of the Clan Thompson against Aberdeen."

She had taken her hands from her face and was now frowning at him. She said slowly, "And you are the young Hawk clansman who stole our horses at the river bank."

He grunted. "And counted coup on three of the Clan Thompson who had been stealing Hawk cattle."

She said, wonderingly, "But you are such a young clansman to have done so much."

There was no answer to that, though he wished he looked older. She was as pretty a lass as he had ever seen, he realized. And it came to him that it would not be too many years before he would be faced with the stealing of a bride from some clan other than the Hawks.

She said, "What will you do with me?" But there was

only the faintest of fear of the unknown, far in the background. The girl was no slink, but, then, she had already proven that.

John said, "First, I will demand you tell me how you are here, under these circumstances."

Her mouth tightened stubbornly, but he held his peace, waiting, and finally she spoke. She said, "I am Alice of the Thompsons."

He nodded to that. "I am John of the Hawks."

"I was but one lass, in a family of five sons."

He couldn't see what that had to do with it. Most families of Caledonia had at least as many children as that, and a large percentage of males was certainly preferable, considering the number of casualties taken by the clansmen in raids and in defense of the flocks.

But she was going on. "It was not a family for a lass. My mother had been captured in a raid from the Edin Phylum, and I was raised by my kin—and my brothers. I was more prone to play with the toy claidheammors than with dolls and other nonsense of girl children. Until I was all but a woman, this was true."

"Go on," John said.

"So it was that when my five brothers were killed in a raid of clansmen from Aberdeen, attempting to protect our herds. . . ."

"Five!" John said blankly "All five in one raid?"

"All five. Two came home that night but with wounds. They died before the week was out, when the fleshrot set in."

"Aiii, lass!" John murmured.

She took a deep breath. "I was still a child but I took an oath that I would have my revengement on Aberdeen. I took it before my clan elders, and none laughed in their pity. But as the years went by, over and over I told all that one day I would have my revengement. And I set aside childhood and practiced as best I could and as best my kin would allow me with claidheammor and skean and carbine, though it was seldom indeed I could cozen a clansman into allowing me to use his firearm."

John of the Hawks was staring at her.

She took another breath. "And always, after I had grown to womanhood, I pleaded with them to take me on their raids. And sent praise to the Holy that it would be so.

"Until, finally, perhaps worried of my health, the sachem

and caciques discussed the matter and one was appointed a spokesman to remonstrate with me, since it had become a scandal in the Caithness Phylum and I made all uncomfortable. When I held to my oath, then he demanded if I would be satisfied with but one raid against Aberdeen, and would then subside, let my hair grow long and participate in the activities of women.''

"Go on," John said, his eyes still wide in disbelief. He had never heard such a tale. Surely it could never happen in Aberdeen amongst his own kin.

She said bitterly, "I was not to find out until later that the raid was a minor one, deliberately planned for my sake. We rode to the outskirts of the heath of Aberdeen. . . ."

"And the preserves of the Clan Hawk," John muttered.

"Yes. And there we proceeded to do no more than round up and butcher the cattle. Far from danger of meeting the clansmen of Aberdeen."

"But that was when I, on a long scout, found you."

"Yes. And counted coup on Will, Raid Cacique of the Clan Thompson, and two of his sagamores."

"*Aiiii!*" John blurted. This would be something to relate to the muster when he was raised up to full clansman.

"So then," she said, "all was forgotten about the original purpose of the raid. The whole party was gathered together and we rode at full pace for Aberdeen—Will, the Raid Cacique, riding ahead in a furious rage."

She shrugged. "You know the rest. Your herds were practically unguarded. We rounded up the horses and each member of the party was given a few head to herd back to Caithness. Will was revenged, at least in part. If mine, alone, of the horses have been recaptured, then it is the biggest raid known in the memory of living clansmen."

"Yours will not be alone," John said sourly. "But I will admit, it was a gigantic raid—and well executed." The last was hard to bring out.

"And now," she said, her voice again bitter, "I suppose you will return me to Aberdeen to become a clanless one in your household."

For a long time he stared at her. Finally, he shook his head. "No. You were never meant to be a kitchen drudge. Before the week was out, you would be stolen from our longhouse by a Clark, or Fielding, or one from the other clans of Aberdeen."

''What difference that to you? They would have to pay the brideright, and a few horses or cattle—I would surely bring a few horses—must be welcome to a clansman as young as yourself. I see that you are already wed. Or is it that you do not find pleasure in my appearance, yourself?'' There was a wistful quality in her voice, as she touched a feminine hand to her hair.

''I am not wed,'' he said gruffly.

''Aiiii,'' she said, her voice bitter still. ''I am not so sure that the clansmen of your Phylum will find me desirable either, John of the Hawks. Undoubtedly, the younger men will think of me as you do. If I am honorably stolen by one of your Aberdeen clansmen, it will be by one of the older, and perhaps incapacitated by wounds, clansmen, who desire a strong lass who can be driven to hard work at his hearth and in his quarters.''

John of the Hawks had come to his feet again. He stared down at her for a moment, then walked over to where he had tethered the horses and returned with the one upon which she had been riding when he had leaped from his ambush.

He held the reins to her.

She looked up at him blankly.

''Return to Caithness,'' he said. ''I am not as yet raised up to full clansman, Alice of the Thompsons, and will not be until the next muster. Thus, I am not eligible to steal a bride. And, if I returned with you to Aberdeen, someone else would take you before it was meet that I could. So, return to your kin, Alice of the Thompsons.''

She looked bewildered.

He added, ''And I will come for you another day.''

She blushed then, as a good lass must. ''If you come, my kin will defend me.''

He twisted his mouth in amusement.

''And if they fail,'' she insisted, her head high, ''I will take my own life with my skean.''

''I have heard of the tradition,'' he said with amused skepticism, ''but I have never heard of it happening. Besides, at the next meeting of the Dail I will ask the Sachem of the Hawks to confer with the Sachem of the Thompsons and honorably arrange for the stealing of Alice of the Thompsons, arranging in advance with her clan for suitable payment of the brideright.''

In a sudden, seemingly uncalled for fury, she raised her hand to slap him.

But he was having none of *that*. He grabbed her strongly, and kissed her full on the mouth. She held tense for a long moment, then her mouth went soft, as though unwillingly. Finally, he released her and stood back, smiling.

She rubbed her hand across her mouth. "But . . . but, I am not your bride," she said in horror. "And it is against the ban."

He grinned at her. "It surely is."

She turned and jumped astride the horse, and glared down at him in feminine rage. "I have been shamed," she snapped.

"I doubt it," he told her. "For none know save you and me."

She dug furious heels into the steed and was gone.

And John of the Hawks stood and watched after the woman he loved until she was long out of sight.

Largely, as he rode back to Aberdeen, herding the recaptured three animals, his mind was on Alice of the Thompsons, as was to be expected of a young man yet to be wed. But he dwelt also on the men from Beyond, and as the distance was passing far for one who rode and herded animals, he had ample time to consider ramifications.

The weapon which the one named DeRudder had demonstrated was cause for thought. On the face of it, the man from other worlds was not adverse to using the frightful thing. And what had he said? *I can wipe them all out with one sweep of this.*

John suppressed a shudder, as unworthy of a clansman, but couldn't help consider what a handful of such weapons could accomplish on a raid. The men from Beyond named themselves explorers, and, if John understood the word correctly, were on a peaceful mission. But suppose they had come in raid? Who could resist them, with such weapons?

There were other aspects. On the face of it, the other-worldlings were far and beyond the Caledonians, whose most advanced vehicle was a simple two-wheeled cart. Even John could envision the span between a horse-drawn cart and a craft that could cross space.

The light was fading rapidly now and his exhaustion came upon him, and he could make it no farther. He drove his animals to a hidden gully, hobbled them, and threw himself to the heather.

When he awakened, it was well toward noon and he was well refreshed though he had slept upon the ground with not even a cloak. Thus is youth, and especially on Caledonia, where, long since, man and nature had eliminated the unfit.

He retrieved his horses, who had not wandered far in their search for graze, in view of the hobbles, and took up again his ride to Aberdeen.

As he drew nearer to the town, he occasionally spotted others, undoubtedly fellow clansmen, heading in the same direction. A few herded horses, but most rode dejectedly without.

Alice of the Thompsons had been correct. It had been a raid of raids and so far as the clansmen of Aberdeen were concerned they had counted few, if any, coups, killed few of the raiders indeed, and had recovered but a fraction of their stolen animals. It was a black day, of which Aberdeen bards would never sing, though most certainly those of Caithness would. He winced to think of the coming Dail, in spite of his own glory.

Closer to the town, he met his friend, Don of the Clarks, who besides the mount he rode, herded another animal before him. It was not a battle steed but an older draft animal, and there was an air of dispirit on the face of the other.

John hailed him, keeping any elation from his voice, for John of the Hawks was maturing rapidly. His own three recaptured steeds were sleek, in their prime, and well trained. Above all, they were not property of related clansmen, and hence it was not necessary to return them to former owners. They were enemy horse, and hence John's own save, of course, the one he rode.

Don asked, "Where did you find them?" He was of John's own age and they had grown up together, shared many an experience in common. However, somehow, he appeared strangely young now to John—callow perhaps.

The other was not a Hawk, so had he willed, John could have lied to him. However, he made a half-truth, realizing only now that he hadn't the slightest idea what story he would tell the sachem and the war cacique of the Hawks.

He said, "I took them from one of the raiders. All except one fast steed upon which the Thompson hurried off in the direction of Caithness, slightly wounded."

"*Aiii!*" Don of the Clarks said in disgust. "If only I had such a story. I spotted not even one. I found this ugly nag, straying. The Holy only knows to whom she belongs."

John nodded. "There will be shame in Aberdeen, this day."

From there on they rode in glum silence.

At the gate, the warder and his men greeted them with compliments, by which John assumed that few indeed were the clansmen who had done even as well as had he.

They turned their mounts and recaptured animals over to youths to be led back to the pastures and headed, after brief farewells, toward their respective longhouses, carrying their horses' harnesses and their weapons and coup sticks.

Bemused, both with thoughts of the action of the day before and his experience with Alice of the Thompsons, John made the same mistake he had on the previous afternoon. He automatically headed for his own family quarters and the room in which he had been quartered for the greater part of his life, forgetful, for the moment, of the fact that the apartment had been turned over to the strangers from Beyond.

He caught himself almost immediately, though evidently the otherworldlings were not using his chamber, the rest of the apartment being ample for their needs. He turned to leave the room by the door which led to the long hall.

But once again he heard voices.

He hesitated. Eavesdropping was beneath the dignity of a clansman, though there was no definite ban nor even an established custom.

However, he told himself, in excuse, they were not members of the Clan Hawk, nor even of the Aberdeen Phylum. And, for that matter, their strangeness was such that they bore looking into.

He pressed his ear to the door that led to the living quarters.

As before, the others were obviously alone and once again in full debate. It would seem that these men from the League, as they called it, were as mystified by the institutions of Caledonia as John and his fellow Phyletics were by the ways of the men from Beyond.

He decided it was DeRudder's voice he was hearing. The second in command of the *Golden Hind* was saying, "And I claim we better get out. Did you hear what their big mucky-muck said at the muster? They've got a traditional three days of hospitality for the traveling stranger. All right. What happens after the three days are up? And that's today, mind you.''

One of the other voices—Harmon?—said sneeringly, ''What could happen? We've awed them. They don't know what to make of us.''

The Skipper's voice said slowly, ''No, we haven't awed them. They don't know what to make of us, but we haven't awed them. You know what they're busily up to now?''

There was no answer to his question and the Skipper went on. ''They're rounding up a raiding party, to replenish their herds of horses.''

DeRudder said, ''You mean they're going to go after this gang that hit them yesterday?''

''No, not at all. One of the war caciques told me that wouldn't do. The Thompsons, or whatever their name was, would be prepared and ready to defend themselves. So they're going to attack another town. They're going to raid somebody else that they haven't had any trouble with recently.''

''Krishna!'' a nervous voice said. ''What a people. I'm in favor of getting back to the ship. I wish we'd brought the skimmer with us instead of the groundcraft.''

Harmon said, ''I'd like to stick around to see if there isn't some way of changing their minds on signing over exploitation rights to their mineral resources. We could offer them just about anything. They're practically poverty-stricken so far as commodities are concerned.''

The nervous one—Perez, John decided—said, ''What would we do with it if we got it?''

It was Harmon's voice again. ''Don't be empty. We'd ditch this so-called exploratory cruise and head for some of the nearest frontier planets, those with early free enterprise type economies. Can you imagine being able to dump an almost limitless amount of platinum onto an open market? And do you realize the scale of living of the really rich on those planets? Why, the Caesars never had it so good.''

The Skipper said thoughtfully, ''Harmon's right. Given the concession, we could find means of profiting by it. The problem is getting the concession.''

John of the Hawks was scowling. About half of this, he didn't understand at all.

It was DeRudder's turn. He said, ''I'm in favor of immediate return to the ship, too. We've already fouled things up here, in trying to learn what makes them tick. We'll have to go on to some other town. Some other Phylum, as they call it. We've got a little background now and can do better. By the way, do you know what Phylum means?''

There was no answer and his voice took over again.

"It means tribe, in this connection, if I'm taking it from the Greek correctly. I would say that they've got a system of several clans that make up each Phylum. These Phyla, in turn, are loosely made up into confederations. From what the old boy said yesterday, there are such confederations all over the planet. He mentioned knowing of twenty-three others.''

"So?" the Skipper said.

"So we'll set down in the territory of some other confederation and start all over again.''

"Start what?" the Skipper asked.

"Subverting institutions, to put it bluntly. Somewhere we'll find a Phylum that's just taken such a licking from a neighbor, that they'll accept our offer of repeating rifles.''

Harmon said, "By the way, where are we getting anything as primitive as repeating rifles and submachine guns? The only place I've ever seen such things was in historical fiction shows.''

"Don't be a dully. We could take half a ton of platinum to any of the frontier planets and they'd tool up and whomp them up for us in a week's time.''

"Why not more sophisticated weapons?" the nervous voice said.

"You're being particularly dense today, Perez. We don't want to give them the sort of firepower that'd enable them to work *us* over.''

"I guess you're right.''

The Skipper's voice said, "And what if we find the same thing elsewhere that we ran into here? That none of these Phyla, or whatever you called them, will sign over their mineral rights?''

DeRudder's voice went suave. "Skipper, there are ways. Obviously, we must abide by the League Canons, but at this distance, that will be no problem. And we can take a page from early Earth history. There are ways, for, ah, civilizing backward peoples if they want to be civilized or not. Remember the European pilgrims and pioneers and the Amerinds? For instance, I note that they have a distilled spirit here they call *uisgebeatha*, and, believe me, it's potent. Very well, where you have potent nip, you've got people who are hooked on it. All we have to do is find a sachem, or so, hooked on *uisgebeatha*, get him binged and have him sign over mineral rights to us.''

Harmon said, his voice expressing interest, "How do you know that under local laws the sachems have such power?''

"What do we care? They're kind of a chief, aren't they? With the papers signed by one or two sachems, we can go to one of the less punctilious planets and get some military beef to back up our legal rights.''

The Skipper said heavily, "Mr. DeRudder, I can see you missed your calling. But what if we can't find any such sachems?''

DeRudder laughed. "In that case, Skipper, maybe we'll elect one or two of our own. Once the chaos starts, who can say who the *legal* sachems are, and who aren't?''

"Just a minute,'' Harmon said abruptly. His heavy boots sounded on the floor, as he moved rapidly across the room in the direction of the door behind which John of the Hawks stood.

V

But some instinct had warned John, a split second before. He spun and scurried across the room to the door to the long hall and was through it before the other could expose him.

In the hall, he shot his eyes up and down, having no immediate plan of action. Where would he find the sachem of the Hawks? Obviously . . .

He was saved the problem.

Through the door to the living quarters of his family stepped DeRudder. On spotting John, he whipped his sidearm from its holster.

"All right, boy," he said. "Step in here.''

John of the Hawks looked at him. "I have no fear of your weapon,'' he said. "A shout and my kinsmen will be upon you.''

"But you will be very dead by that time, boy.''

"I am not afraid to die. I am a Hawk.''

DeRudder hefted the gun up and down. "However, you have seen what the weapon could do. Would you expose your relatives to it?''

John thought about that only briefly. He stepped forward. DeRudder stood to one side, the gun trained, as John entered the room where the others from Beyond were gathered.

He stood there before them, defiantly.

DeRudder closed the door behind him and said, "The overgrown dully's been snooping. What'll we do with him?"

"Let's get out of here," Perez said quickly. "The fat's going to be in the fire before we know it."

The Skipper looked at John, remaining seated in the same chair he had been in the day before. He said, "How much did you hear, son?"

"Do not call me son. I am not kin of yours."

"Oh, belligerent, eh? Not quite the same polite boy you were yesterday." The Skipper looked at DeRudder and then to the other two of his officers. "If you've got anything around here, gather it up quick. We're going back to the *Golden Hind*."

DeRudder jerked his head at John. "What do we do with our empty friend, here?"

The Skipper considered it, his face dour. Finally, "Bring him along. We can use a hostage. Besides, I'd like one of them to question a little more. Half of this whole setup leaves me blank."

"Let's get going," Perez said.

"I refuse to go with you," John said.

DeRudder chuckled. "Boy," he said, "you remember the beam that came out of this gun when I shot it up into the sky? Believe me, with it, in ten minutes I can cut down this whole pint-sized village of yours."

The Skipper said gruffly, "And it's not the only gun we've got on hand, son. Come along."

John said, "Ten minutes is a long time. The clansmen of Aberdeen are not slinks."

Harmon grunted contempt. "And they're not in Aberdeen, either. Practically nobody but women and children are in Aberdeen. Half of your men are still out chasing Thompsons, or whatever you called them. The other half have already taken off to raid another town. You Caledonians seem to spend most of your time butchering each other."

"So," DeRudder said, "if there's any fighting, it'll largely be with women and children, eh? Well boy . . ."

"I will come," John said.

DeRudder made a mocking gesture with the gun. "After

you, John of the Hawks. Our ground car is parked behind the building, in that area you use for your saddle animals that are in immediate use. Take us there by the shortest route. And careful, boy. The slightest trick and we unlimber our artillery and shoot our way out.''

John didn't know what the word artillery meant, but he could guess. He said stiffly, ''I told you I would come. And even though you are not my clansmen, I do not lie to you.''

He led the way, out into the long hall and down it to the entry which led to the paddock. They passed only three or four fellow residents of the Hawk community house as they went, and none of these clansmen. Harmon had been right. The men of the Clan Hawk were highly occupied.

In the paddock, John's eyes widened whether he would or not. The vehicle there was a far cry from anything he had ever expected to see on Caledonia. It was of metal, streamlined and beautiful. There were two doors, one on each side, and several windows. There were no wheels, which mystified him.

Perez opened one of the doors, saying, ''Let's get out of here,'' although obviously that was exactly what they were already doing.

DeRudder said to John, ''Take off that belt, boy. I think we'd better relieve you of that set of toad stickers.''

John kept his shame to himself as he turned over his claidheammor and skean.

The Skipper motioned him inside, and he entered the vehicle from Beyond and took a seat in the rear. There was seating for ten persons, and ample room for luggage, or whatever, to the rear.

The others got in, the officer named Harmon behind a set of bewildering dials, switches and a small wheel. In spite of the position he was in, John of the Hawks was fascinated.

The others settled themselves and Harmon dropped a lever. There was a faint hum and John's stomach turned over in surprised rebellion as the heavy craft lifted slightly from the ground. Harmon trod upon another gadget and they began moving forward.

The vehicle from Beyond progressed slowly to the entry of the paddock and then, as they entered the broad street before the longhouse of the Hawks, sped up. They headed for the Aberdeen main gate, going faster still.

The gate was open and, as they passed through it, John

could see the warder, wide-eyed, staring at them. Only at the last minute did he see that John was in the craft, along with the otherworldlings.

Once in the countryside, Harmon flicked another lever and the craft rose another foot or two and increased speed considerably. They were now progressing as fast as any horse upon which John had ever ridden. He set his facial muscles, hating to show these others that he was amazed. The countryside sped past in bewildering rapidity. In a matter of moments, they had covered ground that would have taken a horseman hours.

DeRudder, who still carried his weapon in his hand, albeit loosely, nonchalantly, grinned at John. "Now if that sachem mucky-muck of yours hadn't been so empty, we might have made a deal to turn over a few of these ground cars in return for platinum rights," he said. "Can you imagine the advantage of taking one of these on one of your raids?"

John said, "Undoubtedly, the Keepers of the Faith would have decided it was against the ban."

The Skipper said to him dourly, "Everything seems to be taboo on this planet. Why should repeating rifles be against the ban?"

"That, as all bans, is in the hands of the Holy," John said without inflection.

"Great," DeRudder grunted. "But somehow the Holy, by whatever name you want to call him, usually makes with his words of wisdom and his threats through the lips of some intermediary or other. Such as your Keepers of the Faith, or bedels, or whatever you call them."

John had never thought of that aspect, but he kept his peace.

DeRudder said in irritation, "So what do your Keepers of the Faith teach you was the reason for a ban against rifles that shoot more than once?"

John of the Hawks had never been particularly reverent; however, he had done the usual amount of reading of the Holy Books when he was taking such schooling as Aberdeen saw fit its youth assimilate.

He said, "It is written that in the misty days, shortly after the *Inverness Ark* came from Beyond . . ."

"The what?" the Skipper said sharply. "What was the name of that ship?"

"Ship?" John said.

"The name of the, well, whatever it was you came in from, uh, Beyond?"

"The *Ark*," John said. "All of the people of Caledonia came in the Holy *Inverness Ark*."

"Krishna!" the Skipper said. "I remember now. Possibly the first pioneer craft ever to be lost in space. Crewed largely by colonists from northern Great Britain."

John didn't know what he was talking about.

DeRudder said, "Go on. Why the ban against a gun that shoots more than once?"

John continued. "In the misty days, there were few people in all the land, and only slowly did the first Phylum multiply. And at that time it is written that there was a strong ban against man raising his hand to man, even though honor was involved. All lived in peace, as all will live in peace when the Land of the Leal is achieved."

DeRudder said, "Great. But about the ban against repeating rifles?"

John said, "But when the people grew so numerous that there was no longer space for all the herds, nor sufficient game for the hunters, then there was a meeting of the sachem fathers, of each clan, and it was decided that half the people, half from each clan, would gather together and move far off to a new land. And so it was. So that now there were two Phyla, rather than one. And time passed and still the people grew in number. So both the new Phyla split, and half their number moved away to new lands."

DeRudder was staring at him. "I'll be damned. So finally, you spread over the whole planet, tribe by tribe, splitting as soon as there got to be so many that your primitive economies were fouled up by overpopulation."

John didn't understand that. For that matter, he was largely reciting what he had always considered legend, or myth, and much of it wasn't clear to him. He went on.

"But then, as the number of the Phyla grew throughout the land, man began to ignore the original ban against raising hand against his fellow man, and the raids began. So it was that the Keepers of the Faith and the bedels gathered and it was revealed to them by the Holy that there must be bans to control the relationships between the Phyla. So it was that it was ruled that it is more glorious to count coup on man than to kill. So it was that the weapons of all were decided upon, and a carbine must fire but one shot at a time, so as to minimize the number that might be killed in a raid. All this so that the population would not be decimated.''

Harmon said, ''There's the ship. Krishna! What's going on?''

They were coming in fast, and John's eyes bugged. The craft was double the length of a longhouse, and all obviously of metal. Could any clansman swallow the nonsense that such an object could fly between the stars?

But while he goggled at the vehicle from Beyond, the others were taking in the clansmen who, concealed by hillocks, or any other cover they could find, were firing their carbines at the huge spaceship.

When the groundcraft approached from the rear, the startled clansmen were up and away, scurrying for new cover, or possibly even for their horses.

''Bruces,'' John said contemptuously.

''What?'' the Skipper said.

''Clansmen of the Clan Bruce,'' John said. ''A whole clan of slinks.''

''If that means coward,'' Perez said, ''I'd hate to see a hero on this planet. Here they are, attacking a spaceship with nothing but single-shot rifles.''

The Skipper said, ''Take her into the port, Harmon. We don't want to get out here, there might be some of those sharpshooters still around.''

As they got nearer to the *Golden Hind* they passed over several kilt-clad bodies, Bruces who must have fallen in a charge on the ship.

To John's amazement, as they approached the rearing otherworld spaceship, it seemed to grow even larger than his first estimate. It was at least, in cubic area, the size of three or four longhouses. And as they drew near, slowing now in speed, one of the metal walls slid open and where earlier he could have seen no indication of an entry port, now there was one, and a ramp of metal to ascend to it.

Harmon expertly jockeyed the groundcraft up the ramp and they slid into the interior.

He flicked his lift lever and the vehicle sank to the metal flooring. Harmon stretched and yawned. ''Home again,'' he said sourly.

Perez opened a door, manually, and stepped out. Another otherworldling came hurrying up. He was dressed as were the four who had come to Aberdeen, but there was a bandage around his head, and his arm was in a sling.

When all, including John of the Hawks, had disembarked, the Skipper scowled at the newcomer. "Where is the Chief?" he growled. "What in the name of Krishna's going on around here, Wylie?"

"The engineer's dead," the one named Wylie said excitedly. "Where've you been, Skipper? All hell's busted loose since you left. We were afraid they'd got you. T. Z. Chu's dead, too. If you hadn't come back, we couldn't even've lifted off."

"Dead?" Perez said in shock.

Wylie said, darting a glance at John, but then coming back to his fellows, "The raids started after you left. It was the first one, got us. They came charging in on horses, shooting, and with these big swords, and they caught the engineer and Chu outside. I tried to come out to help and they nicked me. Jerry and I managed to run them off with flamers, but it was too late for the chief engineer and T. Z."

The Skipper turned to John coldly. "I thought there were three days of hospitality for traveling strangers."

John said, "The kilts on those clansmen outside are those of Bruces. They are not of our Phylum. You are on Aberdeen land. We have granted you the three days of hospitality, in spite of your actions. But the Clan Bruce is not affected by the ban in this case. Do you know nothing at all of honorable usage?"

The Skipper turned from him in disgust and back to the wounded man from Beyond. "What else happened?"

"Jerry and I have been fighting them off ever since. At first we bowled them over like nothing. But they're smarting up now. They don't come within range of small arms, or, at least, not so we can see them. They just lay off and ping away at us."

Harmon said, "What harm can they do?"

Wylie said to him, "Nothing, against the hull of the ship. But we can't go out. They tried to build a big fire up against us last night. I tell you, they're tricky."

John was taking all this in, without overmuch surprise. The men from Beyond were fair game for any clansman save those from Aberdeen, and now that the three days were up, game for Aberdeen, too.

The Skipper grimaced. He thought about it. In irritation he

snapped at DeRudder, ''Put this dully in confinement somewhere, and everybody come on into the lounge.''

DeRudder upped his weapon and motioned to John with it.

John preceded him down a long corridor of metal. John of
the Hawks had never seen so much metal in his life. It gave
him a strange feeling of being shut in, a disturbing feeling.
The halls were very narrow compared with the spaciousness
of those in the longhouses. The ceilings were much lower,
and he felt as though they were squeezing him down. He
wondered how long it must take to come from the Beyond to
Caledonia, and wondered how the otherworldlings could bear
to be confined for whatever time involved. Did they not feel
the demand to dash outside and see the sky above, the
distances stretching away? It would have been a horror to
him. Indeed, it was a horror, even in so short a time.

He was conducted to a small compartment—smaller even
than his young man's quarters in the longhouse—and ushered
inside. The door was closed behind him, and he heard a noise
that was a lock, though this he didn't know, the institution of
locked doors being unknown on Caledonia.

And then came the most trying ordeal in the seventeen
years of John of the Hawks. For confined though the corridor
of the *Golden Hind* might have seemed to him, it was as all
space compared to this small hold which measured little more
than his height, in length, breadth and depth.

His soul screamed against his imprisonment, as that of the
eagle or hawk must when encaged in a space so small it
cannot spread its wings. As that of the timber wolf must when
brought to the zoo, from its woodland range.

All his tendency was to beat with his fists against the metal
door and scream to be released, but the pride of a score of
generations of clansmen came to his aid, and preserved sanity. He refused to play the slink before these foe.

VI

He found some release in closing his eyes and pretending
to be in his own quarters. There was a cot, much too short for
him, but at least he was able to recline. And finally sleep
came.

He was awakened by a noise at the door and at first didn't

comprehend where he was, but then it came flooding back to him.

It was DeRudder and he had his weapon in hand. He said, "Come along, John, the Skipper wants to talk to you."

John came to his feet and followed the other out into the corridor. DeRudder gestured again with the gun. "That way."

They proceeded down the metal hall again, finally to emerge into a fairly large compartment, large enough, at least, so that the awful feeling of confined space was not quite so bad. There were various chairs, tables, and other furnishings and the four spacemen John had originally met were augmented by two others, Wylie and another. John noted with satisfaction that he, too, was wounded. Evidently, the Clan Bruce was doing fairly well—for the Clan Bruce. John slightly altered his opinion of their fighting ability.

The Skipper, who was seated at a table, a glass of some darkish liquid before him, said gruffly, "Sit down, John. We want to talk to you."

"I will stand, Skipper of the Fowlers."

DeRudder said, "Would you like a drink?" He added sarcastically, "Our nip isn't quite up to that *uisgebeatha* of yours, but it'll take the lining off your throat."

John of the Hawks was somewhat taken aback by the offer, but he said, "I will take no hospitality from you. You must realize that there is now vendetta between the Hawks and the Clan DeRudder, and my kinsmen will take revengement of my honor."

The Skipper said, "Don't be empty."

John looked at him. "And you also, Skipper of the Fowlers." His eyes went to Harmon and Perez. "And you two also. My kin will take their revengement on your clans."

Harmon snorted amusement.

DeRudder said, "Among other things, we don't have clans to fight feuds, even if we were primitive enough to have such an institution. We don't use the same type of relationship as you do, boy. You still evidently have a gens system. We of the League have been beyond that for a few thousand years."

"You mean you are clanless? You are without kin?" John's lips were going white. "And you laid hands on me? A Hawk. Dishonored me by taking me prisoner and stripping me of my weapons, rather than letting me face black death in honorable combat? How can my kinsmen take revengement if you are clanless men?"

The one named Perez shook his head. "The words are Earth Basic, but half of what he says doesn't come through. At least not to me."

Harmon leaned forward. "Why should your relatives, your kinsmen, want to revenge you?"

"What else could they do, after my blood has been shed?"

DeRudder wiped the back of his hand over his mouth in frustration. "Look. Nobody is going to shed your blood."

John of the Hawks stared at him in utter disbelief. Finally, "Then what will you do with me?"

"We'll turn you loose, of course."

"To return to Aberdeen, weaponless to the Hawks?"

"Why weaponless? You can have your weapons. All we want to do is ask you a few more questions about how this dully of a planet works."

John shook his head. "Why would you do this to me? What have I done to you that you should desire to make a woman of me? Why not count honorable coup of me, or at least kill me?"

The Skipper, who had remained silent during all this, stirred. "We don't want to kill you, son. We want a little more information, so that when we go up against the next town we'll know more of the customs. You're free to go, sword and all, as soon as we're through."

John said, his voice shaken, "I will follow you. Somehow I will follow you. The word spreads, throughout the countryside, and somehow I will learn where you are and somehow I will follow you until I have killed you all, or you have killed me."

DeRudder rolled his eyes upward, in appeal to higher powers. "Great. So why don't we just kill you here and now, eh? And then we won't have the threat of you coming charging around a corner some day whirling that overgrown cheeseknife."

"This is to be expected," John said evenly. "And then my kin will come to find revengement and you will be killed as clanless ones are killed. And there will be no one to take revengement or pay the bloodright for you."

"It's still going past me," Perez muttered.

The Skipper was interested. He leaned forward. "Look, son, how many of you Hawks are there?"

John said, "We number some fifteen hundred full clansmen."

"All right. Now, suppose they all come charging after us.

You have seen some of our weapons. Believe me, we have more powerful ones. If we were interested in wiping out those dullies outside, we could do it. Maybe we will, later. But if your Clan Hawk came charging up, we'd polish them off.''

"Then,'' John said, "our two sister clans, the Clarks and the Fieldings would take up the vendetta.''

The Skipper grunted. Finally, he shrugged and said heavily, "All right. And what happens when we have polished them off, as well?''

John of the Hawks was obviously taken back by the ignorance of honorable usage these clanless ones showed. He said, "Each clan has two sister clans. We have the Clarks and the Fieldings as our sister clans. The Clarks also have two sister clans, the Hawks and the Davidsons. The Fieldings have two sister clans, the Hawks and the Deweys.''

DeRudder was staring now, as well as the Skipper. "What you mean is, before you're through, the whole Phylum of Aberdeen would be in on the feud, or vendetta, or whatever you call it.''

John looked at him blankly. "But, of course.''

The Skipper sighed his disgust. "All right. Now, what happens if we wipe out the whole village of Aberdeen. Say we dropped a scrambler on it.''

John said, reasonably, "Then our two sister towns, Elgin and Gleneagles, would take their revengement for us. And their sister towns, in turn.''

Harmon closed his eyes in pain. He said, in complaint, "Carrying this on, I suppose ultimately your whole confederation would be involved. O.K. Do you realize that this ship could destroy every town in your confederation, without bothering to come down to the ground?''

"And then, Mister of the Harmons, our two sister confederations would take up the vendetta.''

The six of them, unbelievingly, gaped at him.

At long last, the Skipper shook his head. He said, "This is fantastic. What you're saying is that ultimately a blood feud, what starts with our killing you—in self-defense, by the way—would involve every person on this planet.''

John nodded. "You might slay as many as you say. You might slay by the thousands with your weapons that know no ban. But, if you plan to land anywhere on Caledonia, sooner or later the clansmen would take their revengement. They would charge you on their horses on the heath. They would rush you in the narrowness of the streets of the towns. They would snipe at you from a distance with their carbines. Sooner or later, men from Beyond, they would take their revengement.''

The Skipper was disgusted, all over again. He said, ''If what you say is true, then there wouldn't be a soul left alive on this whole world. Obviously, it's ridiculous. How do you end one of these vendettas, once it starts? It seems easy enough to start. There has to be some way of stopping them.''

John said reasonably, ''Of course. At the first meeting of the Dail, the sachems of the respective clans involved, meet honorably, and arrange for there to be made payment of the bloodright to the kin of the slain. Accounts are balanced. Then all are cleared of the need for vendetta.''

''All right!'' DeRudder said. ''We plan to remain on this planet. We've got some business projects in mind. So we'll confer with your sachem and pay up for making the mistake of, uh, dishonoring you by taking you as a hostage. We'll apologize. We'll end the vendetta before it starts.''

John scowled at him. ''You jest, of course. How can you approach Robert, Sachem of the Hawks? You have admitted that you have no kin. You have no sachem to represent you. It is against the ban for such payment of bloodright to be arranged by other than the sachem of your clan.''

The Skipper ran his palm over his forehead. ''Mari, mother of Krishna!'' he muttered. He looked at DeRudder. ''Throw this dully out!''

John said levelly, ''If you free me, I shall seek you out. I shall inform my clansmen of my dishonor and they will take their revengement. At the next Dail, I will announce my shame and the word will go out. And at the Dails of the other confederations the word will go out that the Hawks' bloodline has been shamed. And from one Dail to the other, the word will go out. Until nowhere on all Caledonia will you be safe from the revengement.''

Harmon said urgently, ''Look, this is completely empty. There must be some way to turn this off. So we're clanless men. O.K. In your towns you have clanless ones. Servants and so forth, evidently. What happens if one of them attacks a clansman? How is the whole thing settled?''

John turned his haughty stare to the youngest of the other

worldlings. "Why, all honorable men unite and kill the shame-less clanless one."

Harmon winced. "I should've known better than to ask," he muttered bitterly.

For a long time, again, the six otherworldlings contemplated him.

DeRudder said, "That warder at the gate saw him go out with us."

No one said anything to that. The implication was obvious. The Skipper's face was working in frustration. Finally, he snapped, "Gentlemen, we have just stopped being entrepreneurs and have become explorers again." He looked at his first officer. "Mr. DeRudder, throw this barbarian out, then prepare the ship for space."

DeRudder looked at him. "We're leaving?"

"Can you think of an alternative?"

Harmon snarled. "It's one big nugget of platinum."

"That will be all, Mr. Harmon."

"Yes, sir."

"Come along," DeRudder growled at John of the Hawks.

John said, his lips white again, "You mean you are not going to honorably kill me?" He snatched his coup stick from his belt and slashed the first officer across the cheek. "I count coup!" he snapped. "Though, indeed, it is a worthless coup, since you are clanless."

DeRudder's face went livid. The gun came up.

"*Mr.* DeRudder, that will be all," the Skipper's voice bit out.

DeRudder conducted him down another corridor and finally to the compartment into which they had entered in the ground car. The first officer of the *Golden Hind* activated the sliding door, which opened in the hull. The ramp snaked out.

He handed John of the Hawks his belt and scabbard, keeping the handgun trained on him, always.

John said flatly, "The Hawks will seek you out. The Clan Hawk of every confederation on all Caledonia will hear of the shame done their bloodline and will be watching for you."

"Shut up!" DeRudder snapped. "Shut up, or I'll burn you down right here. Then your Clan Hawk will have to figure out some way of crossing all space to get at me!"

John turned in dignity and walked down the ramp. He didn't turn to look until he was over the nearest hillock. He was moderately jittery about running into some of the Bruces that had been besieging the *Golden Hind*, armed as he was only with claidheammor and skean, and having no horse.

However, his nervousness was unnecessary. On the far side of the hill were Don of the Clarks and Dewey of the Hawks, along with a dozen more of the younger men of the Phylum. All were flat on their stomachs, on the crest of the hill, staring their amazement at the gigantic ship from space.

Don blurted, "We knew they had you, and were planning the rescue."

"What happened to the Bruces?"

"They made off when we approached. I believe they thought us the full power of Aberdeen."

John squatted down and watched also. "They return from whence they came," he said.

"Why did they take you?" Dewey of the Hawks demanded.

"They wanted more information about the ways of Caledonia, so that they could rob us," John said. He continued to watch the spaceship.

"And what did you tell them?"

John shrugged. "I cozened them. I told them a good deal of nonsense, to make them feel it impossible to remain on Caledonia."

Dewey said, "You mean you *lied?*"

John looked at him coldly. "They are not Hawks. It is not against the ban."

He turned his eyes back to the *Golden Hind*. The spaceship shivered, then slowly, with great dignity, rose into the air.

A sigh went through the ranks of the Aberdeen youths.

When it had reached an altitude of some two hundred feet, the great craft tilted slightly upward and began to progress straight ahead, and up. It gained speed in a geometric progression.

Don of the Clarks stood and, watching still, as were they all, with considerable awe, said, "They have gone."

John was looking off into the sky, at the disappearing dot, as well.

"But they will return," he said, with a wisdom beyond his years. "They, or others like them. For now we have been found and the old days are gone forever."

EDITOR'S INTRODUCTION TO:

THE PREVENTION OF WAR
Stefan T. Possony, Jerry E. Pournelle, and Francis X. Kane

This essay has a long history.

In 1964 I was general editor of a strategic survey of ballistic missile technology in the United States. "Project 75" was written by the Ballistic Systems Division of the US Air Force Systems Command, and was modeled on Air Systems Division's ground-breaking "Project Forecast." The director of "Forecast" was Colonel Francis X. Kane.

"Forecast" and "75" were first efforts to develop a strategy of technology. They looked at present technology; examined the strategic environment; looked ahead to probable strategic environments ten years down the road; and identified technologies that must be developed for the future. These were ambitious goals, but nearly everyone now agrees that "Forecast" and "75" met them.

In 1968 Stefan T. Possony and I began a book called *The Strategy of Technology*, which we published in 1970. When the book was published, Col. Francis X. Kane, Ph.D., was a serving officer in the US Air Force, and already embroiled in the bitter struggle between General Benjamin Schriever of Systems Command and General Curtis LeMay of Strategic Air Command. Kane was a co-author of *Strategy of Technology*, but it was thought expedient that his name not appear on the book.

Strategy of Technology was adopted as a text in the Air Academy, Air War College, and for a short while in the Army War College. It is said to have been highly influential; certainly we do not regret the work we put into it. Duke Kane, Steve Possony, and I are now working on a revised edition. The revisions consist largely of updating the examples; we have found no reason at all to revise the conclusions of the book.

Strategy of Technology argued that the United States is, whether we like it or not, engaged in a decisive Technological War; a "silent and apparently peaceful war, but one which may well be decisive." The book also first introduced the notion that the US ought to abandon the doctrine of Assured Destruction and adopt in its place a doctrine of Assured Survival. To this day I regret that Possony and I were unable to persuade Nixon and Kissinger to make that change. Even so, the idea slowly caught on, as a new generation of military officers and politicians took control; and while no single work brought about the President's "Star Wars" speech of March 23, 1983, *Strategy of Technology* played its part.

"The Prevention of War" was the final chapter of *Strategy of Technology*, and is presented here unrevised, but with my comments [indicated thusly].

In a recent speech, Secretary of Defense Caspar Weinberger said, "To the extent that we in the United States desire true peace with freedom, peace based on individual and sovereign rights and on the principle of resolution of disputes through negotiation, we must acknowledge and follow our interests in creating conditions in which democratic forces can gain and thrive in this world. A world not of our making, but a world in which we must fight to maintain our peace and our strength. And a world in which the very best way to maintain peace is to be militarily strong and thus deter war."

THE PREVENTION OF WAR
Stefan T. Possony, Jerry E. Pournelle, and Francis X. Kane

Why Wars Are Not Fought

The primary stated objective of the United States is to preserve the state we call peace. The Strategic Air Command, which controls more power than all other military organizations throughout history, has as its motto, "Peace Is Our Profession." Our diplomatic machinery is geared to negotiations for peace, and our alliances are defensive. If intentions alone would produce peace, we would have it.

Our pursuit of peace is complicated by two important factors. The first of these is confusion about the meaning of peace. In legal terms we are at peace whenever the Congress has not declared war. Yet we can be actively engaged in a shooting war, and as this book has shown, the Technological War goes on, without regard to legal niceties, as a permanent conflict.

Many of our international legal institutions were conceived and solidified at a time when there was a far greater distinction, even a chasm, between peace and war. In those nearly-forgotten times, when nations went to war they acquired "rights of belligerency," which they could invoke against other nations. Perhaps today there should be some recognition of the rights of cold-war belligerency and the Technological War. If laws ignore the real situations in which people live and reflect fictitious assumptions, the legal order is decaying and society becomes vulnerable. The point is not to curtail rights, freedom, and democracy, but to keep them working during critical times and to provide a reasonable legal basis for the requirements of security.

The other impediment to the achievement of peace is the paradox known since Roman times: "If you would have

peace, prepare thou then for war.'' The unprepared rich
nation without armed allies has never survived for long.
Wealthy nations have ever been forced to depend on their
readiness for war to preserve peace and survival. Yet history
seems to indicate that the greater the state of armaments
acquired, the greater the chance for war; and consequently
many well-meaning people in the contemporary United States
believe that the surest road to peace in the nuclear era is arms
limitations, which may hopefully lead to disarmament.

This misconception stems from an insufficient appreciation
of the modern era. The nuclear weapon has changed the
nature of warfare by providing the defensive power with a
capability to deny victory to the aggressor, even if the aggressor has successfully destroyed all but a small fraction of the
defender's military forces. Unlike conventional weapons, nuclear weapons do not increase the chances of war as both
sides acquire them.

This is so because mutual increases in the nuclear power
available to the superpowers do not cause mutual increases in
their expectations of victory. In fact, the opposite is true. All
but madmen recognize that as mutual capability for destruction increases, the possibility of gain through initiating that
destruction becomes smaller. Whatever the effect of arms
races in conventional weaponry, two-sided arms races in the
nuclear era have a stabilizing effect in so far as the outbreak
of total war is concerned.

Wars are fought because decision makers conclude that
they will be better off after the war than they would be if they
did not engage in it. This has been true whenever rational
decision processes have governed the war decision. The calculation of success is not a matter of objective reality only,
but is in large measure a process in the mind of a strategist
controlling military power. It is not sufficient merely to be
sure that no one can win against you; all those who might
attack must be convinced of it as well. In addition, the
definition of win may be different for a potential aggressor
than for a popularly-elected chief of state; and it is necessarily
different for one aggressor fighting for nationalism or nation-
alist imperialism than for another aggressor who fights for
international Communism or Communist imperialism.

The calculation of chances of success is spoiled by uncertainty; indeed, uncertainty about the outcome of a war is a
powerful deterrent in the absence of clear indication of the

enemy's power. When both sides are engaged in nuclear arms research and deployment, neither will be very certain that he has won the Technological War and can engage in nuclear strikes or blackmail. It is when one side drops out of the race, giving the other a clear shot at technological supremacy, that a strategist can begin to plan on terminating the contest by a nuclear strike.

Deciding on war is also a matter of will, which is essentially willingness to take risks and troubles. Virtually always, the will factors are vastly different for the two parties engaged in conflict. Circumstances that would cause one to initiate a war might not tempt the other. Dictatorial regimes are notoriously generous with human lives; democratic governments fear casualties and usually fight only, and frequently belatedly, to preserve their own security. The will factors change when political systems are on the rise or decline. A dictatorship, for example, is optimistic early in its youth—it may combine determination with caution, or it may be exuberant. But it reacts differently when it is senescent: it then has the rationality of despair, and it may prefer a last chance through war, and even defeat on the battlefield, to ignominious overthrow. World War I would hardly have occurred if Russia, Austria-Hungary, the Ottoman Empire, and China had not been decaying. There will be decaying regimes in the future. In particular, the Communist dictatorships won't last, but the period of their departure will be difficult and dangerous, and the rationality of their last leaders may be influenced less by probabilities of success in a nuclear contest, than by considerations of last chance stratagems, envy, revenge, and pure hatred. There is no such thing as equal rationality for all.

Calculation of military results, then, is only a part of the decision to go to war. Strategy serves as a tool for the political decision maker, and the calculation of military success sets the probable price in blood and treasure that must be paid in war. The political objectives are the factors that determine what price a government is willing to pay; and these objectives are not set in absolute terms. If world domination is the objective, then no price is too high provided that the rulers of the aggressor nation will survive and remain in control and all other countries will be reduced to impotence. Conversely, if the probable result of the war will be the overthrow of the ruling structure, no victory, no matter how cheap in lives and property, is worth the winning.

The calculation of political objectives, and the disparity of objectives between the major powers of the present world, are the primary factors in the decision to begin wars. However, they have received less attention than mathematical calculation of military factors, which has become prevalent. It is supposed by many that even if the political objectives of the USSR can never be understood with certainty, at least the military calculations on which they must base their decisions can be replicated with some assurance. This assumption needs to be examined in some detail.

The Nature of Strategic Decisions

Military calculations must take into account numerous objective factors such as force levels, weapons performance, defense systems, and the like. A strategist's advice will thus be based in part on his predictions of the material factors of battle. Success in war, however, is dependent on the competence of generals and commanders as well as on their equipment. Bad generals can lose wars even though they have the best armies, as witness the performance of the "finest army in Europe" (that of France in 1940), while good generalship can more than make up for numerical and even technical inferiority. The strategist calculates his chances of success on the basis not of statistics but of an operational plan.

His plan must take into account the quantitative factors, but it will also seek to create and exploit opportunities. War is a matter of will as well as equipment, and paralysis of the enemy's will through surprise is one of the most successful of all techniques. In war, there are real uncertainties as well as statistical probabilities. Many factors can never be quantified. The strategist is dealing with the enemy's creative forces, and will counter them with his own. The calculation of destruction by means of slide rule and computer can only be a part of this process.

If this appears vague and uncertain to those more used to scientific calculation, it is because war is uncertain. War is, after all, an operation primarily against the will of the opponent. In some few cases, of course, the opponent is so reduced in capability that his will is no longer an important factor, but most wars have ended long before the loser's capability to damage the victor was destroyed. The great

losses have occurred after surrender, in pursuit or by deliberate execution of prisoners, rather than before the decisive
moment of battle. But once a combatant has lost the will to
fight, his means are unimportant; and often this failure of will
has been caused by surprise, by the opponent doing the
unthinkable, and by so doing producing overwhelming paralysis.

It is generalship, not a calculus of forces, that decides the
outcome of wars. A good general identifies opportunities to
paralyze the will of his opponent and exploits them. Indeed a
good strategist creates such opportunities. Generalship oper-
ates against the enemy's forces as well, of course, but even
then the war is primarily against the will. When the enemy
ceases to fight, the war is over, no matter that the vanquished
may actually be stronger than the victor—as Darius was at
Arbela. Success in war is above all dependent on generalship;
it is not that objective factors such as force relationships do
not count, but that generalship is far more significant. And
generalship means optimal utilization of available strengths
and out-thinking the enemy. Bad generalship is a repeat
performance, whereas good generalship is an act of creation,
hence unpredictable by either side.

Historical experience is explicit on the crucial impact of
generalship: a bad general can lose despite superiority in
material force and a good general can win despite considerable inferiority. Given reasonable means, and sufficient strike
and reserve forces, so that the aggressive side would not be
crushed even if mistakes were committed, the aggressor will
calculate his chances of success not on the basis of statistics,
but on an operational plan, as we have pointed out. If he is a
sound planner, his plan will take into account all the qualitative factors, but go beyond them to employ surprise in all
elements such as strategy, technology, tactics, training, direction, concentration, and phasing. If the would-be aggressor
estimates that the defender will be unable to anticipate his
plan and will not have ready countersurprise operations to
upset the implementation of the operation plan, he will conclude that his chances of success are high.

It is very important to understand that in these matters the
calculus of generalship is far more important than the calculus
of force relations. A homely example would be an investor
who plays the stock market through mutual funds and thus
essentially benefits by or loses from the overall movements of
the market. Such an investor can calculate his probable suc-

cesses on the basis of curves depicting the performance of the market in the past. However, the most successful investors operate both with and against the market. In like manner, a good strategist can identify special situations or opportunities and work out a scheme to take advantage of the openings. Naturally, in a war where there are many opportunities there are only a few that hold great promise of massive success, even if they are exploited with the greatest skill. Furthermore, good opportunities may be fleeting and there may not be enough time to exploit them properly. On the other hand, the strategist who possesses large resources, like the market operator controlling large funds, can create suitable opportunities.

These observations apply to both the offensive and the defensive strategist. Success always depends on more than the resources in hand. It results from a clear knowledge of the objectives to be gained by the particular strategy and from seizing the initiative in carrying out the strategy.

Whether planning aggression or defense against aggression, the strategist must calculate the results of the clashes of forces. He must always remember that he is dealing with human action, the essence of which is creativity. As a consequence, he knows he is grappling with uncertainties, with the basic uncertainties that result from the creativeness of the adversary.

[In these days of high speed computers and complex computer simulations, we often forget that strategy comes from a strategist, and victory and defeat are events in the minds of the victor and the defeated. We shouldn't. JEP 1985]

Offense and Defense

In this interplay of creativities, the aggressor has certain advantages that come from his position. The decision to attack is his. Thus, he knows when hostilities will begin. The defender cannot have this certainty. Every moment can be the moment of the attack. To heighten the effects of his blow, the attacker strives for surprise in as many elements of his strategy as possible. One of the problems of the defender is to prevent his being the surprised. This increases his needs for information about the intent of the enemy and requires him to expend resources on being constantly ready.

The attacker can build his plan for aggression around the

availability of a decisive weapon. This can take the form of a technical surprise for the defender, but it need not. If the aggressor calculates that the defender cannot counter his new advance in time, he can make his decision on the basis of this crucial superiority.

In the present age of total conflict, the aggressor can manipulate the many facets of his strategy to produce a wide variety of threats and opportunities. Political warfare, economic warfare, propaganda, the struggle for technological supremacy, diplomatic maneuverings, subversion, and military operations, taken together or individually, give the aggressor many opportunities. The defender, for his part, must provide a total defense against all these forms of conflict. Most important, he must avoid being second in technical advances that can lead to a decisive military advantage.

The defensive strategist is not without advantages on his side, provided that he does not passively wait for the blow. He can take initiatives to gain and maintain a position of superiority in the various forms of conflict. By having such superiority, he prevents the aggressor from finding the moment for the attack. The defender can plan and execute his own surprises against the would-be aggressor. The combination of initiative and surprise on the part of the defensive strategist produces the creative uncertainty that negates the advantages of the attacker. It is a military truism that strategic offensive and tactical defensive is often a superior position. Sun Tzu says, "Take what the enemy holds dear and await attack."

It is axiomatic that the objectives of the attacker and defender are asymmetric. Thus, the initiatives they take and the advances they make need not and probably should not be of the same kind. They should be chosen for their potential ability to reach the objectives of the strategy.

The Modern Strategic War

The strategy of the United States, and indeed free world strategy, is defensive. We seek no political, economic, or territorial aggrandizement. We do seek to prevent war. These objectives are clearly in direct opposition to those of the Communist bloc. They seek world domination. They create opportunities to use warfare to attain it.

[This was written long before the falling dominoes in Indochina or the Soviet invasion of Afghanistan, and indeed before any but a handful of Western analysts understood the importance of the ideology of conquest in justifying the dominance of the tiny ruling group (known as the *nomenklatura*) over the Soviet masses. JEP, 1985]

We should recognize clearly that our defensive strategy must include initiatives and surprises. Ours need not be a reactive strategy. In fact, the struggle for technological supremacy makes a reactive strategy a most dangerous one. Waiting for clear indications of Soviet initiatives can prevent us from acting in time. We must be constantly on the initiative to anticipate their moves and to create situations to which they must react.

[General Daniel O. Graham first proposed Project High Frontier as a "strategic sidestep into space." In 1981 a Strategic Defense Initiative—*STAR WARS* in popular parlance—was urged by the Citizen's Advisory Council on National Space Policy as a means of seizing the initiative in the Technological War. JEP, 1985]

In the past, we used technology to overcome the advantages of the Soviets both in the resources they control and in the initiatives we conceded them. We succeeded in negating their quantitative superiority by the qualitative advantages we acquired through a superior technology.

The circumstances today are radically different. The Soviets have challenged us in technology. They have enlarged the spectrum of conflict, taking advantage of the inevitable new struggle, the Technological War. No longer are we free to follow an independent course in implementing our strategy. We must meet the technological threat as well as the threats in other forms of conflict.

[Since this was written the Soviets have developed, among other things: neutral particle beams; laser weapons; mobile medium to long range ballistic missiles; satellite destroyers; etc., etc. JEP, 1985]

This form of warfare has become crucial. A technical advance can lead to a decisive military advantage. It is not enough for us to continue past approaches to our total strategy. The strategist must recast his thinking if he is to make his defensive strategy effective. He must find avenues for the initiative in technology. He must prevent the would-be aggressor from attaining a clear advantage in any aspect of technology that could be translated into a decisive military advantage.

Broader horizons are needed in another aspect of the problem of the defensive strategist. Planning methodology and decision processes reflect the past situation. They are no longer adequate. The time has come to break the shackles of science on planning methodology. We need to rehumanize planning and strategy. This process will have a direct impact on decision making. Decision makers can no longer find refuge in the alleged certainties and probabilities that past planning provided them. We are now in an era of creative, dynamic uncertainty. We must have a strong defensive position. But we must also create strategic diversions, feints, deceptions, and surprises.

Only in this way can the defensive strategist ensure that the attacker will choose not to strike. A viable strategy poses insurmountable problems for the aggressor. The nature of some of these problems is illustrated by the following discussion of possible situations.

The Effect of Nuclear Weapons

Nuclear weapons have not changed the nature of strategy; however, they have introduced new complications, just as they have introduced new opportunities. The major new opportunity is that the strategist, once he decides to strike, can apply far more power, over larger areas, than could any of his predecessors who fought with low-energy weapon systems. The main new complication is that the defender, even though deprived of a large portion of his initial strength in the course of the first battle, would still retain enormous firepower to hurt the attacker far more dangerously than it was ever before possible for a defensive force to do. This residual force can be used against the attacker's population, industry, urban areas, government control centers, and armed forces, provided that the defender's will to use it has not failed. The scope of war has grown to include entire populations, not merely military forces.

Also, it is easily conceivable that under some circumstances the attacker, although he may defeat the defender, may achieve only Pyrrhic victory. Or, even if he achieves an unqualified victory, he would not enjoy the fruits because he has paid an excessive price. In fact, he may have lost his country to the blows that his defeated adversary was still able to inflict. Nuclear weapons have not worked totally to the advantage of the attacker.

It would be a grave mistake to assume that this particular strategic problem is new. Even if it were new, the significant aspect is whether the danger of devastating retaliation would prevent war. To put it in different terms, the question is whether such a hazard would prevent the aggressive strategist from planning for war in a rational manner. Obviously a great deal of the strategist's mental effort must be devoted to the security of the aggressor's homeland. If the defender can be induced to leave his weapons unused, the aggressor can still achieve decisive victory.

In order to prevent aggression, the defender must seek safety in strength. He must seek superior technology, modern weapons that can survive attack, and engage actively in the Technological War. He cannot rely on agreements, planned weaknesses, or minimum strength.

In the last analysis, superior strength remains the most reliable insurance for the survival of the defender. The strategist of the superior power has some chance of predicting what his enemy might do; the strategist of a greatly inferior power can only hope. A defensive strategy aiming at superiority in power offers the only dependable hedge against errors in planning.

Force Levels in the Nuclear Era

It is clear that, as the armaments race takes place on high force levels, the aggressor will be hard-put to achieve decisive superiority. The conclusion to draw from this is that relatively low levels of nuclear power are a chief prerequisite for nuclear attack. This is especially true in a period when cities have not been fully dispersed and populations cannot be effectively protected against fall-out. Low levels of force, in being, are more of a danger to the United States than high levels—fears of genocide and the arms race notwithstanding. This is an important finding, which casts a very disturbing light on the recent history of US armaments and armament negotiations.

Of the two belligerents, the one who is able to continue the war beyond the initial strike will have an enormous advantage because the side that does not have this capability will cave in morally and will be unable to reconstitute its force. Such a capability can only be provided by vigorous pursuit of technology, including the design and the deployment of weapons.

The survival force is one key to security. As long as we have secure weapon systems that can ride out the initial and follow-on strikes, we will have the decisive advantage. The in-being power that is still effective after the battles are over will determine the final outcome.

["Project 75" concluded that due to increasing Soviet missile accuracy, by about 1980 the Minuteman force would no longer be able to ride out a full Soviet first strike, and that sometime thereafter the US would be forced to choose between active defense and launch on warning. Launching Armageddon on early warning of attack is not an attractive alternative. As warning times grow shorter, the US is forced seriously to consider computerizing the launch decision. This is even less attractive. JEP, 1985]

Our defensive strategy requires us to have a survivable force. Hardening, dispersal, mobility, and concealment contribute to survival, but they are supporting strategic themes. The single most important element of our defensive strategy is to have in being a clear superiority in effective and reliable numbers. This is the one factor in the strategic equation that is most easily understood, the one the enemy is least likely to misunderstand. Numerical superiority on our side is necessary to convince the aggressor not to strike.

[It is now politically difficult to impossible for the US to engage in a strategic offensive arms race with the Soviet Union, even though the Soviets continue to this moment to operate four different ICBM production facilities three shifts a day. JEP, 1985]

A would-be aggressor, if he were to act rationally, would realize that he cannot cope with high force levels. Therefore, he must make an attempt to bring forces down to a level where he can fight nuclear war—especially if through clandestine armaments of his own he achieves an enormous superiority. It is clear that the aggressor is not particularly perturbed by high force levels of his own, let alone by relative superiority, but is disturbed by a high force level owned by the defender. His problem, therefore, is to achieve a substantial quantitative superiority. To achieve this goal he must persuade the defender to be content with moderate strength.

Another reason why the aggressor needs the low levels of force is that decisive increments in strength are difficult to conceal if they have to be produced within the framework of high force levels. This means that psycho-political strategy is an integral part of nuclear strategy, first to achieve some sort of reduction of armament levels, then to provide a cover to conceal the aggressor's armaments, and third to facilitate nuclear blackmail and prevent retaliation.

Security Through Arms Control

The unending process of armaments has often been criticized as the greatest waste of which mankind is guilty. It is true that if both sides stay in the race and run well, the world situation will remain stable and no war will occur; the weapons will then be thought wasted. The argument is that if both sides agree not to engage in such races, peace would be preserved effectively and at far less cost.

However, we have already seen that by lowering the levels of destruction war would bring, reductions in arms make war thinkable and therefore more likely. This, it would seem, is one major argument against arms control and disarmament. However, it is hardly the only such argument.

Since technology is dynamic, no one can agree to stand still. Force relationships change in the course of armament cycles despite the best planning possible. Sudden accretions of military power can come to a side not even expecting them. New technologies create new power.

It is true that the tempo of this eternal race can be accelerated or slowed. Aside from the technological factors that often determine this tempo, the speed of the process is largely set by political factors, including strategic intentions. If no disturber power is at work, the tempo will slacken almost automatically. If there is a disturber power, explicit or tacit slow-down agreements are at best highly unreliable and temporary. The side that takes the risk of slowing down unilaterally will soon be punished.

The history of disarmament agreements teaches an explicit lesson: international promissory treaties are almost invariably broken and are therefore an utterly undependable instrument of national security.

The fundamental reason for the defender to stay in this

expensive race, and to run hard in it, is to stay alive and not allow the would-be attacker to achieve such an advantage that he might be inclined to break the peace and impose his will on the naive and gullible defender.

So long as the defender must stay in the arms competition, he does not really have the option of running a selective race. He cannot leave open any geographical or technological flanks, or the opponent will take advantage of his opportunities. Thus, the United States does not really have the free choice of saying that it will stop Communism in Europe and defend the East Coast, but ignore Communist advances in Asia. Nor can it say that it will maintain offensive nuclear weapons but not acquire defensive ones, or that it will try to be strong in inner space but will assume that outer space is of no military relevance. Least of all can the United States entrust its security to so-called disarmament treaties, not because it must necessarily and always presuppose bad faith on the part of other nations (although sometimes it must make precisely such an assumption of bad faith), but for the far more elementary reasons (a) that reliable inspection of disarmament agreements is unfeasible, (b) that enforcement against treaty violations requires war, and (c) that disarmament agreements apply to weapons already in existence, but will be speedily outdated and be rendered irrelevant by new weapons, the characteristics of which were unknown at the time the treaty was written.

Security in the Modern Era

As we have seen, security cannot be guaranteed by Soviet intentions; not only do Soviet theorists predict inevitable victory by the USSR, and Soviet generals hasten to install the latest weapons, but, even were we convinced that the USSR is ruled by men who have lost their aggressive drives, there is no guarantee that a new Stalin will not take power.

Security cannot be guaranteed by passive measures. The most modern force purchased at enormous cost will become obsolete in only a few years. Security cannot be guaranteed by agreements to halt the Technological War; the stream of technology moves on without regard for our intentions. The only way to guarantee security is to engage in the Technological War with the intention of winning it. It is as true today as in Roman times that "If you would have peace, prepare thou then for war."

Regardless of the enormous effects of modern weapons, organized brainpower remains the strongest and ultimately decisive factor. The experience of Vietnam, the test ban, and Sputnik have shown that we do not excel in that department. It is not that we lack intelligent people but that we lack an effective organization through which we can optimize our brainpower and collective memory. On the contrary, the more we have overorganized, the more we have reduced brainpower and the more we have forgotten. Secretary MacNamara even organized strategic amnesia.

We must decide to engage in the Technological War, and we must create the planning staff to guide us in this decisive conflict. To do anything short of this is to risk national suicide. At the same time, we must preserve the values that make our society worth defending; we cannot contemplate ending the Technological War by destroying our enemies without warning. Our goal is the indefinite preservation of peace and order, and our hope is that in such an environment the root causes of conflict will slowly wither.

The era of Technological War has not ended conflict, and that millennium may never come. Technological War does, however, have the advantage of being relatively peaceful, so long as the stabilizer powers remain strong. Despite the greatest threat Western civilization has ever known, since 1945 the amount of blood shed to preserve the peace has been quite small—smaller than that shed on the highways. The Technological War can be kept silent and apparently peaceful so long as we continue to engage in it successfully.

Despite fashionable rhetoric, history shows that American supremacy brings relative peace and stability to the world; where the USSR has enjoyed local superiority the results have been quite different. American success in the Technological War is the primary prerequisite for the preservation of world peace.

[In a recent speech Secretary of Defense Caspar Weinberger said, ''To the extent that we in the United States desire true peace with freedom, peace based on individual and sovereign rights and on the principle of resolution of disputes through negotiation, we must acknowledge and follow our interests in creating conditions in which democratic forces can gain and thrive in this world. A world not of our making, but a world in which we must fight to maintain our peace and our strength. And a world in which the very best way to maintain peace is to be militarily strong and thus deter war.'' Of course we agree. JEP 1985]

EDITOR'S INTRODUCTION TO:

THE WEDDING MARCH
Edward P. Hughes

No society could endure if, as is sometimes implicitly assumed, its members became hostile to it by reason of and in proportion to their lowly status within it. Should you so plan a society as to establish and maintain equality in every respect you can think of, there would naturally be a restoration of scarce, desirable positions, by nature attainable only by a minority. You can allot equal time to each member of an Assembly: but you cannot ensure that all will command equal attention. You can chase unequal (more or less log-normal) distributions out of one field after another: they will reappear in new fields. Nor are men so base as to be disaffected from any ordering in which they are low-placed: they are indeed lavish in the precedence they afford to those who excel in performances they value. What exasperates them is a system of qualifying values which seems to them scandalous, a social scaling which jars with their scoring cards.

—Bertrand de Jouvenal, *The Pure Theory of Politics*

Edward Hughes, a communications engineer, lives in Manchester, England. His stories of the village of Barley Cross have been a popular feature of this series.

The skills of the warrior are not those of the king. Nonetheless, Patrick O'Meara, one time Sergeant Major of Her Majesty's Armed Forces, and later Master of the Fist and Lord of Barley Cross, managed to make the transition. The village continued a normal existence in lands ruined by war and destruction; and when O'Meara died, the Mastership passed peacefully enough to his illegitimate son Liam McGrath.

There is no equality in Barley Cross. The happiness and prosperity of the village rests instead on myths—and on the skill of its Lord, who must provide for all the village's needs.

Some are easier than others.

THE WEDDING MARCH
Edward P. Hughes

The entire population of Barley Cross attended the funeral—apart that is, from the guards up at the Fist, Sally Corcoran who was in labour, with Doctor Denny Mallon acting as midwife . . . and . . . the Fintan Dooleys.

Kevin Murphy, slouching along beside the Lord of Barley Cross on the way back from the cemetery, said, "I wonder what's up with old Finty? He was five years at the Fist in the early days, and very close to the Gineral."

Liam McGrath scarcely heard him. General Desmond's death monopolised his thoughts. Could anyone have stopped the General drinking? Larry Desmond had been a forceful character, and not the easiest of citizens to get on with. But his loss would be a hard blow to the village. Someone must be persuaded to take his place.

Celia Larkin, back a little bent, trudged at the Master's other elbow. She said, "Didn't Finty take over the Curry cottage after Liam moved out?"

Kevin Murphy nodded. "Indeed he did. He tried the O'Toole place before that, but it was tumbling down 'round his ears."

Liam came back to the present. He beckoned one of the uniformed pallbearers. "Seamus, nip up to Kirkogue and see if anything's wrong with Finty Dooley or his wife."

Watching the soldier go, Kevin Murphy said, "Have ye anyone in mind for the Gineral's job, me lord? 'Twill have to be filled, ye know. Five years of peace since ye went up the hill don't mean we can relax our vigilance."

Liam sighed. Why hadn't General Desmond nominated his successor! He asked, "Who's next officer in rank?"

Kevin Murphy scratched his head. "Sure it would be Andy McGrath—your stepfather, me lord. I did hear Larry made him a major, or suchlike."

116

Liam kicked flints in the road. "Would the villagers think it was . . . if I . . . ?"

"Nepotism?" Celia Larkin supplied. "Liam, as Lord of Barley Cross you have a perfect right to appoint whom you wish as our General."

Liam grimaced. His stepfather was a good citizen, cheerfully accepting the Master's rule—even such doctrines as his *droit du seigneur*—without question. Such docility would hardly be an asset in a General. He said, "It ain't the legality that bothers me, Celia. It's Andy. With all respect—he ain't exactly brilliant, if you follow my meaning."

Celia Larkin frowned over her spectacles. "Your da is a good, reliable man. He would make a fine General."

Liam blinked. An unexpected vote for his stepfather! He shot a glance at the vet. "Andy McGrath suit you, Kevin?"

Kevin Murphy rubbed a bristly chin. "We don't need brilliance. Andy is a cautious man. I reckon he could do the job."

Liam masked his surprise. Apparently no one shared his opinion of his stepfather. He said, "Okay, I'll have a word with Doctor Denny, then I'll see Andy."

The vet wagged his head in admiration. "See what I mean, Celia? They breed cautiousness at the McGraths."

Liam located Doctor Denny Mallon at the Corcoran cottage. The doctor held a squawking bundle.

Sally Corcoran greeted Liam from the bed, smirking. "Good morning, me lord."

Liam kept an impassive face. Sally's husband, Charlie, was sure to be somewhere about the house. Liam didn't want to annoy him with undue familiarity towards his wife—even though they all knew that the bundle in Doctor Denny's arms had nothing to do with Charlie, and everything to do with Liam.

Denny Mallon laughed jovially. He thrust the child at its mother. "Take her, Sally. Another Barley Cross citizen. And another firm step on our road to the future."

Straightfaced, Liam said, "Congratulations, Sally. I'll send down a present when I get home. Meanwhile . . ." He pulled a shiny medallion from his pocket, and tucked it into the infant's bindings. The trinkets were part of a hoard he had discovered at the Fist, relics of a long-forgotten papal visit, metamorphosed into a successful gimmick since the mothers

had begun looking for them. He kissed the baby's head. Pity
it was a girl. Maybe the next would be a boy.

As they strolled down the Corcorans' path together, Denny
Mallon said, "Andy will do nicely for General. But, consider, Liam, he will be, *ex officio*, a member of the council."

Liam blinked. The idea hadn't entered his mind. Andy
McGrath would never have the nerve to argue with the Lord
of Barley Cross, even though it was his stepson. Liam said,
"So what do we do about it?"

Denny Mallon chuckled. "Ah, get along and ask him, son.
We never educated Larry Desmond. We may have better luck
with your da."

Liam paused at the Corcorans' gate. Seamus Gallagher
pelted down the street towards them.

"Me lord—" Seamus gasped for breath.

"Take your time, man," urged the doctor.

"Me lord—Finty Dooley is lying up at the Curry cottage
with an arrow through his leg, and the Missus Dooley is
gone!"

The council assembled in Liam's parlour. The new General
sat stiffly at Larry Desmond's end of the settee, eyeing
askance the bottle of poteen on the carpet at the other.

Kevin Murphy, seated above the bottle, slopped a tot into a
glass. "Here, Andy. Don't act so formal. We're very easy
here. First names and all that if you've a mind. Knock this
back and tell us what you've done about the Dooleys."

General Andy McGrath held the glass like an unexploded
bomb. He said, "I have sent a three-man patrol up Kirkogue
with instructions to track down whoever abducted Claire
Dooley, and if it's possible, to bring her back." He paused,
forehead shiny. "I have also sent a couple of lads with a litter
to bring Finty down. They'll have to go slow coming back,
but I expect them here inside the half hour."

Denny Mallon clapped. "Good man! Will they be giving
us a shout when they arrive?"

The General nodded. "I told them to report straight to the
guard at the gate."

Celia Larkin put down her knitting. "Why only three men
to track those villains, Andy?"

The General studied his glass for a moment. "Well, Celia,
those raiders didn't try to kill Finty. An arrow through the leg
shouldn't be fatal. I guess they just wanted to run off with his
wife. Now my men are armed with automatic rifles, and

they've plenty of bullets. No bow-and-arrow outfit could stand up to them. But I've told them to report back without engaging if they find themselves seriously outnumbered."

Kevin Murphy thumped the settee. "Can't fault the logic, Gineral."

"Thank you." Andy McGrath turned gravely towards Liam. "Are my dispositions satisfactory to the Master?"

Liam bit off a tart response. Liquor always had a regrettable effect on the vet's tongue. Andy would have to learn to discount it. He turned to his stepfather, "Have your men enough food with them?"

Andy McGrath came to attention, still seated. "Four days supply, sir. Plus fodder for their horses."

Horses, too? Liam glowed inside. And all fixed up within half an hour of being appointed! Maybe they had made a good choice in Andy. He said, gravely, "Thank you, General. Will you keep me informed of progress?"

Andy McGrath relaxed a hair. "As soon as I have something to report, sir."

Liam scanned the room. "Anything else?"

Denny Mallon cleared his throat. "There's this matter of Father Con—"

Celia Larkin interrupted sharply. "There is nothing we can do about that."

The doctor raised a hand. "Let me speak, Celia. Father Con is getting old. I don't count on us having him much longer. Young Adrian Walsh has been helping him—in church as well as in the presbytery. The lad is keen. I wouldn't mind him being our next shepherd. He could start taking over from Father Con—"

The schoolmistress's voice was icy. "There is no way Father Con can make Adrian Walsh into a priest. That is a bishop's job."

Liam held his tongue. So far, but no farther! Just let young Adrian get himself a wife, and Liam McGrath would make a father of him!

The doctor stared at the schoolmistress, hands spread. "But in an emergency?"

Celia Larkin's voice rose higher. "What emergency? We still have Father Con with us, haven't we? Tom O'Connor is making him a wheelchair. I have the children running his errands. We can go to him for a while, instead of him coming to us."

Kevin Murphy said, "What Dinny means is that maybe the good Lord would overlook a small infraction—"

Celia Larkin's voice became painfully shrill. "You've been listening to that *celidh*-dancing set, haven't you? Well you just tell them that *we* don't make the rules. And if there are any infractions, we won't be making them either. If, eventually, we have to do without Father Con, then that is just what we shall do."

"Moreover," Liam interjected, feeling a little diplomacy was in order, "bearing our current surplus of girls in mind, we can't afford to let young Adrian stay celibate. He should get married as soon as he's old enough. Unless—" Liam turned to the schoolmistress. "Do you think Father Con might permit us a married clergy? I believe they used to have them in Europe."

Celia Larkin snorted like a horse. "Those priests that got a dispensation were married before they took Holy Orders—and they never afterwards lived with their wives."

Kevin Murphy wagged his head in mock distress. "Such a sad waste!"

Celia Larkin glared at him. "And Father Con hasn't the authority to give *that* sort of dispensation either!"

Doctor Denny Mallon sighed. "No further business, me lord."

"In that case—" Liam began.

The door behind him opened. His servant, Michael, sidled in. The man bowed to the company. "Word from the gate, sirs and madame. They have Finty Dooley below on a litter."

Fintan Dooley winced as the doctor drew a stitch tight. Kevin Murphy sloshed more poteen into Finty's cup. "Swally that down, lad, and ye won't feel a damn thing."

Finty said, "The pain ain't so bad, Kevin. Me whole leg is gone numb, anyway."

Andy McGrath leaned over the table. "Did you see any of them?"

Finty winced as the needle again punctured his flesh. "Sure, there was three or four of them, Andy. One of the buggers kicked at me door while the others hid out of sight. When I came out a young felly with a ginger beard put the bolt through me pin."

The words "young fellow" rang in Liam's head. "How young was he?" he demanded.

"Eighteen—nineteen?" Finty shrugged. "I reckon none of

them was over twenty. If only I could have reached me shotgun—"

Liam met the doctor's gaze over Finty's head. Eighteen? Nineteen? Liam was twenty-five. And, like the rest of Barley Cross's younger generation, he had been sired by the village's previous ruler. Denny Mallon's mouth shaped a word. "How?"

Liam turned back to Finty. "You sure about their ages?"

Finty groaned. "Would I tell ye a lie, me lord?"

Liam shivered with hope. Was there another village like Barley Cross? A village with someone capable of fathering children? The itch to find another to share his burden became an overwhelming desire. He gripped the doctor's shoulder. "Denny—what if they've got their own O'Meara?"

Denny Mallon had gone pale. He put down his needle, closed his eyes, and bowed his head. "Dear God," he muttered. "Let it be so."

Kevin Murphy, refilling Finty's glass, added, "Amen."

After Finty was put, singing, to bed, the council reconvened.

"We mustn't hurt any of those young men," Celia Larkin declared. "Their lives are too valuable. Someone should go after that patrol of yours, Andy, and tell them so."

Kevin Murphy's eyes gleamed. "You mean it's okay to pot old men like Finty, but not young rascals who'd put a bolt through ye? Sure, that's a quare old point of view."

General McGrath got to his feet. "With your permission, sir, I'll despatch a messenger with fresh orders."

Before Liam could approve, the vet interrupted. "What kind of orders, Andy?"

Andy McGrath turned fractionally towards the other end of the settee. "To refrain from attacking, whatever the provocation. To keep out of sight. To trail the raiders to their base. And to report back here when they know where that base is."

Liam let it go. Andy could be trusted to make the right moves. But steps had to be taken to contact this other village—steps the council would want to discuss and argue about. And, on this subject, Liam wanted no argument. If there was a fertile male living, anywhere, Liam wanted to find him. And, if necessary, Denny, Kevin and Celia would have to be stampeded. He said, "Orders approved, General. And here are a few more. I want half a dozen of our marriageable young ladies informed that they have three days to fix up their trousseaux and be ready to travel. I want the biggest cart you can find converted into a mobile home with enough bedrooms

for the brides, myself and a chaperone. I want an escort of
troopers, armed with automatic weapons. And I want a fancy
rig-out made for myself and my two children—something
royalty might wear, velvet, lace and stuff—can I leave that to
you, Celia?''

They stared at him as if he had gone mad.

He stared back, offering no excuses. This plan was not
subject to their veto, whatever they might think.

Celia Larkin said, hesitant, ''Velvet, Liam?''

He glared at her. ''Cut up my curtains if you have to.''

''Timber for something that big?'' mumbled Kevin Murphy.

Liam swung his glare onto the vet. So timber was scarce in
Connemara? ''Pull a house down for it. There's plenty empty.''

''What if we can't find six girls willing to make a trip with
you?'' Denny Mallon queried.

Liam smiled grimly. ''Just mention there might be a husband for each of them at the end of the journey. They'll be
willing enough.''

''You are planning an expedition?'' the doctor prompted.

Liam hid his relief. That was the argument finished. He
said, ''We have to make friends with the people who raided
the Dooleys. We can't afford to have them as enemies.'' He
paused. ''What if *all* their menfolk are fertile?''

Kevin Murphy looked into his glass. ''Christ—I'd tempt a
few of them to immigrate to Barley Cross!''

Denny Mallon grunted. '' 'Twould be a fine thing for our
future.''

Liam pounced. ''So it's worth any effort we make. And
this expedition might pull it off. I want Celia along to look
after the girls. Andy to command the escort. You and Kevin
stay here, in charge.''

Kevin Murphy snorted. ''An armed escort and Celia? That
don't sound very friendly to me.''

Liam blessed him for the joke. The vet could be thorny
over anything not to his liking. He said, ''We have to be able
to look after ourselves in case they don't feel like being
friends with us. But I think Andy summed them up right—
those lads were looking for wives.''

The vet pulled his lip. ''Reckon I go along with that, me
lord. We must make an attempt to fraternise with them. I'll
sort out a matched team to pull this mobile house for ye.
Praise be we're over the ploughing.''

Doctor Denny thumbed the bowl of his empty pipe, eyes reflective. "I am not keen on your children going."

Liam felt a stab of guilt. Trust Denny to pinpoint his weak spot. But the presence of two genuine children might just swing the deal he planned. And who else's kids dared he risk? He said, "Nor me, Denny. But they're living proof of what we can offer."

"You envisage exchanging your services for theirs?"

"Something like that. If they've only one stag they'll be just as keen for fresh blood as we are."

"And if they've more than one?"

"I've got the girls."

The doctor shrugged. "I'm glad Eileen is your wife, and not mine."

Liam winced. He could imagine Eileen's only too predictable reaction to his taking the children on an expedition. He said ruefully, "That's what you pay me for, isn't it?"

Doctor Denny sighed. "God help us all! Sometimes I wonder if it's all worth it."

Celia Larkin sent her chair skating backwards. "You men! You are all the same! You need guts. If Liam's plan will help the village, it's our duty to back him up."

Liam saw his stepfather flinch. The Larkin contempt was a novel experience for the General. Andy McGrath said stiffly, "I'll get the carpenters on the job immediately, sir. And trust me, you'll have an escort fit for a prince."

Liam got up. He'd had enough discussion. "That was the general idea, Andy. With luck, we'll overawe these raiders."

Kevin Murphy placed his bottle of poteen, untouched, on the table. "By Christ, Liam—you might do just that!"

The mobile home was ready in four days. On the first day Eileen had refused to speak to Liam. On the second he had retaliated with a similar silence. On the third she had demanded to be allowed to join the expedition, and Liam had ordered a larger bedroom. On the fourth day Tom O'Connor put his final nail into the woodwork and let loose the painters. And in the evening Liam surveyed the great green and white contraption which somehow reminded him of a picture of Noah's Ark once seen in a schoolbook.

It was mind-boggling. Cantilevered out on each side of the cart until the wheels were invisible; a row of glazed and curtained windows along each wall; a red-tiled, peaked roof with a stove-pipe chimney—nothing like it could ever have been seen in Connemara before. Was this what he had ordered them to build? Six horses would hardly stir it!

Liam choked on a laugh. God bless Andy McGrath's carpenters! If this didn't overawe the raiders' people, nothing would.

General McGrath's scouts returned on the fifth day, and Liam learned where he was going.

"Achill Island?" mused Denny Mallon. " 'Tis a bleak and draughty place."

"And it'll take a week to get there with your pantechnicon," the vet commented. "Presuming you even get it through the mountains."

Liam watched Michael carefully folding his new outfit. He said, "We'll manage the mountains, Kevin. And Achill won't run away."

Achill Island is reached via a bridge over the Atlantic. At the sight of the viaduct spanning the Sound, Liam brought his caravanserai to a halt. The bridge appeared unguarded, but then that would be how the Achill Islanders hoped it would appear. Magnificent in his parlour curtains, Liam flung his reins to General McGrath and slid from his horse. "Stay here," he ordered. "I'm going ahead with the kids. It's worth the risk if it saves us being ambushed."

Andy McGrath's face grew hard. Liam was forgetting that the kids were also his grandchildren. He said, "Liam—"

Liam's mouth set in a firm line. "Please . . . da?"

The General passed Liam's reins to a nearby trooper. He swung his horse's head 'round. "I'd better get them for you."

The Lord of Barley Cross approached the bridge to Achill in dead silence. His heart was in his mouth, and a trusting infant in each hand. Behind him, his cohorts stood anxious.

A flash of sunlit metal at the far end of the bridge caught his eye. Someone flexing a bow? He called loudly. "Would you shoot at children, then?"

A wild-looking youth wearing a sealskin jacket and trews stepped into sight, bow cocked. He shouted back, "Well, halt—and state yer business!"

Liam halted. He noted that the youth was clean-shaven. At least he wasn't the trigger-happy hooligan who had pinked Finty Dooley. He called, "I've come to trade."

"What sort of trade?"

"Women—seeing as you are short of them."

The youth's face grew suspicious. "What do you know about us being short of women?"

"Enough to offer you a deal."

The voice was still wary, but the bow was lowered. "What kind of a deal?"

He was hooked. Liam opened his arms wide. "Let me talk to your leader. I'm not armed."

"And what's in yonder wagon?"

Liam grinned. "My trade goods—with an escort."

The youth beckoned a number of ruffians out of conceal- ment, and conferred with them. Then he called, "You and the kids can come over, but the rest of your mob, and *that*—" He indicated the Barley Cross juggernaut. "—stays on the far side of the bridge."

Liam shrugged. Inwardly he was not displeased. He didn't want Andy and Celia fussing around until he'd had a chance to sort things out with the youth's boss. He turned to face his troops, making "stay where you are" gestures. Then, clutch- ing his children's hands, he went to meet his fate.

There was a pony and trap concealed in the bushes beyond the bridge. The youth motioned Liam and the children into it. One of his men climbed onto the driver's seat. They set off, the first youth following on horseback.

They drove no more than a mile before turning in at a stone gateway. A gravel drive brought them to the forecourt of a house. The trap halted. Liam saw figures in brown habits working in the gardens around the house, tonsured heads bent over the soil. He said to the driver of the trap, "Is your leader a monk?"

The youth ignored him. The other vaulted from his horse, and entered the house. He reappeared with a tall, elderly man who wore an ankle-length purple habit. A crucifix hung down on his breast. A purple biretta perched on his head.

Liam had seen pictures of bishops. He knew what to do. He got down from the trap, bent a knee, and kissed the ring on the man's gnarled finger. "My lord," he said.

"Get up, son," responded the man. "And call me Zbigniev."

The man didn't *sound* like a foreigner. "You *are* a bishop?" Liam asked, wondering if he had made some mistake.

"For longer than I care to remember," Zbigniev answered. "But not of your country, my son. The riots long ago caught me here on a fishing holiday, and I was never able to go home. Now, tell me what you want.''

Liam tugged at his velvet tunic, wondering if he looked as big a fool as he felt. This was no Achill Island yokel to be dazzled by a show of finery. Any prelate whose conscience permitted him to lead a band of raiders wouldn't impress easily. He said, ''I'm Liam McGrath, the Lord of the village your men visited last week. I have come to take Missus Dooley back home.''

''Missus?'' Zbigniev's intonation mimicked Liam's. He swung on the two youths. ''The woman you took was married?''

''*Is* married,'' Liam corrected. ''We patched her old man up.''

Liam's captor shifted diffidently. ''We didn't know, yer grace. And there wasn't much time for discussion.''

Zbigniev frowned. ''This is not a matter for levity, Dominic. We may be tragically short of women, but—''

The bishop's voice faltered. His mouth opened like a cod on a slab. His eyes were fixed on the children in the trap. He turned enquiringly to Liam. ''How?''

''Mine, your grace. Like you, we still produce offspring in Barley Cross.''

Zbigniev ignored his answer. He rushed towards the trap, arms outstretched to embrace the two infants. ''Glory to God! Are they not a wonderful sight!'' He stood, arms 'round them. ''Surely, Liam, you did not bring these precious mites along just to impress me?''

Liam lowered his gaze. The bishop's guess was too close to the truth for a straight ''yes'' or ''no.'' He said, ''I wanted to demonstrate our peaceful intentions, my lord. I have soldiers back there, but they are only to protect my—er—merchandise.''

''And what is your merchandise?''

Liam took a breath. Zbigniev might have progressive ideas about banditry and still hold old-fashioned notions on sex. But the nettle had to be grasped. He said bluntly, ''I have six young ladies back there. Each willing to marry one of your young men—on condition.''

''Oh? Pray continue. What condition?''

Was the bishop hiding a smile? Liam rushed on. ''First, I want Claire Dooley back. Second—'' Liam hesitated. This was a bishop he was propositioning. It came out in a rush. "Second, I want six rapes committed in Barley Cross."

Zbigniev frowned. "Rapes? That is a harsh word, my son."

Liam stood his ground. "You may describe it how you like, my lord. But I want six pregnancies in exchange for six wives."

Zbigniev raised his eyebrows. "And how may one guarantee even one pregnancy?"

Liam flushed. "You know what I mean, my lord. As far as I know, apart from your village and mine, this whole country is childless. I know where Barley Cross's children come from. And I take it that you are aware how it is managed in yours. I'm offering you a straight swap—six pregnancies for six brides."

Reluctantly Zbigniev released his hold on Liam's children. He turned a regretful face. "My son, I'm afraid you are a little too late with your proposal."

Too late? They had come with the minimum of delay.

Zbigniev bowed his head. "Rory MacCormick perished at sea eighteen years ago. He was the last man on Achill to father children."

Liam felt his hopes drain away. What rotten luck! A generation too late! There could be no deal done with the bishop. And no fresh blood in Barley Cross—unless? He faced the bishop squarely. "Is there a chance any of your young men might have inherited their father's fertility?"

Zbigniev shook his head. "I have no proof, so far, my son. Indeed, I can only guess at which of our youths has Rory for a father. Not all matters are confided to the clergy, you know. But we have almost a dozen unwed young men. Any one of them might be the man you need."

Liam toed the gravel, mind churning. Fat chance of another miracle like him! Still, he had promised to find husbands for his maidens. He said, "Half a deal is better than no deal at all, my lord. With your permission, I'll bring on my dancing girls."

They parked the juggernaut in the centre of the village at the foot of Slievemore. Surf boomed against the nearby cliffs. Seabirds shrieked. The sun shone. Barley Cross and Achill Island citizens mingled under the beaming gaze of Bishop Zbigniev. Claire Dooley was produced, unharmed, and given into the care of Eileen McGrath and Celia Larkin. The woman clutched at them as though they were lost relatives. "How's Finty?" she demanded.

"Och, he'll live," Celia responded. "Doctor Denny put a few tucks into his hide." She dropped a knee to Zbigniev. "Your grace, I suggest you get your eligible bachelors into our caravan, and we let them socialise with our young ladies. Those who don't come out, you can marry."

Liam recalled his *droit du seigneur*, and decided it would be an inappropriate time to bring it up. Instead he went looking for his stepfather. The guards on the juggernaut would need orders to allow Achill Island bachelors entry.

Zbigniev stared hard at Celia. "And you are?"

"Celia Larkin, schoolmistress and chaperone."

Zbigniev nodded sagely. "And you were privy to Liam's plan?"

She coloured. "I was, your grace. And I make no apology. If the good lord had not wanted us to survive, he wouldn't have let us even think up the idea."

Zbigniev winced. "Such charming sophistry. I am sorry there is no way I can make up for our inability to strike a bargain."

Celia Larkin smiled grimly. "Oh but there is a way, my lord . . ."

Later, Liam said to Dominic, "We've spare cottages in Barley Cross if you want to come back with us. But we've little use for fishermen or seal hunters. And any of your spare bachelors can visit us if they fancy their chances of getting a wife. But there are no more girls willing to leave the village."

Dominic slid an arm around a blushing Kathleen Mulroon. "We'll be returning with you, me lord." He grinned slyly. "We might even insist on ye having yer droyt doo seenyer if we don't have no luck on our own."

The council sat again in the Master's parlour.

Kevin Murphy swirled poteen in his glass. " 'Twas a valiant try, Liam. Pity we didn't think of it eighteen years back."

"Och—times were different then." Denny Mallon stuffed dried grass into his pipe bowl. "Sure, two miles out of the village was a war zone, then. We'd never have risked the journey."

"And 'twasn't all a dead loss," Andy McGrath pointed out. "We got four new citizens, and each of them has already volunteered for Fist duty."

Liam said, "There's just a faint hope we might have another O'Meara among them."

The vet tipped poteen recklessly down his throat. "I'd be glad if we have. This village is getting just a wee bit too inbred."

Celia Larkin glowered over her tea cup. "No harm if the stock is good. Think of racehorses."

Kevin Murphy snorted. "It's people we're raising, Celia—not bloodstock!"

She grinned triumphantly. "I'm glad you've reminded me." She jerked the tasselled rope which summoned Michael.

The servant appeared. "More tay, is it, Miss Larkin?"

"No, Michael. Bring in the lad."

Michael shuffled out, to reappear leading a blushing Adrian Walsh. The boy must have been waiting in the yard. He wore a heavy jacket, and a muffler swaddled his neck.

Celia Larkin cooed at him. "Tell the gentlemen what happened to you on Achill."

Liam blinked. Adrian Walsh on Achill? That was news!

The schoolmistress seemed to read his thoughts. "Do you think I'd leave him here at the mercies of those two?" She nodded at the doctor and the vet. "God knows what follies they'd be preaching at him." She turned to the youth. "Go on—speak up, Adrian!"

Adrian began hesitantly. "I—Miss Larkin smuggled me onto the cart-house the night before it left for Achill. I stayed in her bedroom. When we got to Achill, she brought me out to meet the bishop felly. *He* made me lay face down on the ground. Then he put his hands on me head."

"Who did this to ye?" Kevin Murphy demanded.

"The felly with the purple robe and the crucifix."

"And for why would he do all that?" pursued the vet.

"Show him, Adrian," Celia Larkin instructed.

Adrian Walsh opened his coat and pulled off his scarf, revealing a frayed and over-large dog collar encircling his scrawny neck.

Doctor Mallon dropped his pipe. "Holy Mother of God—what have they done at you, son?"

Celia Larkin smirked. "Bishop Zbigniev ordained him. And he's promised to ordain any more lads I send."

Kevin Murphy groaned. "Jasus! Now we'll be overrun with the clergy!"

Celia Larkin gave him a basilisk stare. "Any more remarks like that and I might send girls instead!"

The vet waved his glass wildly. "Boy priests! Sure, I know we were hoping Adrian could take over in time, but this is too much. We're slipping back to the Middle Ages. Does your bishop, by any chance, wear chain mail and carry a sword?"

"Adrian!" Denny Mallon intervened. "You are scarcely fourteen years old. Do you think you'll be able to do Father Con's job in Barley Cross?"

The boy turned grave eyes on the doctor. "Not yet, Mister Mallon. But Father Con can teach me what I need to know. And I am legally ordained. So—when he gets too old . . ." The lad fell silent.

Liam listened. The boy was no fool. Celia Larkin, it seemed, could teach the Master a trick or two. No arguing over a *fait accompli*. And neither Denny, nor Kevin, nor his stepfather would have had the initiative to talk Zbigniev into ordaining the lad. He smiled with satisfaction. Let Celia have her triumph. No point in spoiling it with sour grapes. He smiled with wicked joy. "I reckon Adrian will manage if we give him enough time."

Then he stood, dismissing them and any further argument.

Finty Dooley was waiting in the hall. Finty had a bandaged leg and leaned on a stick. He said, "Just wanted to say thank ye, me lord, for getting me old woman back."

Liam flushed with pleasure. Gratitude was rare, and pleasant to experience. He said, "Sure, Finty, I was only doing my duty."

Finty fiddled with his cap. "Just the same, me lord, Missus Dooley is grateful to be out of the clutches of them crazy Achill lads and their fake bishop."

Liam's heart missed a beat. He stared cautiously around. Adrian and the councillors had dispersed. No one but him could have heard Finty's remark. He leaned forward and whispered. "*Fake* bishop?"

Finty looked embarrassed. "Sure, 'tis what they told the missus. He's a failed priest what came up from Blarney early on in the troubles. He's no more a foreigner than I am. They took him in at the monastery. They reckon he's harmless, apart from the delusions he has. But them Achill lads pretend he runs the village. They let him think he's their leader."

Liam said quickly, "Has Missus Dooley said anything about this to anybody else?"

Finty squirmed. "Sure, she didn't like to open her mouth, sir. Not with Miss Celia being so taken with the felly."

Liam grabbed a coat from the hallstand. He gripped Finty's arm none too gently. "Man, we're going for a walk up Kirkogue. I want a chat with your missus. Then I'll have to find that lad Dominic and his pals."

Limping fast to keep up with the Master, Finty gasped, "What's the hurry, me lord?"

Liam's face was pale. Hurry wasn't the word. At that moment he could have done with being in five places at once. He said, "Finty, no one must ever find out what you've just told me. Neither from you nor your wife. Finty—so help me—if you breathe a word to anyone, I'll have you fired out of the cannon of that tank which stands in front of Fist—and the same goes for Missus Dooley."

Finty's jaw dropped. "What—what's the matter, me lord?"

Liam halted to give Finty his undivided attention. "Listen, man. That fellow Zbigniev was a genuine bishop up to five minutes ago. Well, as far as I'm concerned, he still is a bishop. He made young Walsh into a priest for us, and Adrian is going to stay made. Those lads from Achill can learn to keep their mouths shut, or face my displeasure. In a year or two, when Father Con is gone, Barley Cross citizens will be looking for someone to solemnise their marriages, hear their confessions, visit their sick, christen their children, say their Masses and bury their dead. Well, by God, I'm going to see that Father Adrian Walsh is here to do it for them. And, if the good Lord don't agree, he can take it out of my hide."

Liam tramped on. Finty Dooley panted after him, overawed by the Master's vehemence. Liam had already forgotten him. The Lord of Barley Cross was busy with his thoughts. His village had had a tumultuous past. It looked as though it could expect a stormy future!

EDITOR'S INTRODUCTION TO:

FORD O' KABUL RIVER
by Rudyard Kipling

The camaraderie of the warrior is fragile, for it is the destiny of warriors that one will live and another die. Kipling tells of such an incident in a land far away. Today's soldiers do not cross the Kabul River on horseback; but there remain hazards, for the British were not the last invaders that the hardy *mujahadeen* of Afghanistan have faced.

FORD O' KABUL RIVER
Rudyard Kipling

KABUL town's by Kabul river—
  Blow the trumpet, draw the sword—
There I lef' my mate for ever,
  Wet an' drippin' by the ford.
    Ford, ford, ford o' Kabul river,
      Ford O' Kabul river in the dark!
    There's the river up and brimmin', an' there's 'arf a
      squadron swimmin'
      'Cross the ford o' Kabul river in the dark.

Kabul town's a blasted place—
  Blow the trumpet, draw the sword—
'Strewth I shan't forget 'is face
  Wet an' drippin' by the ford!
    Ford, ford, ford o' Kabul river,
      Ford o' Kabul river in the dark!
    Keep the crossing-stakes beside you, an' they will
      surely guide you
      'Cross the ford o' Kabul river in the dark.

Kabul town is sun and dust—
  Blow the trumpet, draw the sword—
I'd ha' sooner drownded fust
  'Stead of 'im beside the ford.
    Ford, ford, ford o' Kabul river,
      Ford o' Kabul river in the dark!
    You can 'ear the 'orses threshin'; you can 'ear the
      men a-splashin',
      'Cross the ford o' Kabul river in the dark.

Kabul town was ours to take—
  Blow the trumpet, draw the sword—
I'd ha' left it for 'is sake—
  'Im that left me by the ford.
    Ford, ford, ford o' Kabul river,
      Ford o' Kabul river in the dark!
     It's none so bloomin' dry there; ain't you never comin'
       nigh there,
      'Cross the ford o' Kabul river in the dark?

Kabul town'll go to hell—
  Blow the trumpet, draw the sword—
'Fore I see him 'live an' well—
  'Im the best beside the ford.
    Ford, ford, ford o' Kabul river,
      Ford o' Kabul river in the dark!
     Gawd 'elp 'em if they blunder, for their boots'll pull
       'em under,
      By the ford o' Kabul river in the dark.

Turn your 'orse from Kabul town—
  Blow the trumpet, draw the sword—
'Im an' 'arf my troop is down,
  Down and drownded by the ford.
    Ford, ford, ford o' Kabul river,
      Ford o' Kabul river in the dark!
     There's the river low an' fallin', but it ain't no use
       a-callin'
      'Cross the ford o' Kabul river in the dark!

EDITOR'S INTRODUCTION TO:

FIGHTING BACK
Douglas J. Greenlaw and Robert Gleason

> In order for evil to triumph, it is sufficient
> that good men do nothing.
>
> —Edmund Burke

Terrorism seems a characteristic of the age, and for all our power there is seldom anything the United States armed forces can do—for unlike warriors, the terrorists strike from the shadows and creep back into their holes. They do not fight armed warriors; they prey upon the innocent and helpless.

Sometimes the warriors are given an opportunity. As I write this, US Navy aircraft have just forced down an airliner conveying PLO pirates; and the entire nation is cheering.

Alas, such opportunities are rare. I have often thought that one remedy to terrorism might be to require every experienced combat arms officer of the United States to carry, on and off duty, a loaded pistol. Placing ten thousand armed warriors in ships, airplanes, and airports would make life far more difficult for terrorists and common criminals alike.

International terrorists are not the only enemies civilization faces. Some need not be imported; they spring up unwanted from within our society. They are no less dangerous to our society than would-be barbarian invaders.

It is far too seldom that they meet genuine warriors. . . .

FIGHTING BACK
Douglas J. Greenlaw and Robert Gleason

When most people think of TV executives, they flash straight to Robert Duvall in *Network*. In the film, Duvall comes across as the quintessential corporate wheeler-dealer, a button-down cut-throat with the business ethics of a hammerhead shark.

This image of the media VP is, of course, restricted to the skyscraper world of flashing computers and corner-office conspiracies. The Duvall character is a creature of boardroom maneuverings, expense account lunches and sleek stretch limos. We can't quite picture him even taking a subway, let alone chasing mad-dog muggers through those labyrinthine depths. We just can't visualize the Bill Paleys or General Sarnoffs of this world fullbacking into the midtown rush hour crowds, charging through Grand Central's crush, attacking the subway steps, high-hurdling the turnstiles like Edwin Moses and coldcocking the kill-crazed desperado who'd just beaten up an old lady and snatched her purse.

Nonetheless, that is precisely what a New York television executive did not so long ago. His name is Douglas Greenlaw, and he is the Vice President, Sales, of the CBN Cable Network, the third largest cable network in this country. Recently, he witnessed an elderly woman being mugged on 42nd Street in New York City. He saw her get her ankle and nose broken, a cheekbone cracked and two teeth knocked out. Greenlaw, who also received silver and bronze stars in Vietnam, gave chase. He eventually caught and decked the mugger in the New York subways.

Greenlaw, for his efforts, had a piece done on him in the New York *Daily News*. They also gave him a plaque and one thousand dollars which he promptly donated to a fund for police officers' widows and orphans.

136

The mugger, for his efforts, was sent to prison.

When you visit Greenlaw at CBN Cable you find that at age 39, he has an easy-going manner and an engaging smile. He seems surprisingly fit for a New York businessman. Greenlaw comes across as reserved, self-effacing, and when I get down to asking him why he gave pursuit to a violent criminal, he is clearly embarrassed by the question.

"People ask me that, and I never know what to say. We do things because we can do them. In my case, I played the typical high school sports, worked in tractor factories and the Gary, Indiana steel mills while getting through Indiana University, and I saw action in Vietnam—though, come to think of it, that should have discouraged rather than encouraged me. In any event, when I went after him, I had a reasonable expectation of catching him, which is probably why I did it."

I'm curious about 'Nam and ask Greenlaw to expand. . . . "I was in Vietnam for what seemed like an eternity but in fact was there only nine months out of a year tour of duty. I was wounded three times. The first one was minor, a slash on my forearm from a ricochet that seemed to come from no-where during a sniper attack . . . I didn't report it because it is supposedly bad luck to receive Purple Hearts for minor injuries. . . . The second wound was more serious, a rifle shot to the leg. I mended in an 'in country' hospital in Danang for four weeks and was sent back to command a rifle company in the mountains in the north near the DMZ. The third and most devastating wound was caused by a booby-trap. A 155mm artillery shell was trip-wired and hung from a bamboo tree, head high. It killed three men in front of me and one behind. There were serious wounds to the neck, face, legs, buttocks and I had my left arm pinned to my chest with a sliver of the bamboo tree about the size of an arrow."

I asked Greenlaw if he picked up his medals, having heard that some of the Vietnam veterans never bothered. He laughed. "Oh, there wasn't much chance of getting out of that. They had me in the hospital for nine months. I got them lying down."

When I asked him what they were, he hesitated, then said: "Silver Star, two Bronze Stars, two Purple Hearts . . . but that was a long time ago."

I asked Doug if he'd take a crack at describing his pursuit of the mugger. He sent it to me the next day, and I am pleased to note his touch is light.

* * *

The way most of us were raised, if we saw someone in trouble, we thought we were supposed to help. Of course, nowadays a lot of people will tell you this isn't very smart. They will say that it's wiser to look away, walk away, or better still, run away. For whatever it's worth, I recently had a chance to reexamine this old "Good Samaritan" philosophy.

I was walking up 42nd Street toward the CBN offices in New York City, when I witnessed a crime. A young man grabbed an old lady's handbag, knocked her down, kicked her in the face and ran off.

I suppose everyone asks themselves how they should react in that sort of situation. For some unknown reason the crowd on 42nd Street reacted by doing nothing, and for equally mysterious reasons, I took off after the mugger.

In all honesty, I can't say why I did it. At the time I took off after him, my mind was blank. I just did it. One minute I was standing there on the street watching this young man kick a helpless old woman in the face, and the next minute my legs were pumping. I was racing after him toward Grand Central Station, screaming at the top of my lungs: *"STOP, THIEF!"*

In retrospect, I wish I could say I'd had a rational dialogue with myself first—stuff about good and evil, God and man— then done the right thing. But there was none of that. In fact, as he cut across 42nd, darting in and out of the horn-honking, brake-screeching, skidding, swerving trucks, buses and cabs, the only thoughts registering in my brain were: *"You're crazy. You're going to get yourself killed. You're going to be 40 next year. You're too old for this stuff."* And most distressing of all was the thought: *"What are you going to do with him if you CATCH him?"*

But still, there I was, charging into the middle of 42nd Street, banging off bumpers, dodging rear fenders, ears pounding with horn blasts, brake screeches and irate screams. Finally, after failing to halt the west-bound traffic on the opposite side, I ended up careening belly-down across the hood of a candy-apple red Olds Cutlass Supreme, and falling face-first across the sidewalk in front of Grand Central. I looked up from the curb just in time to see the mugger duck into the station and race toward the subway.

Grand Central during lunch hour is a frenzied hive of

activity. People are visiting its stores, cutting through its passageways to save time, getting on and off trains. In short, those packed crowds do not make for *French Connection*-style chase scenes . . . which was probably all that enabled me to keep up with him. Fifteen years ago, it was my fate to slog through the rice paddies of Vietnam; and there a tree mine once had the bad judgment not only to wipe out one of my squads but to blow away half my knee in the process.

So it was just as well that Grand Central was packed. I'm not sure I was up to a serious foot-race. It was all I could do to stumble along fifty or so feet behind the man, shoving my way through the crowd, screaming those dread words at the top of my gasping lungs: "Stop, thief!"

And then it happened.

The crowd parted, and the mugger was in the clear, racing toward the turnstiles. Now that he was in the open again, he was really able to turn on the high-speed, while all I was able to turn on were more complaints from my knee and from the irate passers-by whom I jostled, shoved and grumped at. Even worse, when I got through the crowd, I saw him already slamming through the "Do Not Enter" gate.

I don't know what came over me.

Maybe I thought I was a high school senior playing corner linebacker in the final play-offs. Or maybe I thought that sadistic DI I'd had in OCS was still behind me, lapping me on the quarter-mile Fort Benning track, shouting monstrously terrifying threats. Or maybe I thought my old nemesis, that tree mine, was once again in close pursuit. Whatever it was, the next thing I knew I was kicking out across the subway entrance, vaulting the turnstiles at a dead-run and charging down those steps three at a time. I hit the platform just as the mugger cut through a closing subway door which I got my hand into a split-second before it slammed shut.

Standing there, forcing the door back open, I stared down at the mugger who was now collapsed on the floor, shaking his head in disgust.

Doubled over with exhaustion.

Too out of breath to really struggle.

The police came and got him. Afterward I picked the guy out of a line-up, so I guess justice has triumphed.

However, I was genuinely surprised at the comments from a few of my New York friends. For a couple of days I heard remarks such as: *"What the hell did you do that for?" "You*

*crazy or something?" "You know, you're no kid anymore."
"You better watch that stuff."*

I'm sure that people meant well, but I still feel I did the right thing.

Even if, at the time, I seemed to be a minority of one.

So the week passed. By Friday night the comments had gotten to me, and when I got home I was a little put off. I told my wife about the reactions, and afterward I felt sorry for having said anything.

But later as my wife was putting our son to bed, I heard him ask her from his room: "Mommy, we're not supposed to let bad things happen, are we?"

She said: "No, we're not."

I felt a lot better after that.

EDITOR'S INTRODUCTION TO:

VICTORY
J. P. Boyd

As it was before, it will be again: weapons may win battles, but only warriors can win victory.

VICTORY
J. P. Boyd

The storm clouds were already moving in when Markham checked the ammunition belts and then dumped the maps onto the co-pilot's seat beside him. Against the blue-green sky, so much denser than that of that now mythical world, the earth, one of the old obsolete training zeppelins was circling above the base. Markham tried to tell himself that it was just another mission, that he was an experienced combat pilot and the target he was stalking was slow, fragile, and an easy mark, but he was still frightened. Nonetheless, he had pulled the harness around him and begun his pre-flight checklist when Adarian climbed up on the wing beside him.

"You don't have to go. 341 Squadron is out searching for the reconnaissance plane already. This is a training wing. It's not our job anymore."

Markham's eyes fell on Adarian's left hand, which rested lightly on the lip of the cockpit. Three fingers were missing. Like Markham himself, Adarian had been posted to training after a long spell at the front, but he had earned his retirement honorably. Markham had simply been disgraced.

"I know why you want this one. Over a hundred missions, and not a single confirmed victory. But you have a job *here*. You're the best instructor in the whole wing. Your squadron is always up before anyone else and stays in the air longer than any other. Your kids survive out there because of what you tell them. You want them to have to learn from the likes of Reggie?"

Markham abruptly dropped the clipboard, then retrieved it from between the rudder pedals. His old roommate, Reggie Tooms, had been one of the great pre-war pilots, a member of the Red Dragon stunt team, one of the two pilots on the first nonstop flight from Johanteim to Farl-on-the-Sea. Then he had looped too close to the ground and lost a leg. It was no secret to the wing commander or anybody else that he had a little kaz-wine in the morning, more at lunch, and a whole bottle in the evening. But he was a quiet drunk. With experienced men so short, he had to be risked. Making a tight turn over the Arashim Sea, his plane had collided with a cadet's and both had died.

"The fighters have a long way to go, Rupert. They could easily miss him. If that plane reaches its mothership with its film, the whole coast can expect a major raid within weeks, and hundreds will die. Many of them will be civilians. The Karlans don't yet know how weak our home defenses are. They can bring in their war zeps and drop four thousand tons of bombs in a single night."

Adarian said nothing. Here in this thick, blue-green sky, the zeppelin was king, and heavier-than-air planes were little gnats that huffed and puffed through the dense air at slow speeds only a fraction of the speed of sound, and only a little faster than the steel-hulled monsters that floated serenely below them. As heavy as a sea-going destroyer, even a half-dreadnought or a cruiser could obliterate a city in a single raid if allowed to bomb uncontested. Until three months ago, the coast had been heavily defended, but the war out in the islands, in that giant archipelago where it had all begun, was not going well, and all reserves had to be thrown into a giant push to hang onto the mini-continent of Farsten. If the Karlans knew how thoroughly the coast had been stripped—

"Heavy weather's rolling in. How will you find it?"

Markham shook his head. "I'll need luck. But it's a very big plane, even in the rain."

He laid the clipboard down and started the engine. Adarian looked at him for a few moments and said nothing.

"Torpedo bombers like this don't carry gun cameras. Even if you shoot it down, it will never be officially confirmed."

Markham smiled. "I'll know." He then waved Adarian off the wing and shouted above the sound of the engine: "You'd better climb down."

Adarian nodded, and started to go, then turned back and said, "Good luck, John."

"You've been a good friend, Rupert."

A few moments later, the big recon-bomber was in the air, carrying only a single pilot instead of the usual crew of three, and Markham disappeared into the overcast.

* * *

After he had set his course, Markham had a long time to think, surrounded only by the grey murk and drizzle. His final mission at the front, the one where he had so nearly died, was never far from his mind, and the images kept replaying themselves, over and over.

It had begun as a routine fighter sweep over the Arashim Sea, but they had stumbled upon rich treasure: a Karlan pocket carrier, badly damaged in an air battle over Farsten and left behind by the retreating van. While the squadron leader was calling in four-engined zeppelin destroyers from 518 Squadron, the carrier turned away from them towards the Karlan mainland and dropped its few remaining aircraft, hoping to sacrifice them to cover its own escape.

Lieutenant-Captain Graves had not been fooled. He had sent one flight top-side to shadow the airship for the zeppelin-destroyers and had taken the rest in to tangle with the Karlan heavier-than-air. A few fighters, half a dozen clumsy torpedo-bombers, and even a slow, long-endurance Osprey scout had fallen off the monorail in the zeppelin's belly to offer themselves for the slaughter. Markham went in joyously, hoping to at last end his long drought—and Taisho had turned the wrong way and become separated from the rest of the flight.

In his defense, the boy had never been under fire before, but Markham knew that half of all losses occurred during a pilot's first ten missions, and went after his lost lamb. As had happened half a dozen times before with other rookies, Markham found him and saved his life—but only at the price of firing from extreme long range, driving off Taisho's attacker and in the process passing up an almost sure kill. Moments later, he saw how slowly the Karlan was climbing, sluggishly trying to regain enough height to rejoin the battle, and realized that the enemy must have been damaged in the battle over Farsten.

"Cover my back! I'll get him." Or die trying.

He very nearly *had* died. The Karlan was a veteran, and even in a damaged plane had managed to jink and weave enough to throw Markham's aim off. Four short bursts and Markham had been rewarded only with the flash of a couple of shells exploding against the Karlan's tail—and then his own windshield had exploded.

Markham had ignored the cardinal rule of dogfighting, so obsessed with his victim that he had become an easy mark for another enemy pilot. Half-blinded by his own blood, his instrument panel shattered, only his instincts and experience had kept his plane weaving, dodging—until a wild burst from Taisho had discouraged the Karlan, and Markham had been able to break away.

When he had managed to land his badly damaged plane, he stood beside it, his face covered with dried blood, numbly poking his fist through the hole in the wing. If the shell had hit the main spar, the whole wing would have come off, and he would have cartwheeled three thousand meters into the ocean.

"I'm sorry, Markham. I wanted to give you a little more time." Still staring at his scarred aircraft, he had barely heard the wing commander's words. "By rights, with your seniority you should have a squadron now, but who could follow a man who's never shot down a single enemy plane? I'm posting you to a training squadron—for good."

It had still not sunk in, not even when he was on the transport for the mainland. It was the forty-seventh consecutive mission that his flight had returned without a loss.

"Davidenko Main to Rec One. Where are you?"

The radio crackled with static, but wing commander Rolfe's voice was still recognizable. Markham half smiled, feeling vaguely honored by his concern, and relayed his position.

"341 Squadron is still looking. He may turn south toward Gabila, the way the wind is running. Good luck!"

Markham acknowledged the message and signed off. He was a man with an obsession, but he was also the only pilot on the base who was fully sound of body. Because he had managed to complete a couple of years of the mathematics/physics baccalaureate at Khenov University before the war had plucked him away, he was also that rarity: a fighter pilot who was a good navigator. The wing commander knew all this, and had not tried to talk him out of it when he had burst into Rolfe's office, already in his flying suit, but as they waited in the outer office while the wing Met officer roughed out a quick forecast, Markham's stigma, unspoken, had been much in their thoughts.

Sighing, Markham tried to make himself comfortable, a tall man forever cramped into cockpits of ungenerous size, and forced himself to think of happy memories. For a few minutes, he let his mind roam back to those days when he was a teenager hanging around the airport, finally learning to fly, in the forests and little farms of his native Adar. His home province was deep in the interior of the continent, a region devoid of large cities, and the war had left it little changed, although he had not actually seen it in nearly four years.

Then, he remembered his first meeting with Adarian.

The training zeppelin *Audacious* was tired and slow, one of the last to have a canvas outer hull stretched taut over a duraluminum frame. She was far too fragile for the long-range jousting of modern airships, and so her turrets had been stripped and her hangar enlarged to accommodate the Piradot fighters, now retired from the front themselves, that were used for advance training.

The cadets learned to fly in two-seat trainers with hostilities-only instructors drafted from civilian flying clubs, including a couple of women. Pilots with actual combat experience were too precious to waste on routine flying, but instead gave advanced tactics-and-gunnery training after the cadets had soloed and graduated to single-seaters of their own. In that sense, Markham, Adarian, and Tooms were privileged characters, idolized by the young cubs they taught. Markham did not feel very privileged.

In theory, he was supposed to mess with the other officers in the zeppelin's wardroom, but he no longer felt very hungry. Usually, he hid out at lunchtime in the auxiliary control room in the lower tail-fin of the airship, reading one of the innumerable books he checked out of the village library on his weekend visits off the base while his brother instructors were having a few in the pub.

The tail-fin was rather cramped—it had been adapted to its secondary role merely by fitting a narrow windshield with a hundred and eighty degree field of vision across a slit in the leading edge of the canvas and duraluminum framing, with a rudder wheel mounted just under the glass and the elevator wheel within easy reach to the right. A bank of electric ballast toggles hung overhead and there were three gauges—height, airspeed, and simple compass—mounted on a sheet of plywood just below the windshield. The petty officers who manned it—but only in emergencies—were supposed to control the ship standing up, so Markham had to sit uncomfortably, with his back against the perforated girder that was the main spine of the fin.

"Oh!" Adarian was almost as startled as Markham, who instinctively shut his book and looked guilty.

"Sorry, old man. I'm new on the ship and I didn't know—"

"That's all right." Stiffly, Markham clambered to his feet and put out his hand. Noticing the stylized wings of a heavier-than-air pilot and the two rings of a Senior Lieutenant, he said, "The other instructors are having lunch in the wardroom. It's—"

"No, that's all right." The other man smiled. "My medicine upsets my stomach, and I can't eat for a few hours after I take it, so I have to compensate by gnawing plates and all at supper."

"I'm sorry."

Adarian added cheerfully, "I went a flamer over Astrakhan. Lost these fingers and took a piece of shrapnel in my gut in the bargain. Tummy's better, though; I can eat almost anything now."

Markham looked at his hands; they showed no signs of burns.

As if divining his thoughts, Adarian nodded. "They're okay. You should see my legs, though. You can get out of an aircraft remarkably fast when your fuel supply is coming up through the floor of your cockpit."

Markham laughed in spite of himself, and then stopped abruptly. It had been so long since he had laughed that he had forgotten the sound of it. He had studiously avoided socializing with his brother officers—and would have even if most did not drink so heavily, out of pain or loneliness—and spent his days and nights in a kind of numbness. His disgrace ate at him like a cancer, and though he was reasonably conscientious in the air, for the cadets' sake, he seemed to have lost all emotions, all feelings of his own. Until just then.

Adarian seemed embarrassed when Markham cut his laugh short. "Well, I didn't mean to intrude. I—"

"It's all right. My name is Markham, by the way."

"Rupert Adarian."

Adarian did not return to disturb Markham's privacy the following day, but Markham found himself nodding pleasantly in Adarian's direction at the morning briefings. In time, Adarian responded by striking up a conversation with him now and then, and little by little, Markham began to come out of his shell.

*　　*　　*

What really cemented their friendship was Adarian's habit
of dropping in on Markham's ground school lectures. Usually, the lectures were given in a battered warehouse that had
been converted to a classroom through the addition of graffiti-
scarred desks from a storeroom of the elementary school in
the village, and Markham, as senior instructor, gave most of
them. Adarian first materialized, however, when Markham
had the cadets outside, watching him from above while he
worked down in the firing pit, adjusting his plane's guns for
their edification.

Perched on a stepladder, Markham pulled open the access
panel on the top of a wing and turned around to face his
charges.

"The Piradot, and the faster Tanzers that you'll fly at the
front, have one cannon buried in each wing, set to fire just
outside the propeller arc. Flying is fun, you all want to be
good pilots, but to become an ace, you have to understand
your guns, too.

"The infantry fight with projectile rifles; a powder charge
spits a bit of metal into the air which flies free until it hits
something. Unfortunately, that something is usually the
ground." The cadets laughed. "I think so, too, but to be fair
to them, while our atmosphere isn't nearly as thick as the
ocean, its density is great enough to play all kinds of tricks.

"Our skies are a deep aquamarine because the air scatters
the sunlight, blue and green more than red. Dawn and sunset
are always spectacular, a band of rose and crimson flung
halfway around the sky—it's the air again, fiddling with the
long, slanting rays from a sun just above the horizon. Mirages
over the desert, or sometimes when we look back over the
sun-warmed land when coming back from the cooler sea . . .
the air wrinkles the light to make those, too, and so often that
a good pilot has to learn to allow for the mirages and make
his mind a third eye. And the air slows down a bullet so
quickly that a round is completely spent after a hundred
meters, at most."

He suddenly spotted Adarian standing in the back row and
pointed towards himself. Adarian made a vague gesture as if
to say, "No rush," and Markham collected himself and
jumped into the cockpit. "Our guns fire rocket shells, self-
propelled rounds that keep pushing against the wind until
their fuel runs out. We have much longer range than the
infantry—but the rockets don't solve everything."

Over his shoulder, he called back, "The plane's tail is on a jack, and right now the guns are absolutely horizontal. Watch."

He fired a short burst at the white cloth square a hundred meters in front of him, and missed. The shells exploded on the ground well in front of the target.

He stood up in the cockpit and turned around. "Gravity, gentlemen. To be a good gunner, you have to learn to allow for that drop—five meters in the first second, fifteen more in the second. I and Lieutentant Adarian, who's standing behind you, are going to teach you how to fight. To know how much your shells will drop. To lead a target that's moving left to right, in front of you. And most important of all, how to dodge someone who's shooting at you."

The rest of the lecture was a rather technical introduction to the Mark IX automatic cannon and to the trim screws that could be used to adjust both the horizontal and vertical deflection of the cannons. According to the book, one was supposed to give each wing-gun enough inward deflection that their field of fire would converge at one hundred meters in front of the plane—"But I would recommend fifty, at least to start." All the pilots cranked their guns up a couple of degrees above horizontal to allow for the falling, parabolic trajectory of the rockets, so that the shells would pass through the plane of the wings at the same distance where the two guns converged.

Afterwards, Adarian waited up for him.

"What are you doing here, Rupert?"

"Learning at the feet of the master. You've forgotten more about air-to-air gunnery than I ever knew."

Markham smiled. "But you have four victories."

"Luck. And flying very close to my victims. I once came home with a goodish portion of my late adversary's tail assembly embedded in my port wing. Wing wasn't too pleased."

"Bread-and-water and ten days in the stockade?"

"Well, hardly. A week before, at morning briefing, he'd bellowed and shouted that we should all be more aggressive."

Markham smiled. "Suit yourself."

"I will." Adarian hunched over and jiggled an imaginary joystick. "You never know. I can still fly."

Indeed he could, and he ignored all the flying classes, but ground school in gunnery, tactics, and navigation attracted him like a flame mesmerizing a night-flying insect. Adarian rarely bothered with the brief reading assignments and never with the written quizzes—"An instructor flunk?"—but he squeezed himself into the back row whenever he could.

After Adarian had sat through a talk on snap-aiming and deflection shots, Markham stood him a drink in the officer's club.

"The third time, Rupert?"

"Why not? It's a change from catching a quick one in the club when you've got all the squadrons in the classroom. We all drink too much anyway."

Markham laughed, then turned serious. "You've made me better, Rupert. You can never really teach them what it's like out there. It's so—abstract. But a burning plane isn't."

"No." Adarian played with the handle of his mug. "But good training can give them a chance."

Markham nodded. "And I feel that now. Feel this is important. I'd still jump at a chance to go back to the front, but I feel alive again, like I'm part of the war again."

Peering through the canopy at the overcast, straining to spot the shadow of the Karlan flying boat, Markham felt very much a part of the war. If he found the Karlan, he would have to brave a storm of shells from the flying boat's four turrets, and with or without a fight, it would still take all his skill to find his way home in this foul weather. And yet he felt completely happy for the first time in nearly a year. He was healthy and skillful, and it was right that he should be at risk. The peace and calmness of the training school seemed as remote and phantasmal as a summer daydream.

"Davidenko Main to Rec One. You should be near maximum range. Confirm."

Markham looked at his gauges and sighed. "Rec One to Davidenko Main. Any word from the others?"

"341 Squadron has turned back. Search negative. Over."

"Roger. Tanks half full. Over."

"Davidenko Main to Rec One. You are ordered—"

Markham snapped off the radio. He could always pretend that he had not heard, but the habit of discipline was very strong; it would be easier to ignore an order if he did not permit himself to hear it. It wasn't until the instant of silencing that crackling, static-filled voice that he had realized he might be willing to die just to score one victory.

Dispassionately, he tried to weigh the odds. Of finding the

Karlan, poor. Of ditching and rescue at sea, at best, fair. Of
returning to base if he continued his search pattern, poor to
none. Of the deaths if the Karlan reached its mother-zeppelin,
many thousands. Of the lives spared if he returned and taught
his boys how to survive, who could say? But certainly some.

Markham thought and thought and stared out into the grey
sky. He made his decision.

An hour later, he found the Karlan. The drizzle banged his
canopy like tiny, wet bullets, but the flying boat was huge.
Not the nimble twin-engined Kiriot he had expected, but a
ponderous Wyndan pulled through the air by four huge radi-
als. It cut diagonally in front of him, a shadowy grey blur
only slightly darker than the surrounding clouds, and he was
so startled that he turned late, and almost lost it.

After a quick contact report to Davidenko, he snapped off
his radio, rammed the throttle full forward, and put his plane
into a shallow dive to come up below and behind the flying
boat to strike its vulnerable and unprotected belly.

Adarian had always known the most important rule of
gunnery: get close. As Markham zoomed up towards his
target, he held his fire until he was within a hundred meters.
Bracing his elbows against the sides of his seat, he squinted
through the reflector sight and mentally estimated both the
inward and vertical deflection of the shells, aiming for the
two engines buried in the port wing.

He fired, and fingers of smoke lit at intervals by speeding
dots of brilliant yellow converged from either wing to a point
in front of him. The first few shells flew just high, but then
the stream intersected the wing, and round, bursting flashes
erupted from the engines and the airfoil between them.

At the last moment, Markham shoved the throttle forward—
and for one terrible moment, as the big reconnaissance bomber
nosed down much more slowly than the single-seaters he was
used to, he thought that the big propellers above him would
scythe through his canopy and slice him into pieces. As he
ducked instinctively, the two planes missed by centimeters. A
line of shells flashed above him as the dorsal gunner tried to
kill him, but Markham rolled and turned sharply away as
soon as his tail was clear, and the gunner—trying to train his
gun up and over the interrupter bar that was supposed to keep
him from shooting his own wing off—could not bring his gun
to bear in time.

When Markham came out of his diving turn and split-essed, he saw nothing for a moment, and cursed. Then his eyes, half-blinded by the flash of his own exploding shells, adjusted and he saw a dark shape just at the limit of visibility.

Pursing his lips, Markham made his plans and climbed, staying a safe distance above and behind his target, until it was a dim cross almost directly beneath him—and then fell upon it like a thunderbolt. At the last moment, the gunners saw him, but his shells were already stitching a trail of bursting fire from the tail forward to the wings and nose, and then he was past and below, twisting his clumsy plane into another sharp turn.

As he looked back, he saw no sign that his shots had done any damage at all. He swore and came around for another pass. A quick run at the nose? Too risky in the overcast; even if he avoided a collision, he might still lose contact while turning around after the pass.

His luck was just as bad as ever. His own reconnaissance bomber was lightly armed for so big a plane, and the Wyndan was huge and sturdy. He had drawn within a couple hundred meters, a trail of fire from the tail gunner already falling like a waterfall underneath him, when the port outboard engine exploded.

Markham pulled his own nose up immediately to give the gunner no further chance at him and watched, mesmerized, as the wing section between the engines went up in flames with astonishing abruptness. The inboard engine began to smoke—or so he thought, he could hardly see the plane itself against what suddenly became heavy rain—and then there was a second flash of light and the whole left wing was on fire.

The great flying boat staggered and lost altitude quickly. The pilot was trying to keep it level, but it was handling sluggishly, as if Markham's shells had severed a control line. Suddenly it fell on its side and dropped straight for the water.

Markham dove after it, determined to see the end, to be sure, but as he came closer and closer to the waves, he pulled the nose up a little rather than risk crashing into the sea in the rain. The fiery beacon continued to fall before him, and then seemed to right itself for a moment just a few meters above the ocean. Markham lined up for a shot while still far away, but the flying boat slammed into the choppy waves before he could fire.

The damaged wing ripped off completely, and the boat

went up on its nose, then leisurely fell back, right-side up. Markham reached down for the toggle and dropped a parachute flare. If the crew were quick, some of them might still get out.

The boat sank only five minutes later, after Markham had dropped the remainder of his flares, and he turned for home.

He remembered that this plane, unlike the fighter he had flown in the islands, was not equipped with a gunsight camera. Probably, his victory would never be confirmed.

Somehow, that didn't seem important. *He* knew, and he would go back to his cadets with a clear conscience.

Too excited to sleep after filing his report and telling an excited Adarian the good news, he spent the rest of the evening walking along the beach, listening to the pounding surf and unwinding. Adarian finally found him there well after midnight.

"Where the heck have you been? I've been hunting all over for you. You lucky bastard! A coastal cutter picked up a couple of crewmen from the Wyndan. Your victory will be confirmed."

Markham started laughing, and his ribs ached by the time he finally regained control of himself.

"Thanks, Rupert. I mean it. It's very nice."

"There's one thing I don't understand."

"What?"

"The cutter was only a few kilometers off shore. How did they drift so far so fast?"

"They didn't. The flying boat must have trusted to the bad weather and stayed close to the coast. I don't really know. But I didn't run into it until long after I had turned back."

"Turned back?"

Markham nodded, and picked up a wave-polished twig to heave into the surf.

Adarian threw up his hands and said feelingly, "Victory!" but it was not at all obvious which conquest he meant.

EDITOR'S INTRODUCTION TO:

THE WAR AGAINST "STAR WARS"
by Robert Jastrow

Robert Jastrow was the founder of the Goddard Institute for Space Studies, as well as the first chairman of NASA's Lunar Exploration Committee. He received his Ph.D. in theoretical physics from Columbia University, and is currently Professor of Earth Sciences at Dartmouth University. His books on astronomy have been widely read, and he is recognized as one of the nation's foremost experts in space science. He has received the Flemming Award for outstanding service in the federal government.

Dr. Jastrow's introduction to his own essay can hardly be bettered. I'll reserve my remarks for an afterword.

THE WAR AGAINST "STAR WARS"
Robert Jastrow

PRESIDENT REAGAN offered a new strategic vision to the American people in his "Star Wars" speech of March 23, 1983. The policy he had inherited from his predecessors relied on the threat of incinerating millions of Soviet civilians as the main deterrent to a Soviet nuclear attack on our country. The President was troubled by the moral dimensions of this policy. He said: "The human spirit must be capable of rising above dealing with other nations and human beings by threatening their existence." And he called on our scientists to find a way of defending the United States against a Soviet nuclear attack by intercepting the Soviet missiles before they reached our soil.

When I first heard the President's speech, I thought he had a great idea. I wrote an article commenting favorably on the proposal[1] and then, a little later, I traveled to Washington to hear a talk by Dr. George Keyworth, the President's Science Adviser, on the strategic and technical implications of the President's plan.

Since Dr. Keyworth was rumored to have made a major contribution to the thinking behind the "Star Wars" speech, I felt that I would be getting an insider's view of the technical prospects for success in this difficult undertaking. That was particularly interesting to me, because several of my fellow physicists had expressed the gravest reservations about the technical feasibility of the proposal. In fact, Dr. Hans Bethe, a distinguished Nobel laureate in physics, had said bluntly, "I don't think it can be done."

Dr. Keyworth started by describing the circumstances that had led to the President's speech. Then he got into the

---

[1] COMMENTARY, January 1984.

technical areas I had come to hear about. "For more than five months," he told us, "some fifty of our nation's better technical minds [have] devoted their efforts almost exclusively to one problem—the defense against ballistic missiles." This group of specialists, which included some of the most qualified defense scientists in the country, had concluded that the President's goal was realistic—that it "probably could be done."

"The basis for their optimism," Dr. Keyworth went on, "is our tremendously broad technical progress over the past decade." He pointed specifically to the advances in computers and "new laser techniques." He also mentioned the promising new developments that might enable us to protect the vitally important satellites carrying all this laser weaponry and computing equipment, and prevent the Soviets from knocking these critical satellites out as a preliminary to a nuclear attack on the United States. "These and other recent technical advances," Dr. Keyworth concluded, "offer the possibility of a workable strategic [missile] defense system."

That was pretty clear language. Defense experts had given the President's proposal a green light on its technical merits. I went back to New York with a feeling that the President's vision of the future—a future in which nuclear weapons would be "impotent and obsolete"—was going to become a reality.

The following month, a panel of university scientists came out with a report that flatly contradicted Dr. Keyworth's assessment. According to the panel, an effective defense of the United States against Soviet missiles was "unattainable." The report, prepared under the sponsorship of the Union of Concerned Scientists (UCS),[2] leveled numerous criticisms at the "Star Wars" proposal. It pointed out, *inter alia*, that thousands of satellites would be needed to provide a defensive screen; that one of the "Star Wars" devices under consideration would require placing in orbit a satellite weighing 40,000 tons; that the power needed for the lasers and other devices proposed would equal as much as 60 percent of the total power output of the United States; and that, in any case, the Soviets would be able to foil our defenses with a large bag of

---

[2] *A Space-Based Missile Defense*, March 1984; The Fallacy of Star Wars, based on studies conducted by the Union of Concerned Scientists, edited by John Tirman, Vintage, 293 pp., $4.95.

relatively inexpensive tricks, such as spinning the missile to prevent the laser from burning a hole in it, or putting a shine on it to reflect the laser light.

The signers of the report included physicists of world renown and great distinction. The impact of their criticisms seemed absolutely devastating.

Around the same time, another study of the feasibility of the "Star Wars" defense came out with more or less the same conclusion. According to that report, which had been prepared for the Office of Technology Assessment (OTA)[3] of the Congress, the chance of protecting the American people from a Soviet missile attack is "so remote that it should not serve as the basis for public expectations or national policy."

These scientific studies, documented with charts and tables, apparently sounded the death knell of missile defense. Scientists had judged the President's proposal, and found it wanting. According to *Nature*, the most prestigious science journal in the world:

> The scientific community knows that [the President's proposal] will not work. The President's advisers, including his science adviser, Dr. George Keyworth, know it too, but are afraid to say so.
>
> Dr. Keyworth is employed to keep the President informed on these technical matters, but sadly, there is no evidence that he is willing to give Mr. Reagan the bad news.

A few weeks later, I received unclassified summaries of the blue-ribbon panels appointed by the Defense Department to look into the feasibility of a United States defense against Soviet missiles.[4] These were the documents on which Dr. Keyworth had relied in part for his optimistic appraisal. The reports by the government-appointed consultants were as different from the reports by the university scientists as day is from night. One group of distinguished experts said no funda-

---

[3] *Directed Energy Missile Defense in Space:* A Background Paper, April 1984.
[4] *Ballistic Missile Defense and U.S. National Security:* A Summary Report, Prepared for the Future Security Strategy Study, October 1983; *The Strategic Defense Initiative:* Statement by Dr. James C. Fletcher Before the House Committee on Armed Services, March 1984.

mental obstacles stood in the way of success; the other group, equally distinguished, said it would not work. Who was right? According to the UCS report, "any inquisitive citizen" could understand the technical issues. I decided to look into the matter. This is what I found.

Missiles usually consist of two or three separate rockets or "stages," also called boosters. On top of the uppermost stage sits the "bus" carrying the warheads. One by one, the stages ignite, burn out, and fall away. After the last stage has burned out and departed, the bus continues upward and onward through space. At this point it begins to release its separate warheads. Each warhead is pushed off the bus in a different direction with a different velocity, so as to reach a different target. The missiles with this capability are said to be MIRVed (MIRV stands for multiple independently targetable reentry vehicle).

Most of the discussion of the "Star Wars" defense assumes a many-layered defense with three or four distinct layers. The idea behind having several layers is that the total defense can be made nearly perfect in this way, even if the individual layers are less than perfect. For example, if each layer has, say, an 80 percent effectiveness—which means that one in five missiles or warheads will get through—a combination of three such layers will have an overall effectiveness better than 99 percent, which means that no more than one warhead in 100 will reach its target.[5]

The first layer, called the boost-phase defense, goes into effect as the Soviet missile rises above the atmosphere at the beginning of its trajectory. In the second layer, or mid-course defense, the booster has burned out and fallen away, and we concentrate on trying to destroy or disable the "bus" carrying the nuclear warheads, or the individual warheads themselves, as they arc up and over through space on their way to the United States. In the third layer, or terminal defense, we try to intercept each warhead in the final stages of its flight.

The boost-phase defense offers the greatest payoff to the defender because at this stage the missile has not yet sent any

---

[5] The explanation is that 20 percent get through the first layer; 20 percent of that fraction, or a net of 4 percent, get through the second layer; finally, 20 percent of that 4 percent, or 0.8 percent, get through the third layer. The overall effectiveness of the three layers is 99.2 percent.

of its warheads on their separate paths. Since the largest Soviet missiles carry ten warheads each, if our defense can destroy one of these missiles at the beginning of its flight, it will eliminate ten warheads at a time. The defense catches the Soviet missiles when they have all their eggs in one basket, so to speak.

But the boost-phase defense is also the most difficult technically, and has drawn the most fire from critics. How can we destroy a Soviet missile, thousands of miles away, within seconds or minutes after it has left its silo?

At the present time, one of the most promising technologies for doing that is the laser, which shoots a bolt of light at the missile as it rises. Missiles move fast, but light moves faster. A laser beam travels a thousand miles in less than a hundredth of a second. Focused in a bright spot on the missile's skin, the laser beam either burns a hole through the thin metal of the skin, which is only about a tenth of an inch thick, or it softens the metal sufficiently so that it ruptures and the missile disintegrates.

Another very promising technology for the boost-phase defense is the Neutral Particle Beam, which shoots a stream of fast-moving hydrogen atoms at the missile. The atoms travel at a speed of about 60,000 miles a second, which is less than the speed of light but still fast enough to catch up to the missile in a fraction of a second. The beam of fast-moving atoms is very penetrating, and goes through the metal skin of the missile and into the electronic brain that guides it on its course. There the atoms create spurious pulses of electricity that can cause the brain to hallucinate, driving the missile off its course so that it begins to tumble and destroys itself. If the beam is intense enough, it can flip the bits inside the brain's memory so that it remembers the wrong things; or it can cause the brain to lose its memory altogether. Any one of these effects will be deadly to the Soviet missile's execution of its task.

The Neutral Particle Beam can also play havoc with the circuits in the electronic brain that guides the bus sitting on top of the missile. The mischief created here may prevent the bus from releasing its warheads; or it may cause the bus to send the warheads in the wrong directions, so that they miss their targets; or it may damage the electronic circuits in the warheads themselves, after they have been pushed off the

bus, so that when they reach their targets they fail to explode.[6]
The Neutral Particle Beam can be lethal to the attacker in the
boost phase, the mid-course phase, and the terminal phase.
All in all, it is a most useful device.

Now for an important point: to be effective, the laser or the
Neutral Particle Beam must have unobstructed views of all
the Soviet missile fields. One of the best ways of achieving
that is to put the device that produces these beams on a
satellite and send it into orbit.

So this, then, is the essence of the plan for a boost-phase
defense against Soviet missiles: a fleet of satellites, containing equipment that generates laser beams or Neutral Particle
Beams, circles the earth, with enough satellites in the fleet so
that several satellites are over the Soviet missile fields at all
times—a sufficient number to shoot down, in the worst case,
all 1,400 Soviet missiles if they are launched against us
simultaneously.

The plan looks good on paper. Yet according to the UCS
report, it has absolutely no practical value. This study shows
that because of the realities of satellite orbits, the satellites
needed to protect the United States against Soviet attack
would "number in the thousands." The report's detailed
calculations put the precise number at 2,400 satellites.

Now, everyone acknowledges that these satellites are going
to be extremely expensive. Each one will cost a billion dollars
or more—as much as an aircraft carrier. Satellites are the
big-ticket items in the plan for a space-based defense. If
thousands are needed, the cost of implementing the plan will
be many trillions of dollars. A defense with a price tag like
that is indeed a "turkey," as a spokesman for the UCS called
it.

If the numbers put out by the UCS were right, there would
be no point in looking into the plan further. But after the UCS
report hit the papers, I began to hear rumors from professionals in the field that the numbers were not right. Since the
whole "Star Wars" plan rested on this one point, I thought I

---

[6] Nuclear explosives, unlike ordinary explosives, do not detonate if you
drop them or hit them with a hammer. A series of precisely timed steps,
controlled by electronic circuits in the warhead, has to occur before the
explosion can happen. If the circuits are damaged, and the steps do not
occur, or their timing is off, the warhead will not explode.

would just check out the calculations myself. So I got hold of a polar-projection map of the northern hemisphere and a piece of celluloid. I marked the positions of the North Pole and the Soviet missile fields on the celluloid, stuck a pin through the North Pole, and rotated the celluloid around the Pole to imitate the rotation of the earth carrying the missile fields with it. Then I played with the map, the moving celluloid, and different kinds of satellite orbits for a day or two, to get a feel for the problem.

It was soon clear that about 50 evenly spaced satellite orbits, with four satellites in each orbit, would guarantee adequate coverage of the missile fields. In other words, 200 satellites would do the job, and "thousands" were certainly not needed. I could also see that it might be possible to get down to fewer than 100 satellites, but I could not prove that with my celluloid "computer."

I talked again with my friends in the defense community and they told me that my answers were in the right ballpark. The experts had been looking at this problem for more than ten years, and the accurate results were well known. As I had suspected, a hundred or so satellites were adequate. According to careful computer studies done at the Livermore laboratory 90 satellites could suffice, and if the satellites were put into low-altitude orbits, we might get by with as few as 45 satellites.[7]

So the bottom line is that 90 satellites—and perhaps somewhat fewer—are needed to counter a Soviet attack. That cuts the cost down from many trillions of dollars to a level that could be absorbed into the amount already earmarked by the government for spending on our strategic forces during the next ten or fifteen years. It removes the aura of costliness and impracticality which had been cast over the President's proposal by the Union of Concerned Scientists' report.

The scientists who did these calculations for the UCS had exaggerated the number of satellites by a factor of about twenty-five. How did they make a mistake like that? A modicum of thought should have indicated that "thousands" of satellites could not be the right answer. Apparently the members of the panel did begin to think more carefully about

---

[7] These numbers depend on the power of the laser beams and the sizes of the mirror used to focus them. All the studies described here make the same assumptions—a 20- or 25-million-watt laser and a 30-foot mirror.

the matter later on—but only after they had issued their report—because in testimony before a congressional committee a UCS spokesman lowered his organization's estimate from 2,400 satellites to 800 satellites.[8] In their most recent publication on the matter, the members of the panel lowered their estimate again, to 300 satellites.[9] That was getting closer. Another factor of three down and they would be home.

But the Union of Concerned Scientists never said, to the press or the Congress: "We have found important mistakes in our calculations, and when these mistakes are corrected the impact is to cut the cost of the missile defense drastically. In fact, correcting these errors of ours has the effect of making the President's idea much more practical than we thought it was when we issued our report." Months after the publication of the report, *Science 84*, published by the American Association for the Advancement of Science, was still referring to the need for "2,400 orbiting laser stations."

The work by the Union of Concerned Scientists on the question of the satellite fleet is the poorest that has appeared in print, to my knowledge. The report prepared for the Office of Technology Assessment, which does a better job on this particular question, says that 160 satellites are needed for our defense. That is only about double the accurate result that came out of the computer studies at Livermore.

But the report to the OTA has a different failing. Because of an error in reasoning—an extremely inefficient placement of the satellites in their orbits—it concludes that if the Soviets were to build more missiles in an effort to overwhelm our defense, the United States would have to increase the number of its satellites in orbit in direct proportion to the increase in the number of Soviet missiles.[10]

---

[8] The scientist explained that his panel had forgotten that Soviet missile fields are spread out across a 5,000-mile arc in the USSR, and had put all the missiles in one spot. This made it harder for the satellite lasers to reach all the missiles, and meant more satellites were needed.

[9] *The Fallacy of Star Wars*, Chapter 5. The explanation offered by the UCS for this correction is that its experts belatedly realized some satellites are closer to their missile quarry than others, and can polish the missile off in a shorter time. That means each satellite can kill more missiles, and, therefore, fewer satellites are needed to do the whole job.

[10] The report assumed the American satellites would move through space in tight bunches, instead of being spread out around their orbits. By bunching them together this way, it kept the satellites from being used

This seems like a technical detail, but it has a cosmic impact. It means that if the Soviets build twice as many missiles, we have to build twice as many satellites. If they build four times as many missiles, we have to build four times as many satellites. Since our satellites are going to be expensive, that can be a costly trade-off. In fact, it could enable the Soviets to overwhelm our defense simply by building more missiles. As the *New Republic* said: "They could just roll out more SS-18's" (the SS-18 is the biggest and most powerful missile in the Soviet arsenal).

But some fine work by the theoretical physicists at Los Alamos has shown that the report to the OTA is seriously in error. The Los Alamos calculations, which have been confirmed by computations at Livermore, show that the number of satellites needed to counter a Soviet attack does *not* go up in direct proportion to the number of Soviet missiles. It turns out instead that the number of satellites goes up approximately in proportion to the *square root* of the number of missiles.

That also seems like a fine point—almost a quibble—but consider its significance. The square root means that if the Soviets build *four* times as many missiles, we only have to build *twice* as many satellites to match them. Suppose the United States built a defensive screen of 100 satellites that could shoot down—as a very conservative estimate—80 percent, or four-fifths, of the Soviet missiles. And suppose the Soviets decided they wanted to build enough missiles so that the number of missiles getting through our defensive screen would be the same as the number that would have reached the United States if we had no defense. That is what "overwhelming the defense" means. To do that, the Soviets would have to build more than 5,000 additional missiles and silos.[11]

---

effectively, and overestimated the number of satellites we would have to put up to counter an increased Soviet deployment of missiles. The theorists at Livermore and Los Alamos assumed the satellites were spread out evenly in their orbits when they did their calculations. I did also, when I took a look at the problem. Anyone trying to figure out how to build the best defense for the United States at the lowest cost to the taxpayer would do the same.

[11] The Soviets have 1,400 missile silos and missiles. To get five times this number and make up for the losses suffered in penetrating our defense, they would have to build another 5,600 missiles and silos.

The Los Alamos "square-root" rule tells us that if the Soviets went to that trouble and expense, the United States could counter those thousands of new missiles with only 100 additional satellites.

With numbers like that, the cost trade-offs are bound to favor the defense over the offense. If the Soviets tried to overwhelm our defense, they would be bankrupted before we were.

The report to the OTA has other defects. One is a peculiar passage in which the author exaggerates by a factor of roughly 50 the requirements for a terminal defense, i.e., a defense that tries to destroy the Soviet warheads toward the end of their passage, when they are already over the United States. Current planning assumes that as the warheads descend, they will be intercepted by smart mini-missiles with computer brains and radar or infrared "eyes" which maneuver into the path of the warhead and destroy it on impact. A smart missile of this kind destroyed an oncoming enemy warhead at an altitude of 100 miles on June 10, 1984, in a successful test of the technology by the Army.

The question is: how many smart missiles are required? Professionals sizing up the problem have concluded that at most 5,000 intercepting missiles will be needed. The answer according to the report to the OTA: 280,000 smart missiles. Though these smart missiles will not cost as much as aircraft carriers, they are not exactly throwaways. Thus the effect of this calculation, as with the studies by the Union of Concerned Scientists on the size of our fleet of laser-equipped satellites, is to create the impression that a defense against Soviet missiles will be so costly as to be impractical.

How did the report to the Office of Technology Assessment arrive at 280,000 missiles? First, the report assumed that about 1,000 sites in the United States—missile silos, command posts, and so on—need to be defended. That is reasonable.

Second, the report assumed the Soviets might choose to concentrate·their whole attack on any one of these 1,000 sites. This means that every single site would have to have enough intercepting missiles to counter the Soviet attack, if the entire attack were aimed at this one location.

That is not reasonable. Why would the Soviets launch thousands of warheads—their entire nuclear arsenal—against one American missile silo? This is known in the trade as a

GIGO calculation (garbage in, garbage out). The theorist makes an absurd assumption, does some impeccable mathematics, and arrives at an absurd answer.

When theoretical physicists joust over ideas, a factor of two hardly counts; a factor of three matters a bit; factors of ten begin to be important; factors of 100 can win or lose an argument; and factors of 1,000 begin to be embarrassing. In a study of the practicality of the Neutral Particle Beam—that most promising destroyer of Soviet missiles and warheads—the panel of the Union of Concerned Scientists made a mistake by a cool factor of 1,600. As in the case of the panel's estimate of the size of our satellite fleet, the direction of its error was such as to make this promising "Star Wars" technology seem hopelessly impractical.

According to the scientists who wrote the UCS report, the device—called a linear accelerator—needed to generate the Neutral Particle Beam would weigh 40,000 tons. To be effective, this enormous weight would have to be placed in a satellite. Of course, the idea of loading 40,000 tons onto an orbiting satellite is absurd. By comparison, the NASA space station will weigh about 40 tons. This finding by the Union of Concerned Scientists makes it clear that the plan to use the Neutral Particle Beam is ridiculous.

But the UCS's study panel made a mistake. The correct result for the weight of the linear accelerator is 25 tons, and not 40,000 tons. Now, 25 tons is quite a practical weight to put into an orbiting satellite. It is, in fact, about the same as the payload carried in a single flight of the NASA shuttle.[12]

A UCS spokesman admitted his organization's rather large error in congressional testimony some months ago.[13] But when he made the admission he did not say: "We have made a mistake by a factor of more than a thousand, and the correct weight of the accelerator for this Neutral Particle Beam is not 40,000 tons, but closer to 25 tons." He said: "We proposed to increase the area of the beam and accelerator, noting that would make the accelerator unacceptably massive for orbital

---

[12] The shuttle's payload is 33 tons in the orbits currently in use. It would be about 20 tons in the orbits needed for the defensive screen against Soviet missiles.

[13] Hearings Before the Senate Committee on Armed Services, April 24, 1984.

deployment. Our colleagues have pointed out that the area could be increased after the beam leaves the small accelerator.''

That was all he said about the mistake in his testimony.

Now, this cryptic remark does not convey to a senator attending the hearing that the scientist has just confessed to a mistake which changes a 40,000-ton satellite into a 25-ton satellite. There is nothing in his remark to indicate that the UCS's distinguished panel of scientists had reached a false conclusion on one of the best "Star Wars" defenses because the panel had made a whopping error in its calculations.

The report prepared for the OTA also makes a mistake on the Neutral Particle Beam, but this mistake is only by a factor of fifteen. According to the report, the Soviet Union can protect its missiles and warheads from the Neutral Particle Beam with a lead shield about one-tenth of an inch thick. The shield, the report states, would not weigh too much and therefore could be "an attractive countermeasure" for the Soviets.

But scientists at Los Alamos have pointed out that a layer of lead one-tenth of an inch thick will not stop the fast-moving atoms of the Neutral Particle Beam; they will go right through it. In fact, a table printed in the OTA report itself shows that the lead shield must be 15 times thicker—at least 1½ inches thick—to stop these fast-moving particles.

A layer of lead as thick as that, wrapped around the electronics in the missile and its warheads, would weigh many tons—considerably more than the total weight of all the warheads on the missile. If the Soviets were unwise enough to follow the advice offered them in the report to the Office of Technology Assessment, their missile would be so loaded down with lead that it would be unable to get off the ground.

That would be a great plus for American security, and a nice response from our defense scientists to the President's call for ways of making the Soviet missiles "impotent and obsolete."

Other suggestions for the Soviets can be found in the report by the Union of Concerned Scientists. They include shining up the Soviet missiles, spinning them, attaching "band-aids" and "window shades," as the UCS report calls them, and launching "balloons" as fake warheads. I am not an expert in this dark area of "countermeasures," but I have talked with the experts enough to understand why the professionals in the defense community regard many of these proposals as bordering on inanity.

Putting a shine on the missile sounds like a good idea, because it reflects a part of the laser beam and weakens the beam's effect. However, it would be a poor idea for the Soviets in practice. One reason is that the Soviets could not count on keeping their missiles shiny; during the launch the missile gets dirty, partly because of its own exhaust gases, and its luster is quickly dulled. But the main reason is that no shine is perfect; some laser energy is bound to get through, and will heat the surface. The heating tends to dull the shine, so more heat gets through, and dulls the shine some more, and still more heat gets through . . . and very soon the shine is gone.

Spinning the missile spreads the energy of the laser beam over its whole circumference, and is a better idea than putting a shine on it. However, it only gains the Soviets a factor of pi, or roughly three, at most. And it does not gain them anything at all if the laser energy is transmitted in sharp pulses that catch the missile in one point of its spin, so to speak. The experts say there is no problem in building a laser that sends out its energy in sharp pulses.

Now to the other proposals by the scientists on the UCS panel. The "band-aid" is a metal skirt which slides up and down the outside of the missile, automatically picking out the spot that is receiving the full heat of the laser beam, and protecting the metal skin underneath. The "window shade" is a flexible, metallized sheet which is rolled up and fastened to the outside of the missile when it is launched, and then unrolled at altitudes above fifty miles. It is supposed to protect the missile against the X-ray laser, which is another exotic but promising defense technology.

The trouble with these suggestions is that they do not fit the realities of missile construction very well. A missile is a very fragile object, the ratio of its weight empty to its weight loaded being 10 or 15 to 1—nearly the same as an eggshell. Any attempt to fasten band-aids and window shades on the outside of the missile, even if their contours are smoothed to minimize drag, would put stresses on the flimsy structure that would require a major renovation of the rocket and a new series of test flights. If the Soviets tried to carry out all the suggestions made by the UCS's scientists—putting on band-aids and window shades, spinning their missiles and shining them up—their missile program would be tied up in knots. That would be another fine response from our scientists to the President's call for a way of rendering the Soviet weapons useless.

The "balloon" is still another trick to foil our defenses. The thought here is that after the boost phase is over, and the booster rocket has fallen away, the bus that normally pushes out the Soviet warheads will instead kick out a large number of "balloons"—light, metallized hollow spheres. Some balloons will have warheads inside them, and some will not. Since the empty balloons weigh very little, the Soviets can put out a great many of these. Not knowing which among this great multitude of balloons contain warheads, we will waste our mid-course defenses on killing every balloon in sight, empty or not.

A friend who works on these matters all the time explained to me what was wrong with this idea. He said that a modest amount of thought reveals that it is possible to tell very easily which balloons have warheads, and which do not. All the defense has to do is tap one, in effect, by directing a sharp pulse of laser light at it, and then observe how it recoils. An empty balloon will recoil more rapidly than a loaded one. Once the loaded balloons—the ones with the warheads—are picked out, we can go after them with our Neutral Particle Beams, or other warhead-killers.

This list of proposed countermeasures is not complete, but it is representative. The ideas put forward by the UCS—the band-aid, the window shade, the shining and spinning rockets, and the balloon—remind one of nothing so much as a group of bright students from the Bronx High School of Science getting together to play a game in which they pretend to be Soviet scientists figuring out how to defeat American missile defenses. The ideas they come up with are pretty good for a group of high-school students, but not good enough to stand up to more than a thirty-minute scrutiny by the defense professionals who earn their living in thinking about these matters.

Of course, there is no harm in these proposals. The harm comes in offering shoddy work—superficial analyses marred by errors of fact, reasoning, and simple carelessness—as a sound scientific study bearing on a decision of vital importance to the American people. The work seems sound enough on casual examination, with its numbers, graphs, and theoretical arguments. Certainly the New York *Times* was impressed when it described the UCS report as "exhaustive and highly technical." It is only when you penetrate more deeply, and begin to talk with knowledgeable people who have thought long and hard about these problems, that you realize something is wrong here.

How did published work by competent scientists come to have so many major errors? A theorist reviewing these reports on the feasibility of the President's proposal cannot help noticing that all the errors and rough spots in the calculations seem to push the results in one direction—toward a bigger and more costly defense, and a negative verdict on the soundness of "Star Wars" defense against Soviet missiles. If the calculations had been done without bias, conscious or otherwise, you would expect some errors to push the result one way, and other errors to push it the other way.

But all the errors and omissions go in one direction only—toward making the President's plan seem impractical, costly, and ineffective.

This is not to say that the errors were made in a deliberate, conscious effort to deceive. I do not think that for a moment. What happens is quite different, and every theorist will recognize the phenomenon. When you finish a calculation, you check your result against your intuitive feeling as to what the situation should be. You ask yourself: "Does this result make sense, or not?" If the result does not make sense, you know either that you have made a great discovery which will propel you to Stockholm, or you have made a mistake. Usually you assume the latter, and you proceed to check your calculations very carefully. But if the result seems to be in good agreement with everything you expected about the behavior of the system you are investigating, you say to yourself, "Well, that looks all right," and you go on to the next step.

Of course, a careful theorist always checks his calculations anyway, whether the answer seems sensible or not. But he is apt to check them just a mite less carefully if the results agree with what he expected, than if they do not.

I think this is what must have happened to the theorists who wrote the report for the Union of Concerned Scientists. Clearly they had a strong bias against the President's proposal from the beginning, because they believed that a defense against Soviet missiles would, in their own words, "have a profoundly destabilizing effect on the nuclear balance, increasing the risk of nuclear war," and that such a defense against missiles "could well produce higher numbers of fatalities" than no defense at all.

So, when the calculations by the panel yielded the result that thousands of laser-equipped satellites would be needed to counter a Soviet attack—which meant that for this reason alone the whole plan was hopelessly impractical—the members of the panel were not surprised. Their technical studies had simply confirmed what they already knew to be true for other reasons, namely, that the President's idea was terrible.

Now, I would like to wager that if the theorists studying the matter for the UCS had found that only 10 satellites could protect the United States from a massive Soviet attack—if they had gotten a result that indicated the President's proposal was simple, effective, and inexpensive to carry out—then they would have scrutinized their calculations very, very carefully.

What is one to make of all this?

When I was a graduate student in theoretical physics, we revered some of the men who have lent their names to the report by the Union of Concerned Scientists. They are among the giants of 20th-century physics—the golden era in our profession. Yet these scientists have given their endorsement to badly flawed calculations that create a misleading impression in the minds of Congress and the public on the technical feasibility of a proposal aimed at protecting the United States from destruction.

Lowell Wood, a theorist at Livermore and one of the most brilliant of the younger generation of defense scientists, made a comment recently to the New York *Times* about what he also saw as a contradiction between the research talents of Dr. Hans Bethe—the most prominent physicist associated with the Union of Concerned Scientists—and the negative views of that great theorist on the technical merits of the proposal to defend the United States against Soviet missiles. Dr. Wood said:

> Is Hans Bethe a good physicist? Yes, he's one of
> the best alive. Is he a rocket engineer? No. Is he a
> military-systems engineer? No. Is he a general? No.

Everybody around here respects Hans Bethe enormously as a physicist. But weapons are my profession. He dabbles as a military-systems analyst.

It seems to me that Dr. Wood has part of the answer. I think the remainder of the answer is that scientists belong to the human race. As with the rest of us, in matters on which they have strong feelings, their rational judgments can be clouded by their ideological preconceptions.

EDITOR'S AFTERWORD TO:

THE WAR AGAINST "STAR WARS"

There have been few changes in the US intellectual scene since the publication of Dr. Jastrow's essay. The Union of Concerned Scientists and other such groups have not changed their opinions, and have gained prestigious new recruits. In the fall of 1985 Dr. Isaac Asimov, in a letter mailed under the aegis of Americans For Democratic Action, called the President's Strategic Defense Initiative "fantastic," and said the President did not know the difference between science and science fiction.

He proceeded to describe a system no one has ever advocated, and impute to the President and Department of Defense impossible goals no one would ever implement. He doesn't know what *STAR WARS* (as he insists on writing it throughout his letter) will cost, but he hears "guesses" and the guesses he hears run from five hundred billion to a trillion dollars—"and from all our recent experience with weapons systems, it almost invariably takes far greater sums of money to complete the job than is anticipated."

In other words, the President and his supporters are for some bizarre reason embarked on a mad scheme to bankrupt the nation in order to provide an unworkable defense.

That appears to be the hypothesis of that letter.

I am Chairman of the Citizens Advisory Council on National Space Policy (an organization that includes astronauts like Buzz Aldrin, aerospace managers like George Merrick, space scientists like Max Hunter, military people like Daniel O. Graham, laser experts like Dennis Reilly, high energy physicists like Lowell Wood and Gregory Benford, engineers like Harry Stine and Gordon Woodcock, and a host of other experts). The Council not only advocates strategic defense but takes pride in having provided some of the papers on which

172

the President based his speech of March 23, 1983. I know of no such conspiracy. I think Strategic Defense—*STAR WARS* if you like—is, in Robert Heinlein's words, "the best news since VJ Day," and I think the President and his advisors believe that too.

In the Council at least we have done our homework, and while we may be wrong, we've not seen any serious analysis to convince us of that. You can prove anything if you can make up your data. So far as I can tell, the opponents of Strategic Defense continue to give us confirming instances of that elementary proposition.

EDITOR'S INTRODUCTION TO:

FINAL SOLUTION
by Ames MacKenzie

Some stories would be ruined by an introduction. This is one of them.

FINAL SOLUTION
by Ames MacKenzie

Lala was an impetuous boy and not to be gainsaid.

"Grandfather," he begged in piping Hindee, "please tell me the story!"

The old man sighed. "Very well, small one," he said, "but quickly, for the great Giver of Life drowns in the Black Water and thou must rest!

"How came we to this green and gracious land? Once another race dwelt here, the sons and daughters of mighty warriors and the makers of wonderful songs.

"But their creeds divided this people, for they worshipped different gods or different aspects of the same god, like unto the myriad sects of the children of Allah.

"The followers of each belief were determined that their faith should be supreme in the land. So both sides formed secret bands, not unlike the dreaded Thugs of old, to terrorize and murder till the other would do submission."

"The White Queen—" broke in Lala.

"Hush, 'tis come!" chided his grandsire. "The soldiers of the White Queen came to bring order to her province. They spent much of their blood and her treasure to no avail. Till, at last, the Queen and her councillors declared to the makers of discord, 'Thou art not fit to have such a land! Begone and trouble it no more!' And so they were made to leave, every man, woman and child of them. The White Queen gave them gold to ease their way, but 'tis said it was a bitter parting.

"Yet was not their lot better than our own? We, the lost children of Hind, whose father and fathers' fathers had gone to be the keepers of papers and dealers in goods in the Southern land? When the White Queen freed her dark servants, the children of Ham cast us out, calling us leeches and worse.

"Aye, we had the White Queen's ticket, saying we might dwell in her house. There we were good enough to sweep her streets and carry her filth, nought but untouchables' work could we find. And the Queen's poor children among whom we lived loved us not. They did not understand our ways, nor we theirs.

"So when the Queen banished her erring sons and daughters and left this country unsettled, we came hither at her bidding and made it a bit of Hind in the Western Sea, where all now dwell in peace and contentment under the White Queen and the Lord Vishnu."

"The name, grandfather, the name!" demanded the youngling.

"Name? Why 'tis New Hindustan, as thou knowest right well," teased the elder.

"The old name, grandfather, the funny one!"

"I know, my child, 'tis a peculiar name, truly. 'Twas called *Northern Ireland*, as thou are called 'He-Who-Should-Be-In-Bed'! Now, off with thee!"

EDITOR'S INTRODUCTION TO:

MASTERPLAY
by William F. Wu

War is not necessarily, has not always been, what we see today.

In the time of Napoleon only the men of military age were taken —and not all of them, for as a general rule the Emperor would call up only half a class. All the rest of the population were left, apart from having to pay war taxes of moderate size, to lead their normal lives.

In the time of Louis XIV less still was taken: conscription was unknown, and the private person lived outside the battle.

We may say, then, that it is not an unavoidable result of an outbreak of war that every member and every resource of society must be involved in it: may we also say that the circumstances of the outbreak [of total war] of which we are at once the spectators and the victims are due to chance? Assuredly not . . .

—Bertrand de Jouvenal, *On Power*

De Jouvenal continues his analysis to show that "the total war of today is only the logical end of an uninterrupted advance toward it, of the increasing growth of war."

We can speculate on what might happen if that trend were reversed; if the world, weary of total war, turned to some other means for settling disputes.

The problem with this is contained in a passage in the life of Alexander the Great when, as a young prince, he was sent on campaign into the Balkans. As he approached the front he saw the refugees streaming back toward Macedonia. Most were women and children. The few men were ancient or deformed or badly wounded. Nearly all the women had been raped, and they carried all they owned on their backs. As the Macedonians rode forward, one of the generals said to Alexander: "This is defeat. Avoid it."

Human history goes through cycles. In some of those cycles defeat has not been so terrible, nor victory so final. Dr. William F. Wu writes of a time when the world has wearied of war but is not yet ready to turn to justice; of a time when victory is better than defeat, but defeat is better than real warfare. In such a time governments might turn to other means to settle disputes.

MASTERPLAY
by William F. Wu

Ken Li leaned toward the window of the luxurious shuttle-copter and squinted into the bright sunlight. Below him, the World Headquarters of the Gaming Masters' Guild was growing larger, no longer a dot lost in the sprawling city, but now resembling an architectural model like those displayed in hospital lobbies. He continued to watch as the shuttlecopter descended toward the rooftop heliport, so he could enjoy his excitement and anticipation to the fullest.

This was it. At age twenty-nine, after years of first apprenticeship and then later gaming in the Master class, he had finally made his way to the center of his profession. A rare opening had occurred here at WHQ and over two hundred Master Gamers had competed for it in a tournament stretching across fifteen months.

Ken Li was the only survivor.

When the shuttlecopter had landed gently, Ken stood up in the aisle and looked down at himself. He had dressed carefully for this occasion, in a loose white dress shirt of some silky synthetic, worn open at the collar, and a hand-tailored, solid-turquoise sport jacket with silver buttons. Dark blue dress slacks and white loafers completed the picture—an extreme one, that made him smile with self-conscious irony as he smoothed the sides of his jacket. He knew the message conveyed by his appearance, that he was professional, successful, vain, and a bit eccentric.

Well, he reflected, that message was fairly honest. With a big grin for the pretty, wide-eyed, redhaired flight attendant who opened the door, he picked up his empty briefcase, slung the strap of his black shoulder bag over his shoulder, and stepped out to descend the steps.

With an unerring but amused sense of drama, Ken strode

regally down the metal steps with his back erect, looking out across the paved rooftop with apparently casual interest. The wind from the propellor overhead blew his hair forward. Two men stood at the bottom of the steps, awaiting the flight's only passenger.

As Ken neared the bottom, he looked directly at his hosts for the first time. He recognized one as Kirk Emerald, director of the Guild's executive committee and one of the founders of the Guild. Ken was pleasantly shocked, and then humbled. He hadn't expected *him*.

"Master Li." Kirk Emerald, a tall, slender man with a full head of white hair tossed in the shuttlecopter's stiff breeze, extended his hand. "I'm Kirk Emerald. Welcome to World Headquarters."

"Thank you. I'm glad to be here." Ken shook hands, smiling up at the man who towered over him.

"This is Lou Crandall." Emerald gestured to the man beside him.

"Oh, of course. Pleased to meet you." Surprised again, Ken shook hands with the heavyset man in his forties.

"Ken, I'm glad to meet you, too. After all the corresponding we've done, it's about time. I'm honored to be your new contractor."

Ken wasn't fooled. Crandall was one of the top contractors in the business, and he could do more for Ken than Ken could do for him. "*I'm* honored to be able to sign with you. Thanks for meeting me. I really appreciate it." He included Emerald in his eye contact. "Thanks very much."

Lou took a cigar wrapped in cellophane out of his inside jacket pocket and started tearing at the wrapper with his teeth. "That's the great part of having this heliport on the roof, Ken; you don't have to go very far to meet people." He laughed good-naturedly.

Kirk Emerald clapped Ken on the shoulder as they turned and started to walk. "No need to be formal any more. You're one of us now."

So Ken Li came to World Headquarters.

Ken was introduced at the Guild Hall reception desk, an impressive black marble structure in the main lobby; after that, his hosts said farewell and a reception clerk escorted him up to the suite of rooms that the Guild was providing for free, temporarily. Most of his belongings were somewhere on the way from Ann Arbor, Michigan, in a van; now, he simply set down his empty briefcase, his shoulder bag of books and cameras, and one suitcase of clothes.

The suite was large, spacious, and airy. One wall of the sunken living room was a huge window, looking out over the city. The furnishings were contemporary modular rectangles of pastel orange, yellow, and blue. The video screen on one wall could be keyed for any of the games being played in the Guild Hall, provided public access had been granted. In addition, old tapes could be called up from the Guild Hall library. The bedroom contained a huge, firm bed and an entire wall of entertainment consoles, for video, film, radio, or audio pastimes. The kitchen was fully equipped with electronic appliances. The refrigerator, bar, and pantry were fully stocked, not only with staples, but also with champagne, black caviar, dim sum, and sushi.

Ken explored with a mixture of amazement and giddiness. He laughed aloud at the large sunken tub and the shag carpeting in the bathroom, and then, shaking his head at the wonder he felt, he washed up and changed into a clean, light blue shirt. Then he checked his watch, composed himself with a deep breath, and went out to see the Guild Hall. His giddiness would remain in the suite, as it would not befit a Master Gamer of the World Headquarters.

Later, just before 5.30 P.M., Ken wandered casually down a wide, carpeted hallway to the Summer Palace banquet room, where the reception in his honor was to take place. It was decorated in the style of the opulent Summer Palace in Beijing. Ken smiled to himself, amused that they had chosen this banquet hall, out of many, to honor him. Quite a crowd was already visible in the room, through the open doorway, where shelves of ancient Chinese antiques and art lined the walls under glass.

"Well, well." He spoke aloud to himself, grinning. Then he stuck his hands into his pockets and walked up to the short line at the door. As he waited, he gradually became aware that everyone inside the banquet room, and everyone ahead of him in line, was wearing a long red ribbon. When his turn came, he inclined his head toward the people filing into the room. "Where, uh, do I get a red ribbon?"

A young, slender man in a black tuxedo looked up at him. He had a green ribbon reading "hospitality" on his lapel. "You should have received it over a week ago, sir. That is, you did preregister, didn't you? We don't have registration here at the door."

"Well, I was told to be here at 5:30." Ken smiled amiably, not wanting to cause the young man any trouble. "I'm Ken Li, and—"

"*Oh!* Master Li?" The young man's eyes grew wide, and his face suddenly started turning pink. "Uh—well . . . just a moment, Master." He stuck his head inside the door of the banquet room and shouted in a hoarse stage whisper. "Donna! I need help!"

Ken smiled awkwardly and glanced behind him. The line was still forming. He hadn't meant to cause a problem, and the young man's discomfiture embarrassed him. When he turned to face forward, the young fellow had been joined by a stunningly pretty woman also wearing the green hospitality ribbon.

"Can I help you? I'm Donna Wong." She smiled and held out her hand.

"Glad to meet you. I'm Ken Li." Ken shook her hand, which was small and warm and gripped his firmly.

Donna was about five feet four, with high, even cheekbones and a square jaw. Her lips were full and her nose was straight and a little wide. Wavy, shoulder-length black hair framed her face as her eyes met his. She had a strong Cantonese look, he thought.

"*Oh*—Master Li. I'm sorry if there was a mix-up. Um—we were expecting you to come down with Lou Crandall." She waited for a response, watching his face with an open, pleasant smile.

"Ah—that's my fault. I forgot all about it. He did tell me he'd swing up to my room to get me. I was exploring the Guild Hall and just came over here when it was time."

Donna nodded, without taking her eyes off his face. "I see. Well, Lou has your ribbon." Her smile remained as she gazed at him.

Ken realized, suddenly, that even though she seemed impressed with his looks—or his status, more likely—and even though she was not going to embarrass him outright, she also had no intention of letting him in just because he claimed to be the guest of honor. He laughed lightly and reached for his wallet. "May I show you some identification?"

"I—wait. There's Lou, now." Donna looked past him and waved.

"Ken!" Lou called out as he came striding down past the rest of the line. "Hi. Came down early, eh?"

"I'm sorry, Lou. I forgot you were coming up to my room."

"No harm done. Here, pin this on." Lou handed him a red ribbon. "Okay, hon?"

"You know my name, Lou." Donna spoke firmly.

"Aw, yeah, all right. Sorry." Lou gripped Ken's shoulder. "C'mon, let's go in."

"Okay." Ken grinned at Donna, gave a little shrug, and followed the contractor.

The room was already crowded. Lou worked his bulk slowly along the wall toward the bar, and Ken took advantage of the trail he blazed. The big contractor looked back over his shoulder and waved him forward.

"C'mon, Master Li! Don't be shy. What do you drink, anyhow?"

"White wine." Ken laughed at Lou's bluff and friendly manner. His personality would be an asset for their working together.

"White wine it is. Yeah, here you are." Lou handed him a cold glass. "Well, you'll get a formal introduction to the crowd later. In the meantime, here's a toast."

"Oh?" Ken grinned and raised his glass.

"Here's to the new arrangement that brought you here—to the Gaming Act. May we all prosper." Lou clinked glasses with Ken and took a healthy swallow.

"Ah, yes. Here's to it." Ken sipped the sweet white wine and turned to survey the crowd. He was certain that he had heard of many of the Master Gamers present, but he didn't know them by sight any more than Donna Wong had known him.

Richard Ross was looking at him.

Deep in the crowd, a tall, lanky man with reddish blond hair stood with his long, lean arms folded across his chest, a glass of beer clutched in one hand at an awkward angle. He was watching Ken with a self-conscious smile. As soon as their eyes met, Ken began weaving his way through the crowd toward him, and he started toward Ken.

"See you later," Lou said quietly, behind Ken. "He gives me the creeps."

Ken, jostled by someone in the press of people, still managed to reach out and shake with Richard.

"Welcome to World Headquarters," Richard said with that familiar strange tone of his that seemed to hint at sarcasm.

"Thanks. I'm glad to be here. Back in the old home town again."

Richard waved his glass of beer slightly in his other hand. "Let's see . . . we haven't seen each other since I was visiting the Detroit Guild Hall a couple of years ago. You've, uh, been moving up in the world."

Ken shrugged, uncomfortable with an apparent compliment from his old friend. "I have to say, this Guild Hall makes the others look like outhouses."

Richard laughed shortly. "Yeah. Trouble is, everyone here knows it." He tilted his head back for a sizeable swallow of beer. "You realize, of course, that you've got it made, now, just by being a Master Gamer slotted in this Guild. You can do anything here but fail."

"Well, I guess that's true. It's true in any Guild Hall, though." Ken shrugged.

"Not like it is here." Richard sneered and waved his glass around at the crowd. "Our esteemed colleagues have the souls of circling buzzards. I've been here, what, over eleven years and I've never been rated lower than six in the entire world. They know it, too—and every one of them would like my slot near the top."

"Or at the top, frequently." Ken grinned.

Richard laughed genuinely, then. "Yeah, sometimes." He frowned again. "Just keep in mind—no one here even discusses failure. Success is expected, and to hear people talk, that's all that happens here. We all know better, but that doesn't matter. Every Master here just says . . . it's a *good* life." He laughed and shook his head. "I guess you'll have to be here a while to feel it, but it'll come."

Ken nodded, watching his childhood friend take another long draught of his beer. Richard had been a young phenom when he had attained Master status at age 19. He had always been extremely competitive, with his anxiety and insecurity about winning always near the surface. Yet his knowledge of military history and tactics was unmatched by any other Master, past or present.

On the other hand, Ken was not exactly in the habit of discussing failure—or even considering it—himself.

"Ironically," said Richard, "I won't be under the gun quite as much any more. Now it's your turn."

"What? How so? If anything, people have been falling all over themselves to welcome me."

Richard laughed with a sarcastic twist to his smile. "Oh, yeah. They'll always be like that on the surface. Do you realize why you're here—in depth, I mean?"

Ken was in no mood to guess. "Suppose you tell me."

"All right." Richard shrugged. "Before the Guild Act was passed, we had a fairly stable number of games contracted. One slob gets mad at some other jerk; their lawyers can't work it out, and so they mutually hire Masters to play for their dispute. The old trial by combat, right? You with me so far?"

"Get on with it." Ken raised an eyebrow in annoyance. "I don't need lectures. What's the point?"

"Now, under the old rules, we were only contracted by mutually agreeable private parties—the government had nothing to do with it. With the Guild Act passed, the very same slob can now sue the very same jerk for a game, and under certain provisions, a judge may grant it, whether or not the defendant agrees to trial by combat."

"You haven't told me one single item yet that's new to me. Every Master who reads the trades knows all this."

Richard eyed him tightly. "And you still don't get it? What it means to you?"

"The Guild expects more games to be contracted than before, and has opened new slots in Guild Halls all over the country. I got the one here. That's all."

Richard laughed derisively. "Not hardly. *You* are the new gunslinger in town. Every Master here will be gunning for you. And the members of the public who hate us for the Guild Act will center on you as the most visible representative of the new order."

Ken looked down at his glass. "Hmm. I hadn't thought of that. I remember reading that some people are against the Guild Act. I don't see why, really. Nobody likes being sued. Why should getting sued for a game be any worse than getting sued for anything else?"

Richard waved his free hand in dismissal and finished his beer with the other. "You got me. I don't care, anyway. Plenty of people love watching our games and betting on them and making us celebrities. That's good enough for me."

"I still think you're being too hard on the other Masters. I was friends with lots of my colleagues back in Michigan."

"That was Michigan. You notice how no one has approached you while we've been talking? They must know who you are. I mean, you do rather stand out in a crowd."

Ken grinned. "I just thought they were avoiding *you*."

Richard laughed, and his pale face flushed slightly. "Could be, at that." He raised his empty glass. "I'm going for a refill. Want one?"

"No, thanks. Think I'll mingle."

Richard vanished into the crowd, and Ken turned to look around. The crush of well-dressed men and women were talking in the normal fashion for any cocktail party, but he could see people occasionally glancing at him as they spoke. That made sense; the reception was in his honor, after all.

Donna Wong, in a striking dress of lavender lace, was circulating, talking to people briefly with a quick smile and then moving on. Ken hesitated, then began working his way toward her. He intended to make running into her look like an accident, but when she saw him, she changed direction to meet him.

Ken stopped where he was, smiling at her, and watched. Her dress was long, made of lace over satin, with white trim. She seemed to be of a medium build, but the cut of her dress really disguised her traits below the neck. Meanwhile, he noticed with amusement, she was looking him over, too—this outfit he had so carefully selected to make the impression he wanted.

Judging from the look on her face, it had worked just fine.

"Master Li. Can I get you another?" Donna gestured to take his glass, with a big smile.

"Oh—no, thanks. This is fine."

"You haven't turned red." She put her upper teeth on her lower lip in a teasing expression.

"It hasn't been long enough yet; that's all." Ken laughed. "And call me Ken, will you?"

"Sure."

Ken kept on smiling at her, feeling just a little awkward. Her eyes were so plainly enjoying looking at him that he wasn't sure how to act. He was tempted to gaze at her with equal enthusiasm, but then nobody would talk.

Just before the pause became a burden, he nodded toward her green ribbon. "Are you catering? Or are you associated with the Guild?"

"I'm an Apprentice Gamer." Her tone was proud. "I came to it later than most, but I'm perking right along."

"Oh, really?" Ken was more interested, now. "How far along are you?"

"I've already applied for a qualifying game. Right now, all the Masters here are so backlogged that none of them are playing qualifiers. I'll get it eventually, though. In the meantime, I'm practicing a lot and passing the time with projects like this."

"That sounds like a good program." Ken realized, suddenly, that he could offer to play against her in a game that would test her ability to become a Master, since he was unbooked. He immediately dismissed the idea, since he wanted to get to know her better. Becoming her opponent would only be an obstacle.

"Now." Donna took his arm. "I'd like to escort you up to the front, where Master Emerald is getting ready to introduce you to the assembled multitude. You don't have to do much. Just smile and wave at the right time, and it'll all be over."

"Yes, Lou explained it to me this afternoon." Ken responded to the pressure of her on his arm and started moving toward the front of the room. "Well, even if I'm in a room full of future opponents and competitors, at least I feel like it's a family. You know what I mean? The Guild is like home."

Donna looked up at him, and her face was close to his. Her full lips were pursed in a tight smile. "Well, Ken . . . Master Li. Perhaps you should know that some of us are very much against the Guild Act that brought you here."

Ken glanced at her in surprise. "Even gamers are against it?"

Donna nodded. "Not very many—in fact, here in town, I may be the only one."

"But . . . you're really against it? Seriously?"

"Definitely."

"I don't understand how anyone—"

"Shh." She laughed and put a finger to her lips. "Master Emerald is about to start. We'll talk some other time."

Early the next morning, freshly showered and breakfasted, Ken hurried down a silent, carpeted, dimly-lit corridor after Richard, whose steady, long-legged stride set a brisk pace. They passed long rows of heavy closed doors and kept turn-

ing corners set at irregular angles. Ken could see brass name-
plates on each door, shining slightly in the weak overhead
light. Finally, after Ken had completely lost his way, Richard
stopped to open one of the doors with a key.

Without speaking, Richard snapped on the room light and
walked inside. He had worked himself into a fierce competitive mood for their practice game, Ken realized, and would
not be sociable again until after they had finished. Ken waited
for Richard to choose one side of the big room, then took the
other for himself.

The practice room was a large rectangle, just a bit bigger
than the ten-meter square playing field outlined in black on
the floor. The playing field itself was a plain white synthetic
substance that took holograms particularly well; Ken could
never remember what they called the stuff, nor did he really
care. Outside the square, the room was luxuriously carpeted
and furnished with a multiple beverage dispenser and private
restroom.

Ken sat down in the padded chair centered along one side
of the playing field. It had a console that allowed him to
adjust the softness or firmness of the seat, back, and arms,
and to shift all their angles to the minutest degree. Ken liked
a hard seat and back, with the back straight up behind him.
Years ago, in high school, his Latin teacher—a silver-haired
woman who had corrected students' mistakes without the
need to consult her text—had decreed that no one could
"cerebrate" if he was comfortable. As near as Ken's own
cerebrum could tell, she had been right.

Across the field from Ken, Richard was adjusting his own
seat. Above the center of the field, Ken could see the opening
in the ceiling that housed the projectors. He reached down to
his left and brought up the keyboard on a swiveling steel arm.
It held twelve horizontal rows of keys, twelve keys to a row,
plus larger buttons and dials running vertically down each
side. Across the top, a small video screen completed the
board.

Across the way, Richard glanced up at him with an intense
scowl. Trying not to laugh nervously—he was too knotted up
inside to be truly amused—Ken waved a hand. Richard hit a
button and the game opened.

The field was suddenly lit up from above with three-
dimensional miniatures. A city from ancient times sat on the
coast of a large sea or ocean; the surrounding region held two

sizeable armies, still some distance from each other. The terrain was generally flat and rolling slightly, covered by the green of plowed fields and patches of forest separated by open country.

Since this was a practice game, both gamers had sixty seconds before the game would come alive in a computerized simulation of tactical warfare. Ken read on his video screen: "Tunis. 255 B.C. Carthaginians. Xanthippes." Officers' names, Victory Conditions, and odds for the battle followed. That was all the system would tell him.

Ken was taking the place of the Spartan mercenary, Xanthippes, who had come to Carthage and taken command of the Carthaginian army. As Master Gamers, both Ken and Richard were expected to know all the details of the battle, including the personalities of individual officers who were on record historically and the abilities and cultural tendencies of the troops. These were all programmed into the game.

Tunis, Ken thought. His heart was pounding. This battle had been fought in the Punic Wars, well before the time of Hannibal. Xanthippes had defeated a Roman army led by its consul Atilius Regulus, whose decisions would now be made by Richard.

Ken flexed his fingers nervously. He, as Xanthippes, had units representing four thousand cavalry, twelve thousand foot soldiers, and one hundred elephants. The battlefield would be on level ground. He sat quivering with intensity, not certain that he could defeat Richard even now, but anxious to play him close, at the very least. As the seconds passed, he could feel his confidence ebb, to be replaced by an old familiar feeling of intimidation.

The game activated.

Ken's Carthaginian army was on the near side of the screen, represented by tiny figures. They were too small to discern clearly with the naked eye as individuals, but they functioned most of the time in military units that were fairly easy to identify.

Ken picked up the metal sensory band from its hook on the arm of the chair. He fitted it around his head, turning it so that the transparent eye pieces and small audio speakers were properly placed. The sensory band was controlled by the keyboard; unless he activated it, he would see and hear normally.

The Carthaginian armies were usually comprised of foreign

mercenaries led by Carthaginian officers. Ken remembered
that this army was an exception. The Romans had landed
outside Carthage, isolating the city from its recruiting field
and part of its food supply. So two-thirds of Ken's army were
Carthaginian citizens with training but limited experience, led
this time by a mercenary.

Ken began tapping the keys to arrange his units. On the far
side of the field, Richard was setting up his Roman legionaries. He had a slight numerical advantage, with fifteen thousand
infantry and five thousand horse. However, the Carthaginian
cavalry had possessed more fighting quality, and the figures
had greater combat power to reflect this.

Since Carthage had won the real battle, Ken did not tamper
with the Spartan's plan. Like Xanthippes, he put his elephants
in the front line as shock troops, followed by his infantry,
with his cavalry on the wings. It was a fairly standard arrangement: the elephants, charging across the level plain,
should trample the front lines of legionaries and throw the rest
into confusion, to be finished off by the Carthaginian infantry. The mobility of the cavalry would prevent any flanking
movement by the more numerous Romans. Richard's numerical superiority could be nullified by the elephants.

Ken activated his sensory band and moved into the battle
scene as Xanthippes. The great gray elephants lumbered forward, raising their trunks and trumpeting. He could choose
between an on-scene viewpoint, from the spot where his
game persona was at any given time, or he could use the
larger perspective of the gaming seat, with a near-total loss of
detail.

Ken hesitated, then pulled out of the sensory band again. It
was most useful at crisis points, but had little to offer when
the large pattern of the battle was still developing. He happened to enjoy it a great deal, but that was a matter of
pleasure, not business.

Behind the elephants, the lines of infantry began to move
forward. Both wings of cavalry fanned out slightly to prepare
for action. Ken would meet any flanking motion by the
Roman cavalry with his own, but he doubted Richard would
try it. The two sides were too closely matched for such a
move to work on level ground.

The Romans marched forward. Even with his naked eye,
Ken could see the red hairline that was the great red plumes
of dyed horsehair worn by the Roman legionaries. The forma-

tion looked a little odd to him, but on close examination he found the different units to be in conventional order. He selected the combination of keys he wanted and directed his elephants, through the tiny figure of Xanthippes on the field, to charge.

The front line of Carthaginians began to move out ahead of the others. The Roman infantry halted its forward progress. Ken held his breath, watching.

The gray line of Carthaginian elephants advanced up the field, meshed with the lines of Roman infantry, and continued to charge forward, between the files of legionaries. Ken's stomach tightened. The elephants, now rampaging out of control of their drivers, were stampeding harmlessly through gaps in the formation. The Romans closed files behind them and resumed marching.

Ken swallowed. The Roman formation had looked odd because Richard had spread the files apart, while keeping the positions of his troops otherwise conventional. Ken remembered that the Romans had used this technique on other occasions, though not at this battle. Gamers had the option of such authentic tactics and Richard, of course, knew better than anyone when to use them.

The two front lines of infantry clashed and Ken concentrated on the screen and his keyboard. The computer considered morale factors, and the Romans gained an advantage from surviving the elephant charge intact, while the Carthaginians lost morale for the same reason. Ken's infantry held but did not move forward. The wings of cavalry met on each side and spread out farther as they fought for position against each other.

Ken hit the keyboard as quickly as he dared, holding back a little speed for fear of making a mistake. His confidence had been rattled. He watched his front line carefully. Through Xanthippes, he encouraged the mercenaries to hold their ground. The Carthaginian left, in particular, was hard pressed by the Romans. Ken's right was advancing slightly, but he was not sure what to do next. In the real battle, the Carthaginian elephants had thrown the Romans right into chaos and the Carthaginian infantry had crushed them. Here, the balance was still undetermined.

On the wings, the Carthaginian cavalry was commanded by two separate officers programmed by the computer. As Xanthippes, Ken could issue them new orders, but if he did not, those officers and their men would perform as they had historically. Ken's cavalry, with a fighting superiority that more than offset their fewer numbers, threatened to drive their Roman counterparts from the field. He figured he should not interfere.

All at once, then, he realized that the Romans were trying to disengage themselves. It was a complicated maneuver; if the Romans retreated too quickly, their formation would break and become a rout. In these circumstances, with the Carthaginians still strong and aggressive, that was nearly inevitable. Richard, however, was pulling his legionaries back in good order, despite the pressure from Ken's lines. The Carthaginians began to score even better, destroying their retreating enemy at a faster rate than before. Still, the Roman infantry, anticipating help, maintained their fighting order. The game computer allowed this because of the renowned discipline of the Roman legions and Richard's delicate handling, Ken surmised, of the necessary orders.

Both wings of Roman cavalry, fleeing the Carthaginians, fought their way between the two bodies of infantry and slowed the Carthaginian advance. The retreat of the Roman infantry gave their cavalry room to maneuver. Then, as the Carthaginian cavalry closed on the Roman cavalry from each side, the mounted Romans fought a holding action to allow their infantry time to escape.

Ken ground his teeth as he punched the keyboard. He was seriously damaging the Roman cavalry, but his own infantry could no longer close with the retreating legions. Ken hated losing and his stomach felt cold as he watched the Roman infantry pull away.

It was a risky and costly maneuver on Richard's part, and not one he was likely to try in a real game. He had tried it just to find out if he could sacrifice his cavalry to save his infantry. In a way, he was just playing around—experimenting. Ken realized that the insult to him was unintentional, but he was still disturbed by the fact that Richard could succeed even though he had not taken Ken very seriously.

Resigned, Ken halted the advance of his units. His refusal to pursue the fleeing Romans activated an assessment by the computer. After a wait of thirty seconds, during which the two gamers could resume new maneuvers, the field froze. The game results appeared on the video screen above Ken's board.

Ken read them with disgust for himself.

"Victory Conditions: None.

"Tactical position: Stalemate, advantage Carthage.

"Strategic position: Stalemate, advantage Rome."

The list went on, giving statistics and elapsed time, but Ken ignored the rest. He was angry with himself and embarrassed.

Richard punched a button and erased the game, leaving only the blank playing field again. He visibly relaxed and lounged back in his chair. Then he remembered his sensory band and leaned forward a moment to pull it off. "You lost," he called out, grinning. His bushy blond hair was sweaty. "Welcome to World Headquarters."

Ken swung his own keyboard out of the way and took off his sensory band. "Stalemate, actually." He adjusted his seat to lean back and fell onto it, aware that he was hot and soaked in sweat.

"Technically true." Richard turned to one side and hung a long leg over the arm of the chair. "Actually, though, the strategic position favors Rome. Atilius Regulus still has enough of an army to keep Carthage isolated, and the Romans can get new horses from the surrounding country. Carthage is still threatened, and would have to fight again under these circumstances. If the Romans wait for the return of their reinforcements in the spring, Carthage could be finished."

Ken shrugged and shook his head in concession. At this point, he just wanted to forget it.

Suddenly Richard jumped up. "Never mind! I'm celebrating. Let's run down to the Club for brunch, on me. Champagne time."

"Okay." Ken slid out of the chair. He understood that Richard had been unable to make friendly conversation before the game, when he had been in a competitive frenzy. "What's the celebration about? Not beating me, surely."

Richard laughed. "Are you kidding? Let's get settled downstairs, and I'll tell you all about it."

Again, Ken followed him through the labyrinth of Guild hallways. They had been deliberately constructed this way to increase the privacy of gamers who often did not wish their colleagues to know when they were practicing, or with whom. No formal rules governed such information, but a tradition of discretion in the Guild had a rigidity bordering on that of law.

The Guild Club was a formal dining room and lounge on

one of the lower floors. It offered linen and sterling silver for
the settings, a staff in black tie and tails, crystal goblets, and
fresh flowers clustered around scented candles. Heavy curtains adorned the walls; they proved to be, Ken found, copies
of famous medieval European tapestries. Money was not
exchanged here; only Masters who gamed out of this Guild
Hall could eat or host meals here, and the staff was expected
to know them by sight and to accept their signatures without
further verification.

When they had ordered an elaborate brunch, Richard flipped
out his napkin and set it in his lap. "Gene called me early this
morning—uh, that's Gene Graham, my contractor. He's wran-
gled an offer for me to play in the very first game contracted
under the provisions of the Guild Act. Hey, I'm going right
back to the top."

Ken was impressed, though a pang of envy hit him, no
doubt strengthened by his disappointment over the morning's
practice game. "Really? That *is* grounds for celebration.
Let's see—you're rated number two right now?"

"Yep—whatshisname, DuVeau, is number one at the moment. They tried to get him first, of course, but apparently
he's booked four or five months ahead."

"I don't know much about him, but he must be good."
Ken watched as the immaculately dressed waiter wheeled up
an ice cart, carrying a bottle of champagne.

Richard frowned and shook his head. "Naw—he's a flash
in the pan. I was in the top ten long before he was, and I'll be
here long after. Matter of fact, he's older than we are."

Richard nodded his approval of the champagne, and they
both watched as the cork was popped and the bottle poured.
When the waiter had retired, Ken lifted his glass. "Congratulations. Here's to Victory Conditions."

Richard clinked glasses with him. "Ah, yes—here's to
Victory Conditions. Thank you."

Brunch arrived promptly, and Richard devoted his attention
to it with a nervous, energetic earnestness that Ken remembered well. As they ate in silence, he began wondering if the
pressure to win had gradually created an obsession with winning in his old friend. It was not easy to tell, because Richard
had always been ferociously competitive, and he may have
simply thrived here in a naturally conducive environment.

Another thought occurred to Ken about their practice game.

"That maneuver you were trying with me earlier. Are you, uh, working on a masterplay?"

Richard looked up in surprise, hesitated, and then grinned self-consciously. He reddened as he finished a mouthful of food. "No, not exactly. To be honest, it's hard to plan a masterplay. If people could figure them out in practice games, at their leisure, they'd do it all the time."

"And then they wouldn't be masterplays." Ken nodded. "You have, what, three of them?"

"Four."

"Two more than anyone else. That's a major contribution to the field." Ken was not being generous; this was the plain truth.

"Actually, masterplays will become a problem if they're ever common. Think of it—a masterplay is a maneuver that always works in the game it's developed for. So—"

"Given that the opportunity develops. It may not—"

"Yeah, yeah, of course," Richard snapped. "But, like I was saying, *if* the situation for a masterplay develops in a game, and the maneuver is already in our professional repertoire, then the game is essentially over. We'll have standard solutions for every game, and I guess they'd have to be reprogrammed or something."

Ken nodded. "Right now, though, there aren't very many masterplays in the books, are there?"

Richard grinned again and shook his head. "Well, no. It's a long way off." He returned to his plate.

A masterplay, thought Ken. It was a special mark of prestige, a pure artistic accomplishment that went beyond winning games and charging fees and drawing clients and crowds. A Master with a mediocre career would always be known for creating a masterplay; a Master with an otherwise stellar career might never feel completely fulfilled without one. Richard's place in Guild history was already assured. Only the extent of his prestige had yet to be established.

Throughout their childhood and teen years, Richard had always been Ken's closest friend. Yet their personalities had never fit the age-old metaphor of gears meshing; Ken suppressed a grin as he thought instead of gears grinding, disengaging, and grinding again. For Ken, the competitive tension between them had been stronger because Richard had always been in the lead. At the same time, his life had always been more narrow.

*   *   *

At the age of fourteen, Richard had been hunkered over his
small personal screen on the desk in his bedroom. He was
even thinner back then, but he already had most of his height.
While he played the Battle of An Shr Chong, between the
Tang Dynasty of China and Korea, Ken sprawled on Richard's bed, re-reading *Knight's Castle*, by Edward Eager.

"Stupid!" Richard pounded his fist on his desk in frustration. "I did it again, the same stupid mistake. I'm gonna beat
this computer yet, though." He punched a button and ended
the game. "No sense playing out this monstrosity now."

Ken had not looked up from his book.

"You still reading that kiddie stuff?" Richard demanded.

"It's not kiddie stuff. It says 'juvenile' on it, and that's
uh—me."

"We both read it when we were eight years old." Richard
dismissed the book with a contemptuous wave.

"So we were the only kids reading juvenile novels at that
age. So what?" Ken laughed, and Richard joined him. Their
intelligence, and intellectual interests, had drawn them together early.

"I thought you liked war games."

"I do. I also like this." Ken waved the red, battered
hardback with his finger in it marking his place. "For that
matter, I like watching football games, too."

"Ha. That's barbaric." Richard turned back to his screen
and started a new game.

Ken had started to read again, but his mind had wandered
to a girl in his English class.

Later that evening, Donna drew her feet up onto the couch
and wrapped the hem of her long flannel nightgown over
them. "Really, Sharon, it just sort of happened. I mean, *I*
don't believe in love at first sight. I really don't." She
laughed and wrinkled her nose playfully. "Except, I do now."
She knew she'd get a rise out of her friend with that.

Sharon Wills rolled her eyes and put her fists on her hips in
an exaggerated gesture. She was sitting on the floor by the
coffee table and her broad-shouldered, angular frame threw
an intimidating shadow across Donna's bright colorful painting of Fa Mulan, on the far wall. "It's not that I'm not
interested, but you asked me to run you through this exercise.
Mooning about a total stranger won't help you get Master

status." Sharon laughed, then, and sighed. "All right. I'll put
water on. Do you still have some of that—what do you call
it? The expensive imported tea, from high altitudes?"

"Monkey-picked tea. Sure." Donna slid her feet into her
embroidered red silk slippers. "Just remember *why* it's so
expensive—just think of all the poor monkeys that pitched
over the edge of cliffs trying to reach those hard-to-get tea
bushes. You can use up a lot of monkeys that way."

Sharon laughed and stood up, smoothing her rust-colored
turtleneck down over the waistband of her jeans. "That's
terrible. But, uh—speaking of hard to get . . . you know
what I mean?"

Donna followed the taller woman into the kitchen. "Yeah,
I suppose. I just don't want to play any games. I used to do
that with men and it ruined everything. Always. I'd rather be
honest."

"I'm not arguing with that." Sharon raised her voice as
she ran water into a white plastic container over the sink.
"You could find a middle ground, though, couldn't you?"
She opened the transparent door of the flasher and set the
two-liter container of water inside. Then she stepped back and
winced as she pushed a button. The flasher lit up, buzzed,
and went off.

"What are you afraid of?" Donna asked. "I've seen you
do that before. It's all sealed and insulated and everything."
She opened the door and took out the boiling water.

Sharon took the lid off Donna's elaborate blue and white
Ming-style teapot and sprinkled leaves inside. "You trust
those damn contraptions too much. They told you it was
sealed, but for all we know, it's flashing us at the same time
it's flashing the water."

Donna picked up two cups and started back to the living
room. "Maybe you don't trust enough. I trust my instincts
about Ken, too." She hesitated, debating whether to say her
next thought. It was nothing new to Sharon, anyway. "I'm
not exactly without experience, you know." She smiled tightly.

"I know. That's what I'm worried about." Sharon knelt
and began to pour.

Stung, Donna said nothing.

"You like it weak, right? I'll let mine steep longer."

"Yes, thank you. Um—okay, I'm going to start the exercise. Illegitimate foreign duke, by right of conquest."

Sharon consulted her sheet of paper. "Right. Second son, by specific inheritance."

Donna leaned forward from the couch to accept her cup of tea. "Younger brother."

"Nephew."

"Cousin once removed, plus war and signed agreement."

"Son." Sharon sighed. "All right, wait a minute. I give. Somehow, your love life does seem a little more pressing than the right by which medieval rulers of England took the throne. You still want to tell me about him?"

"Sure!" Donna spoke earnestly. "Sharon, I'm really not the way I used to be anymore. I'm not. I have a lot more self-confidence and direction and everything. Really, Sharon. I'm not looking to be used again. It's been a long time since I was into that really self-destructive phase of my life."

Sharon sipped her tea and then gazed into it thoughtfully. "All right, I'm sorry. But I'm still worried about you. The way you talk, you sound so vulnerable. You're just so . . . gushy over this guy. I haven't seen you like this in a long time." She looked up with a smile. "You aren't going to revert on me, are you?"

"No." Donna shook her head. "I won't revert. I know who I am now. I'm Donna Wong and I'm an Apprentice Gamer and I'm going to be a Master. That's a far cry from the confused mess I used to be. And I came out of it the hard way, too, all by myself. I won't revert."

"I'm glad to hear you say so. But, uh, what about him? Didn't you say he was this new guy the Guild brought into town after some big elimination tournament?"

Donna nodded enthusiastically. "He impresses the hell out of me. He's the last survivor out of two hundred Masters from around the world. But you know—I didn't realize who he was when I first came out and saw him. That's when it really happened—the moment I laid eyes on him. It really did."

Sharon sighed. "I just wish you'd stop saying it was love at first sight. Call it infatuation, lust, anything else. But you can't love him when you don't even know him."

"I intend to know him. And I don't mean the way I used to, either. He knows I'm an Apprentice, and we'll get acquainted as one gamer to another."

"Maybe I have him confused with someone else, but . . . isn't he the one who represents everything you're against?"

"Well. . . ." Donna wrinkled her nose again, this time uncomfortably. "He's the one you mean. That's true. It's just that, well, political opinions can change. I'll just have to change his mind." She looked up apologetically and laughed lightly. "That's all. I'll just have to change his mind."

Sharon gave her a reluctant grin. "I don't know about you, sometimes. You're incurable, I guess."

"Yeah. I'm also determined."

Ken tossed the morning paper down on the couch next to him and looked around the Guild Hall lobby. The city was full of comfortable, affordable places to live—but none were available anywhere near the Guild Hall. The Guild Hall wouldn't be the only location in his life, he knew, but until he made more friends in town and learned his way around the area, his career was about all he had. Finding a place to live nearby was only sensible.

The problem was, he couldn't find one. Well, the Guild would continue to put him up without charge for at least a month, and probably longer if he convinced them that he was seriously looking. In the meantime, his suite upstairs was opulent, even decadent, but also empty and boring.

So was his morning, for that matter.

People had been bustling through the lobby ever since he had settled there, after having breakfast served to him in his sunken bathtub up in the suite. That idea, too, had been overrated, but he had wanted to try it upon learning that the Guild Club offered room service. He had been reading the paper here in the lobby ever since.

People were still weaving briskly around the black marble pillars and tall potted plants placed throughout the lobby. Most of them stopped at the reception desk before hurrying on. The gold carpet was deep and new; Ken reflected that a lot more foot traffic would have to pass through before it became worn. He suspected, however, that it was replaced regularly, long before any wear became obvious.

"Ken? You busy?" A woman spoke near his ear, from a little behind him.

Deeply grateful for someone to talk to, Ken turned and found Donna Wong coming around the end of the couch.

"Well, hello!" He smiled and started gathering the newspaper to move it out of the way. "No, I'm not busy. Would you like to sit down?"

"Are you sure? I don't want to take up your time." Donna sat down gracefully, though, and crossed her knees.

Ken laughed. "I wish someone would. It's been a dull day so far; I can tell you that."

"Really? You mean you've moved into a new place and everything already? And now you don't have anything to do."

"No, no. I'm looking for a spot near the Guild Hall and the decent places around here are all taken. So right now, I don't have much looking to do." Ken became aware, again, that she was gazing at him with a smile that seemed unrelated to anything either of them was saying.

"Yes, I'm afraid the area is saturated with gamers. I live just a few blocks from here myself. It's a nice area." She nodded sympathetically.

"It's funny. Right now, I have the most outrageously fancy suite I've ever seen. The trouble is, it's too much. It doesn't seem like a place to live. It looks more like a set for a movie."

"Have you been meeting people and all? Getting acquainted?"

Ken laughed. "No, not at all. Lou introduced me to a few people at the reception last night after my formal introduction to the crowd, but that's about all."

"Are you shy?"

Surprised, Ken laughed lightly again. "No, I wouldn't say so. On the other hand, I haven't been collaring people in the lobby just to say hello, either."

Donna flashed a bright, pretty smile of amusement. "Oh, that's not what I meant. But everyone knows who you are. I'm sure it would be easy if you got started."

"Maybe later in the day. This morning, everyone coming through here has been pretty preoccupied." Ken shifted on the couch to face her. "Can I ask you something? You said last night that you came to gaming late. How did you get involved in gaming?"

"Speaking of last night, I meant to say good night to you when the party was breaking up. I got caught up in hospitality duties, though."

"That's okay. I was pretty tired after traveling and all. Uh—"

"Oh, sorry. Yes, I . . . well, it sounds like such a cliché. But I had never watched a game until I was twenty-three. A friend took me to be a spectator at a game played over some kind of huge corporate merger or something. Anyway, it was the Battle of Zama. I was fascinated.''

"Really? That's all it took?''

"The very next day, I started calling around to find out what it took to become a gamer.'' Donna spoke with pride.

"I've never known anyone who actually became a Master from that kind of start. It's a cliché for spectators to identify with gamers, and to dream about gaming, but hardly any of them ever make that decision in adulthood. Those of us who make it usually start as kids.''

"I'm the exception, then.'' Donna nodded. "I've almost reached Master status, but I have a long way to go before I reach your level.''

Ken grinned and shook his head. "You wouldn't say that if you'd seen me yesterday.''

"Oh, I doubt that. What happened? Nothing serious, I hope.''

"Well, not really. Richard Ross and I played. He beat me badly, as usual.''

"As usual? You just beat out two hundred other Masters for this position. I know you're good. So does everyone else in the Guild.''

Ken laughed. "Correction—I beat one hundred ninety-nine other Masters. I was the two-hundredth.''

"Touché.'' Donna closed her eyes with a smile and shook her head tightly. "Of course.''

"Actually, Richard and I are old childhood friends. He's always beaten me, as a matter of fact. That's why he made it into the Guild Hall at World Headquarters long before I did.''

Donna watched him, still smiling, without saying anything.

"Uh . . . as a matter of fact, I thought about asking him to put me up until I find a place, but I decided it would be a mistake. He's too intense.'' Ken tried to force a laugh. "I'll have to suffer here, in lonesome luxury.''

"You can stay with me.''

"What?'' Ken wasn't sure he had heard her right.

Donna smiled warmly. "No obligations, no strings attached. I have a nice two-bedroom condo. You'd have to sleep on the couch in the living room, though. The second bedroom is full of junk.''

"Uh . . .'' Ken smiled and sort of shrugged.

"To tell the truth, I wouldn't mind a little company for a change. It would break the routine."

"Well . . ." Ken still didn't know what to say.

Donna shrugged, though she was still smiling. "You don't have to decide now. And if you don't want to, that's fine. It's just a suggestion. Oh, and remember, you'll still have the suite here to fall back on. So think about it. I'm not going to pressure you."

"Okay. Sure." Ken nodded, finally gathering his wits. "I do appreciate the offer."

"I think I've taken enough of your time. As a matter of fact, one of the reception clerks has been trying to get your attention for the last couple of seconds. I suppose you ought to see what he wants." Donna uncrossed her legs and rose.

Ken looked back over his shoulder and saw a clerk waving the earpiece to a videophone. "Oh! Uh, yeah. I've got a call. Okay, thanks for the, um, offer. Would—would you like to have dinner with me tonight?" It was an impulse.

She smiled apologetically. "Actually, I would, but I have a girlfriend coming over. She's helping me keep my history fresh. Maybe another time?"

"Sure. Gotta go. Bye!" Ken gave her a big smile and hurried toward the reception desk. He could feel her gaze following him as he crossed the lobby. When he took the earpiece from the clerk he made a point of not turning around. He didn't want to see her quit watching and walk away.

"Hello?" Ken shifted the small videophone screen toward him and saw Lou's broad, smiling face. He had a freshly lit cigar, long and thick, between his teeth.

"Ken, I got a hot one for ya." Lou was obviously excited. "You sittin' down?"

Ken laughed. "I don't have anything to sit on except the floor. What is it, Lou?"

"All right, bucko. You're the celebrity hotshot they brought into town on account of the Guild Act, right?"

Ken shook his head, but he managed to keep smiling. He didn't feel he knew Lou well enough yet to hurry him along. "I guess that's who I am. If you say so."

"So, it's only right that you play in the very first game contracted under the new Act, isn't it?" Lou laughed gleefully. "I got you the offer, bucko. Great, huh?"

"Yeah." A flood of mixed emotions came over Ken.

"Uh—wow. You got me a contract already?" He was fumbling for words.

"Not *a* contract; *this* contract. You, uh . . . you do understand what I'm talking about, don't you? You don't seem too excited."

"No! I am. I understand. Really, Lou. Yeah, of course I want to do it." Ken tried to sound enthusiastic, but he could feel his confidence ebbing. Yet only yesterday he had gotten off the shuttlecopter ready to take on the entire Guild.

"That's better. Tell you what. Swing by my office any time today and we'll go over the details. The sooner the better, though. Okay?"

"I'll be up soon. Right away. Bye." Ken handed the headset back to the clerk and sighed, watching the small screen go blank. This was what he had played for, fought for, and worked for. He was in World Headquarters, playing the most important game the Guild had offered in many years. Even now, he knew that he could probably defeat almost any Master.

The problem was, he would be playing Richard.

Ken started his practice schedule with no changes in his usual routine. He hoped to take the approach that this game was no different, at least on the gaming level, than any other. The charade failed as he found himself making simple mistakes in his practice games and having lapses of judgment that he had outgrown long ago. At first he blamed the problem on moving; he accepted Donna's invitation to move in with her and put considerable effort into being a decent guest. She was a flexible apartment mate, however, and seemed to be hinting that they could be more. Ken was reluctant to trust his own appraisal of those hints, though, and afraid that he might just be misinterpreting her gestures of friendship.

As the date of his formal game neared, Ken had to admit to himself that his sloppy practice games were due to his feeling of intimidation by Richard. Once he faced that, the situation seemed to get even worse. One day, in the lobby of the Guild Hall, he overheard two masters talking, and one said that in a practice game, Richard as King Roderick of the Goths had actually fought the Arabs to a standstill in Wadi Bekka.

Ken had never heard of anyone doing that before.

The day before the game, Ken played one final practice game. Normally, he took a rest the day before a formal game,

but by now he was frantic. By the end of the game his arms
were stiff and weary as he punched the last sequence of keys.
The move sent the scant remainder of his Arab army into
retreat under General Ziyad ibn-Salih.

The game had been a disaster. Ken had been pressing too
hard for a victory, and again made amateurish mistakes. His
opponent, playing the Tang Dynasty General Gao Xianzhi,
had brilliantly escaped a pincer movement by Ken's Arabs
and an army of Karluk Turks led by a computer-programmed
personality. The retreat would give Victory Conditions to his
opponent, but it would constitute a better performance than if
he simply kept fighting until the Arabs were routed or
slaughtered.

Ken watched the screen, imagining the lightly-armed Arabs
galloping away across the dusty hills, robes flying out behind
them, with bows slung on their shoulders and bloody scimi-
tars still in their hands. In July of 751, the Flame of Islam had
met the Golden Age of China on the banks of the Talas River
near Aulie-Ata. A huge conflict had decided, perhaps for all
time, whether Central Asia would be part of the Islamic world
or remain under the sway of Chinese culture. Historically, the
Arabs had marched north and the Karluks had marched south
to trap the immense Chinese host between them. They had
destroyed the Chinese army and had taken thousands of prisoners on the wastes of Central Asia north of Sogdiana. Yet
Ken's Arabs were in frantic flight.

Several seconds passed and the computer froze the screen
with "Victory Conditions: Tang Empire." It was the worst
defeat Ken had ever suffered. Shaken, he gave his opponent a
quick congratulations and hurried away.

That evening, Ken went up to the roof of Donna's building
to be alone for a while. He found a beat-up, rusted metal
chair and sat down gingerly. The summer sun was still high,
and the air was humid and heavy. The bugs were never bad
up here, though, and from this height the city was pretty.

Ken propped his feet on an overturned paint can. In the
distance, he could see the old Union Station, where Pretty
Boy Floyd had once had a shoot-out with federal agents.
Beyond it, tall modern buildings gleamed in the sunlight. Ken
leaned back and gazed at them, studying the lines of architec-
ture, the flight of occasional birds, and the sweep of the
billowing white clouds.

The time passed easily, and the slant of the sunlight grew sharper.

"Just sitting here?" Donna asked.

Ken jumped in surprise, then grinned awkwardly. "Uh, yeah. Hi. I didn't hear you."

"I'm sorry to bother you. One of the neighbors said you came up here a long time ago, and I just wondered, well, if you were here."

Ken squinted into the sunlight, looking up at her. The breeze was blowing her hair into her face, and she held it out with one hand. She was wearing a turquoise sleeveless t-shirt and white shorts that emphasized her tan. Her legs and feet were bare, and he made a point of looking away from them.

"Do you want to be alone?" She started to turn away.

"No! Not necessarily, I mean." Ken realized that he wanted her to stay. "Listen, did you ever see a movie called *The Golden Horde*? It's old. I saw it when I was a kid."

"No, I don't think so. Some epic about Mongol Russia, I suppose."

"Supposedly. It was no more accurate than most historical films. It suggested that the Mongols merely overwhelmed their enemies with numbers and never made any real military contributions."

Donna squatted Asian-style next to him. "That sounds like typical Hollywood. Why do you ask?"

"Oh . . . I've just been thinking about how I got to this point—being a master, and getting to World Headquarters and all. It's a little frustrating, coming all this way and still carrying around an old childhood fear."

"It's awfully irrational, too." She smiled gently. "I guess you know that."

"Yeah." Ken nodded. "If you weren't a gamer, what would you be?"

Donna looked away and stood up. "I don't know. Not much, certainly."

Ken wished he and Donna were closer. He suddenly wanted a hug, as in childhood, but he could tell that she had become leery of the conversation after his last question. He decided to change the subject a little. "I'm also trying to face the fact that I'm going to lose."

"Hey!" She put a fist on her hip in exaggerated disapproval. "You can't talk like that. You haven't even started playing yet. That's even more irrational than feeling intimidated by Richard. At least, we all admit he's very good. But you can't just give up before you start."

Ken lowered his head. "Guess I just need moral support."

For a moment, neither of them spoke.

"You need a good dinner, too, and some rest." Donna took his arm and pulled him up, then let go. "It's late. Let's eat."

"Yeah, okay." Ken followed her back downstairs.

They heated up leftovers for dinner. Afterward, though, Ken could not sit still. He paced around the apartment and finally went for an extended walk just to burn up his nervous energy. This was the first time he had felt this tense before a game since his very first formal contest. Even the elimination tournament that had brought him here had not thrown him off his stride this much. In fact, his confidence had been a large part of his success there.

Eventually, Ken decided he was tired enough to go to bed. "See you in the morning."

"All right." Donna looked up from her book as she sat on the couch with her feet drawn up beneath her. "Tell you what; I'll treat you to breakfast out tomorrow. Interested?"

Ken grinned appreciatively. "It's a date. Thanks."

Once Ken was in bed, however, he did not sleep well. In the darkness, his mind wandered on the verge of sleep, just beyond conscious control. Thundering hoofbeats and clanging swords accompanied the constant glow of blue and orange lines of battle, flexing and shifting across the sky. Rivers flowed on the edge of battlefields, running red with blood instead of water. Inca warriors dressed in feathers and gold battled burnoosed Bedouin. Vikings in furs and leather assaulted the stone towers of Zimbabwe. When he finally slept, he dreamed.

He dreamed that he walked the narrow ledge atop a winding castle wall that wandered in and out of the clouds. Howling winds threatened to carry him away, but he kept his balance. A full-length mirror appeared in front of him, reflecting his own slender frame, with slanted eyes and wind-tossed black hair.

What kind of career is this? he asked his image. *Even if it is for important issues, it's still a game.*

What's the difference between Varus and Verus? asked his reflection. What about Pax Sinica and bar sinister?

Around the mirror and himself, a lavish baroque ballroom

took shape, shining with gold leaf, marble statuary, and chandeliers.

Do you have to win all the time? If you can't win, will you pout and go home? Where does your ego lie? he asked the face in the mirror.

This room is ugly, said his reflection.

It vanished, to be replaced by the dry mountain walls of Tassili N'Ajjer in the Central Sahara. Paintings of cattle over eight millennia old listened to Ken say, *Winning is the glamorous side of these wars, but you can't have winners without losers.*

Can you tolerate being a loser? sneered his reflection. If you lose, it's desolation city.

The empty, wasted mountains grew forests and jutting crags. High, heavy walls of carefully cut stone sprang from the rocky soil. The thin, cold air of the Andes blew through ruined Machu Picchu.

Ken shivered. *It was cold, this business. You did your work all alone, despite the crowds and friends and colleagues. The real work went on in your head, where no one else could help. When game time came around, it was just you and the keyboard and the screen.*

Is the Temple of the Moon really the Haram Bilkis, as Yemenis say? Who cares? Did Hui Shen and his monks really reach Teotihuácan? Does it really matter to anyone?

I don't have to win.

You do.

I'm not good enough to win.

That, of course, could be.

Thanks a lot.

Clouds roiled up around the dead bones of the Andean city. Ken's image in the mirror put on a gray cowboy hat and tipped it.

Goodbye.

The dream faded to a fitful sleep.

When the moment finally arrived, Ken found himself sitting in his game seat on the floor of the Guild's formal Marathon Gaming Arena. On all four sides, spectators packed the rows of theater seats up to a height far above him. A giant video screen was embedded in each wall over the highest row, so that if spectators could not follow the holograms clearly on their own, they could watch an overview close-up on the screen opposite them.

Ken waited patiently while an attendant adjusted the keyboard's position in front of him. Then he fitted the sensory band on and looked across the white playing field. Richard was also prepared.

To Ken's left, seated on a high platform, another attendant waited for both Masters to raise their hands. When Ken and Richard had both done so, he pushed a button. The playing field lit up with color.

Ken's keyboard screen read, "Bosworth Field. 1485. Richard III."

Ken felt a pang of disappointment, followed by a seizure of panic. *Richard III.* From what he knew about Bosworth, where the Plantagenet Dynasty of England had come to an end with the death of Richard III, the best way to beat the role would be to get the king away from the battlefield alive. But the computer would not be impressed with a hapless retreat.

Since this was a formal game, they had only fifteen seconds of orientation before the game activated. Ken lost a few more seconds wiping his palms on his shirt. Then he studied the battlefield.

His army, led by him as Richard III, was divided into three sections. The units in the van, led by the Duke of Norfolk as a programmed personality, stood in position around the northwest slope of Ambion Hill. On the crest behind them, Richard III commanded the main body of his army. Altogether, the royal units represented eight thousand men. That included reserves of about three thousand under the Earl of Northumberland, a mile to the rear.

The disposition of forces resembled a four-sided card game. Henry Tudor, the Lancastrian heir to the throne, advanced from the west with three thousand French mercenaries and two thousand Welsh supporters. His van, led by the Earl of Oxford as a programmed personality, slid along Redmore Plain on their way to Ambion Hill, skirting the north side of a large marsh that separated the rebel and royal armies. Sir William Stanley, a supposed vassal of King Richard, held two thousand mounted knights to the northwest. His brother, Lord Thomas Stanley, stood about a mile to the south with units of another two thousand men. Ken, as Richard III, nominally had the combat power of twelve thousand men ready to take the field against five thousand in the rebel cause.

Ken's royal units also represented better fighting men than Tudor's mercenaries and had greater combat power in the computer as a result. However, the loyalty of both Stanleys, and also of Northumberland, was suspect. The Stanleys had prospered during the Wars of Roses by keeping a careful eye on the main chance. Lord Stanley had changed sides six times in the preceding twenty years, always aligning himself, just in time, with the dominant side as the situation fluctuated. The Stanleys had neglected to challenge Tudor's entry into England from Wales through Stanley lands, neither joining him nor obstructing him. As the battle approached, they remained in neutral positions.

Thanks to Ken's childhood play and enthusiastic study, he had remembered the situation quickly. However, the screen activated before he figured out what to do. He doubted that either his opponent, Richard, or his historical *persona*, Richard III, shared that problem.

Oxford led the rebel van resolutely forward. Ken made minor adjustments in his own van through orders sent from King Richard to the Earl of Norfolk. His van stretched in a line across the northwest slope, with the flanks curving slightly forward in a pincer shape. Those flanks were chained serpentine guns—early cannon. The units of mounted knights waited some distance behind the guns in two wings. In the body of the line, units of longbowmen were clumped at intervals with handgunners and pikemen between them.

Ken keyed his sensory band on, to check its perspective. Instantly, he, as King Richard, looked down the slope toward Norfolk's men. Their heavy plate-steel armor shone in the sun, blooming with the red badges of Norfolk's livery. This particular perspective offered no special advantage, so he keyed off the band, aware that he would later be counting on it in crucial moments.

The rebel van advanced in a triangle, with its base forming a straight front line and the body of the triangle tapering to a point in the rear. Historically, Oxford's tactic had been to hurl every man forward as fast as possible. Since it had worked, Ken expected Richard would allow the tactic to stand.

Ken watched anxiously as the enemy units advanced. As they entered the range of Norfolk's field guns, he remembered a little rhyme from the day before the battle: "Jock of Norfolk, be not too bold, for Dickon thy master is bought and sold." The two Stanleys had agreed with Tudor to enter the battle on his side and Northumberland had agreed not to take the field at all. In the game, those three roles were programmed personalities whose decisions would be made by the computer.

Ken just had time to feel another wave of hopelessness, and to wonder if Richard III had shared one. No, he realized with embarrassment—of course the king's despair had been much worse. He had been fighting for his life, his kingdom, and his house; Ken was playing a game.

Oxford's van cleared the marsh. The two sides exchanged cannon fire and then volleys of arrows. Holes opened in both front lines and were filled by the lines behind. Norfolk ordered his units to advance when the line of rebels started up the slope. The royal van eased forward at a trotting speed in close order, well-disciplined. If necessary, Ken could send new orders down, still.

Ken searched the screen. The key to the battle was the action of the Stanleys. If they could somehow be induced to stay out of the battle, then Ken's royal forces still outnumbered the rebel army.

The game program would include the secret agreement betraying the king, but also the Stanleys' instinct for self-preservation. The only small advantage Ken had was that his opponent Richard, in the position of Henry Tudor, could not totally trust the Stanleys either.

Norfolk's center was wavering under the onslaught. The only response Ken could think of was to follow the example of Richard III. He sent units forward from the main body of the army to bolster the sagging center, in groups of one hundred men at a time. Yet if he continued to use the tactics of his predecessor, he was likely to suffer the same defeat as his predecessor. He had to think of something new, and effective.

Ken sent more men forward in blocks of one hundred.

Richard III had been an experienced and highly successful general, as well as a ferocious fighter personally. Ken was not sure he could improve on the king's tactics. Again, now, he saw that he would have to imitate Richard III.

Ken's units on the hilltop were dwindling and the time had come to call Northumberland and Lord Stanley forward. Ken sent out two messengers, but did not waste one on Sir William Stanley.

Ken had one slight chance that either Lord Stanley or Northumberland would respond. It lay in the near impossibility of some blunder by his opponent that was known to the computer already but not yet apparent on the field. That was hardly likely, but Ken had to consider the possibility.

As the battle raged, holding Ken's career in the balance, he tried to anticipate the coming developments. The next logical step was an even greater jamming of the densely packed and quickly shifting units on the slope of Ambion Hill, as the two main bodies of troops pushed toward each other behind their front lines. That would begin the critical phase in which the entrance of the Stanleys and Northumberland on the royal side could crush the rebels.

That phase never fully developed. In one of the variations open to the computer, Lord Stanley decided to attack. His two thousand men charged from the south, directly toward the left flank of the royal army.

Ken gasped quietly, angrily, and realized that his flank would probably be turned and possibly crushed. He forgot his previous expectations and chose his last resort.

King Richard himself had always been a fine combatant, but in this battle he had been desperate. Ken sent in the royal unit and keyed on his sensory band.

Suddenly, Ken was looking out over the great, nodding head of White Surrey, the king's charger, as he led a thundering charge of reserve knights in support of their own left flank. His lance angled out ahead, fluttering with his pennon. Ahead, Stanley's men smashed into the royal line, driving it back and sideways. Seconds later, the king's lance shattered against the shield of some nameless Stanley knight. He cast the useless handle aside and unslung his huge, trusty axe. As White Surrey plunged and reared, with hooves flailing, the king swung his axe two-handed, furiously, in the crush of steel and bodies and horses.

The king's men surged around him. Those before him pressed on, rather than feel their fighting king close on their backs; those behind him shouted their battle-cries and came on to join the fray. Ken's greatest asset was the king himself, but if he should fall in the fighting, Ken would lose instantly. That was the way of dynastic struggles.

Historically, Northumberland had not moved against the

king's rear; too many of his northern men favored the king. Yet even if the computer repeated that abstention, King Richard alone could not save the left wing. Ken keyed off his sensory band and pulled the king out of combat, back up onto Ambion Hill.

The royal lines were crumbling. Any second Sir William Stanley would order the killing blow. Ken felt that he shared a feeling of desperation with the real king, even though that was presumptuous.

Also like the king, Ken wanted to win, not just to survive. In the real battle, King Richard had located his personal rival, Henry Tudor, observing the struggle from a small hill to the right and rear of his line. The king had gathered his household knights and other somber volunteers, over a hundred in all, for a charge to the standard of the Lancastrian heir. The danger: the charge would carry the royal contingent right in front of Sir William Stanley and his two hundred horse just to the north.

Historically, the king had fought his way through the surprised party around Tudor and, with great effort, reputedly even fought him hand-to-hand briefly. However, Sir William Stanley had seen the charge and its purpose. The Stanley knights had roared forward to protect Tudor. The force of their charge had swept the king from his rival; he had been unhorsed and killed. The royal forces had fled and the Lancastrian heir had founded the Tudor Dynasty as Henry VII.

Ken had King Richard gather his household knights and call for volunteers. All of the royal party must have felt a special anger, Ken thought. If Northumberland or even one of the Stanleys had held to his oath of allegiance, the battle would have been very different.

Ken himself was outraged, watching the five thousand men under Northumberland and Sir William Stanley who should have been fighting for the king. Tudor, at least, was an openly avowed enemy.

Ken's chance to win, like the king's had been at this point, now lay entirely in the possibility of killing Tudor himself. That figure still stood on the same hill where the real Tudor had stood; Ken's opponent had kept him there so he could observe the battle.

Ken keyed his sensory band back on. It looked hot there on Ambion Hill, with the blazing summer sun shining on their heavy plate-steel armor. The king sat high on White Surrey, his visor open, sweat running down into his eyes. His personal followers crowded around; if the sensory band had allowed it, they would have sent up the varied smells of horses, leather, blood, and sweat. The wounded slid off their mounts with help, others unbuckling their armor for them. Someone raised a bulging water skin up to the king. He took two long draughts and handed back the empty skin. Then, when he took a new lance that was offered up, the knights around him, too, strengthened their resolve and grasped fresh lances.

King Richard turned White Surrey and waved for his axe. The charge they were about to make would end these long civil wars, finally—the king wore a golden crown outside his helmet and would either die as a king or triumph as one. Then, as a party of more than a hundred knights gathered behind him, he made a sweeping arm gesture toward their goal: the red dragon banner of Wales, atop a distant hill behind the lines, ringed with a reserve bodyguard. Everyone could also see the formation of Stanley horse waiting to the north.

Suddenly Ken thought of an additional tactic. He directed one of his captains to withdraw another troop of knights from the struggling lines. The royal lines were about to break anyway, but Tudor's death would give them the victory if the gamble worked.

Ken ordered that the second block of one hundred charge behind the royal contingent at an interval, and farther out in a wing to the right under the very noses of the Stanley traitors. Both maneuvers were likely to be suicidal, but if they succeeded, the battle was won.

The royal center was disintegrating. Ken could not wait longer. Blinking sweat away from his eyes, he led the charge down Ambion Hill.

The way was open; the right flank of the royal line held the rebel left committed, and the king's charge thundered around them. Ahead, Tudor's bodyguard saw the charge and prepared for the impact, jamming themselves around the person of their proclaimed king. King Richard's knights smashed into them, and Ken gritted his teeth as he heard the splintering of lances and human screams in his mind. The action at close quarters was too fast for logical thought; all was reflex, pressing forward, smashing and slashing, always toward Tu-

dor himself. One by one, King Richard hacked away those
who rose before him, swinging his axe with lethal abandon,
eyes always on Tudor—who suddenly pulled away, behind
his line. He was no fighter and simply turned on his charger
and ran for his life, with a meager escort of two knights
galloping behind him. Even his standard bearer was hemmed
in by the furious fighting on the hilltop, and abandoned. King
Richard held his breath, swinging his axe with both arms
straight, chopping against the wall of flailing steel around
him—and then, suddenly, the sensory band went off.

Ken sat away from the keyboard and looked at the field.
The king was gone—dead.

Ken tried to blink sweat away, then had to wipe his eyes
with one hand. He had been so involved in the scene . . . and
now the game was lost. His screen read, "Victory Conditions: Lancaster."

Ken heard applause vaguely around him, but did not react.
He leaned toward the field again, still breathing heavily, to
peer at the motionless figures. The position of forces at the
end of the game was still visible.

Someone's hand plucked at his arm, but he shook it off. He
located Tudor on the screen, a short distance from the hill
where the king had fallen. Then he found the important
information—behind the remains of the king's first contingent, whose survivors were scattered like confetti as the
charge of the Stanley horse held motionless in mid-gallop.
There Ken found his second wing of charging knights. They
were scattered also, their momentum smashed by the force of
the Stanley sweep. However, from the positions still evident
on the screen, Ken knew that the tactic had worked. It had
partially broken the Stanley attack and delayed them very
slightly. In the real battle, King Richard had been only seconds away from cutting down Tudor. Ken had found a way to
gain those seconds. Even though he had failed to destroy the
Lancastrian heir, his ploy had fulfilled its purpose.

Ken let out a long breath of relief and fell back into his
seat. A moment later, an attendant came up to move aside his
keyboard. The applause was continuing; Ken became aware
for the first time just how enthusiastic it was.

The attendant helped him to his feet, and down the steps to
a wheelchair. As Ken was being wheeled out, he looked
around at the crowd and realized that many of the people in

the audience were looking at him, applauding for him, as well as for Richard. Surprised, he smiled wryly.

Across the arena, Richard was also being wheeled out. Ken felt a cold pang in his stomach at seeing him. He hated losing, and he especially hated losing to Richard.

Donna was already waiting for him in the reception room, standing next to the long refreshment table with a cold glass of white wine for him.

"Ken! That was wonderful." Donna handed him the glass and knelt next to him for a kiss. "It really was. And the finish was so exciting."

"Yeah, well, I still lost." Ken accepted the glass and hooked his other elbow around her neck to draw her close. He hesitated, first to gaze at her full, waiting lips, and then, amused, to look at her eyes as she watched his own mouth. Then he kissed her suddenly, and long.

"Consolation prize?" Richard's sardonic voice came from the other side of Ken's wheelchair.

Ken and Donna both started laughing, and she stood up. Ken turned and extended his hand to Richard, whose own wheelchair had pulled up alongside. "Congratulations."

"Thanks." Richard shook his hand briefly, chuckling with a sudden, embarrassed shake of his head. "You know, that final ploy of yours was incredibly ruthless—sending all those guys to certain death on that extra wing. Matter of fact, it was pretty sharp, too."

Ken shrugged. "Almost worked. Not quite, though." He sighed.

"You may have a masterplay on your hands, there."

Ken looked at him sharply, ready to find Richard's edged sarcasm mocking him. Instead, he found Richard in his professional mood. "What did you say?"

"Well, it's not proven, but that wing tactic of yours just might turn out to be the masterplay for Bosworth. You created it, even if you didn't execute it properly. It'll have to be tested by other Masters, but if it proves out, you're on record as devising it." Richard reached up to accept a glass of red wine from someone.

Ken felt a warm sense of accomplishment building in him, as Richard's appraisal sank in. Gradually, Ken realized what he had acquired since arriving here by helicopter. He had Donna's affection, a dimension Richard's life lacked; he had honest praise from his old friend, a quality he had rarely received; he had, perhaps, a masterplay to his credit. All three were victories, despite the official outcome of the game.

Ken spoke quietly to Richard. "It *is* complicated, isn't it?"

Richard grinned and clinked his glass against Ken's. "Welcome to World Headquarters."

EDITOR'S INTRODUCTION TO:

DEFENSE IN A N-DIMENSIONAL WORLD
TECHNOLOGICAL SURPRISE MUST BE PREVENTED
Stefan T. Possony

Dr. Stefan T. Possony, Senior Fellow Emeritus of the Hoover Institution on War, Revolution and Peace, was for some twenty years an intelligence officer of the United States. He received his Ph.D. from the University of Vienna at the age of twenty, and shortly after entered Austrian politics. He was instrumental in the anti-Nazi movement; when the German panzers entered Austria his name was high on the Gestapo's wanted list. After many adventures he came to the United States.

One of his projects was a study of the Soviet nuclear effort; he received a medal for correctly predicting the first Soviet nuclear test.

The Protracted Conflict, by Robert Strauss-Hupe, Stefan Possony, and William Kintner was one of the most penetrating analyses of Soviet strategy ever published, and remains essential for a true understanding of the modern world.

In 1970 Possony and I co-authored *The Strategy of Technology*. This book has been used as a text in the US Air Force Academy and the Air War College. In the early sixties, Dr. Possony correctly predicted that beam weapons and beam technologies—"beamology" as he liked to call it—would be of inestimable military importance. He has had similar success in spotting the potential of other key technologies before any one else—scientist or strategist—has recognized their importance.

Dr. Possony considers this one of his most important essays.

DEFENSE IN A N-DIMENSIONAL WORLD: TECHNOLOGICAL SURPRISE MUST BE PREVENTED
Stefan T. Possony

For good reasons the US adopted a defensive military strategy. Concurrently it should have decided to adopt sub-strategies to ensure the success of the defense, in the sense that hostile offense would be foreclosed. This did not happen: No systematic strategy to forestall surprise and thereby to prevent aggression was developed. The Strategic Defense Initiative constitutes the first step toward a rational peace preservation strategy. Hopefully, second and third steps will follow.

There are three major types of surprise which must be avoided: 1. sudden transformation of friends into foes, and of foes into friends; 2. operational surprise, such as an unexpected geographical center of attack, unexpected timing, and unexpected numbers and reserves; and 3. technological surprise such as unexpected weapons and extraordinary performance.

Ad 1. The US is well informed about the politics of its major allies but it tends to be confused about the distribution of friendly and hostile groups both in allied and in enemy countries.

Ad 2. Originally the US was not much worried about operational surprise, but when the USSR moved into space, the US followed suit and established warning systems and surveillance from orbit. Though space reconnaissance is not foolproof—no system is—the hazard of operational surprise has been managed efficiently. Consequently, the would-be attacker must compensate for his presumed operational inability to strike like a bolt from the blue. Technological shock would be the most promising substitute.

Ad 3. The US has been holding the technological lead for a long time, during which it acquired major advantages in nucleonics, astronautics, electronics, and computers. Given this leverage, the danger of technological surprise for the US has been downgraded. The Pentagon did not think it was necessary to assign high priority to the anticipation and prevention of technological miracles. Also, the blades of scientific endeavor were not honed on the edges of technological surprise. Indeed, much scientific work was performed without thought being given to the possibility that what was created for peace may help the attacker unless it can be used first by the defender. Has high energy physics military significance? For years the very topic was totally taboo.

This low assessment of technological ambush is visibly reflected in the Strategic Defense Initiative which apparently is linked to an estimate that the US has 10 to 20 years before it needs modernized defenses. A leisurely time-table is being established, despite the fact that the Soviets began their charged particle beam program some five years before the US got wind of it. This Soviet effort ran for another five years before the US decided, on its part, to do a little work on particle beams. Thus, there exists at least one major technology in which the Soviets have gained a substantial lead. This American handicap arose in the very field of strategy where the US intends to put an end to the specter of unending nuclear menace.

True, particle beams are just one of several technologies through which the defense initiative can be implemented. But is the question properly posed when charged particle beams are conceived as merely one of many technologies? Is it not conceivable that sub-atomic particles lined up as accurate beams would turn out to be a dominant technology? If this were the case, might a lead in this area not be decisive by itself, if only because it would prime virtually all other technologies?

US Air Intelligence discovered the Soviet particle beam program. This discovery came as a total surprise, both to the intelligence and the military-scientific "communities," and it was discounted, ridiculed, and disbelieved for years. Testing was delayed and financially starved. After the new reality was accepted, reaction was slow and evaluations were reductionist; to a point where the advance into the sub-atomic realm was treated as a normal routine—just one little step forward at this time. That major and entirely unprecedented potentialities may be involved in the sub-atomic dimension was not recognized, even though such a perspective is implied or explicitly discussed in modern textbooks.

Numerous physicists have stated that the four dimensions of space-time are not sufficient to comprehend nature, and that many additional dimensions are needed. Yet explicit recognition by the military of new dimensions, with new potentialities and new dangers, was not disclosed. If such recognition did not occur, this would not be because of failures in intelligence. It would result from a *carence intellectuelle*.

Given modern intelligence systems, how might technological surprise occur? Let us assume two protagonists "share" scientific information through the processes of research and exchange. In this case, one side might fail to develop one or the other opportunity either because of an oversight or because capabilities of exploitation are lacking.

However, there may be the more profound reason that one side rejects new information or misinterprets data because those do not conform with principles or beliefs regarded as correct or unchallengeable. Once upon a time, prominent American scientists denied that powered flight was feasible, and an authoritative scientific magazine lost two years before it deigned to acknowledge that the first powered flight at Kitty Hawk was not a hoax.

Sometimes scientists "forget" disturbing facts and accept uncritically what they learned in school or read in dictionaries. They don't always live up to their professed ethos. Example: The velocity of light is a "constant," and as such basic to much of physics. Yet the actual figure of 300,000 kilometers per second is an average of numerous different measurements; strangely enough, this average has remained unchanged. Worse, Soviet scientists discovered that light is faster in a vacuum on earth than in space, remote from planetary masses. American scientists are reported not to believe this. Since "it can't be so," this discovery is simply ignored. A very important effect (which will be discussed later) was discovered by one well-known American physicist, a protégé of Einstein, together with an Israeli graduate student. In 1959 the information was published in *The Physical Review*, one of the leading refereed physics organs. The date when the manuscript was received was duly marked, just as the date of the receipt of the revised text (which shows that the paper had been refereed, and that defects or errors were discovered and corrected). Within two months, the paper was published as a lead article. The asserted effect was verified experimentally by a third physicist in 1960.

This background suggests that the findings of this paper should be accepted as valid, and the information would normally be so handled. Yet the effect which was disclosed in 1959 remained largely unknown, and reportedly was and is being totally ignored in military technology. Nobel prize laureate Richard P. Feynman, in specific reference to the effect in question, ascribed the neglect of 25 years to "prejudices of what is and is not significant."

Directed energy was anticipated—or rather invented—by Nikola Tesla, more than 80 years ago. As the inventor of the alternating current, Tesla was once regarded as the world's outstanding theoretician and practitioner of electromagnetism. He refused the Nobel prize, which had been offered jointly to him and Edison. Tesla viewed the methods of selecting laureates as incompetent and dishonest. Problems of primacy pitted him against Marconi and Edison, and financial problems turned Tesla into a black sheep: Alternating current was threatening huge investments in direct current. His experiments on "free" electric energy showed him up as crazy among "school" physicists.

In short, we like to criticize the communists for turning historical figures like Trotsky into non-persons and throwing them into memory-holes. Yet we are capable of doing precisely the same, with scientists, rather than policemen, performing as executioners. Scandalous though such events are, they were easily and routinely covered up.

Tesla was the foremost victim among American scientists. His work is ignored in textbooks and curricula. The investigations which he started were dropped. The resulting damage to the US was substantial and durable.

The American scientific body is covered with numerous "Tesla tumors." To be sure, treatment by means of downgrading, silencing, and forgetting is not an American specialty. It is an inborn affliction of all scientific communities, and it is visible in the history of Nobel prizes. Fortunately, after a lapse of time, the trouble tends to be self-correcting; or so we hope.

However, danger tends to lurk high if science and research are undertaken for the Armed Forces under monopolistic direction, and with dogmatic and arrogant scientific advisory boards sticking to biases. As a result, major technologies may be blotted out, and unexpected opportunities ignored or denied. A catastrophe can ensue if the opponent does not suffer from the identical bias, but develops a technology which exploits the opponent's "bias" which, actually, is nothing but an ignorant and fatal error.

I am neither writing a historico-philosophical essay, nor do I wish to rekindle the Tesla controversy. I am talking about what I conceive to be a most dangerous and concrete risk for American security: namely, scientific blindness caused by dogma. I do not claim competence in high energy physics; it is the job of physicists to solve problems in physics. But I am competent to decide whether a big problem is being investigated seriously by scientists, or else is given the heave-ho. If unscientific judgments are enunciated by scientists pretending to act scientifically, alarm clocks need to be rung.

For more than 15 years strange "phenomena" have been observed in many parts of the world, whose nature has not been deciphered. (I am not alluding to "flying saucers," although those could be peripherally involved.) The "phenomena" to which I am referring, include flashes, fireballs, aerial blasts at high altitude, very loud booms, brightening skies, arcs in the sky, expanding globes of light, giant underwater sounds, possibly anomalous earthquakes, and abnormal weather patterns.

Some of the phenomena have been more military than theatrical. For example, radar invisibility was achieved, alerting us that a stealth capability may exist years in advance, before the American realization of this revolutionary technology is due.

Singular long-distance communication signals were received: The strength of the signals was stunning. Dubbed "woodpeckers" by US intelligence, the sounds were explained by the very powerful over-the-horizon "Henhouse" radars which are deployed in the western Ukraine. Some analysts were wondering whether the Soviets were trying to upgrade radars to actual weapons. Since Henhouse is merely a very modern radar, this seems to be an artificial speculation. Also, it is not known that the signals actually originated in those or any radars. After many years, the woodpeckers remain mysterious.

The "discovery" by Vela satellites of two seeming nuclear

tests which were falsely attributed to the Republic of South Africa was another episode in the series of inexplicable phenomena. An impressive "phenomenon" happened on April 9, 1984, when a mushroom cloud, with the astounding diameter of 150 miles, rose to an altitude of 60,000 feet within two minutes. This occurred south of the Kuriles, 200 miles from Tokyo and 350 miles from a Soviet missile test ground. A nuclear explosion? Five Boeing 747's flew through and near the cloud, and found no radioactivity. The plume was neither nuclear nor volcanic. Instead, the cloud was much colder than the ambient air. Satellite photography recorded 78 similar mushrooms since 1974, many of those in the Arctic.

Late in 1975 infrared sensors on US satellites were temporarily disabled in four incidents. In one case a sensor was blinded during four long hours. This incident demonstrated not only that an operation was mounted with effective equipment (not with blueprints), and with astounding accuracy. It also indicated that a power source was available for sustained attack against satellites. Nothing is known about the equipment and the power supply, and neither the accuracy nor the duration of the weapon's effect are understood—nine years after the occurrence. The incident is subjected to "protracted silent treatment." Yet the event may indicate that US space warning systems are becoming vulnerable.

The mysterious phenomena have in common that they are not natural but technical and deliberate. They are electrical and electromagnetic, probably are caused by beams, and they have multiple military implications. The many phenomena evidently represent tests of different applications. All of those tests required enormous energies whose nature, versatility, range, and origin remain enigmatic.

In spite of their variability, the different phenomena seem to be caused by a single, basic technology which as yet continues entirely unknown in the West. Circumstances suggest that the USSR is familiar with this technology, and that the "phenomena" or tests are carried out by Soviet scientists, technologists, and soldiers.

The press has published reports on several of the unusual observations. Yet little was done to confirm geographic origins or to identify the apparatus which enacted the phenomena. The fact that one Tesla-type weapon was identified at Sary Shagan, the Soviet R & D center on strategic defense weapons, seems to have attracted very little attention.

The official reaction was and still is marked by lethargy and disinterest: "We don't know, and we don't know anybody who would know." This line needs to be re-written: "We won't ask those scientists of whom their 'mainstream' colleagues disapprove." For as long as this attitude persists, a rather sudden and far-reaching surprise operation should not be astounding.

With this background, let us look at the effect whose neglect was deplored by Richard Feynman. This effect was discovered by David Bohm and Y. Aharonov in 1959, and verified in 1960 by R.G. Chambers. It shows that in the absence of electrical and magnetic fields, the potentials still can exist and cause real effects to occur in field-free regions. Bohm's summary of the basic paper described "the significance of electromagnetic potentials in quantum theory" this way:

> Contrary to the conclusions of classical mechanics, there exist effects of potentials on charged particles, even in the regions where all the fields (and therefore the forces on the particles) vanish.

In the discussion, the following statements appear:[1]
> In quantum mechanics, the fundamental physical entities are the potentials, while the fields are derived from them by differentiations.
> The potentials are richer in properties than the fields.
> The potentials must, in certain cases, be considered as physically effective, even when there are no fields acting on the charged particles.
> The classical notion "that the potentials cannot have any meaning, except insofar as they are used mathematically to calculate the fields, . . ." cannot be maintained for the general case.

Those statements of 1959 were enlarged in 1980. A summary of the new version reads as follows:[2]

> Empty space . . . is not empty at all; it's full, an immense sea of energy on top of which matter as we know it is only a "small quantized wavelike excitation . . . rather like a tiny ripple."

> The entire universe of matter . . . is to be treated as a comparatively small pattern of excitation on the energy sea.

Bohm is a physicist of world reputation, even though some of his work is disputed. He co-authored another important paper with Nobel laureate Louis de Broglie, who developed the wave nature of electrons, and who is considered one of the champions of modern physics. Much more could be said about Bohm but, briefly, this physicist cannot be ignored. For that matter, Tesla, Bohm's predecessor two generations removed, must be rescued from oblivion.

Bohm's effect was corroborated, and so far, it has not been falsified. Hence the effect is valid.

At this juncture, the effect is beginning to be noted. During the 1984 Annual Meeting of the American Association for the Advancement of Science, I heard three references to the effect, one in connection with neutrons, and another in an astrophysical discussion. In the third case a plasma specialist, who contributed to a panel on security, was asked: "What is the military significance of the Bohm-Aharonov effect?" His extremely speedy and testy answer: "None." Whatever the pertinence of this answer may be, the man was familiar with the problem, and he was distinctly uneasy about the question.

Since the Bohm-Aharonov effect disproves the tradition which regards electrostatic and magnetostatic potentials as being of negligible importance, and which treats them as purely mathematical conveniences, it follows that the potentials are real entities. Hence the potentials can "directly affect and control charged particle systems even in a region where all the fields and hence the forces on the particles have vanished," to quote T.E. Bearden, a leading expert on the subject, who wrote the only extant analysis in Western literature of the military implications of the effect.[3]

Creation and annihilation of quanta mark the observable passage of an object through time. Fundamentally, this quantum change is controlled by the invisible substructure of matter, specifically by subquantal ("virtual") actions and interactions.

The First Order of Reality, which is observable, emerges from vector interactions of electromagnetic energy with matter. There is a more fundamental Second Order of Reality which is "unobservable." This reality consists of "virtual" vectors and conditions. This Second Order was discovered by Tesla (using a different terminology).

The notion that a vacuum is not total emptiness, but denotes merely the absence of mass, is no longer in serious dispute. A vacuum is a charge, more exactly a charge-flux, without mass. Accordingly, the physics of today regard all observable forces to be generated by virtual particle reactions. The well-known British physicist Paul Davies stated that modern theories of the vacuum reveal that empty space is "seething with activity."

Bearden explains that such activity in and through a point constitutes a "potential" at that point. Hence the vacuum should be regarded as a potential field. Put differently, there are spaces without matter, or vacua, but there are no spaces without potentials, which are virtual particle reactions.

Particle physicists believe that physical reality consists of "internested virtual levels" of ever finer structure, and that those unobservable structures of "spinning particles" carry, or are, massless charge-fluxes in constant acceleration. In this context, Einstein, who transformed the three-dimensional world into a four-dimensional world, was "overtaken" by modern physicists who propose models of 8, 11, 32, and still more dimensions.

While particles provide the substructure of the visible reality, they also can occupy the invisible reality in hidden form. Their hidden realm is known as the "Dirac Sea," after P.A.M. Dirac, one of the founders of quantum theory who predicted the electron spin. Bearden associates each virtual level with a "hyperspace," a concept adapted from J.A. Wheeler, expert on spacetime physics. Still another concept is that of the "neutrino sea," which has been promoted by astrophysicists. The bewilderment exceeds that which reigned when electricity was discovered.

Tesla discovered that waves and beams of pure potential, without observable electric and magnetic fields, could easily be made and utilized. Since this Tesla wave was his fundamental and forgotten secret, the name "Tesla Reality" for the Second Order of Reality might be most fitting.

There are differences between those various concepts, but they all seem to agree that the invisible particle substructure is of the utmost importance and cannot, therefore, be handled as a simple observable zero. On the contrary, this substructure is, or contains, huge magnitudes of energy pitted against one another, and it influences or determines the force vectors in the observable reality. All observable forces arise in, on, and of the actual sub-structure of accelerating particles. Note that all fundamental particles are charged both internally and externally, i.e. they are dynamic assemblages of smaller, charged particles. Moreover, they are constantly changing from one kind of particle into another, forming a sort of "charged cloud."

This vast complex has so far only been adumbrated. At present, high energy physics remain mainly concerned with subatomic particles, and the inter-relationships between the particles and the atomic and molecular worlds are as yet largely unexplored. To recapitulate the preceding discussion: The space vacuum is the sum total of all "virtual things." It is in constant flux, and hence it is totally charged. Yet it is still being assigned a hypothetical zero charge.

By contrast, on the basis of up-to-date interpretations, Bearden estimated that the potential of the space vacuum may run up to 200 million volts per point in a n-dimensional space, with "n" being greater than 4.

One interpretation assumes no charge, another postulates charge of incalculable magnitude. What an exhibition of confusion! Evidently, military technologists can no longer, or should not, ignore the sub-structure in their strategic investigations and weapon-equipment designs.

What might be done with the potential?

Given the Second Reality, "beams of pure potential without observable vector force fields may be deliberately produced and intersected at a distance to cause observable effects in the interference zone," according to Bearden who has proposed and experimented with mechanisms for doing so.

To achieve military effects, two Tesla waves may be launched through the vacuum plasma to achieve interference through their crossing in the target area. The two waves are non-Hertzian longitudinal waves of electrostatic potential. The waves move in the vacuum charge flux and exert stress on four-dimensional space-time.

Each wave is composed of two or more interlocked Hertz waves of identical frequencies, with cancellation of their opposing magnetic and electric fields, so that the externally observable vector fields sum to zero. The two crossing waves in spacetime are related to four or more virtual waves in the sub-structure. The working energy is not transported from the operational base through space to the interference zone, but directed to arise there from the interfering sub-structures of the intersecting Tesla waves. That is, instead of transmitting energy, the input energy is transformed into potentials which are interfered at a distance, modifying and producing the energy again in the interference zone.

In the interference zone energy can be released like a pulse or a high temperature explosion. Alternatively, energy can be withdrawn from the interference zone, producing a cold explosion. Precision is needed for the locating of the interference zone. Good accuracy can be achieved through narrow beams and a substantial input of energy resulting in high energy density in the interference zone.

The energy which is needed to do military work in the target area is pumped into the two waves at their launch base. The working energy at the distant zone will be approximately as large as the injected energy, Except for leakages and imperfections, no energy will be lost to the process.

Tesla two-wave interference weapons may be substantially cheaper than current and currently projected systems.

Tesla weapons can be used for non-lethal as well as for lethal purposes. They possess defensive and offensive utilizations.

A ''Tesla weapon system'' represents a highly advanced form of directed energy. Yet many of the problems which bedevil particle beams on their passage through the atmosphere will not be significant in the new technology. Tesla-type directed energy weapons promise to have a uniquely broad spectrum of military (and industrial) relevance.

Tesla weapons and/or equipments are expected to be fit for anti-avionic purposes like jamming, for under-water communications and the locating of submarines, for strategic defense, for strategic warfare, for operations in space, and for large-scale and catastrophic weather modifications. Interferometers will be the principal element of a Tesla weapon, and may be the core of Soviet devices and weapons.

Tesla weapons need explosive power generators (a branch of technology in which the Soviets are highly proficient), special power units to produce energy from vacuum, translators to create and alternate waves, Fourier transform computers and transmitters, and aiming-pointing instruments, etc.

If the Second Order of Reality is correctly recognized and can be entered as predicted, the military gear may be neither large nor complicated. This might enhance the present danger. But it also might facilitate the task of quickly countering the unexpected threat.

What's the message?

First, the world in which we live has undergone a major transformation. We learned that we live in two orders of existence, the Einstein and Tesla realities. The first is known as space-time, and the second as the sub-structure of matter and vacua. Space-time is four-dimensional, and the two realities together are at least six-dimensional.

This transformation has come as a major surprise. The surprise is behind us as a fact and as an occurrence. But the comprehension of the fact is still ahead of us.

Second, the USSR knows about the six or n-dimensional world, and it seems to possess various interferometric equipments usable for directed energy operations. This means that a strategic surprise may be in the making, possibly a decisive surprise.

Third, the exploitation of unilateral surprise is based on superior knowledge and equipment. It can take different forms ranging from psycho-political panics to military disasters. Soviet actual choices, if any, depend on their concrete capabilities, about which I do not care to speculate. However, I wish to warn against aprioristic assumptions that no such capabilities are in being, or can as yet exist.

Fourth, a prudent reader will understand that the discovery of a danger must be supplemented by its measurement. This task must be performed without delay by knowledgeable, wise—and young—experts in intelligence, science and technology, and military planning.

Fifth, Tesla weapons must be designed and procured promptly, and the impact of the novelty on existing and emerging armaments be assessed.

Neither panic nor flight from reality will help, and the typical advisers who belittle or deny innovations should not be expected to be useful.

If the danger is real, Tesla weapons will mean a military transformation whose magnitude will exceed that of the nuclear and the electronic space revolutions. But the effect of those weapons will depend on the energy which is fed into them. Furthermore, hypothecating that tests have been going on, those weapons must be produced and deployed, and crews must be trained to operate them. Every surprise has its limits.

Our task, therefore, is not insoluble. On the contrary, an extraordinary chance to discover entirely unprecedented opportunities for security may be arising.

The Pentagon includes specialists who are knowledgeable about the demise of the old vacuum and the emergence of novel dimensions. But they don't believe the "political atmosphere" is receptive to such novelties.

No realist should expect bureaucracies to champion technological upheavals, let alone total transformations.

Notes

1. *The Physical Review*, Second Series, Vol. 115, No. 3, August 1, 1959, pp. 483 and 490.
2. For a recent discussion of Bohm and his work, see John Briggs and F. David Peat, *Looking Glass Universe, the Emerging Science of Wholeness*, New York, Simon & Schuster Cornerstone Library, 1984, chapter 2, e.g. p. 140. See also p. 132: "In one cubic centimeter of empty space the amount of energy is much greater than the total amount of energy of all the matter in the known universe."
3. Those who wish to study the scientific basis of this story, to understand various concepts of weaponry, and to familiarize themselves with the mysterious phenomena should consult the writings by T.E. Bearden, published by Tesla Book Company (1580, Magnolia Ave, Millbrae, CA 94030). Bearden, a weapons analyst and nuclear engineer, is at present developing an Artificial Intelligence "expert system" for command and control. His previous work dealt with technological requirements of Nike-Ajax, Nike-Hercules, Hawk, and Patriot missiles, and high energy laser weapons. He holds advanced degrees in mathematics and nuclear sciences. A retired lieutenant colonel, he graduated from several US Army artillery and missile schools, and from the US Army Command and General Staff College.

EDITOR'S INTRODUCTION TO:

THREE POEMS

A. E. Housman died before the modern era; but he well understood the virtues—and sins—of the warrior.

Timothy Sarnecki is new to this series. I hope to publish more of his work in future volumes.

EPITAPH ON AN ARMY OF MERCENARIES
by A. E. Housman

These, in the day when heaven was falling,
   The hour when earth's foundations fled,
Followed their mercenary calling
   And took their wages and are dead.

Their shoulders held the sky suspended;
   They stood, and earth's foundations stay;
What God abandoned, these defended,
   And saved the sum of things for pay.

THE ORACLES
by A. E. Housman

'Tis mute, the word they went to hear on high Dodona
    mountain
  When winds were in the oakenshaws and all the cauldrons
    tolled,
And mute's the midland navel-stone beside the singing fountain,
  And echoes list to silence now where gods told lies of old.

I took my question to the shrine that has not ceased from
    speaking,
  The heart within, that tells the truth and tells it twice as
    plain;
And from the cave of oracles I heard the priestess shrieking
  That she and I should surely die and never live again.

Oh priestess, what you cry is clear, and sound good sense I
    think it;
  But let the screaming echoes rest, and froth your mouth no
    more.
'Tis true there's better boose than brine, but he that drowns
    must drink it;
  And oh, my lass, the news is news that men have heard
    before.

The King with half the East at heel is marched from lands of
    morning;
  Their fighters drink the rivers up, their shafts benight the
    air.
And he that stands will die for nought, and home there's no
    returning.
  The Spartans on the sea-wet rock sat down and combed
    their hair.

233

THE LAST THREE DAYS
by Timothy P. Sarnecki

The last three days a hot wind has blown
Up from the south; a blood-letting wind,
Breathing hot, angry breath into the night.
The walls of my room, drawn in by the heat,
Turn my face into my pillow, it stained
By the cup, poured to forget, overturned.
The wind from the steppes blows cold by the tent,
Where three stern, cold men drink hot blood and wine,
Dipping their knives in the gilded skull-cup.
In the morning they ride to the hilltop
To meet Darius and die; or, to win,
For which they bleed themselves and drink their pact.
Then heat-brought sweat in the wind makes me cold,
Like Scythian horsemen, buried in gold.

EDITOR'S INTRODUCTION TO:

THE INTERROGATION TEAM
David Drake

The still uncouth City which Hannibal came over to attack numbered a mere million men at the time that it put into the field against him at Cannae an army of more than 85,000 men. But when its armies clashed at Pharsalia, the Republic, though by then it was spread out over the whole of the Mediterranean basin, could not put in the field more than 65,000 men in all. When Tiberius strained every nerve to avenge the legions of Varus, he could send the future Germanicus but 50,000 men. Marcus Arelius seems to have had not many more in Parthians. When Julian checked the Alemanni near Strasbourg, he had 13,000 men, and Belisarius was given 11,000 to win Italy back from the Goths. . . .

The smallest province in the Empire, had its inhabitants still been trained to arms, could have wiped out the Goths and Vandals who were but small nations in arms. Assuredly, Alaric could have no more taken the Rome of old than Genseric the Carthage of old.

—Bertrand de Jouvenal, *On Power*

Machiavelli warned republics against reliance on mercenaries. If they are incompetent, he said, they will ruin you by losing battles; and if they are competent, they will be tempted to turn against the state and become its conquerors.

De Jouvenal argues that the "natural evolution of a people which is rising in the scale of civilization" is toward smaller armies, fewer warriors, and more citizens. Machiavelli convinces us that we cannot entrust our fate to mercenaries. This presents an obvious dilemma. Whatever we do, we are in danger.

We cannot destroy liberty in order to preserve it. Robert Heinlein and others have argued that a nation which cannot defend itself without conscription does not deserve to live; and while I cannot accept that absolute judgment—in this world we must often choose among undesirable alternatives—I do find the argument appealing. We must not destroy liberty in order to preserve it; we must not forever construct Power in order to oppose our enemies. And yet—without organization which can only be provided by a strong government, we may be rendered helpless.

Perhaps the answer is not to expect so much from government; to splinter Power before it enslaves us. The United States has never been in danger from its own citizens. It is particularly in no danger from conscript armies, which are merely the citizens in arms. It is the ceaseless striving toward domestic perfection that renders unto Washington not only those things which are Caesars, but everything else.

Our intentions may be good and noble, but when we build Power we build what Benjamin Franklin said was "like fire, a dangerous friend and a fearful master." History knows few cases of a wealthy republic whose citizens would defend themselves.

It is worse for those who would establish empires, or defend far frontiers. The temptation to turn to mercenaries can become nearly overwhelming—but it is seldom wise to succumb. Warriors are warriors, and the glories and sins of the warrior are universal. There is a fatal flaw in hiring one's defense; for even if we hire competent mercenaries and keep them under tight control, their interest is not ours. La Legion Etrangère could and did fight fiercely and die bravely for a government which it held in contempt; but most mercenaries are not like that.

Certainly Hammer's Slammers are not. . . .

THE INTERROGATION TEAM
David Drake

The man the patrol brought in was about forty, bearded, and dressed in loose garments—sandals, trousers, and a vest that left his chest and thick arms bare. Even before he was handed from the back of the combat car, trussed to immobility in sheets of water-clear hydorclasp, Griffiths could hear him screaming about his rights under the York Constitution of '03.

Didn't the fellow realize he'd been picked up by Hammer's Slammers?

"Yours or mine, Chief?" asked Major Smokey Soames, Griffiths' superior and partner on the interrogation team—a slim man of Afro-Asian ancestry, about as suited for wringing out a mountaineer here on York as he was for swimming through magma. Well, Smokey'd earned his pay on Kanarese. . . .

"Is a bear Catholic?" Griffiths asked wearily. "Go set the hardware up, Major."

"And haven't I already?" said Smokey, but it had been nice of him to make the offer. It wasn't that mechanical interrogation *required* close genetic correspondences between subject and operator, but the job went faster and smoother in direct relation to those correspondences. Worst of all was to work on a woman, but you did what you had to do. . . .

Four dusty troopers from A Company manhandled the subject, still shouting, to the command car housing the interrogation gear. The work of the firebase went on. Crews were pulling maintenance on the fans of some of the cars facing outward against attack, and one of the rocket howitzers rotated squealingly as new gunners were trained. For the most part, though, there was little to do at midday, so troopers turned from the jungle beyond the berm to the freshly-snatched prisoner and the possibility of action that he offered.

"Don't damage the goods!" Griffiths said sharply when the men carrying the subject seemed ready to toss him onto the lefthand couch like a log into a blazing fireplace. One of the troopers, a non-com, grunted assent; they settled the subject in adequate comfort. Major Soames was at the console between the paired couches, checking the capture location and relevant intelligence information from Central's data base.

"Want us to unwrap 'im for you?" asked the non-com, ducking instinctively though the roof of the command car cleared his helmet. The interior lighting was low, however, especially to eyes adapted to the sun hammering the bulldozed area of the firebase.

"Listen, me 'n' my family *never*, I swear it, dealt with interloping traders!" the York native pleaded.

"No, we'll take care of it," said Griffiths to the A Company trooper, reaching into the drawer for a disposable-blade scalpel to slit the hydorclasp sheeting over the man's wrist. Some interrogators liked to keep a big fighting knife around, combining practical requirements with a chance to soften up the subject through fear. Griffiths thought the technique was misplaced: For effective mechanical interrogation, he wanted his subjects as relaxed as possible. Panic-jumbled images were better than no images at all; but only *just* better.

"We're not the Custom's Police, old son," Smokey murmured as he adjusted the couch headrest to an angle which looked more comfortable for the subject. "We're a lot more interested in the government convoy ambushed last week."

Griffiths' scalpel drew a line above the subject's left hand and wrist. The sheeting drew back in a narrow gape, briefly iridescent as stresses within the hydorclasp readjusted themselves. As if the sheeting were skin, however, the rip stopped of its own accord at the end of the scored line.

"What're you doing to me?"

"Nothing I'm not doing to myself, friend," said Griffiths, grasping the subject's bared forearm with his own left hand so that their inner wrists were together. Between the thumb and forefinger of his right hand he held a standard-looking stim cone up where the subject could see it clearly, despite the cocoon of sheeting still holding his legs and torso rigid. "I'm George, by the way. What do your friends call you?"

"You're drugging me!" the subject screamed, his fingers digging into Griffiths' forearm fiercely. The mountaineers living under triple-canopy jungle looked pasty and unhealthy, but there was nothing wrong with this one's muscle tone.

"It's a random pickup," said Smokey in Dutch to his partner. "Found him on a trail in the target area, nothing suspicious—probably just out sap-cutting—but they could snatch him without going into a village and starting something."

"Right in one," Griffiths agreed in soothing English as he squeezed the cone at the juncture of his and the subject's wrist veins. The dose in its skin-absorbed carrier—developed from the solvent used with formic acid by Terran solifugids for defense—spurted out under pressure and disappeared into the bloodstreams of both men: thrillingly cool to Griffiths, and a shock that threw the subject into mewling, abject terror.

"Man," the interrogator murmured as he detached the subject's grip from his forearm, using the pressure point in the man's wrist to do so, "if there was anything wrong with it, I wouldn't have split it with you, now would I?"

He sat down on the other couch, swinging his legs up and lying back before the drug-induced lassitude crumpled him on the floor. He was barely aware of movement as Smokey fitted a helmet on the subject and ran a finger up and down columns of touch-sensitive controls on his console to reach a balance. All Griffiths would need was the matching helmet, since the parameters of his brain were already loaded into the data base. By the time Smokey got around to him, he wouldn't even feel the touch of the helmet.

The dose was harmless, as he'd assured the subject, unless the fellow had an adverse reaction because of the recreational drugs he'd been taking on his own. You could never really tell with the sap-cutters, but it was generally okay. The high jungles of York produced at least a dozen drugs of varying effect, and the producers were of course among the heaviest users of their haul.

By itself, that would have been a personal problem; but the mountaineers also took the position that trade off-planet was their own business, and that there was no need to sell their drugs through the Central Marketing Board in the capital for half the price that traders slipping into the jungle in small starships would cheerfully pay. Increasingly violent attempts to enforce customs laws on men with guns and the willingness to use them had led to what was effectively civil war—which the York government had hired the Slammers to help suppress.

It's a bitch to fight when you don't know who the enemy is; and that was where Griffiths and his partner came in.

"Now I want you to imagine that you're walking home from where you were picked up," came Smokey's voice—but Griffiths was hearing the words only through the subject's mind. His own helmet had no direct connection to the hushed microphone into which the major was speaking. The words formed themselves into letters of dull orange which expanded to fill Griffiths' senses with a blank background.

The monochrome sheet coalesced abruptly, and he was trotting along a trail which was a narrow mark beaten by feet into the open expanse of the jungle floor. By cutting off the light, the triple canopies of foliage ensured that the real undergrowth would be stunted—as passable to the air-cushion armor of Hammer's Slammers as it was to the locals on foot.

Judging distance during an interrogation sequence was a matter of art and craft, not science, because the "trip"—though usually linear—was affected by ellipses and the subject's attitude during the real journey. For the most part, memory was a blur in which the trail itself was the major feature, and the remaining landscape only occasionally obtruded in the form of an unusually large or colorful hillock of fungus devouring a fallen tree. Twice the subject's mind—not necessarily the man himself—paused to throw up a dazzlingly sharp image of a particular plant, once a tree and the other time a knotted, woody vine which stood out in memory against the misty visualization of the trunk which the real vine must wrap.

Presumably the clearly-defined objects had something to do with the subject's business—which was none of Griffiths' at this time. As he "walked" the Slammer through the jungle, the mountaineer would be mumbling broken and only partly intelligible words, but Griffiths no longer heard them or Smokey's prompting questions.

The trail forked repeatedly, sharply visualized each time although the bypassed forks disappeared into mental fog within a meter of the route taken. It was surprisingly easy to determine the general direction of travel: Though the sky was rarely visible through the foliage, the subject habitually made sun-sightings wherever possible in order to orient himself.

The settlement of timber-built houses was of the same tones—browns, sometimes overlaid by a lichenous gray-green—as the trees which interspersed the habitations. The village glowed brightly by contrast with the forest, however, both because the canopy above was significantly thinner, and because the place was home and a goal to the subject's mind.

Sunlight, blocked only by the foliage of very large trees which the settlers had not cleared, dappled streets which had been trampled to the consistency of coarse concrete. Children played there, and animals—dogs and pigs, probably, but they were undistinguished shadows to the subject, factors of no particular interest to either him or his interrogator.

Griffiths did not need to have heard the next question to understand it, when a shadow at the edge of the trail sprang into mental relief as a forty-tube swarmjet launcher with a hard-eyed woman slouched behind it, watching the trail. The weapon needn't have been loot from the government supply convoy massacred the week before, but its swivelling base was jury-rigged from a truck mounting.

At present, the subject's tongue could not have formed words more complex than a slurred syllable or two, but the Slammers had no need for cooperation from his motor nerves or intellect. All they needed were memory and the hard-wired processes of brain function which were common to all life forms with spinal cords. The subject's brain retrieved and correlated the information which the higher centers of his mind would have needed to answer Major Soames' question about defenses—and Griffiths collected the data there at the source.

Clarity of focus marked as the subject's one of the houses reaching back against a bole of colossal proportions. Its roof was of shakes framed so steeply that they were scarcely distinguishable from the vertical timbers of the siding. Streaks of the moss common both to tree and to dwelling faired together cut timber and the russet bark. On the covered stoop in front, an adult woman and seven children waited in memory.

At this stage of the interrogation Griffiths had almost as little conscious volition as the subject did, but a deep level of his own mind recorded the woman as unattractive. Her cheeks were hollow, her expression sullen, and the appearance of her skin was no cleaner than that of the subject himself. The woman's back was straight, however, and her clear eyes held, at least in the imagination of the subject, a look of affection.

The children ranged in height from a boy, already as tall as his mother, to the infant girl looking up from the woman's arms with a face so similar to the subject's that it could, with hair and a bushy beard added, pass for his in a photograph. Affection cloaked the vision of the whole family, limning the faces clearly despite a tendency for the bodies of the children to mist away rather like the generality of trees along the trail; but the infant was almost deified in the subject's mind.

Smokey's unheard question dragged the subject off abruptly, his household dissolving, unneeded to the answer, as a section of the stoop hinged upward on the end of his own hand and arm. The tunnel beneath the board flooring dropped straight down through the layer of yellowish soil and the friable rock beneath. There was a wooden ladder along which the wavering oval of a flashlight beam traced as the viewpoint descended.

The shift was seventeen rungs deep, with a further gooseneck dip in the gallery at the ladder's end to trap gas and fragmentation grenades. Where the tunnel straightened to horizontal, the flashlight gleamed on the powergun in a niche ready to hand but beneath the level to which a metal detector could be tuned to work reliably.

Just beyond the gun was a black-cased directional mine with either a light-beam or ultrasonic detonator—the subject didn't know the difference and his mind hadn't logged any of the subtle discrimination points between the two types of fuzing. Either way, someone ducking down the tunnel could, by touching the pressure-sensitive cap of the detonator, assure that the next person across the invisible tripwire would take a charge of shrapnel at velocities which would crumble the sturdiest body armor.

"Follow all the tunnels," Smokey must have directed, because Griffiths had the unusual experience of merger with a psyche which split at every fork in the underground system. Patches of light wavered and fluctuated across as many as a score of simultaneous images, linking them together in the unity in which the subject's mind held them.

It would have made the task of mapping the tunnels impossible, but the Slammers did not need anything so precise in a field as rich as this one. The tunnels themselves had been cut at the height of a stooping runner, but there was more headroom in the pillared bays excavated for storage and shelter. Flashes—temporal alternatives, hard to sort from the multiplicity of similar physical locations—showed shelters both empty and filled with villagers crouching against the threat of bombs which did not come. On one image the lighting was

uncertain and could almost have proceeded as a mental arti-
fact from the expression of the subject's infant daughter,
looking calmly from beneath her mother's worried face.

Griffiths could not identify the contents of most of the
stored crates across which the subject's mind skipped, but
Central's data bank could spit out a list of probables when the
interrogator called in the dimensions and colors after the
session. Griffiths would do that, for the record. As a matter
of practical use, all that was important was that the villagers
had thought it necessary to stash the material here—below the
reach of ordinary reconnaissance and even high explosives.

There were faces in the superimposed panorama, villagers
climbing down their own access ladders or passed in the close
quarters of the tunnels. Griffiths could not possibly differenti-
ate the similar, bearded physiognomies during the overlaid
glimpses he got of them. It was likely enough that everyone,
every male at least, in the village was represented somewhere
in the subject's memory of the underground complex.

There was one more sight offered before Griffiths became
aware of his own body again in a chill wave spreading from
the wrist where Smokey had sprayed the antidote. The subject
had seen a nine-barrelled powergun, a calliope whose ripples
of high-intensity fire could eat the armor of a combat car like
paper spattered by molten steel. It was deep in an underground bay from which four broad "windows"—firing slits—
were angled upward to the surface. Preparing the weapon in
this fashion to cover the major approaches to the village must
have taken enormous effort, but there was a worthy payoff:
At these slants, the bolts would rip into the flooring, not the
armored sides, of a vehicle driving over the camouflaged
opening of a firing slit. Not even Hammer's heavy tanks
could survive having their bellies carved that way. . . .

The first awareness Griffiths had of his physical surround-
ings was the thrashing of his limbs against the sides of the
couch while Major Soames lay across his body to keep him
from real injury. Motor control returned with a hot rush,
permitting Griffiths to lie still for a moment and pant.

"Need to go under again?" asked Smokey as he rose,
fishing in his pocket for another cone of antidote for the
subject if the answer was "no."

"Got all we need," Griffiths muttered, closing his eyes
before he took charge of his arms to lift him upright. "It's a

bloody fortress, it is, all underground and *cursed* well laid out.''

"Location?" said his partner, whose fingernails clicked on the console as he touched keys.

"South by southeast," said Griffiths. He opened his eyes, then shut them again as he swung his legs over the side of the couch. His muscles felt as if they had been under stress for hours, with no opportunity to flush fatigue poisons. The subject was coming around with comparative ease in his cocoon, because his system had not been charged already with the drug residues of the hundreds of interrogations which Griffiths had conducted from the right-hand couch. "Maybe three kays—you know, plus or minus."

The village might be anywhere from two kilometers to five from the site at which the subject had been picked up, though Griffiths usually guessed closer than that. This session had been a good one, too, the linkage close enough that he and the subject were a single psyche throughout most of it. That wasn't always the case: Many interrogations were viewed as if through a bad mirror, the images foggy and distorted.

"Right," said Smokey to himself, or to the hologram map tank in which a named point was glowing in response to the information he had just keyed. "Right, Thomasville they call it." He swung to pat the awakening subject on the shoulder. "You live in Thomasville, don't you, old son?"

"Wha . . . ?" murmured the subject.

"You're sure he couldn't come from another village?" Griffiths queried, watching his partner's quick motions with a touch of envy stemming from the drug-induced slackness in his own muscles.

"Not a chance," the major said with assurance. "There were two other possibles, but they were both north in the valley."

"Am I—" the subject said in a voice that gained strength as he used it. "Am I all right?"

Why ask us? thought Griffiths, but his partner was saying, "Of course you're all right, m'boy, we said you would be, didn't we?"

While the subject digested that jovial affirmation, Smokey turned to Griffiths and said, "You don't think we need an armed recce then, Chief?"

"They'd chew up anything short of a company of panzers," Griffiths said flatly, "and even *that* wouldn't be a lotta fun. It's a bloody underground fort, it is."

"What did I say?" the subject demanded as he regained intellectual control and remembered where he was—and why. "Please, *please*, what'd I say?"

"Curst little, old son," Smokey remarked. "Just mumbles—nothing to reproach yourself about, not at all."

"You're a gentle bastard," Griffiths said.

"Ain't it true, Chief, ain't it true?" his partner agreed. "Gas, d'ye think, then?"

"Not the way they're set up," said Griffiths, trying to stand and relaxing again to gain strength for a moment more. He thought back over the goose-necked tunnels; the filter curtains ready to be drawn across the mouths of shelters; the atmosphere suits hanging beside the calliope. "Maybe saturation with a lethal skin absortive like K3, but what's the use of that?"

"Right you are," said Major Soames, tapping the console's preset for Fire Control Central.

"You're going to let me go, then?" asked the subject, wriggling within his wrappings in an unsuccessful attempt to rise.

Griffiths made a moue as he watched the subject, wishing that his own limbs felt capable of such sustained motion. "Those other two villages may be just as bad as this one," he said to his partner.

"The mountaineers don't agree with each other much better'n they do with the government," demurred Smokey with his head cocked toward the console, waiting for its reply. "They'll bring us in samples, and we'll see then."

"Go ahead," said Fire Central in a voice bitten flat by the two-kilohertz aperture through which it was transmitted.

"Got a red-pill target for you," Smokey said, putting one ivory-colored fingertip on the holotank over Thomasville to transmit the coordinates to the artillery computers. "Soonest."

"Listen," the subject said, speaking to Griffiths because the major was out of the line of sight permitted by the hydorclasp wrappings, "let me go and there's a full three kilos of Misty Hills Special for you. Pure, I swear it, so pure it'll float on water!"

"No damper fields?" Central asked in doubt.

"They aren't going to put up a nuclear damper and warn everybody they're expecting attack, old son," said Major

Soames tartly. "Of course, the least warning and they'll turn it on."

"Hold one," said the trooper in Fire Control.

"Just lie back and relax, fella," Griffiths said, rising to his feet at last. "We'll turn you in to an internment camp near the capital. They keep everything nice there so they can hold media tours. You'll do fine."

There was a loud squealing from outside the interrogators' vehicle. One of the twenty-centimeter rocket howitzers was rotating and elevating its stubby barrel. Ordinarily the six tubes of the battery would work in unison, but there was no need for that on the present fire mission.

"We have clearance for a nuke," said the console with an undertone of vague surprise which survived sideband compression. Usually the only targets worth a red pill were protected by damper fields which inhibited fission bombs and the fission triggers of thermonuclear weapons.

"Lord blast you for sinners!" shouted the trussed local. "What is it you're doing, you blackhearted devils?"

Griffiths looked down at him, and just at that moment the hog fired. The base charge blew the round clear of the barrel, and the sustainer motor roared the shell up in a ballistic path for computer-determined seconds of burn. The command vehicle rocked. Despite their filters, the vents drew in air burned by exhaust gases.

It shouldn't have happened after the helmets were removed and both interrogator and subject had been dosed with antidote. Flashback contacts did sometimes occur, though. This time it was the result of the very solid interrogation earlier; that, and meeting the subject's eyes as the howitzer fired.

The subject looked so much like his infant daughter that Griffiths had no control at all over the image that sprang to his mind: the baby's face lifted to the sky which blazed with the thermonuclear fireball detonating just above the canopy——and her melted eyeballs dripping down her cheeks.

The hydorclasp held the subject, but he did not stop screaming until they had dosed him with enough suppressants to turn a horse toes-up.

EDITOR'S INTRODUCTION TO:

A TIME OF MARTYRS
by Jim Fiscus

The Levant has been at war for a thousand years. The League of Nations attempted to impose peace by giving Britain and France mandated control over large areas; one result was that when World War II broke out and France sundered into the Vichy regime collaborating with the Nazis and the Free French of de Gaulle, *La Légion Etrangère* was also divided. The divisions of the Foreign Legion fought each other bitterly and without quarter in Syria. After WW II ended, Arab and Zionist fought both each other and the British; and they but continued wars that were old in the time of the Crusades.

In the late 1970's the Shah of Iran, having been abandoned by his allies in the West, fled the country. Although he did not officially abdicate the throne, he left behind an autonomous government dedicated to constitutional principles. That government lasted no more than days; and after its overthrow by the fanatic Ayatollah Khomaini, the constitutionalists and republicans of Iran were savagely butchered alongside the pacifist Baha'i.

The Shah had commanded the best army in that part of the world. After his fall, the Iraqi government thought it saw an opportunity to take—or recover, depending on your view—a strategic waterway and other territory of the Tigris-Euphrates delta. Thus was born the Iraq-Iran war which continues to this day, and, it is safe to predict, will not soon be ended.

Thus was also born the period of the Tehran hostages, and our humiliation in the Iranian desert. From the same roots sprang a more pleasant memory, of the United States Navy's capture of the pirates of the *Achille Lauro*. The incidents are illustrative: The Iranian adventure was controlled from Washington, with President Carter insisting on knowing every detail as it happened; while the Navy's capture of the pirates was ordered by a President confident enough to leave the rest to the warriors.

There is more to learn. In this original work, James Fiscus shows graphically just how difficult it is to understand the politics of the Levant, where there are warriors in plenty, but few statesmen.

A TIME OF MARTYRS
By Jim Fiscus

The enemy stormed in a ragged wave across the dry, shell-cratered mud of Mesopotamia. Dust rose from beneath their feet to meet the driving heat of the sun. A torrent of children swept across the wide plain, once ruled by the city-states of Sumer, toward the guns and trenches of the Iraqi Fourth Army. At least ten thousand Iranian troops were charging our lines. Fowler wanted me to stop them in their own past. I swung around to watch the attack against the battalion entrenched slightly forward on our right flank.

I focused my glasses on the center of the advancing army of martyrs. Ropes lashed many together into small bunches. Few were armed. As they neared the first line of barbed wire, the wave of bodies faltered, crested, and flooded onward with new vigor to the second line of wire. Spirits of dust and smoke marked the explosion of mines within the Iranian lines. The attackers were scarcely three hundred meters from the first bunkers. The Iraqis still had not begun to fire. "Holding it a bit long, aren't they, Major Salam?"

"No, Mr. Koch. Not at all." He spoke quietly in nearly perfect American English. "Look now to the rear of the first wave."

I lowered my glasses and followed his directions. Three hundred meters behind the first of the Iranian troops, squat M-60 tanks pushed over a ridge, driving the children forward. Between the tanks came the regular troops of the Revolutionary Guard, shackled only by their fanaticism. Fountains of dust and flesh flowered into the air as mortar and artillery rounds tore gaps in the attacking formations.

"Now, Mr. Koch, it is time for the real slaughter."

The front of the Iranian wave was only one hundred meters from the bunkers when the Iraqi machine guns and quad anti-aircraft mounts began firing. A scythe swept across the plain. Thousands fell, or faltered. Others pushed on. In a few places, regular troops reached the line of trenches, only to die in seconds. "You do a slick job of it, Major." In the face of the heavy artillery fire, the prodding tanks too fell back.

"We do our job, Mr. Koch." He swung around to stare at me.

"You must enjoy the chance to kill Iranians, Major. You should hate them more than I do."

"My hate only survived the first ten thousand my men killed. We kill them, we do not hate them."

I nodded, as if I understood him, and walked over to where Fowler stood against the far wall of the trench. "Gooks killing gooks. Best game I've seen in a year. I love it."

"You would, Koch." Fowler was wearing khaki fatigues, their creases still sharp and crisp, though heavy with dust. Shades and a bush hat polished his image. He wore no military insignia.

"Why stop them, Fowler? They want to die, let them die. Screw the sand niggers."

Fowler stepped closer, shoving his face within centimeters of mine. "Koch, use that term again and I'll find someone else for the job."

"Sure you will. You'll just walk into MIT or Cal Tech and ask one of the boys to drop over to Iraq and escort you on a little trip through time."

"If you knew anything about the people . . ." Fowler turned aside. "I thought that if you saw the fighting, you'd want to help stop the slaughter."

"You pay well, Fowler. I'm tired of third rate engineering jobs." I also missed working in a timeflow lab. "But I don't see how you hope to stop Khomaini with the controller. You won't be able to change the timeflow seriously."

"Not drastically change events, no. We only need to nudge them a bit and we can destroy the doctrinal basis of Khomaini's power." He pulled me into the shade of a sandbagged bunker. "We've made small changes already." The bunker muffled the thud of the artillery.

"Then you have men who know more than I do."

"We did have them. The lab team was killed by an Iranian suicide pilot a month ago. Fortunately, we have their records. They had made small changes in the past, killing men a few days earlier than recorded, or in different ways."

"History is too complex for any change to have much of an impact on later events, Fowler. Year adds to year, all building inertia into the timeflow."

"The possible gain is . . ."

"Mr. Fowler, Mr. Koch, please come to the trench," Major Salam called quietly from the door of the bunker.

I blinked hard against the stabbing glare of the sun, and slipped my sunglasses back on. Shells hurled by our artillery screamed overhead toward the enemy. The Iraqi troops were all at the forward edge of the trench, staring over the parapet, their Kalashnikovs sighted on the enemy.

"It is our turn to kill," Major Salam said.

I stared over the shoulder of an Iraqi machinegunner. Again, the ragged advance of wave after wave of running figures. This time, they were coming straight down our throats.

"You should not need that, Mr. Koch."

"What?" I realized my hand had dropped to my .45 automatic. I glanced along the line of Iraqi guns. "No, I imagine you're right, Major." And then I saw the Iranian tanks pushing forward over the crest of the next hill. One by one, they rocked back sharply as their guns fired.

The blast of concussion swept down the trench, and I staggered against the back wall. The air was filled with dust and the screams of men. I stood, leaning against the sandbags, and tried to focus my mind.

The heavy firing of our machineguns pulled me back to the trench. Fowler was next to me, shoving a canteen in my face. "Thanks." I choked down the stale water. "What happened?"

"Round hit the quad mount in the next bunker."

"Oh shit!" The acrid smoke from the explosion burned my throat. I stared past Fowler. The tanks were falling back under the pounding of the Iraqi artillery. Through the dust, near us, came the running specters of several dozen Iranian infantry. Some Iraqis jumped to the top of the trench to meet them, others backed away and continued firing.

A few Iranians reached the top of the trench and fired into the Iraqis to my left, as others, unarmed, jumped into our midst. I saw one reach for a fallen rifle. He was a boy, twelve, maybe thirteen years old. My .45 slid out of its holster, almost on its own.

I stared at the boy across the barrel of the .45. He started to raise the Kalashnikov.

"Stop," I yelled, hesitating, myself, to bring death. "Surrender!"

But how could a village boy from Iran understand me? The rifle continued to swing up.

There was terror in the boy's face, and in my heart. I stared into his eyes and fired. The pistol smashed back into my hand twice. I turned as the body fell back, and swung the .45 for another target.

Six or seven Iranians lay on the parapet, one or two inside the trench. One of the Iraqis was trying to cover a fist-sized hole in his own chest with his cap.

I turned back to the boy as Fowler knelt by the body. "Good shot, Koch." Fowler let the back of his hand rest lightly on the boy's cheek, and looked up at me. "You got your own."

"My own?" I looked at the boy. His face was smooth and unlined, marred only by a smear of dirt on one cheek. He was still alive. I stared again into his eyes as he died. And we were in hell together.

"Your trophy, Koch, you should be feeling proud. You got a sand nigger."

"Better that little motherfucker than me," I said automatically.

Fowler examined our car. All the tires had been flattened by shrapnel. "Come on, Koch, we walk back to Sector HQ and catch a truck to Baghdad."

"Look, Fowler," I followed him to the road, "it's time you told me what the Colonel is paying me to do. I want details."

"Agreed." Heat broiled down from above and reflected back from the road. The world seemed afire. Fowler pulled his sweat-soaked sleeve across his forehead. "What do you know about the differences between Shia and Sunni doctrine?"

"The Sunni are the majority and the Shi'i the minority of Moslems. But who cares what the differences are? A gook is a gook, eh?" I smiled and watched Fowler hold his anger in check.

"The two sects connect religious authority to political legitimacy in different ways. Shia doctrine supports the role of the clergy in determining political legitimacy and thus serves as the basis of Khomaini's power." A line of trucks crept toward us on the narrow, mine-free, strip of road. We edged to the side to let them pass. " 'Shia' means no more than 'party,' by the way," Fowler said.

"Yeah, right, the Shia supported Muhammad's son-in-law, Ali, to be caliph." I knew the history, Rossanna had told me before she went home. "Arabs had themselves a nice little civil war over who would be the fourth caliph after the Prophet, but I don't give a damn."

"Koch, where did a bigoted asshole like you ever learn about Islam?" The trucks picked up speed as they passed.

"An Iranian broad I knew . . . everybody screws up from time to time. It was my turn." I covered my nose and mouth with an old handkerchief, and tried to filter out the dust blown up by the convoy. "But, knowing one sect of Islam from the other won't help you change time." Let Fowler talk and breathe this junk, I thought.

"Everything follows from the difference between them, Koch. And that gives us a real chance. One group, they became the Sunni, argued that the consensus of the community could properly determine the caliph."

"Sure, they kicked out Ali and founded the Umayyad Caliphate." I glanced at him. "Don't tell me you're going to try to depose a dynasty." Sweat, hot and salty, stung my eyes.

"No, the plan is subtler. The Shia favored designation. They argued that Ali had been designated by Muhammad as his successor before his death, and that the Prophet's will should be followed. Later, the Shi'i argued that Ali's descendants were the proper leaders of the community . . . as descendants of the Prophet's family, they were closer to God. Ali was assassinated, and the Umayyads suppressed his family and followers."

"Get to the point, Fowler. I don't need a lecture on religion. What do you want me to do with the damn time machine?"

"Try and contain your enthusiasm for ignorance, Koch. The Shia became the political opposition and were viewed, rightly, as fomenters of rebellion."

"Finally, you approach the fucking point."

Fowler ignored my comment. "This is where the political argument turns religious. The Sunni believe that Moslems can be guided to correct actions in life by following the Book, the Koran."

I stopped walking, pulled out my canteen, and took a sip of

water, letting the hot liquid wash the inside of my mouth before swallowing. I glanced across the naked, broken ground. Heat shimmered in the air. I handed the canteen to Fowler.

"Thanks." He drank and gave me back the canteen. "The Shi'i say this is not enough. Man must have the Law inspired by God. It is the role of the Imam, inspired by God, to give the community guidance. They have come to consider the Imams infallible."

"Quaint. The gooks need an infallible religious leader. Don't have the guts to decide for themselves." I smiled, chuckled slightly, and said, "Did they steal the idea from the Catholics, or did the Catholics steal it from the Shi'i?" I was becoming interested. "And the Iranians say Khomaini is the current Imam, right?"

"In this sense, no. The term is applied to him only as a title of respect. He is not *the* Imam. There hasn't been one for over a thousand years."

"So where's Khomaini's authority come from?" His authority to murder.

"From the Imam."

"But you said that there is no Imam."

"Exactly. The Shia have developed the idea that the Ulama, the learned clergy, are delegated to speak for the Imam and interpret the law." Fowler whirled as a heavy engine roared from behind us. We jumped aside, barely escaping a truck that sped past. "Bastard."

"Gooks will kill us yet," I mumbled. Dust rose in a thick, choking cloud around us.

"There were disputes over the line of succession to the Imamate," Fowler said. "Some Moslems still claim authority from the Third Imam, the Seventh Imam or others."

"The Iranians are called Twelvers, I know, but I never got around to asking why."

"The last Imam in their line to serve publicly was the eleventh, al-Askari, who died in 874 A.D. Because they had been held under house arrest by the caliph, al-Askari and his immediate predecessor used deputies to communicate with their followers."

"If he was the Eleventh Imam, and the last, where does the Twelfth Imam come in? Can't they count?"

"Al-Askari is said to have had a son who was hidden from the caliphate by his Shi'i followers. They feared that if he were publicly known, he would be assassinated. The Twelvers have converted this political problem into a matter of doctrine. The Twelfth, or Hidden, Imam is in Occultation awaiting the proper time to return and lead his followers to a golden age of justice . . .''

"Justice my ass. Revenge is more likely. Revenge against the whole world."

"A little of each, from what they say. In any case, the Imam's rule will be an era of a true and pure Islam. The Imam is not a prophet . . .''

"Muhammed was the last prophet. That belief is key to all Islam," I said, interrupting, not sure why I was letting myself be drawn into a discussion.

Fowler nodded. Sweat and dust had combined to streak his face with mud. "But the Imam does have divine knowledge equal to the Prophet's. He is the Mahdi, the promised one, the Messiah."

"And because he vanished without trace, the Twelver clergy can use the Hidden Imam as a source of authority. Slick. They have a phone line to the man who has a line to God."

"Correct. This deputized authority has led to two of the major differences between the Shia and the Sunni. The Shi'i claim that only the rule of the Hidden Imam can be a truly legitimate government." Fowler paused to wipe sweat from the back of his neck. The crease had long since left his pants and shirt. His uniform had wilted in the heat.

"And without the Hidden Imam, no government or state can be fully legitimate. They're all caretakers, right?" I turned to glance at Fowler. "But wouldn't that apply to Khomaini as well? If he is not the Imam, his authority, too, has to be illegitimate?"

"Yes, a good point. The source of his moral, and political, influence is the delegated authority of the Imam. The key point is that Khomaini is not the Imam, and because of that, his regime can not be fully legitimate."

"Has the bastard ever claimed to be the Hidden Imam? That could be an easy way out of his dilemma."

"In fact," Fowler answered, "Khomaini has denied rumors that he was the Hidden Imam."

"And the other difference between the Shi'i and the Sunni you mentioned, what the hell is that?" I turned and looked back down the road through a haze of dust and the shimmer of heat, hoping for a truck.

"Each Shi'i has to select a living religious scholar and obey only his interpretation of the religious law."

"The mujtahids. Right, Fowler?"

Fowler turned and glanced at me. "Yes, and in a very nice twist of reasoning, the interpretation of a living cleric takes precedence over that of any dead mujtahid."

"Great job security."

Fowler continued, "They try to determine the will of the Hidden Imam. The mujtahids are not infallible, as the Imam is, but they will always come closer to the truth than any temporal ruler. Remember, they have religious authority delegated from the Imam. The mujtahids can exercise tremendous charismatic leadership. And it all started after the Twelfth Imam vanished."

"His loyal followers protected him, eh? What did they really do, toss the little bastard down a well?" I held up my hand to flag down another truck nearing us from the front lines. This driver began to brake and pull to the edge of the road.

"That, actually, is one of the better historical guesses. The deputies would have lost much of their authority had he lived. They needed the mystery."

"I think I see your idea." I paused to consider the idea, then continued. "If the Hidden Imam dies in public . . . that would undercut Khomaini's power by striking at the source of his deputized authority. No line to God, eh."

Fowler actually beamed at my flash of insight. "Correct. We've sent back a number of remote sensors and located the boy. Al-Askari's son did exist, and he was hidden by his followers. Koch, the boy is the linchpin to a large section of the timeflow."

"How do you plan to attack him?"

"We've identified a day when he was moved through Baghdad. He and his escorts barely escaped capture by the caliph's guards. We want him to die in public, while in the custody of the authorities." Fowler stopped talking as the truck slid to a stop several meters ahead of us.

We ran toward the back of the truck and jumped onto the wide bumper. Neither of us tried to climb into the bed of the vehicle. The truck was packed with the dead, wounded and rotting remnants of the weeks' fighting. The stench of death and the cries of the wounded swept around us as we clung to the tailgate of the bouncing truck.

*　　　*　　　*

Ghosts drifted out of my past to haunt my mind. I lay without light, looking into the darkness of a small room. The eyes of the boy I had shot stared back at me. I tried to imagine him playing in his village, running through the dust and kicking stones, or perhaps herding the family goats. I failed, and could not change my memory of his body, and his eyes.

The springs of the cot creaked under me as I rolled onto my back. The air was still and heavy in the Iraqi army guest room. We had driven from Baghdad late in the evening, arriving at the military compound north of the city just after twilight had passed into night. No work until morning, Fowler had said, so I hit the sack to fight my jet lag. Half the night had passed before I slept and was free of the boy's image. But I slept only to dream of my 45 firing again and again into the boy.

"Koch. Get moving," Fowler's voice boomed through the door of my room, pulling me awake. "The Colonel's aide is arriving in an hour to talk about the operation."

I rolled over and stared at the chipped grey paint of the closed door. I was tired, and needed to sleep for six or seven more hours. "Damn. Where'd he come from?"

Fowler stuck his head into the room. "He flew in from Tripoli last night."

After a fast shower and a quickly eaten breakfast, I was ready to face our Libyan paymaster. We left the guest quarters and stepped into the dust and heat of the early morning. I looked around the compound that had been hidden in darkness the evening before. We were in the ruins of an old fort. Mud brick walls towered around us, and mud or timber buildings were arranged around a central parade ground. "Who built this place, Fowler?"

"The Ottomans, I suspect." He chuckled. "Or maybe the Persians. They've been here enough times."

The buildings were ancient, but the machine guns and twin AA mounts on the walls were manned by troops who stared alertly outward . . . except for the half dozen men who watched us, their Kalashnikovs casually following our progress. Dust swirled across the open ground, creating a brown haze as we crossed to the mud brick HQ building.

Four guards flanking a door in the far wall stiffened to attention as we entered the first room. A fifth man stepped to meet us. "Mr. Fowler, Mr. Koch, our visitors wait inside."

"Major Salam." I turned toward him. "Thought you'd still be on the front line."

"That is my wish, Mr. Koch." He moved toward the far door. "The army wishes me here, though. You see, I know something of your field."

"Do you, now? Where did you . . ."

"I worked at the European timeflow laboratory for two years. . . . But our guests wait."

Two men stood in the next room, studying a wall map of the Iran-Iraq border. They turned as we entered. The shorter man wore a black business suit, of European cut and clearly expensive. The taller man was dressed in a khaki uniform.

Salam nodded to the uniformed man. "Lieutenant Colonel al-Hajjaj. He has been chosen to do the job," Salam turned to the man in the fancy suit, "and his aide, Lieutenant Muhallab." He swung back toward us. "Mr. Fowler and Doctor Koch," he used my title for the first time.

Fowler smiled as we shook hands with the Libyans. "Was your flight smooth?"

"It was." Al-Hajjaj turned to me. His eyes were cold. "Doctor Koch . . ."

"I don't use 'doctor' anymore, Colonel."

"No? I thought you academicians lived for your honors." He glanced at his companion. "A scientist who is different, Muhallab. But then he had to be different to work with us on the project, did he not? Please, do not become angry, Mr. Koch. You work for me, remember."

"With you, Colonel al-Hajjaj. After all, there are colonels, and there is the Colonel. And you are not the Leader."

"Gentlemen, please, we have an enemy in common." Major Salam stepped to the Libyan's side. "Remember, it is Khomaini we are to fight. . . ." His voice was overpowered by the sudden, engulfing roar of jet engines.

An explosive shock wave smashed the door open and drove me to my knees. I fell forward as a second shock swept through the building. For several seconds I stared at the ancient bricks of the floor, then shook my head and slowly stood. The room swam in a circle around me.

I let the wall support me and looked for Fowler. He was using the far wall to pull himself to his feet. The three officers were also slowly climbing off the floor. I turned and tried to see the guards in the outer room. Dust obscured my

vision, and I needed several seconds to locate the broken and
scattered pieces of their bodies.

"You hurt, Koch?" Fowler swept his glance across the
debris that had been four men.

"No."

Major Salam pushed past Fowler and moved uneasily to a
gaping hole in the front wall. "Bomb craters outside." He
touched the jagged edge of broken bricks. "The Turks built
well, or we would be dead." Fowler and I followed Salam
out of the building. Salam continued, "Iran has only a few
planes that can still fly. And we will soon have our own air
cover." He pointed to three specks streaking toward us from
the east. "These should be our planes now."

I watched the specks grow into planes within seconds.
"Don't hold your breath, Major. Those are Phantoms. I saw
enough of them in Vietnam." I turned to Salam. "And I
don't think Iraq has any. They have to be Iranian." I looked
around the devastated compound. "You know any hole we
can climb into?"

"There's a new bunker at the corner of the rear wall." He
turned and shouted in Arabic back into the HQ.

Fowler and I ran for the rear of the compound. I glanced
back over my shoulder. Salam was starting across the parade-
ground, the two Libyans just coming out of the door. The
attacking planes swept toward us.

Cannon shells tore into the ground, steps ahead of Salam.
He whirled, shouted into the wind, and dove back toward the
shelter of the damaged HQ. The projectiles sent a dancing
line of dust across the compound.

"Move, Koch!" Fowler yelled from the sandbagged bunker.

I started to run, jerking my head up as the first F-4 tore
through the air a hundred meters overhead, blocking out the
sun for a heartbeat. I stopped cold. And stared at the next
plane as it shot over us. The torrent of sound from the
Phantom nearly drove thought from my mind. But I saw very
clearly the Star of David on its wing. "Oh, shit." A second
three-plane group was nearly on us. I ran.

The bunker was unfinished and without a roof. I vaulted
the low wall of sandbags. My leap became a tangled somer-
sault and I was driven into the soft, sandy floor of the bunker
by a shock wave from exploding bombs.

"You all right, Koch?" Fowler edged over to sit next to
me.

"I think so." Four Iraqi soldiers were pressing themselves against the sandbags. One of them bled from a gash in his left arm. "We're being hit by the Israelis, Fowler. What the fuck is going on?"

"I saw them," Fowler said, quietly.

"I can understand the Israelis wanting to stop an Iraqi time machine. It could be turned against them next, but how did they know? You said the last team was killed by an air strike. Are you sure the planes were Iranian?" I massaged my left shoulder.

"Yes, but some bastard's telling people where we are." Fowler stood and looked into the sky. "No more planes, I think."

"Good. Still, you have a spy to catch."

"And little chance of doing it, Koch. The leak is probably in Tripoli, or Baghdad."

We pressed against each other and the cool concrete walls of the deep tunnel as the heavy vault door swung open. Fowler led me, and the three Arab officers, into the time vault. The antechamber lights glared after the dark tunnel.

The main strike of the Israeli raid had missed our compound and hit another old fort several miles away. Their information had not really been as good as it should have been, and the opening to the control lab was undamaged.

Colonel al-Hajjaj pulled his sunglasses from his uniform pocket. "What do we do now?"

"Walk into the next room, Colonel, and de-sync." Fowler started across the room.

"Please, explain this to me." Lieutenant Muhallab stood uncertainly by the far door, his once dapper suit torn and wrinkled.

Al-Hajjaj turned sharply. "You were given information. You should know this, Muhallab."

"I am sorry, Colonel. There was not time for me to gain technical knowledge." Only the slightest deference colored his voice.

"Headquarters should have let Idris come as planned. You are of no value," al-Hajjaj said.

"I work for the survival of the Jamahiriya, Colonel," Muhallab glanced at me and added, "The People's Nation, Mr. Koch, Libya."

I nodded, walked to the inside door, and began to explain.

"The control lab must be locked out of synchronization with the normal timeflow. Otherwise, any change we do make in the past will also affect us, and change our memories. When we de-sync, we pull ourselves slightly out of the timeflow and into alignment with the lab."

"What happens when we return to normal . . . sync, and leave the lab?" Muhallab asked.

"We remember our real pasts, we remember the changes we made, we remember everything that happens. . . ." I closed my eyes a moment, and I could hear Rossanna's screams. I forced my attention back to the conversation.

"I see, Mr. Koch." Muhallab walked toward the far door. "We must be careful of the memories we create for ourselves."

We moved into the de-sync room. There was no furniture in the small chamber. I stepped to the control module and examined the readings on the three digital clocks. From left to right, they showed the normal, outside timeflow; the time in the sync chamber; and the time inside the control lab. The lab was one second behind the outside world. I turned to Fowler. "Ready?"

"Yes."

Salam and al-Hajjaj were both calm. Muhallab displayed the tension of a first-time visitor to a time lab. The best nerves in the world react to the thought of being yanked about in time. I snapped the control switch from left to right.

The room began to hum, and the air seemed to vibrate. My body tingled. A sharp, nervous chill shot down my spine, and I shivered. The hum stopped.

"That is it?" Muhallab asked.

"Sorry, nothing more to offer. No electric shocks, no blinding lights." I swung open the inner door and led them into the lab.

Fowler pointed to one of several doors. "The control room is in there. Full manuals, and notes from the last team. You go review the equipment, Koch. I suspect there've been a few changes since your last work in a lab. I'll show our associates the living quarters."

I nodded, and started toward the control room.

Al-Hajjaj glanced at Fowler. "Living quarters? There are no living quarters in our training lab."

"No doubt, Colonel. But the plan, you see, is for us to stay in the lab until the job is done. It should take about a week."

"You are starting now? My equipment is not with me. We must wait."

"Everything you need is in the lab, Colonel. The last team was assassinated. We will take no more chances," Fowler said.

"No, it was agreed to act next month." Al-Hajjaj swung to face Salam. "Major, do your superiors know of this?"

"It was felt wise to attack on our own schedule, not your grand Colonel's." Salam smiled. "Our leaders share limited interests, they do not share trust."

I spent the afternoon alone in the control room familiarizing myself with the equipment and reading the notes of the last team. Finally, I started to check the time displacement booth itself. I barely heard Fowler enter the room.

"Is the lab in order, Koch?"

"So far. The equipment is newer than the last lab I worked in . . . but then it should be. That was six years ago."

"Are the notes detailed enough to tell you what the last team was planning?" Fowler sat on a padded, brown-plastic chair.

"Yes, there's full data." I sat on the edge of the console. "They had found the boy, the Hidden Imam. . . ."

"Right."

"The team was able to fix a tracer into his clothes."

"That's the first step, anyway," Fowler said.

"They had also managed to use a remote unit to plant a time-lock stabilizer in the boy's hair. All we have to do is feed the stabilizer's code into the machine, and we can manipulate the boy's time and location."

"Will it stay in place? Might it not fall out?"

"Only if his head is shaved, judging by the diagram of the attachment." I flipped open the team's notebook and pointed to the drawing. "But, we have a deadline. The stabilizer's battery will only be good for another week and a half of lab time."

"Could you plant another one on the Imam?"

"Not likely. Operating a remote unit is a very special skill. It's rather like building a ship in a bottle, with gloves on, in the dark." I closed the notebook. "That, at least, is what Joe Curry at Cal Tech always said. And I believe him."

"Koch," Fowler paused to pour a cup of coffee, and

continued, "The Cal Tech lab fired you three years ago. Why?"

"That is not your concern, Fowler."

"Koch, you were the number two man in the lab. I have to know if you were fired for a reason that would affect this operation."

"You should have been able to dig the information out of Cal Tech."

"There wasn't time. We had to move quickly when the first team was killed." Fowler looked directly at me and said softly, "I have to know."

I sat silently for a moment. "Yes, all right." I stared at the floor as I talked. "You know I was engaged to an Iranian professor?"

"Yes."

"Rossanna was from Isfahan. We met while she was doing post-doctoral work in chemistry at Cal Tech. She was not involved in politics." I cleared my throat, and continued. "When the Shah was overthrown, Rossanna said she had to go home and help her country rebuild. After all, it was now free."

"Iran has never been free. That's the great tragedy of the country," Fowler said.

"About a year after Rossanna left, I learned that she had been arrested, held for about two weeks in prison, and executed." I stared at the green geometric patterns on the grey floor tiles and forced myself to keep talking. "I became obsessed with finding her in the timeflow, in a time before she had died. I wanted to save her."

"With the machine at Cal Tech?"

I nodded. "I found Rossanna's cell in the Tehran prison, and talked Joe Curry into planting a stabilizer on her." I pushed myself off the console. I had to move. "It took him six hours of lab time to do the job. It was really rather easy, compared to most stabilizer plants, because she couldn't move. They had hung her from the ceiling by her hands . . . the guards could torture her more easily."

"I'm sorry, Koch."

I stopped and turned to face him. "It's so damn hard to place a stabilizer. Even with my position we only had the lab during a term break. We had to finish the job while we had the chance." I started to walk again, using a steady rhythmic pace on the hard floor.

"What happened?"

"I decided to kill the judge who had condemned her, to kill him before her trial. I saw a Majahedin agent plant a bomb in the judge's car. A guard found it and disabled it. I was able to create a diversion, the guard was late, and the bomb killed the Mullah."

"It didn't save your lady, I assume."

"Right. The new judge also condemned her. I tried twice more. Each time killing an official whose replacement might have let her go." I stopped pacing and leaned against the wall. "We stayed in the lab a week. When we came out, the only change was that Rossanna had been tortured for five weeks instead of for two."

"Is that the last time you were in a control lab?"

"Yes. Partly by choice, I didn't want to go into a lab again. I didn't contest my firing."

"Why take this job?"

"To kill as many Iranians," I stopped, realizing I hadn't called them sand niggers or gooks since killing the boy. I started again, "To kill as many as I could by changing the timeflow. Even if I only took a few hours off their lives, I would be killing them myself." I drank from my own cup of coffee, now cold. "I've been doing a lot of thinking about Rossanna since I arrived in Iraq. I turned my own feelings of loss into hatred of an entire people who are themselves victims. Let those who are dead, remain dead, and let those who are alive, live."

"It will work this time, Koch. I understand enough about the theory of the timeflow to see that. You just weren't able to find the key event. Knock the linchpin out of the timeflow, and you can change history. We can destroy Khomaini."

"I am just not sure, Fowler. The last team's calculations do offer a possibility of success." I thought back over the figures and nodded slowly. "Don't worry. I'll go through with the plan. It might even save Rossanna."

"We have at least one advantage you didn't have. We have the lab tied into a new, world wide, timeflow monitoring system," Fowler said.

"I know about it. Based on time stabilizers and monitors placed around the globe."

"Right. We'll be able to tell what changes have occurred without leaving the facility." Fowler glanced over his shoulder at the control room door. It was closed, as he had left it earlier. "Look, Koch, you know we have a bad situation here."

"The Libyans?"

"They pay us, but we don't really know what they want. You can be sure that their Colonel, Qaddafi, wants a strong and independent country, but beyond that, it's up in the air."

"Look, you're doing this for the money, and so am I. But I don't understand Qaddafi attacking another revolutionary state," I said.

"The Colonel has had several Shi'i leaders killed in the past, that we do know. Also, Khomaini is a powerful rival for leadership in the radical section of the Islamic world."

"So Qaddafi is a natural ally against Khomaini, despite his rhetoric of leftist solidarity."

Fowler smiled. "Right."

"Look, Fowler, you speak Arabic, don't you? I might be able to use the controller to check on their briefings in Libya. It would take a few hours to find them."

"I speak both Arabic and Farsi, but it won't work. You've been out of the field too long. About a year ago MIT managed to convert a stabilizer into a field damper." He held up his wrist watch. "With the damper on, a timeflow controller can't be focused on the area the damper protects."

"Very neat. Another new gadget." I dropped into a chair. Its wheels squeaked as I pulled up to the console. "Any of your people on the outside likely to send you any useful information on al-Hajjaj? And what about Muhallab?"

"Al-Hajjaj is regular army and the commander of their time lab. Muhallab, I suspect, is with Qaddafi's security force. I have some hope of hearing something soon, about both of them."

The five of us stood in the control room of the time lab. Fowler, al-Hajjaj, and I were near the displacement booth. Salam sat at the console, monitoring the stabilizer planted on our target, the boy, the Hidden Imam. Lieutenant Muhallab was watching from the far side of the room.

"Yes, this is the right weapon." Al-Hajjaj held a long rifle in his left hand and opened the breach. He had changed his uniform for a dark jumpsuit. Turning to me, he held out the rifle. "You would be interested, Dr. Koch." He was acting the complete professional.

I took the rifle from him and examined it for several

minutes. It was an air rifle: single shot, breach loading. It was two meters long, but I could balance it easily at the trigger guard, thanks to the large gas cylinder fitted into the frame stock and the light weight of the resin-fiber barrel. Heavy wires ran from the stock to a belt-mounted battery pack and a stabilizer control.

"Well, Dr. Koch, your opinion? Can you guess its full purpose?" Al-Hajjaj's voice dripped with smug superiority.

"Rather a straightforward device, Colonel." I slid my hand along the barrel, feeling the tiny spiral ridges of imbedded wires. "The barrel is a de-sync chamber, powered by the belt-pack." I glanced at Fowler. "Right?"

"So far."

"The assassin," I looked at al-Hajjaj, "and the weapon would be out of sync with the target—he'd have to use a translator helmet to aim. When the rifle is fired, the projectile passes through the de-sync chamber of the barrel and is adjusted to the target's timeflow. I suspect that the only part of the system that would be visible in the target's time would be the front tip of the barrel." Looking again at Fowler and ignoring al-Hajjaj, I asked, "Do you have one of the darts?"

"Here." He handed me a small open box.

Six bullet shaped darts, each a centimeter long and about four millimeters across, lay in the box. The front half of each was metallic, the rear looked like black plastic. The bullets were mounted on white plastic rods three centimeters long.

"The white rod is only to make loading easier, it separates after the projectile is in the breach." Fowler used his pen to point to the bullets. "The tips are made of osmium for mass. The back of the unit is a mix of water and fat soluble resins, impregnated with a nerve poison."

"How fast does it kill?"

"About a minute. The symptoms of this poison are consistent with brain damage from a beating. The target jerks for about a minute before he dies. We know the Imam was roughed up a bit." Fowler glanced up.

"Have you had any problem with the dart's velocity driving it through the target?" I asked.

"We did at first. The tech boys added a minute explosive charge between the tip and the resin. It detonates on entry, and ensures separation. Even if the tip passes on out of the target, it fragments into dust when it hits anything solid." Fowler turned to al-Hajjaj. "Well, Colonel, the timeflow controller is locked on the boy and ready." He nodded to the displacement booth. "Jump in, you should be finished in five minutes."

"And Twelver Shi'ism will never have existed." Muhallab was standing near the far wall of the control room. "There will be total victory over the apostates." He spat out the words.

"No, Muhallab. The followers of the Mahdi will not be damaged. It is your Colonel who will die." Al-Hajjaj stepped back from the displacement booth, and slid an automatic pistol from his jumpsuit.

Muhallab jerked open his suit jacket and grabbed for his own pistol. Al-Hajjaj fired twice. Muhallab took half a step back, hand still on his pistol, and bumped against the wall. He stood for a moment, then slid down the wall and flopped over onto his side.

"No movement, please." Al-Hajjaj's voice displayed the habit of command. "I have no cause to kill any of you." He stepped to the body and removed Muhallab's gun from its belt holster. He glanced at Salam, who was now standing by the console. "Salam, I will need your help."

"My help? Colonel al-Hajjaj, give me your gun, please. I will see that you are not punished if you do, insallah."

"Salam, you are Shi'i. You follow the Imam Mahdi. You must help me." He waved his free hand at Muhallab. "Our glorious Colonel forced this dog upon me as an aide. The man who was to have come with me is no doubt dead."

"Colonel al-Hajjaj, I am Iraqi, and I am Arab before I am Shi'i." Salam slowly sat down on the edge of the console. "I have seen too many die in this war. There must be an end to the blood. I cannot help you."

"You must help, Salam," al-Hajjaj demanded. "We must use the machine to kill Qaddafi. . . ."

"Your own palace coup, Colonel?" Fowler spoke for the first time since the attack on Muhallab. He kept both hands in clear view, away from his clothes. "You plan to replace one Colonel with another?"

"We pave the way for the coming of the Mahdi. No more."

"That would be enough," Fowler said quietly. "Did you tip off the Israelis?"

Al-Hajjaj spat violently. "No."

"Yes, you had to have told them." Salam slowly put one foot up on a chair. "You must be a spy for the Zionists."

Watching al-Hajjaj's eyes, I thought Salam was going to die in that instant, but he did not. After a moment al-Hajjaj said, "There is no time to talk. I did not tell the Israelis. I told only SAVAMA."

"SAVAMA?" I glanced at Fowler.

"Iranian Intelligence, the successor to SAVAK. A lot of the professionals carried over." Fowler shook his head very slightly. "And SAVAMA still works with MOSSAD, when they need to. Professionals working with professionals. But your hands are clean, Colonel?"

Salam bent his knee, pulling the chair closer to him. He was staring at al-Hajjaj.

"MOSSAD, that's Israeli intelligence. Don't kid yourself, Colonel," I turned toward the Libyan, "you do work for the Israelis. Are you a closet Zionist?"

He whipped the automatic around, centering it on my stomach. "If I did not need you . . ." The high squeak of the chair wheels screamed for his attention. He whirled back to Salam and fired once, an instant before the chair smashed into his legs.

Fowler's gun slipped out of his back holster. As the gun centered on al-Hajjaj and began to rise, Fowler fired. The first round whined off the concrete underlying the floor tiles. The second drove into the Colonel's groin. The third and fourth struck him in the chest. I began to breath again as the last echo reverberated around the room.

"Mr. Koch, please . . ."

Salam was lying on the floor, clutching his right shoulder. I moved to him and slowly pulled his hand away from the wound. It was high on the chest, just below his shoulder joint. "I won't ask how you feel." The sharp scent of cordite filled the room.

"It is not bad. With the small automatics, you must be accurate. . . ." Salam gasped as I examined the wound.

"Let me patch him up." Fowler moved me aside and lay a first aid kit on the floor. Within minutes, he had cleaned and bandaged the small entrance and exit wounds. "Koch, check the console, see if the bullet damaged anything."

"I have. The tracer circuit is all right, but he hit the stabilizer controls. We're still locked on to the boy, but the readings are shifting. The overload safety might be damaged. I don't think we can remain locked to the Imam long."

"Mr. Koch, try. You must go back and kill the Twelfth Imam." Salam shifted his position, and winced. "We must try and stop the deaths."

"I'm not an assassin." I stood up. I felt trapped, but I was free compared to Salam. He was trapped between his religion, his nation and his Arab heritage. "I can run the lab while Fowler goes back."

"Won't work, Koch." Fowler looked up at me, "The de-sync tube in the gun might need adjustment when you get back there. I know nothing about it. It has to be you, with Salam running the lab."

"No, Fowler. I don't even think your plan will really work."

"But if it does, Koch, it might save your lady." He paused. "Neither I nor Salam can do the job. Damn it, I know you fired expert in the Army."

"This can't help Rossanna. The timeflow is too rigid. You can only change part of it once."

"Directly, yes, but this change is so remote from your efforts to save her that it can work."

"Perhaps. . . . All right." I didn't want to go back, but I had to try again to help Rossanna. "I'll get into the spare jumpsuit and test fire the rifle in the hall." I knelt a moment by Salam. "You can run the lab?"

He nodded.

"While I change, get me a picture of the timeflow at the moment I'm to shoot the Imam."

The helmet was a little tight, but it would work. I slid the de-sync visor down and up to be sure it moved smoothly, then walked over to the control console. The main wall screen showed my target, locked in time by the stabilizer. The scene was a large city plaza. The details were unclear, the picture fuzzy, but the plaza was surrounded by tall mud brick buildings. It was filled with the stalls of a market, and a large crowd of shoppers.

Most of the people were unclear. But at the center of the view, a small group stood out sharply, locked in focus by the time stabilizer. A half-dozen guards with chain mail, helmets and swords surrounded a robed and turbaned man of middle age and a boy of about eight.

"The last lab team was able to delay the escape of the boy Imam until the Caliph's guards had captured him," Fowler said. "The man is known to the crowd, most of whom are Imamites. He was the major deptuy of al-Askari, the Eleventh Imam. They suspect the boy to be the new Imam."

"Anything else?" I put on the battery pack and controller and picked up the rifle.

"No."

"Then let's do the job." I stepped into the displacement booth. "Salam, give me a few seconds, and hit it." I saw him nod. Then I closed the door and sat on the small stool, the rifle on my lap. The booth darkened, and my skin began to tingle. Again, a chill ran down my spine. The sensation intensified.

Light began to filter through a heavy fog. The booth was gone. I saw the marketplace, and I saw the boy Imam. I raised the rifle. I took a moment to adjust the de-sync barrel, then sighted down at the boy. He was too far away. I changed the magnification on my helmet's de-sync visor.

The Imam's face filled my vision. I stared. He was so damn young, with a bruise on one cheek. I lowered the rifle, centering the sights on his chest. Slowly, I squeezed the trigger.

Across the sights of the air rifle I saw not the boy who was the Twelfth Imam, not the Mahdi, but the ghost of the boy I had killed in battle. As the gun puffed death, I whispered, "No." The barrel jumped slightly.

The boy jerked, and was engulfed in a ball of light that faded in a heartbeat. The boy was gone. The crowd stared, and the guards and the deputy looked for the Imam. But he had vanished.

"What the bloody hell happened, Koch?" Fowler loomed behind me as I studied the console. "Where is the damn Imam?"

As I studied the stabilizer record, I could smell a trace of ozone in the air. "Here. The dart must have hit the stabilizer planted on the boy. That caused an overload loop back to the main controller. It fed the full power of the machine into the kid."

"The Twelfth Imam has not gone into occultation in hiding, Mr. Fowler," Salam too examined the record, "he has vanished in a blinding flash in the middle of a crowd of believers.''

"Well where the hell is the boy? Where did he go?''

"He'll likely drop back in sync at a point of affinity in the timeflow, and within a thousand miles of us. But he could be anywhere, Fowler, anywhere in time.''

"Can you fix the machine?''

"No luck, Fowler. The controller overloaded. It's dead.'' I checked the secondary board. "Wait a minute . . . luck is with us, the tracer is still working. But I can't quite get a fix on it, it's too close in time to us.''

"I'll check the data from outside and see what we did,'' Fowler said. Fifteen minutes later, he turned from his work. "Looks as if political and geographical factors held pretty firm. Same nations, and the same general borders. There do seem to be about the same number of Shi'i as Sunni, however. And Libya itself is now Shi'i.''

"The war?'' Salam asked.

"There is none, at the moment. But Khomaini is still leading Iran through a reign of terror.''

I thought of Rossanna, closed my eyes a moment, and turned back to the tracer controls. A green light began blinking on the board. "I have him!''

"Put it on the wall monitor.'' Fowler shoved his chair around to watch the display.

"Coming up now.'' The two meter wall screen was filled with a picture of a large city square filled with a mob. "Something familiar about that.'' The main crowd consisted of men and boys, many waving rifles or machineguns. Dotted throughout the square were black-robed mullahs.

"It is Tehran, Dr. Koch,'' Salam said. "Near the University, I think.''

"Can you bring up the sound?'' Fowler stared at the screen. "There, in the center, a clear area around a few men.''

"If I can back up . . . now.'' The picture blinked. The open area was now filled with men. The crowd was turned toward a speaker on a far platform. It was Khomaini. The sound switched in, and the Ayatollah's voice filled the control room. I glanced at Fowler.

"It's Farsi, but I understand most of it. The bastard is calling for a holy war against the Iraqi devils.''

A bright flash of light glared in the center of the crowd.

The packed mob shoved away from the light, sending ripples of motion outward. As the light faded, I saw a lone figure standing in a small open space in the center of the crowd. It was the boy, the Hidden Imam.

"Oh shit." Fowler watched at the screen.

The boy whirled in a tight circle, staring at the crowd. His eyes were filled with fear. He began to babble in Arabic.

"Translate, damn it, Fowler."

"I understand most of it. He's asking where he is, and who the people are." A black-robed mullah pushed through to the boy. They stood alone at the center of the clear circle, the boy cowering as the mullah shouted at him. "The cleric speaks Arabic. He's calling the Imam a spy . . . a spy for the murderers of Ali, for the Sunni leadership of Iraq."

The boy turned sharply at the mention of Ali. He called to the mullah and the crowd, holding his hand to his own chest, "Al-Askari, ibn-Askari!"

"Ibn-Askari? He's identifying himself as the son of al-Askari," Fowler said. "The mention of Ali told him that he's among fellow Shia. . . ."

The mullah stared a moment. He turned, pointed to a man with an M-16 rifle, and jerked his hand back at the boy. The automatic rifle swung toward the Twelfth Imam.

A burst of fire ripped into the boy, smashing him back into the mob where he fell to the ground. Bright blood soaked his clothes and ran onto the dirt. Men began to kick the body.

"Insallah," Salam said quietly. "Yes. Al-Askari was his father's name, but in both Arabic and Farsi askari also means soldier. They thought the Hidden Imam, the Mahdi, was boasting of being a spy."

EDITOR'S INTRODUCTION TO:

THE ROAD NOT TAKEN
by Harry Turtledove

Harry Turtledove works in the Los Angeles County Office of Education, where his studies of Byzantine history come in handy in understanding what's going on. His forthcoming series from Ballantine Books chronicles the exploits of one of Caesar's legions transported in time to the late Byzantine Empire just prior to Manzikert, that disastrous battle that destroyed Byzantium and brought the Turks to Anatolia.

Other things being equal, courage and the warrior spirit will be decisive; but sometimes other things are not equal. Herewith a delightfully improbable story . . .

THE ROAD NOT TAKEN
by Harry Turtledove

Captain Togram was using the chamberpot when the *Indomitable* broke out of hyperdrive. As happened all too often, nausea surged through the Roxolan officer. He raised the pot and was abruptly sick into it.

When the spasm was done, he set the thundermug down and wiped his streaming eyes with the soft, gray-brown fur of his forearm. "The gods curse it!" he burst out. "Why don't the shipmasters warn us when they do that?" Several of his troopers echoed him more pungently.

At that moment, a runner appeared in the doorway. "We're back in normal space," the youth squeaked, before dashing on to the next chamber. Jeers and oaths followed him: "No shit!" "Thanks for the news!" "Tell the steerers—they might not have got the word!"

Togram sighed and scratched his muzzle in annoyance at his own irritability. As an officer, he was supposed to set an example for his soldiers. He was junior enough to take such responsibilities seriously, but had had enough service to realize he should never expect too much from anyone more than a couple of notches above him. High ranks went to those with ancient blood or fresh money.

Sighing again, he stowed the chamberpot in its niche. The metal cover he slid over it did little to relieve the stench. After sixteen days in space, the *Indomitable* reeked of ordure, stale food, and staler bodies. It was no better in any other ship of the Roxolan fleet, or any other. Travel between the stars was simply like that. Stinks and darkness were part of the price the soldiers paid to make the kingdom grow.

Togram picked up a lantern and shook it to rouse the glowmites inside. They flashed silver in alarm. Some races, the captain knew, lit their ships with torches or candles, but glowmites used less air, even if they could only shine intermittently.

Ever the careful soldier, Togram checked his weapons while the light lasted. He always kept all four of his pistols loaded and ready to use; when landing operations began, one pair would go on his belt, the other in his boot tops. He was more worried about his sword. The perpetually moist air aboard ship was not good for the blade. Sure enough, he found a spot of rust to scour away.

As he polished the rapier, he wondered what the new system would be like. He prayed for it to have a habitable planet. The air in the *Indomitable* might be too foul to breathe by the time the ship could get back to the nearest Roxolan-held planet. That was one of the risks starfarers took. It was not a major one—small yellow suns usually shepherded a life-bearing world or two—but it was there.

He wished he hadn't let himself think about it; like an aching fang, the worry, once there, would not go away. He got up from his pile of bedding to see how the steerers were doing.

As usual with them, both Ransisc and his apprentice Olgren were complaining about the poor quality of the glass through which they trained their spyglasses. "You ought to stop whining," Togram said, squinting in from the doorway. "At least you have light to see by." After seeing so long by glowmite lantern, he had to wait for his eyes to adjust to the harsh raw sunlight flooding the observation chamber before he could go in.

Olgren's ears went back in annoyance. Ransisc was older and calmer. He set his hand on his apprentice's arm. "If you rise to all of Togram's jibes, you'll have time for nothing else—he's been a troublemaker since he came out of the egg. Isn't that right, Togram?"

"Whatever you say." Togram liked the white-muzzled senior steerer. Unlike most of his breed, Ransisc did not act as though he believed his important job made him something special in the gods' scheme of things.

Olgren stiffened suddenly; the tip of his stumpy tail twitched. "This one's a world!" he exclaimed.

"Let's see," Ransisc said. Olgren moved away from his spyglass. The two steerers had been examining bright stars one by one, looking for those that would show discs and prove themselves actually to be planets.

"It's a world," Ransisc said at length, "but not one for us—those yellow, banded planets always have poisonous air, and too much of it." Seeing Olgren's dejection, he added, "It's not a total loss—if we look along a line from that planet to its sun, we should find others fairly soon."

"Try that one," Togram said, pointing toward a ruddy star that looked brighter than most of the others he could see.

Olgren muttered something haughty about knowing his business better than any amateur, but Ransisc said sharply, "The captain has seen more worlds from space than you, sirrah. Suppose you do as he asks." Ears drooping dejectedly, Olgren obeyed.

Then his pique vanished. "A planet with green patches!" he shouted.

Ransisc had been aiming his spyglass at a different part of the sky, but that brought him hurrying over. He shoved his apprentice aside, fiddled with the spyglass' focus, peered long at the magnified image. Olgren was hopping from one foot to the other, his muddy brown fur puffed out with impatience to hear the verdict.

"Maybe," said the senior steerer, and Olgren's face lit, but it fell again as Ransisc continued, "I don't see anything that looks like open water. If we find nothing better, I say we try it, but let's search a while longer."

"You've just made a *luof* very happy," Togram said. Ransisc chuckled. The Roxolani brought the little creatures along to test new planets' air. If a *luof* could breathe it in the airlock of a flyer, it would also be safe for the animal's masters.

The steerers growled in irritation as several stars in a row stubbornly stayed mere points of light. Then Ransisc stiffened at his spyglass. "Here it is," he said softly. "*This* is what we want. Come here, Olgren."

"Oh my, yes," the apprentice said a moment later.

"Go report it to Warmaster Slevon, and ask him if his devices have picked up any hyperdrive vibrations except for the fleet's." As Olgren hurried away, Ransisc beckoned Togram over. "See for yourself."

The captain of foot bent over the eyepiece. Against the black of space, the world in the spyglass field looked achingly like Roxolan: deep ocean blue, covered with swirls of white cloud. A good-sized moon hung nearby. Both were in approximately half-phase, being nearer their star than was the *Indomitable*.

"Did you spy any land?" Togram asked.

"Look near the top of the image, below the ice cap," Ransisc said. "Those browns and greens aren't colors water usually takes. If we want any world in this system, you're looking at it now."

They took turns examining the distant planet and trying to sketch its features until Olgren came back. "Well?" Togram said, though he saw the apprentice's ears were high and cheerful.

"Not a hyperdrive emanation but ours in the whole system!" Olgren grinned. Ransisc and Togram both pounded him on the back, as if he were the cause of the good news and not just its bearer.

The captain's smile was even wider than Olgren's. This was going to be an easy one, which, as a professional soldier, he thoroughly approved of. If no one hereabouts could build a hyperdrive, either the system had no intelligent life at all or its inhabitants were still primitives, ignorant of gunpowder, fliers, and other aspects of warfare as it was practiced among the stars.

He rubbed his hands. He could hardly wait for landfall.

Buck Herzog was bored. After four months in space, with five and a half more staring him in the face, it was hardly surprising. Earth was a bright star behind the *Ares III*, with Luna a dimmer companion; Mars glowed ahead.

"It's your exercise period, Buck," Art Snyder called. Of the five-person crew, he was probably the most officious.

"All right, Pancho," Herzog sighed. He pushed himself over to the bicycle and began pumping away, at first languidly, then harder. The work helped keep calcium in his bones in spite of free fall. Besides, it was something to do.

Melissa Ott was listening to the news from home. "Fernando Valenzuela died last night," she said.

"Who?" Snyder was not a baseball fan.

Herzog was, and a Californian to boot. "I saw him at an old-timers' game once, and I remember my dad and my grandfather always talking about him," he said. "How old was he, Mel?"

"Seventy-nine," she answered.

"He always was too heavy," Herzog said sadly.

"Jesus Christ!"

Herzog blinked. No one on the *Ares III* had sounded that excited since liftoff from the American space station. Melissa was staring at the radar screen. "Freddie!" she yelled.

Frederica Lindstrom, the ship's electronics expert, had just gotten out of the cramped shower space. She dove for the control board, still trailing a stream of water droplets. She did not bother with a towel; modesty aboard the *Ares III* had long since vanished.

Melissa's shout even made Claude Jonnard stick his head out of the little biology lab where he spent most of his time. "What's wrong?" he called from the hatchway.

"Radar's gone to hell," Melissa told him.

"What do you mean, gone to hell?" Jonnard demanded indignantly. He was one of those annoying people who think quantitatively all the time, and think everyone else does, too.

"There are about a hundred, maybe a hundred fifty, objects on the screen that have no right to be there," answered Frederica Lindstrom, who had a milder case of the same disease. "Range appears to be a couple of million kilometers."

"They weren't there a minute ago, either," Melissa said. "I hollered when they showed up."

As Frederica fiddled with the radar and the computer, Herzog stayed on the exercise bike, feeling singularly useless: what good is a geologist millions of kilometers away from rocks? He wouldn't even get his name in the history books—no one remembers the crew of the third expedition to anywhere.

Frederica finished her checks. "I can't find anything wrong," she said, sounding angry at herself and the equipment both.

"Time to get on the horn to Earth, Freddie," Art Snyder said. "If I'm going to land this beast, I can't have the radar telling me lies."

Melissa was already talking into the microphone. "Houston, this is *Ares III*. We have a problem—"

Even at light-speed, there were a good many minutes of waiting. They crawled past, one by one. Everyone jumped when the speaker crackled to life. "*Ares III*, this is Houston Control. Ladies and gentlemen, I don't quite know how to tell you this, but we see them too."

The communicator kept talking, but no one was listening to her any more. Herzog felt his scalp tingle as his hair, in primitive reflex, tried to stand on end. Awe filled him. He had never thought he would live to see humanity contact another race. "Call them, Mel," he said urgently.

She hesitated. "I don't know, Buck. Maybe we should let Houston handle this."

"Screw Houston," he said, surprised at his own vehemence. "By the time the bureaucrats down there figure out what to do, we'll be coming down on Mars. We're the people on the spot. Are you going to throw away the most important moment in the history of the species?"

Melissa looked from one of her crewmates to the next. Whatever she saw in their faces must have satisfied her, for she shifted the aim to the antenna and began to speak: "This is the spacecraft *Ares III*, calling the unknown ships. Welcome from the people of Earth." She turned off the transmitter for a moment. "How many languages do we have?"

The call went out in Russian, Mandarin, Japanese, French, German, Spanish, even Latin. ("Who knows the last time they may have visited?" Frederica said when Snyder gave her an odd look.)

If the wait for a reply from Earth had been long, this one was infinitely worse. The delay stretched far, far past the fifteen-second speed-of-light round trip. "Even if they don't speak any of our languages, shouldn't they say *something*?" Melissa demanded of the air. It did not answer, nor did the aliens.

Then, one at a time, the strange ships began darting away sunwards, toward Earth. "My God, the acceleration!" Snyder said. "Those are no rockets!" He looked suddenly sheepish. "I don't suppose starships would have rockets, would they?"

The *Ares III* lay alone again in its part of space, pursuing its Hohmann orbit inexorably toward Mars. Buck Herzog wanted to cry.

As was their practice, the ships of the Roxolan fleet gathered above the pole of the new planet's hemisphere with the most land. Because everyone would be coming to the same spot, the doctrine made visual rendezvous easy. Soon only four ships were unaccounted for. A scoutship hurried around to the other pole, found them, and brought them back.

"Always some water-lovers every trip," Togram chuckled to the steerers as he brought them the news. He took all the chances he could to go to their dome, not just for the sunlight but also because, unlike many soldiers, he was interested in planets for their own sake. With any head for figures, he might have tried to become a steerer himself.

He had a decent hand with quill and paper, so Ransisc and Olgren were willing to let him spell them at the spyglass and add to the sketchmaps they were making of the world below.

"Funny sort of planet," he remarked. "I've never seen one with so many forest fires or volcanoes or whatever they are on the dark side."

"I still think they're cities," Olgren said, with a defiant glance at Ransisc.

"They're too big and too bright," the senior steerer said patiently; the argument, plainly, had been going on for some time.

"This is your first trip offplanet, isn't it, Olgren?" Togram asked.

"Well, what if it is?"

"Only that you don't have enough perspective. Egelloc on Roxolan has almost a million people, and from space it's next to invisible at night. It's nowhere near as bright as those lights, either. Remember, this is a primitive planet. I admit it looks like there's intelligent life down there, but how could a race that hasn't even stumbled across the hyperdrive build cities ten times as great as Egelloc?"

"I don't know," Olgren said sulkily. "But from what little I can see by moonlight, those lights look to be in good spots for cities—on coasts, or along rivers, or whatever."

Ransisc sighed. "What are we going to do with him, Togram? He's so sure he knows everything, he won't listen to reason. Were you like that when you were young?"

"Till my clanfathers beat it out of me, anyway. No need getting all excited, though. Soon enough the flyers will go down with their *luofi*, and then we'll know." He swallowed a snort of laughter, then sobered abruptly, hoping he hadn't been as gullible as Olgren when he was young.

"I have one of the alien vessels on radar," the SR-81 pilot reported. "It's down to eighty thousand meters and still descending." He was at his own plane's operational ceiling, barely half as high as the ship entering atmosphere.

"For God's sake, hold your fire," ground control ordered. The command had been dinned into him before he took off, but the brass were not about to let him forget. He did not really blame them. One trigger-happy idiot could ruin humanity forever.

"I'm beginning to get a visual image," he said, glancing at the head-up display projected in front of him. A moment later he added, "It's one damn funny-looking ship, I can tell you that already. Where are the wings?"

"We're picking up the image now too," the ground control officer said. "They must use the same principle for their in-atmosphere machines as they do for their spacecraft: some sort of antigravity that gives them both lift and drive capability."

The alien ship kept ignoring the SR-81, just as all the aliens had ignored every terrestrial signal beamed at them. The craft continued its slow descent, while the SR-81 pilot circled below, hoping he would not have to go down to the aerial tanker to refuel.

"One question answered," he called to the ground. "It's a warplane." No craft whose purpose was peaceful would have had those glaring eyes and that snarling, fang-filled mouth painted on its belly. Some USAF ground-attack aircraft carried similar markings.

At last the alien reached the level at which the SR-81 was loitering. The pilot called the ground again. "Permission to pass in front of the aircraft?" he asked. "Maybe everybody's asleep in there and I can wake 'em up."

After a long silence, ground control gave grudging assent. "No hostile gestures," the controller warned.

"What do you think I'm going to do, flip him the finger?" the pilot muttered, but his radio was off. Acceleration pushed him back in his seat as he guided the SR-81 into a long, slow turn that would carry it about half a kilometer in front of the vessel from the spacefleet.

His airplane's camera gave him a brief glimpse of the alien pilot, who was sitting behind a small, dirty windscreen.

The being from the stars saw him, too. Of that there was no doubt. The alien jinked like a startled fawn, performing maneuvers that would have smeared the SR-81 pilot against the walls of his pressure cabin—if his aircraft could have matched them in the first place.

"I'm giving pursuit!" he shouted. Ground control screamed at him, but he was the man on the spot. The surge from his afterburner made the pressure he had felt before a love pat by comparison.

Better streamlining made his plane faster than the craft

from the starships, but that did not do him much good. Every time its pilot caught sight of him, the alien ship danced away with effortless ease. The SR-81 pilot felt like a man trying to kill a butterfly with a hatchet.

To add to his frustration, his fuel warning light came on. In any case, his aircraft was designed for the thin atmosphere at the edge of space, not the increasingly denser air through which the alien flew. He swore, but had to pull away.

As his SR-81 gulped kerosene from the tanker, he could not help wondering what would have happened if he'd turned a missile loose. There were a couple of times he'd had a perfect shot. That was one thought he kept firmly to himself. What his superiors would do if they knew about it was too gruesome to contemplate.

The troopers crowded round Togram as he came back from the officers' conclave. "What's the word, captain?" "Did the *luof* live?" "What's it like down there?"

"The *luof* lived, boys!" Togram said with a broad smile.

His company raised a cheer that echoed deafeningly in the barracks room. "We're going down!" they whooped. Ears stood high in excitement. Some soldiers waved plumed hats in the fetid air. Others, of a bent more like their captain's, went over to their pallets and began seeing to their weapons.

"How tough are they going to be, sir?" a gray-furred veteran named Ilingua asked as Togram went by. "I hear the flier pilot saw some funny things."

Togram's smile got wider. "By the heavens and hells, Ilingua, haven't you done this often enough before to know better than to pay heed to rumors you hear before planetfall?"

"I hope so, sir," Ilingua said, "but these are so strange I thought there might be something to them." When Togram did not answer, the trooper shook his head at his own foolishness and shook up a lantern so he could examine his dagger's edge.

As inconspicuously as he could, the captain let out a sigh. He did not know what to believe himself, and he had listened to the pilot's report. How could the locals have flying machines when they did not know contragravity? Togram had heard of a race that used hot-air balloons before it discovered the better way of doing things, but no balloon could have reached the altitude the locals' flier had achieved, and no balloon could have changed direction, as the pilot had violently insisted this craft had done.

Assume he was wrong, as he had to be. But how was one to take his account of towns as big as the ones whose possibility Ransisc had ridiculed, of a world so populous there was precious little open space? And lantern signals from other ships showed their scout pilots were reporting the same wild improbabilities.

Well, in the long run it would not matter if this race was as numerous as *reffo* at a picnic. There would simply be that many more subjects here for Roxolan.

"This is a terrible waste," Billy Cox said to anyone who would listen as he slung his duffelbag over his shoulder and tramped out to the waiting truck. "We should be meeting the starpeople with open arms, not with a show of force."

"You tell 'em, Professor," Sergeant Santos Amoros chuckled from behind him. "Me, I'd sooner stay on my butt in a nice, air-conditioned barracks than face L.A. summer smog and sun any old day. Damn shame you're just a Spec-1. If you was President, you could give the orders any way you wanted, instead o' takin' 'em.''

Cox didn't think that was very fair either. He'd been just a few units short of his M.A. in poli sci when the big buildup after the second Syrian crisis sucked him into the army.

He had to fold his lanky length like a jackknife to get under the olive-drab canopy of the truck and down into the passenger compartment. The seats were too hard and too close together. Jamming people into the vehicle counted for more than their comfort while they were there. Typical military thinking, Cox thought disparagingly.

The truck filled. The big diesel rumbled to life. A black soldier dug out a deck of cards and bet anyone that he could turn twenty-five cards into five pat poker hands. A couple of greenhorns took him up on it. Cox had found out the expensive way that it was a sucker bet. The black man was grinning as he offered the deck to one of his marks to shuffle.

Riffff! The ripple of the pasteboards was authoritative enough to make everybody in the truck turn his head. "Where'd you learn to handle cards like that, man?" demanded the black soldier, whose name was Jim but whom everyone called Junior.

"Dealing blackjack in Vegas." *Riffff!*

"Hey, Junior," Cox called, "all of a sudden I want ten bucks of your action."

"Up yours too, pal," Junior said, glumly watching the cards move as if they had lives of their own.

The truck rolled northward, part of a convoy of trucks, MICV's, and light tanks that stretched for miles. An entire regiment was heading into Los Angeles, to be billeted by companies in different parts of the sprawling city. Cox approved of that; it made it less likely that he would personally come face-to-face with any of the aliens.

"Sandy," he said to Amoros, who was squeezed in next to him, "even if I'm wrong and the aliens aren't friendly, what the hell good will handweapons do? It'd be like taking on an elephant with a safety pin."

"Professor, like I told you already, they don't pay me to think, or you neither. Just as well, too. I'm gonna do what the lieutenant tells me, and you're gonna do what I tell you, and everything is gonna be fine, right?"

"Sure," Cox said, because Sandy, while he wasn't a bad guy, was a sergeant. All the same, the Neo-Armalite between Cox's boots seemed very futile, and his helmet and body armor as thin and gauzy as a stripper's negligee.

The sky outside the steerers' dome began to go from black to deep blue as the *Indomitable* entered atmosphere. "There," Olgren said, pointing. "That's where we'll land."

"Can't see much from this height," Togram remarked.

"Let him use your spyglass, Olgren," Ransisc said. "He'll be going back to his company soon."

Togram grunted; that was more than a comment—it was also a hint. Even so, he was happy to peer through the eyepiece. The ground seemed to leap toward him. There was a moment of disorientation as he adjusted to the inverted image, which put the ocean on the wrong side of the field of view. But he was not interested in sightseeing. He wanted to learn what his soldiers and the rest of the troops aboard the *Indomitable* would have to do to carve out a beachhead and hold it against the locals.

"There's a spot that looks promising," he said. "The greenery there in the midst of the buildings in the eastern—no, the western—part of the city. That should give us a clear landing zone, a good campground, and a base for landing reinforcements."

"Let's see what you're talking about," Ransisc said, elbowing him aside. "Hmm, yes, I see the stretch you mean. That might not be bad. Olgren, come look at this. Can you find it again in the Warmaster's spyglass? All right then, go point it out to him. Suggest it as our setdown point."

The apprentice hurried away. Ransisc bent over the eyepiece again. "Hmm," he repeated. "They build tall down there, don't they?"

"I thought so," Togram said. "And there's a lot of traffic on those roads. They've spent a fortune cobblestoning them all, too; I didn't see any dust kicked up."

"This should be a rich conquest," Ransisc said.

Something swift, metallic, and predator-lean flashed past the observation window. "By the gods, they do have fliers, don't they?" Togram said. In spite of the pilots' claims, deep down he hadn't believed it until he saw it for himself.

He noticed Ransisc's ears twitching impatiently, and realized he really had spent too much time in the observation room. He picked up his glowmite lantern and went back to his troopers.

A couple of them gave him a resentful look for being away so long, but he cheered them up by passing on as much as he could about their landing site. Common soldiers loved nothing better than inside information. They second-guessed their superiors without it, but the game was even more fun when they had some idea of what they were talking about.

A runner appeared in the doorway. "Captain Togram, your company will planet from airlock three."

"Three," Togram acknowledged, and the runner trotted off to pass orders to other ground troop leaders. The captain put his plumed hat on his head (the plume was scarlet, so his company could recognize him in combat), checked his pistols one last time, and ordered his troopers to follow him.

The reeking darkness was as oppressive in front of the inner airlock door as anywhere else aboard the *Indomitable*, but somehow easier to bear. Soon the doors would swing open and he would feel fresh breezes riffling his fur, taste sweet clean air, enjoy sunlight for more than a few precious units at a stretch. Soon he would measure himself against these new beings in combat.

He felt the slightest of jolts as the *Indomitable*'s fliers launched themselves from the mother ship. There would be no *luofi* aboard them this time, but rather musketeers to

terrorize the natives with fire from above, and jars of gunpowder to be touched off and dropped. The Roxolani always
strove to make as savage a first impression as they could.
Terror doubled their effective numbers.

Another jolt came, different from the one before. They
were down.

A shadow spread across the UCLA campus. Craning his
neck, Junior said, "Will you look at the size of the mother!"
He had been saying that for the last five minutes, as the
starship slowly descended.

Each time, Billy Cox could only nod, his mouth dry, his
hands clutching the plastic grip and cool metal barrel of his
rifle. The Neo-Armalite seemed totally impotent against the
huge bulk floating so arrogantly downwards. The alien flying
machines around it were as minnows beside a whale, while
they in turn dwarfed the USAF planes circling at a greater
distance. The roar of their jets assailed the ears of the nervous
troops and civilians on the ground. The aliens' engines were
eerily silent.

The starship landed in the open quad between New Royce,
New Haines, New Kinsey, and New Powell Halls. It towered
higher than any of the two-story red brick buildings, each a
reconstruction of one overthrown in the earthquake of 2034.
Cox heard saplings splinter under the weight of the alien
craft. He wondered what it would have done to the big trees
that had fallen five years ago along with the famous old halls.

"All right, they've landed. Let's move on up," Lieutenant
Shotton ordered. He could not quite keep the wobble out of
his voice, but he trotted south toward the starship. His platoon followed him past Dickson Art Center, past New Bunche
Hall. Not so long ago, Billy Cox had walked this campus
barefoot. Now his boots thudded on concrete.

The platoon deployed in front of Dodd Hall, looking west
toward the spacecraft. A little breeze toyed with the leaves of
the young, hopeful trees planted to replace the stalwarts lost
to the quake.

"Take as much cover as you can," Lieutenant Shotton
ordered quietly. The platoon scrambled into flowerbeds, snug-
gled down behind thin treetrunks. Out on Hilgard Avenue,
diesels roared as armored fighting vehicles took positions
with good lines of fire.

It was all such a waste, Cox thought bitterly. The thing to

do was to make friends with the aliens, not to assume automatically they were dangerous.

Something, at least, was being done along those lines. A delegation came out of Murphy Hall and slowly walked behind a white flag from the administration building toward the starship. At the head of the delegation was the mayor of Los Angeles: the President and governor were busy elsewhere. Billy Cox would have given anything to be part of the delegation instead of sprawled here on his belly in the grass. If only the aliens had waited until he was fifty or so, had given him a chance to get established—

Sergeant Amoros nudged him with an elbow. "Look there, man. Something's happening—"

Amoros was right. Several hatchways which had been shut were swinging open, allowing Earth's air to mingle with the ship's.

The westerly breeze picked up. Cox's nose twitched. He could not name all the exotic odors wafting his way, but he recognized sewage and garbage when he smelled them. "God, what a stink!" he said.

"By the gods, what a stink!" Togram exclaimed. When the outer airlock doors went down, he had expected real fresh air to replace the stale, overused gases inside the *Indomitable*. This stuff smelled like smoky peat fires, or lamps whose wicks hadn't quite been extinguished. And it stung! He felt the nictitating membranes flick across his eyes to protect them.

"Deploy!" he ordered, leading his company forward. This was the tricky part. If the locals had nerve enough, they could hit the Roxolani just as the latter were coming out of their ship, and cause all sorts of trouble. Most races without hyperdrive, though, were too overawed by the arrival of travelers from the stars to try anything like that. And if they didn't do it fast, it would be too late.

They weren't doing it here. Togram saw a few locals, but they were keeping a respectful distance. He wasn't sure how many there were. Their mottled skins—or was that clothing?—made them hard to notice and count. But they were plainly warriors, both by the way they acted and by the weapons they bore.

His own company went into its familiar two-line formation,

the first crouching, the second standing and aiming their muskets over the heads of the troops in front.

"Ah, there we go," Togram said happily. The bunch approaching behind the white banner had to be the local nobles. The mottling, the captain saw, was clothing, for these beings wore entirely different garments, somber except for strange, narrow neckcloths. They were taller and skinnier than Roxolani, with muzzleless faces.

"Ilingua!" Togram called. The veteran trooper led the right flank squad of the company.

"Sir!"

"Your troops, quarter-right face. At the command, pick off the leaders there. That will demoralize the rest," Togram said, quoting standard doctrine.

"Slowmatches ready!" Togram said. The Roxolani lowered the smoldering cords to the touchholes of their muskets. "Take your aim!" The guns moved, very slightly. "Fire!"

"Teddy bears!" Sandy Amoros exclaimed. The same thought had leaped into Cox's mind. The beings emerging from the spaceship were round, brown, and furry, with long noses and big ears. Teddy bears, however, did not normally carry weapons. They also, Cox thought, did not commonly live in a place that smelled like sewage. Of course, it might have been perfume to them. But if it was, they and Earthpeople were going to have trouble getting along.

He watched the Teddy bears as they took their positions. Somehow their positioning did not suggest that they were forming an honor guard for the mayor and his party. Yet it did look familiar to Cox, although he could not quite figure out why.

Then he had it. If he had been anywhere but at UCLA, he would not have made the connection. But he remembered a course he had taken on the rise of the European nation-states in the sixteenth century, and on the importance of the professional, disciplined armies the kings had created. Those early armies had performed evolutions like this one.

It was a funny coincidence. He was about to mention it to his sergeant when the world blew up.

Flames spurted from the aliens' guns. Great gouts of smoke puffed into the sky. Something that sounded like an angry wasp buzzed past Cox's ear. He heard shouts and shrieks from either side. Most of the mayor's delegation was down, some motionless, others thrashing.

There was a crash from the starship, and another one an instant later as a roundshout smashed into the brickwork of Dodd Hall. A chip stung Cox in the back of the neck. The breeze brought him the smell of fireworks, one he had not smelled for years.

"Reload!" Togram yelled. "Another volley, then at 'em with the bayonet!" His troopers worked frantically, measuring powder charges and ramming round bullets home.

"So that's how they wanna play!" Amoros shouted. "Nail their hides to the wall!" The tip of his little finger had been shot away. He did not seem to know it.

Cox's Neo-Armalite was already barking, spitting a stream of hot brass cartridges, slamming against his shoulder. He rammed in clip after clip, playing the rifle like a hose. If one bullet didn't bite, the next would.

Others from the platoon were also firing. Cox heard bursts of automatic weapons fire from different parts of the campus, too, and the deeper blasts of rocket-propelled grenades and field artillery. Smoke not of the aliens' making began to envelop their ship and the soldiers around it.

One or two shots came back at the platoon, and then a few more, but so few that Cox, in stunned disbelief, shouted to his sergeant, "This isn't fair!"

"Fuck 'em!" Amoros shouted back. "They wanna throw their weight around, they take their chances. Only good thing they did was knock over the mayor. Always did hate that old crackpot."

The harsh *tac-tac-tac* did not sound like any gunfire Togram had heard. The shots came too close together, making a horrible sheet of noise. And if the locals were shooting back at his troopers, where were the thick, choking clouds of gunpowder smoke over their position?

He did not know the answer to that. What he did know was that his company was going down like grain before a scythe. Here a soldier was hit by three bullets at once and fell awkwardly, as if his body could not tell in which direction to twist. There another had the top of his head gruesomely removed.

The volley the captain had screamed for was stillborn. Perhaps a squad's worth of soldiers moved toward the locals, the sun glinting bravely off their long, polished bayonets. None of them got more than a half-sixteen of paces before falling.

Ilingua looked at Togram, horror in his eyes, his ears flat against his head. The captain knew his were the same. "What are they doing to us?" Ilingua howled.

Togram could only shake his head helplessly. He dove behind a corpse, fired one of his pistols at the enemy. There was still a chance, he thought—how would these demonic aliens stand up under their first air attack?

A flier swooped toward the locals. Musketeers blasted away from firing ports, drew back to reload.

"Take that, you whoresons!" Togram shouted. He did not, however, raise his fist in the air. That, he had already learned, was dangerous.

"Incoming aircraft!" Sergeant Amoros roared. His squad, those not already prone, flung themselves on their faces. Cox heard shouts of pain through the combat din as men were wounded.

The Cottonmouth crew launched their shoulder-fired AA missile at the alien flying machine. The pilot must have had reflexes like a cat's. He sidestepped his machine in midair; no plane built on earth could have matched that performance. The Cottonmouth shot harmlessly past.

The flier dropped what looked like a load of crockery. The ground jumped as the bombs exploded. Cursing, deafened, Billy Cox stopped worrying whether the fight was fair.

But the flier pilot had not seen the F-29 fighter on his tail. The USAF plane released two missiles from point-blank range, less than a mile. The infrared-seeker found no target and blew itself up, but the missile that homed on radar streaked straight toward the flier. The explosion made Cox bury his face in the ground and clap his hands over his ears.

So this is war, he thought: I can't see, I can barely hear, and my side is winning. What must it be like for the losers?

Hope died in Togram's heart when the first flier fell victim to the locals' aircraft. The rest of the *Indomitable*'s machines did not last much longer. They could evade, but had even less ability to hit back than the Roxolan ground forces. And they were hideously vulnerable when attacked in their pilots' blind spots, from below or behind.

One of the starship's cannon managed to fire again, and quickly drew a response from the traveling fortresses Togram got glimpses of as they took their positions in the streets outside this parklike area.

When the first shell struck, the luckless captain thought for an instant that it was another gun going off aboard the *Indomitable*. The sound of the explosion was nothing like the crash a solid shot made when it smacked into a target. A fragment of hot metal buried itself in the ground by Togram's hand. That made him think a cannon had blown up, but more explosions on the ship's superstructure and fountains of dirt flying up from misses showed it was just more from the locals' fiendish arsenal.

Something large and hard struck the captain in the back of the neck. The world spiraled down into blackness.

"Cease fire!" The order reached the field artillery first, then the infantry units at the very front line. Billy Cox pushed up his cuff to look at his watch, stared in disbelief. The whole firefight had lasted less than twenty minutes.

He looked around. Lieutenant Shotton was getting up from behind an ornamental palm. "Let's see what we have," he said. His rifle still at the ready, he began to walk slowly toward the starship. It was hardly more than a smoking ruin. For that matter, neither were the buildings around it. The damage to their predecessors had been worse in the big quake, but not much.

Alien corpses littered the lawn. The blood splashing the bright green grass was crimson as any man's. Cox bent to pick up a pistol. The weapon was beautifully made, with scenes of combat carved into the grayish wood of the stock. But he recognized it as a single-shot piece, a small arm obsolete for at least two centuries. He shook his head in wonderment.

Sergeant Amoros lifted a conical object from where it had fallen beside a dead alien. "What the hell is this?" he demanded.

Again Cox had the feeling of being caught up in something he did not understand. "It's a powderhorn," he said.

"Like in the movies? Pioneers and all that good shit?"

"The very same."

"Damn," Amoros said feelingly. Cox nodded in agreement.

Along with the rest of the platoon, they moved closer to the wrecked ship. Most of the aliens had died still in the two neat rows from which they had opened fire on the soldiers.

Here, behind another corpse, lay the body of the scarlet-plumed officer who had given the order to begin that horrifyingly uneven encounter. Then, startling Cox, the alien moaned and stirred, just as might a human starting to come to. "Grab him; he's a live one!" Cox exclaimed.

Several men jumped on the reviving alien, who was too groggy to fight back. Soldiers began peering into the holes torn in the starship, and even going inside. There they were still wary; the ship was so incredibly much bigger than any human spacecraft that there were surely survivors despite the shellacking it had taken.

As always happens, the men did not get to enjoy such pleasures long. The fighting had been over for only minutes when the first team of experts came thuttering in by helicopter, saw common soldiers in their private preserve, and made horrified noises. The experts also promptly relieved the platoon of its prisoner.

Sergeant Amoros watched resentfully as they took the alien away. "You must've known it would happen, Sandy," Cox consoled him. "We do the dirty work and the brass takes over once things get cleaned up again."

"Yeah, but wouldn't it be wonderful if just once it was the other way 'round?" Amoros laughed without humor. "You don't need to tell me: fat friggin' chance."

When Togram woke up on his back, he knew something was wrong. Roxolani always slept prone. For a moment he wondered how he had got to where he was . . . too much water-of-life the night before? His pounding head made that a good possibility.

Then memory came flooding back. Those damnable locals with their sorcerous weapons! Had his people rallied and beaten back the enemy after all? He vowed to light votive lamps to Edieva, mistress of battles, for the rest of his life if that was true.

The room he was in began to register. Nothing was familiar, from the bed he lay on to the light in the ceiling that glowed bright as sunshine and neither smoked nor flickered. No, he did not think the Roxolani had won their fight.

Fear settled like ice in his vitals. He knew how his own race treated prisoners, had heard spacers' stories of even worse things among other folk. He shuddered to think of the refined tortures a race as ferocious as his captors could invent.

He got shakily to his feet. By the end of the bed he found his hat, some smoked meat obviously taken from the *Indomitable*, and a translucent jug made of something that was neither leather nor glass nor baked clay nor metal. Whatever it was, it was too soft and flexible to make a weapon.

The jar had water in it: *not* water from the *Indomitable*. That was already beginning to taste stale. This was cool and fresh and so pure as to have no taste whatever, water so fine he had only found its like in a couple of mountain springs.

The door opened on noiseless hinges. In came two of the locals. One was small and wore a white coat—a female, if those chest projections were breasts. The other was dressed in the same clothes the local warriors had worn, though those offered no camouflage here. That one carried what was plainly a rifle and, the gods curse him, looked extremely alert.

To Togram's surprise, the female took charge. The other local was merely a bodyguard. Some spoiled princess, curious about these outsiders, the captain thought. Well, he was happier about treating with her than meeting the local executioner.

She sat down, waved for him also to take a seat. He tried a chair, found it uncomfortable—too low in the back, not built for his wide rump and short legs. He sat on the floor instead.

She set a small box on the table by the chair. Togram pointed at it. "What's that?" he asked.

He thought she had not understood—no blame to her for that; she had none of his language. She was playing with the box, pushing a button here, a button there. Then his ears went back and his hackles rose, for the box said, "What's that?" in Roxolani. After a moment he realized it was speaking in his own voice. He swore and made a sign against witchcraft.

She said something, fooled with the box again. This time it echoed her. She pointed at it. " 'Recorder,' " she said. She paused expectantly.

What was she waiting for, the Roxolanic name for that thing? "I've never seen one of those in my life, and I hope I never do again," he said. She scratched her head. When she made the gadget again repeat what he had said, only the thought of the soldier with the gun kept him from flinging it against the wall.

Despite that contretemps, they did eventually make progress on the language. Togram had picked up snatches of a good many tongues in the course of his adventurous life; that was one reason he had made captain in spite of low birth and paltry connections. And the female—Togram heard her name as Hildachesta—had a gift for them, as well as the box that never forgot.

"Why did your people attack us?" she asked one day, when she had come far enough in Roxolanic to be able to frame the question.

He knew he was being interrogated, no matter how polite she sounded. He had played that game with prisoners himself. His ears twitched in a shrug. He had always believed in giving straight answers; that was one reason he was only a captain. He said, "To take what you grow and make and use it for ourselves. Why would anyone want to conquer anyone else?"

"Why indeed?" she murmured, and was silent a little while; his forthright reply seemed to have closed off a line of questioning. She tried again: "How are your people able to walk—I mean, travel—faster than light, when the rest of your arts are so simple?"

His fur bristled with indignation. "They are not! We make gunpowder, we cast iron and smelt steel, we have spyglasses to help our steerers guide us from star to star. We are no savages huddling in caves or shooting at each other with bows and arrows."

His speech, of course, was not that neat or simple. He had to backtrack, to use elaborate circumlocutions, to playact to make Hildachesta understand. She scratched her head in the gesture of puzzlement he had come to recognize. She said, "We have known all these things you mention for hundreds of years, but we did not think anyone could walk—damn, I keep saying that instead of 'travel'—faster than light. How did your people learn to do that?"

"We discovered it for ourselves," he said proudly. "We did not have to learn it from some other starfaring race, as many folk do."

"But *how* did you discover it?" she persisted.

"How do I know? I'm a soldier; what do I care for such things? Who knows who invented gunpowder or found out about using bellows in a smithy to get the fire hot enough to melt iron? These things happen, that's all.''

She broke off the questions early that day.

''It's humiliating,'' Hilda Chester said. ''If these fool aliens had waited a few more years before they came, we likely would have blown ourselves to kingdom come without ever knowing there was more real estate around. Christ, from what the Roxolani say, races that scarcely know how to work iron fly starships and never think twice about it.''

''Except when the starships don't get home,'' Charlie Ebbets answered. His tie was in his pocket and his collar open against Pasadena's fierce summer heat, although the Caltech Atheneum was efficiently air-conditioned. Along with so many other engineers and scientists, he depended on linguists like Hilda Chester for a link to the aliens.

''I don't quite understand it myself,'' she said. ''Apart from the hyperdrive and contragravity, the Roxolani are backwards, almost primitive. And the other species out there must be the same, or someone would have overrun them long since.''

Ebbets said, ''Once you see it, the drive is amazingly simple. The research crews say anybody could have stumbled over the principle at almost any time in our history. The best guess is that most races did come across it, and once they did, why, all their creative energy would naturally go into refining and improving it.''

''But we missed it,'' Hilda said slowly, ''and so our technology developed in a different way.''

''That's right. That's why the Roxolani don't know anything about controlled electricity, to say nothing of atomics. And the thing is, as well as we can tell so far, the hyperdrive and contragravity don't have the ancillary applications the electromagnetic spectrum does. All they do is move things from here to there in a hurry.''

''That should be enough at the moment,'' Hilda said. Ebbets nodded. There were almost nine billion people jammed onto the Earth, half of them hungry. Now, suddenly, there were places for them to go and a means to get them there.

''I think,'' Ebbets said musingly, ''we're going to be an awful surprise to the peoples out there.''

It took Hilda a second to see what he was driving at. ''If that's a joke, it's not funny. It's been a hundred years since the last war of conquest.''

"Sure—they've gotten too expensive and too dangerous. But what kind of fight could the Roxolani or anyone else at their level of technology put up against us? The Aztecs and Incas were plenty brave. How much good did it do them against the Spaniards?"

"I hope we've gotten smarter in the last five hundred years," Hilda said. All the same, she left her sandwich half eaten. She found she was not hungry any more.

"Ransisc!" Togram exclaimed as the senior steerer limped into his cubicle. Ransisc was thinner than he had been a few moons before, aboard the misnamed *Indomitable*. His fur had grown out white around several scars Togram did not remember.

His air of amused detachment had not changed, though. "Tougher than bullets, are you, or didn't the humans think you were worth killing?"

"The latter, I suspect. With their firepower, why should they worry about one soldier more or less?" Togram said bitterly. "I didn't know you were still alive, either."

"Through no fault of my own, I assure you," Ransisc said. "Olgren, next to me—" His voice broke off. It was not possible to be detached about everything.

"What are you doing here?" the captain asked. "Not that I'm not glad to see you, but you're the first Roxolan face I've set eyes on since—" It was his turn to hesitate.

"Since we landed." Togram nodded in relief at the steerer's circumlocution. Ransisc went on, "I've seen several others before you. I suspect we're being allowed to get together so the humans can listen to us talking with each other."

"How could they do that?" Togram asked, then answered his own question: "Oh, the recorders, of course." He perforce used the English word. "Well, we'll fix that."

He dropped into Oyag, the most widely spoken language on a planet the Roxolani had conquered fifty years before. "What's going to happen to us, Ransisc?"

"Back on Roxolan, they'll have realized something's gone wrong by now," the steerer answered in the same tongue.

That did nothing to cheer Togram. "There are so many ways to lose ships," he said gloomily. "And even if the High Warmaster does send another fleet after us, it won't have any more luck than we did. These gods-accursed humans have too many war-machines." He paused and took a long, moody pull at a bottle of vodka. The flavored liquors the locals brewed made him sick, but vodka he liked. "How is it they have all these machines and we don't, or any race we know of? They must be wizards, selling their souls to the demons for knowledge."

Ransisc's nose twitched in disagreement. "I asked one of their savants the same question. He gave me back a poem by a human named Hail or Snow or something of that sort. It was about someone who stood at a fork in the road and ended up taking the less-used track. That's what the humans did. Most races find the hyperdrive and go traveling. The humans never did, and so their search for knowledge went in a different direction."

"Didn't it!" Togram shuddered at the recollection of that brief, terrible combat. "Guns that spit dozens of bullets without reloading, cannon mounted on armored platforms that move by themselves, rockets that follow their targets by themselves . . . And there are the things we didn't see, the ones the humans only talk about—the bombs that can blow up a whole city, each one by itself."

"I don't know if I believe that," Ransisc said.

"I do. They sound afraid when they speak of them."

"Well, maybe. But it's not just the weapons they have. It's the machines that let them see and talk to one another from far away; the machines that do their reckoning for them; their recorders and everything that has to do with them. From what they say of their medicine, I'm almost tempted to believe you and think they are wizards—they actually know what causes their diseases, and how to cure or even prevent them. And their farming: this planet is far more crowded than any I've seen or heard of, but it grows enough for all these humans."

Togram sadly waggled his ears. "It seems so unfair. All that they got, just by not stumbling onto the hyperdrive."

"They have it now," Ransisc reminded him. "Thanks to us."

The Roxolani looked at each other, appalled. They spoke together: "What have we done?"

EDITOR'S INTRODUCTION TO:

DELUSIONS OF SOVIET WEAKNESS
by Edward N. Luttwak

It is axiomatic that one must never underestimate the enemy If the Soviets are not giants, neither are they midgets.

They do have weaknesses, and in recent years a spate of books showing those weaknesses have enjoyed wide popularity. One, Tom Clancy's *The Hunt For Red October*, was one of the most enjoyable books I've read this year. There was also General Hackett's series of works in which the West loses all the battles of World War III, but eventually triumphs because of internal stresses within the Soviet Empire.

I fervently hope that these books reflect the true state of affairs inside the Soviet military machine; but I am much afraid that there is an element of wishful thinking at work here.

Without military power the Soviet Union is no more than a rather large conglomerate of backward and undeveloped countries. Despite spectaculars like the Moscow subway, their rail and surface road net is primitive. They have yet to achieve the agricultural triumphs of Czarist times. Industrial production is low and quality of goods is lower.

We see this and naturally assume that military structure is equally fouled up. Alas, that may well be no more than hope, and dangerous hope at that. Fortunately we have Edward Luttwak to give us warning.

It is not often that scholars have great influence in their own lifetimes. Professor Edward Luttwak is an exception. His *The Pentagon and the Art of War* (1984, Simon and Schuster, ISBN 0-671-52432-1) has become widely read, not only among military people, but in Congress and the White House; and is required reading for those who would understand the current ferment among strategic planners.

Dr. Luttwak is a Senior Fellow in Strategic Studies at Georgetown University's Center for Strategic and International Studies, and includes among his previous works *The Israeli Army*, and *The Political Uses of Sea Power*.

In summer, 1985, my wife and I traveled extensively in Europe. The trip was made much more enjoyable by my copy of Luttwak's *The Grand Strategy of the Roman Empire*, for with its help I found and understood the peculiar boundaries of Roman power from Frankfurt to the Danube.

DELUSIONS OF SOVIET WEAKNESS
Edward N. Luttwak

In recent years, entire books have appeared which argue that the Soviet armed forces are much weaker than they seem. Citing refugee accounts or personal experience, they depict the pervasive technical incompetence, drunkenness, corruption, and bleak apathy of officers and men. Drunken officers and faked inspections, Turkic conscripts who cannot understand orders in Russian drowning in botched river-crossing tests, the harsh lives of ill-fed, ill-housed, and virtually unpaid Soviet conscripts, and a pervasive lack of adequate training fill these accounts.

It is odd how all these stories (each true, no doubt) contrast with the daily evidence of the routine operations of the Soviet armed forces. Merely keeping its warships seaworthy and supplied in distant and often stormy waters demands a great deal of discipline and expertise from the officers and men of the Soviet navy. Even more skill is needed to carry out successfully the missile launches and gunnery trials that are also part of the Soviet naval routine. Likewise, we have the evidence of Soviet air operations; they too require a great deal of competence, both in the daily training sorties of the fighters and in the long-range flights of the bombers and transports.

Nor can the Soviet army fake all the disciplined maintenance, tight planning, and skills needed to assemble, move, and operate the many thousands of complicated armored vehicles, hundreds of helicopters, and countless smaller weapons in its exercises. It only takes a little drunken inattention or technical incompetence, or mere apathy by maintenance crews, to cause an aircraft to crash; a little more can sink a ship; and the delicate gear box of a battle tank is easily wrecked.

It is true that at fairly regular intervals we learn of spectacular failures in the upkeep of the Soviet armed forces. Breakdowns at sea lead to much photography of submarines adrift in the ocean and to much speculation over possible radiation leaks. Word of plane crashes reaches us now and then, and most recently there was solid evidence of huge explosions in the weapon stores of the Northern Fleet in the Kola peninsula. It is perfectly probable that Soviet standards of maintenance are lower than those of the United States, but the difference is scarcely of dramatic consequence. All armed forces, including those of the United States, have their collisions, their air crashes, their catastrophic breakdowns. The Soviet armed forces may well have more than their share. Yet it was never by superior efficiency that first Russia and then the Soviet Union became so very powerful, but rather by a combination of numbers, persistent strategies, and a modest technical adequacy.

When the actual record of war is assessed, not from official accounts but from the testimony of those who were there, it becomes quite clear that battles are not won by perfection but rather by the supremacy of forces that are 5-percent effective over forces that are 2-percent effective. In peacetime, when all the frictions of war are absent, when there is no enemy ready to thwart every enterprise, effectiveness may rise to dizzy levels of 50 or 60 percent—which means, of course, that filling in the wrong form, posting to the wrong place, supplying the wrong replacement parts, assigning the wrong training times, selecting the wrong officers, and other kinds of errors are merely normal. Matters cannot be otherwise, because military organizations are much larger than the manageable groupings of civilian life that set our standards of competence; and because their many intricate tasks must be performed not by life-career specialists like those who run factories, hospitals, symphony orchestras, and even government offices, but by transients who are briefly trained—short-service conscripts in the case of the Soviet armed forces.

Actual alcoholism, in the severe, clinical sense, is now epidemic in the Soviet Union, where so many lead bleak lives, no longer alleviated by the once vibrant hope of a fast-approaching better future. So drunkenness is no doubt pervasive in the Soviet armed forces. But Russians have always been great drinkers. Drunk they defeated Napoleon, and drunk again they defeated Hitler's armies and advanced all the way to Berlin. All these stories of corruption are also undoubtedly authentic. But no great military empire is likely to be undone by generals who procure villas through corrupt dealings, nor by sergeants who take the odd ruble off a conscript; Anglo-Saxon morality makes much of these things, history much less. Corruption in the higher ranks can demoralize the troops—but not if it is accepted as a normal part of life.

On the question of loyalty, even less need be said. Should the Soviet Union start a war, only to experience a series of swift defeats, it is perfectly possible that mutinies would follow against the Kremlin's oppressive and most unjust rule. But if the initial war operations were successful, it would be foolish to expect that private disloyalty would emerge to undo victory and disintegrate the armed forces. There will always be a small minority of lonely heroes with the inner resources to act against the entire power of the world's largest and most complete dictatorship. The rest of us weaker souls will stay in the safety of the crowd—and the crowd will not rebel against a uniquely pervasive police system at the very time when successful war is adding to its prestige, and the laws of war are making its sanctions more terrible.

Only one claim can be allowed: it is true that the ethnic composition of the Soviet population is changing, with non-Russians making up an increasing proportion of the total. This creates problems of loyalty that are unknown in the United States, because in the Soviet Union, distinct nationalities persist with their own languages, ethnic sentiments, and sometimes strong antagonism to the Russian master-people. As the proportion of non-Russian conscripts increases, language problems also increase, and because many of these conscripts come from backward nationalities, they are harder to train in modern military skills, even if they do know the Russian language. There is also a greater potential for ethnic strife, already manifest in barrack-room fights.

In the *very* long run it is possible and even likely that the non-Russians, or at least the larger non-European peoples—the Uzbeks, Kazakhs, Tadzhiks, and so on—will demand full national independence and struggle for it, eventually causing the dissolution of the Soviet empire, which is the last survivor of the European empires that dominated much of the entire world until a generation ago. Demography is indeed a powerful and relentless force, but slow in effect. In 1970, out of a total Soviet population of 242 million, 74 percent was Slavic and 53 percent actually Russian. (Some of the fiercest antagonisms are between Russians and other Slavs.) In that year, there were 35 million people of Muslim origin (mostly Turkic), just under 15 percent of the Soviet total. By the year 2000 it is projected that the Muslims will account for more than a fifth (21–25 percent) of the total population of 300 million, with Russians at 47 percent and all Slavs at 65 percent. Naturally the change will be felt sooner and more strongly in the younger groups of military age. For example, out of the 2.1 million males projected to be at the conscription age of eighteen in 1985, the non-Slavs will account for more than 35 percent, and quite a few of them will not know enough Russian to obtain the full benefit of training.

But of course the armed forces of a multinational empire know a thing or two about managing diverse nationalities. Those with a high percentage of dissidents, such as the Estonians, Western Ukrainians, and Jews, can be safely employed in military-construction battalions, which are virtually unarmed, or in other support units far from combat; those with many illiterates or conscripts whose Russian is poor, such as the Kirghiz, Turkmen, and Tadzhiks, can be placed in the undemanding mechanized infantry of second-line divisions. There are problems, but they remain quite manageable. The real problem of national self-assertion is for the distant future.

So far nothing precise has been said about the most obvious attribute of the Soviet armed forces: their sheer numerical strength. The gross totals are well known, and mean little. As against the 30 large divisions of the US army and marine corps, active and reserve, the Soviet army has 194 divisions, smaller by a third on average but just as heavily armed. One-third are fully manned, one-third are half and half, and the rest are mostly manned by reservists—but all Soviet divisions are fully equipped, even if not with the latest and best, and all have a full-time professional cadre, even when their line units are manned by reservists. The Soviet tactical air force has some 6,000 strike aircraft, fighters, and fighter-bombers, less advanced on average but also of more recent vintage than the 5,600 or so equivalent aircraft of the US air force, navy, and marines. Another 1,250 interceptor-fighters serve in the territorial air defenses (along with more than 9,600 anti-aircraft missiles), and the Soviet navy's land-based aviation also includes some fighter-class aircraft.

For the Soviet navy, one ship list prepared by the US navy shows 1,324 "surface combatants," as against its own 285 surface warships; 367 submarines, as against 99; and 770 auxiliaries, as against its own 105 logistic and support ships. The figures are of course grossly inflated, but even the most sober count that excludes the old, the inactive, and the small would still list 290 major Soviet surface warships, 119 nuclear and 157 diesel-attack submarines, and 360 land-based naval bombers, of which 100 are modern machines of transoceanic range.

No true military balance is made of mere lists, however. The place and the time, the allies present on each side, and the circumstances of the nation and of the particular theater of war will govern what can be achieved, and indeed what forces can be deployed at all. No estimate can be made for expeditionary ventures in undefined theaters of hypothetical war—except to say that the power of the Soviet military wanes drastically as the distance from the Soviet Union increases, much more so than does that of the American forces, which are far better equipped to reach and fight in faraway places. But we can make rather solid estimates for the continental theaters of war directly adjacent to the Soviet Union—in Europe, the Middle East, and northeast Asia. The results are grim.

In the five possible war theaters of the North Atlantic alliance—northern Norway, the "central" front in Germany, northeast Italy, the Thrace frontier of Greece and Turkey with Bulgaria, and the Turkish border with the Soviet Union in remote eastern Anatolia—it is clear that the ground forces of both the United States and its allies, those already deployed in peacetime and those to be mobilized, would be outnumbered, outgunned, or both. By adding absolutely everything on the books—including Turkish infantry and the American National Guard, in addition to the manned forces actually in place—the total number of alliance divisions for the five theaters rises to 144, as against a combined Warsaw Pact total of 170. That is scarcely a catastrophic imbalance, and the situation looks even easier for the alliance when we recall that the Warsaw Pact total includes the divisions of rebellious Poland, unwilling Hungary, restive Czechoslovakia, doubtful East Germany, and uncooperative Rumania.

If we make a somewhat finer comparison, however, including only tank and mechanized divisions on the alliance side, thus removing a mass of ill-armed and immobile infantry forces of low military value, while at the same time eliminating *all* the non-Soviet forces of the Warsaw Pact, 80 divisions of the alliance remain, while the Soviet army alone has 109—*after* leaving 78 Soviet divisions to face the Chinese border, occupy Afghanistan, and control Iran's long border. These 109 Soviet divisions are smaller than the Western divisions, but no longer by much, and they do belong to one army under one central authority, whereas the Western total is split among the armies of the United States, Canada, Britain, Norway, Denmark, West Germany, Holland, France, Portugal, Italy, Greece, and Turkey—and the French divisions are not under alliance command and not necessarily available, the Greek divisions are of uncertain allegiance, and the American reserve forces must first be mobilized, then filled out and updated in training, then transported across the ocean.

If we include the non-mechanized forces of high military value (such as the American and Soviet airborne divisions), and exclude alliance forces not rapidly available for reinforcement, the realistic alliance count is on the order of 56 divisions, the Soviet, 114.

The situation in the air over the European fronts is similar: by the fullest count, the Soviet Union alone could muster 4,700 fighters, fighter-bombers, and interceptors, without reinforcement from other theaters; the Western air forces in Europe hold a total of 3,045, of which not more than two-thirds can be considered modern, including all the 594 American fighters and fighter-bombers.

To consider the military balance in the Persian Gulf, with Iran as the possible theater of war, no computation is even needed: against a maximum of four or five American divisions that could eventually be deployed with great difficulties and greater risk, the Soviet Union could send 20 with great ease.

On the last of the "continental" fronts, which cuts across the peninsula of Korea—where sudden war is all too possible, but where a large Soviet intervention now seems most unlikely—it is the Korean forces on both sides that now make the balance. But should Moscow choose to do so, it could add much more to the North Korean strength than the United States could add to that of South Korea.

Thus on every possible major front we encounter the powerful arithmetic of the Soviet army. By integrating reserves with active units and providing full equipment, the Soviet army is a very effective producer of armor-mechanized divisions. Not at all suited for overseas expeditions, dependent on rail transport for large movements between the different fronts separated by several thousand miles, these divisions are nevertheless powerful instruments of offensive war wherever the Soviet Union may seek to enlarge its empire.

With Western air power now offset to a large degree by Soviet air defenses, and with naval power only relevant in the less critical theaters remote from Europe, the Middle East, and East Asia, the ground forces are the basic currency of East-West strategy. Because of the Soviet Union's energetic countering efforts, its advantage in ground forces can no longer be offset by Western strengths in other forms of military power, including (as we shall see later) nuclear.

The combat value of the mass of the Soviet armed forces remains untested by the terrible urgencies of war. But it is possible to estimate their organizational, operational, and tactical competence—if not their fighting spirit—by observing exercises, which show quite clearly that the Soviet armed forces can now execute complicated military operations on a very large scale.

Specifically, we know that the Soviet army can assemble, supply, and send out its long columns of armor and considerable artillery to defeat enemy fronts, not in a steamroller action of costly head-on attacks, as in the past, but rather in quick probes—to find gaps and weak sectors, and to follow with fast-paced penetrations into the rear to achieve great encirclements; to overrun forward air bases, depots, and command centers; to "hug" cities so that tactical nuclear attacks against Soviet advancing forces would hit allied population centers (and would thus be inhibited); and to seize large extents of territory in so doing.

At the same time, raiding forces of the airborne divisions, of the special helicopter-assault brigades, of the "diversionary" and commando units of both military and civilian intelligence, can fly into, parachute into, or infiltrate the deep rear in order to seize nuclear-weapons storage sites, attack headquarters and communications centers, sabotage aircraft in their hangars and fire across crowded runways, ambush road convoys, and spread havoc by their mere presence—and by the inevitable tide of false reports about their doings and undoings.

We know that the Soviet air force has enough aircraft, enough bases, and enough quality in men and machines to deny air supremacy to whatever Western air forces it might meet in Europe, the Persian Gulf, or East Asia. Its fighter-interceptors, along with their anti-aircraft defenses, could keep Western air forces from doing much harm to the Soviet army; its long-range strike fighters could reach and bomb Western airfields even in the deepest rear, and its fighter-bombers and ground-attack aircraft could disrupt if not seriously reduce Western ground forces. In theory, Western air forces could eventually prevail in the contest for air supremacy—if the Soviet ground forces had not by then overrun their airfields. One thing is certain: Western air power can give little help to the ground forces in the first days of a war—precisely when air support would be needed most urgently.

We know that the Soviet navy can send out its aircraft, group its ships, and deploy its attack submarines in a concerted worldwide action to stage simultaneous missile strikes on American carrier task forces at sea, certainly in the Indian Ocean, eastern Mediterranean, and northeast Pacific, and possibly in the Atlantic and eastern Pacific as well. Though lacking the floating air power that remains the costly center-piece of the American navy, the Soviet Union can neverthe-less soberly estimate that *if* it attacked first, it could destroy the main fighting strength of the American navy actually at sea. In any event, Soviet attack submarines would endanger the sea connection between the United States and American forces overseas.

So far, not a word has been said about the entire subject of Soviet nuclear weapons. This separation and implied down-grading of the matter corresponds to the strategic logic of the Soviet position against the West. Moscow's protestations of reluctance to use nuclear weapons against the West (China is another matter) may be perfectly sincere. Just as the invader is always peaceful—for he seeks only to advance and not to fight, while it is his victim who causes war by resisting—so the Soviet Union has every reason to avoid nuclear war, because it is now stronger than the West in non-nuclear military forces. Fully able to invade Europe, Iran, or Korea without having to use nuclear weapons, the Soviet Union now needs its nuclear weapons mainly to neutralize the nuclear deterrence of the United States, Britain, and France. Just as it is always the victim who must make war to resist aggression, so the West must rely on the fear of nuclear war to obtain security, by threatening nuclear attacks against invading Soviet forces if they cannot be stopped by non-nuclear means.

To deter such "tactical" attacks—that is, to inhibit the first level of the Western nuclear deterrent in order to restore the full value of its armies for intimidation or actual invasion—the Soviet Union has built up its own "tactical" nuclear forces, in the form of artillery shells, rockets, short-range missiles, and bombs for fighter-class aircraft and strike bombers. The Soviet Union can therefore reply in kind should its invading armies have their victories spoiled by nuclear attacks.

If the West begins to strike at invading Soviet columns with tactical nuclear weapons, the Soviet Union can, in a simple military calculation, use its own tactical nuclear weapons to blast open paths through the alliance front, so that even badly reduced and shocked invasion columns can continue to advance, eventually to reach and "hug" the cities—thereby forcing the alliance to stop its nuclear attacks. In the far more meaningful political calculation, the mere existence of large and very powerful Soviet tactical nuclear forces should inhibit to some extent any Western use of the same weapons.

But the alliance has a most significant advantage that arises from its purely defensive character: at this first level, the entire onus of beginning a war rests on the Soviet Union; it is by *its* decision that the movement of the armies would begin; it is by *its* decision that the invasion of Western territory would continue so that tactical nuclear weapons would be used against its forces, raising the conflict to the second level. Hence the Soviet tactical nuclear forces are not sufficient to dissuade Western use of the same weapons. The Soviets could only use them to achieve physical results (blasting gaps through the front) that would not begin to remedy the catastrophic deterioration of their position from a successful nonnuclear invasion to a nuclear conflict in which no good result could be achieved.

Therefore, to inhibit Western tactical nuclear forces much more powerfully, the Soviet Union maintains another category of nuclear weapons of longer ("intermediate") range, which threaten the cities of Europe, as well as large military targets in the deep rear, such as air bases. At present, the celebrated SS-20 ballistic missile is the main weapon in this category, which also includes Soviet strike aircraft such as the Su-24 ("Fencer"). With these weapons the interaction be-

tween Soviet and Western military power reaches its third
level.

Of late, the alliance has begun to deploy intermediate-range
cruise and Pershing-2 missiles in Britain, West Germany, and
Italy (more are to be deployed in Belgium and Holland).
Because they are widely regarded as an entirely different
category of weapons, they *are* different politically: the huge
controversy surrounding their deployment may enable the
cruise and Pershing-2 missiles to have a counter-intimidation
impact since public opinion views them as an answer to the
SS-20's. To that extent, they are *politically* distinct from the
far more abundant aircraft bombs and all the other nuclear
weapons officially described as tactical. In addition, the new
missiles may be more reliable in reaching their targets than
strike aircraft with nuclear bombs.

But *strategically* the cruise and Pershing-2 missiles are *not*
different from the tactical nuclear weapons of the alliance:
they too serve to neutralize the non-nuclear strength of the
Soviet army, and they too are neutralized in turn by the
Soviet nuclear counterthreat against the cities of the alliance.
As a matter of physical fact, the cruise and Pershing-2 missiles do not threaten anything not already threatened by alliance weapons classified as tactical; specifically, they do not
threaten Soviet cities any more than the tactical nuclear bombs
of longer-ranged alliance strike aircraft. Both those aircraft
and the new missiles could reach cities in the western part of
the Soviet Union; neither is meant to be used against those
cities; for both, the relevant targets are Soviet military forces
and their bases and command centers.

To neutralize the Soviet third-level threat against the alliance cities in Europe, the new missiles would have to
counterthreaten Soviet cities with an equal certainty of complete destruction; because of their vulnerability and range
limits, the new missiles cannot do that. Hence the new missiles cannot take the strategic interaction to a fourth level,
where the Soviet invasion potential is once again neutralized.
The third level thus leaves the Soviet Union in control of the
situation, because with or without the cruise and Pershing-2
missiles, the alliance can protect its frontal defenses only at
the risk of provoking Soviet nuclear attacks against the cities
that those same frontal forces are supposed to protect.

It takes a fourth level to restore a war-avoiding balance, in

which this Soviet third-level nuclear threat is itself deterred
by American intercontinental nuclear forces capable of inflict-
ing catastrophic destruction on the Soviet Union. Then the
Western "tactical" nuclear forces can once again deter a
Soviet (non-nuclear) invasion, and the Soviet Union's invasion potential yields neither war options nor the power to
intimidate the European allies of the United States.

The Soviet response would be to seek a fifth level of
strategic interaction, where the American deterrent would be
neutralized by the threat of destroying the intercontinental
nuclear force if any were used against Soviet military forces,
and American cities if any Soviet cities were destroyed. If the
United States government would withdraw its threat of a
nuclear attack on the Soviet Union in response to a Soviet
attack on European cities, or if American intercontinental
nuclear forces could not plausibly threaten the Soviet Union,
the strategic interaction would revert to the third level, in
which the Soviet threat against the cities of the allies inhibits
the West from using its tactical nuclear forces, thus making
the world safe for the Soviet army.

One hears it said endlessly that the competition between
American and Soviet intercontinental nuclear forces is not
only costly and dangerous but also futile, because each side
can already destroy the population of the other "many times
over." That, however, is a vulgar misunderstanding. It is not
to destroy the few hundred cities and larger towns of each
side—easy targets neither protected nor concealed—that intercontinental nuclear forces continue to be developed. The
purpose is not to threaten cities and towns already abundantly
threatened, to "overkill" populations, but rather to threaten
the intercontinental nuclear forces themselves: the missiles in
their fortified housings, the bomber bases and missile-submarine
ports, and the centers of military command and communication for all those forces. Thus there are several thousand
targets, as opposed to a few hundred cities and towns, and
many of those targets can only be destroyed by very accurate
warheads.

At the fifth level of interaction, each side strives to reduce
the nuclear-attack strength of the other, by defenses when
possible (notably anti-aircraft, against the bombers), but mainly
by offensive weapons accurate enough to destroy the weapons
of the other side. And it is not enough to be able to threaten

the destruction of the weapons: to make the threat effective it is also necessary to demonstrate the ability to destroy them without at the same time destroying the nearby population centers. For if that happens, then all the strategy and all rational purposes come to an end, as the victim will respond by launching his surviving weapons (there will always be some, perhaps many) against the cities of the attacker. For the United States, the competition at this point is driven by the goal of keeping the strategic interaction at the fourth level, where the Soviet army stands deterred; for the Soviet Union, the goal is to reach the fifth level, where American nuclear deterrence is itself deterred.

Because of the goals now pursued, contrary to widespread belief, intercontinental nuclear weapons are steadily becoming *less* destructive in gross explosive power. The goal of each side is to make its forces more accurate and more controllable so that they can destroy small and well-protected targets, and no more. During the 1960's, the United States was still producing weapons of 5 and 9 megatons, while the Soviet Union was producing 20-megaton warheads; nowadays, most new American warheads have yields of less than half a megaton, while most Soviet warheads are below one megaton. As new weapons replace old, the total destructive power of the two intercontinental nuclear arsenals is steadily declining. (A "freeze," incidentally, would put an end to that process.)

The state of the American-Soviet intercontinental nuclear balance is the basic index, the Dow-Jones, of world politics. Directly, or through sometimes subtle hopes and fears, it shapes much of what American and Soviet leaders feel free to do in world affairs. Two things are quite obvious about the current intercontinental nuclear balance. Both sides can easily destroy the cities and larger towns of the other. And neither can launch an all-out strike that would fully disarm the other's weapons. The competition is now between these two extremes, as each side seeks to protect as many of its weapons as possible while threatening the other's weapons.

Although the United States is by no means inferior across the board, category by category, it is impossible to extract an optimistic estimate from the numbers. There are 1,398 Soviet intercontinental ballistic missiles in underground housings, as against 1,000 American Minuteman missiles; some of the latter have been modernized and others have not, but the Soviet missiles are much larger, with many more warheads (almost 6,000 versus 2,100), which are no longer less accurate than their American counterparts (as was the case till quite recently). No expert disputes the accuracy and reliability of the more modern Soviet ballistic missiles—the four-warhead SS-17 (150 in service), the huge SS-18, with as many as ten warheads (308 in service), and the slightly less modern but more abundant six-warhead SS-19 (330 in service). The combined Soviet force clearly out-matches the 450 one-warhead Minuteman 2's and 550 three-warhead Minuteman 3's. Specifically, the Soviet land-based missiles could now destroy all but a fraction of their American counterparts, while the latter could not hope to do the same to the Soviet force.

The remaining defect of the Soviet land-based ballistic-missile force is that its warheads are not yet small enough to make the threat of a "clean" disarming strike believable. (The smallest warheads are of half-megaton size, and some are almost a full megaton.) The Soviet Union is now developing an entire new group of land-based ballistic missiles: undoubtedly they will be more accurate, and their warheads will be smaller. The new American MX missiles now in production are also meant to be more accurate, although their original purpose was greater survivability, which is dubious, since they will be placed inside fixed housings, though they were built for mobility.

The Soviet force of submarine-carried ballistic missiles is also much larger than the American, with 980 missiles as opposed to 640, but the quality difference is still so great that the American force remains superior. In the first place, most Soviet submarine-launched missiles are still one-warhead weapons, while their American counterparts have multiple warheads. As a result, the Soviet Union has fewer than 1,000 separate warheads in its submarine force, as against more than 5,000 (much smaller) American warheads.

A greater defect in a force that is, or should be, the ultimate strategic reserve, the best-protected of all in the intercontinental category, is the fact that all the Soviet submarines, except perhaps the very latest, are much noisier and thus more easily detected than their American counterparts.*

---

*Among the 80 Soviet ballistic-missile submarines in service, some 22 are ancient diesel and early vintage nuclear boats that have every right to

This is all the more striking because the Soviet submarines are much newer on average: between 1974 and 1984 the Soviet Union built 35 Delta-class submarines and one huge Typhoon, as against just four bigger still Ohio-class submarines built by the United States. On the other hand, the latest Soviet submarine-launched missile, the SS-N-20, has such a long range (8,300 kilometers) that it can reach most targets without requiring the submarine carrying it to leave safe waters near the Soviet northern coasts.

Throughout the long years of strategic competition, the Soviet force of intercontinental bombers remained much smaller, and its aircraft much inferior, though this may be about to change. In the latest count, the 297 American bombers, mostly ancient but much modernized B-52's, can be compared to a total of 273 Soviet bombers, including roughly 130 Backfires that are modern and supersonic, but not quite sufficient in range (5,500 kilometers), as well as a greater number of Tu-95's, an aircraft as old as the B-52 but much inferior in every way. Only recently has the Soviet Union started producing a true modern intercontinental bomber, the Blackjack, which is externally similar to the new American B-15, and is destined to be electronically less advanced but also much faster.

For all their technical inferiority, Soviet bombers are still formidable, simply because the United States has very weak air defenses. While American bombers would have to contend with 1,250 Soviet interceptor-fighters and almost 10,000 anti-aircraft missiles to reach their targets, Soviet bombers would virtually have a free ride against 90 air force and 180 National Guard interceptors, and not a single missile.

The Soviet Union's destruction of the Korean airliner (flight KAL 007), on September 1, 1983, has been interpreted by some as proof of the incompetence of Soviet territorial air defenses. In one version, which assumes that the attack was made in error, the Soviet radar network is judged grossly incompetent for having failed to distinguish between KAL 007 and the very much smaller RC-135 electronic-reconnaissance aircraft (supposedly the intended victim). In a second version, the mere fact that KAL 007 was not actually shot down until

be noisy, but these account for fewer than 60 of the 980 missile tubes. The bulk of the force should be much less noisy than it is, raising some interesting questions about Soviet design, or perhaps strategy.

two-and-one-half hours after it first entered Soviet airspace over the Kamchatka peninsula is treated as a failure of the system, regardless of whether the aircraft was correctly identified.

These interpretations illustrate very well the difficulty of making operational judgments in a vacuum; the mere fact that the Korean airliner *was* found and reached by a Soviet fighter, that a missile was launched correctly, that it detonated and destroyed a large aircraft is simply taken for granted, as if these were easy things. And indeed they should be for any air-defense system at war, operating day in and day out, with all the habits of combat operations. But on September 1, 1983, until KAL 007 arrived on the scene, Soviet air defenses were at peace, as they have been for almost forty years. To monitor the air space closely, to have the fighters ready at the end of the runway, to have pilots find the target, to have missiles fully operational—to have all this when the action suddenly starts after decades of inaction is not easy at all. The interception of KAL 007 should be compared to the non-interception by American air defenses of more than one Cuban airliner that violated US flight corridors on the Havana-Mexico City route.

Even a delay of two-and-one-half hours would not be significant. But as it happens, the delay was nowhere near so long; KAL 007 first penetrated and then left Soviet airspace (over Kamchatka), before reentering Soviet airspace (near Sakhalin). Its first penetration was very brief, a matter of minutes and forgivable even by the Soviet Union. Its second led to its destruction in short order.

The misidentification theory takes for granted that a 747 can very easily be distinguished from an RC-135. That is simply not the case; identification depends, among other things (size, aspect, frequencies, type of radar and displays), on atmospheric conditions. But as it happens, it is certain that the Soviet air-defense controllers knew exactly what they were destroying; this is one case where the negative evidence prevails. As in the Sherlock Holmes story, the dog that did not bark is definite proof: though Soviet air-defense controllers could have confused the KAL 007 radar image with that of an RC-135, the scheduled Korean Air Lines flight from Anchorage, Alaska, to Seoul, Korea, which Soviet radar would routinely track, had to be *somewhere* on the radar screens. If it was not, only two possibilities remained—either that KAL 007 had crashed into the sea without any signal at all, or else that the aircraft being intercepted was in fact KAL 007. So to believe in the misidentification theory, we have to assume that Soviet air-defense controllers not only confused the two radar images but believed that KAL 007 had mysteriously fallen out of the sky without even a few seconds in which to transmit a "mayday" call. Thus once again we must resist the seductive urge to believe in Soviet ineptness.

The Soviet Union continues to make a large effort in strategic defense, maintaining costly forces to fight what can be fought (the bombers and cruise missiles), doing all it can to develop anti-ballistic-missile defenses, and keeping up a nationwide civil-defense program combining highly realistic with merely symbolic arrangements, from shelters to evacuation. The United States by contrast is pursuing innovation in offensive weapons (cruise missiles for the bombers, surface ships, and attack submarines, and Trident-2 submarine-launched missiles) and exploring many highly advanced defensive schemes based on satellite-mounted weapons, but it has no serious civil defense.

One could add details and nuances to the estimate of the Soviet Union's intercontinental nuclear strength and homeland defenses, but the result would not change, for the two forces do not have the same task. The United States must rely on believable threats to use its intercontinental nuclear forces to offset the Soviet Union's non-nuclear superiority and "tactical" nuclear parity. Otherwise matters would stand at the third level, where there is nothing to stop Soviet military intimidation of America's allies—who then could scarcely remain allies. The Soviet Union by contrast need only make the American intercontinental nuclear threat unbelievable in order to recover the invasion potential of its armies, thus restoring their power to intimidate or actually invade. To do that the Soviet Union does not even need intercontinental nuclear superiority, which it is striving so hard to achieve. But the United States does need a margin of intercontinental nuclear strength merely to keep the overall military balance duly balanced.

Hence "parity" (shorthand for strategic-nuclear parity) is or should be fundamentally unacceptable to the United States. Any true parity between the intercontinental nuclear forces of each side must leave the United States militarily inferior in all the continental theaters where the Soviet army can muster its power—namely Europe, Iran (and thus the Persian Gulf), and Korea. And that is the situation that now prevails, the true cause of today's anxieties for world peace.

EDITOR'S INTRODUCTION TO:

THE DAY AND THE HOUR
by Duncan Lunan

Duncan Lunan is, in no particular order, an astronomer, a Scot, an artist, scientist, and author. He has built, in a park in Glasgow, Scotland, the first working "stonehenge," stone circle astronomical computer constructed since pre-historic times. His *New Worlds for Old* and *Man and the Planets* soberly discuss spacecraft and the colonization of other worlds; I highly recommend them.

When Duncan was last in the United States, Larry Niven and I spent a delightful evening with him, during which we consumed immense quantities of single malt scotch whiskey and discussed the universe, from the birth of stars to psychic experiences. It was an evening I will not forget, and one I hope some day to repeat.

In Volume Four of this series (*Day of the Tyrant*) we examined the view of English author John Brunner, who believes that Britain would do better to divest herself of nuclear weapons. He would rather see Britain "an indigestible lump in a communist empire" than a nuclear battlefield; a sentiment it's hard to disagree with if those are the only choices.

Duncan Lunan writes of a time when this has happened; when the Soviets have swept across Europe and have enjoyed their day in the sun; of a time when the warriors of Scotland may once more come down from their hills.

THE DAY AND THE HOUR
by Duncan Lunan

There was no snow to delay the unit's journey north from Salisbury. Though the stratosphere was still hazed with ice crystals, long-lived reminders of the jet aircraft now so scarce, and though veils of dust persisted still higher from the aftermath of World War Three, as the second century after the war wore on the 'years without a summer' were becoming less common. The transporter and escorts travelled all night, and came into Derby under a grey morning sky.

Johnson was taken to the General almost at once, and that in itself showed the seriousness of the situation. He had tried for years to gain the attention of the upper ranks in the British People's Army, to point out the implications of his discoveries and gain recognition and priority for the research, but always he had been blocked far down the chain of command. Major Gregory, as he then was, had been one of the first disbelievers to bar Johnson's way. Since then Gregory had changed his name to Gregori, and risen through the higher echelons into supreme command of the remaining British forces. Now some twist in the national emergency had reminded Gregori of Regressive Ballistics, and Johnson was being rushed to this meeting as if he alone could save the State.

"Captain Johnson, sir." The aide saluted and withdrew.

"You've made good time from Wiltshire, Captain. Come in, take a chair." Promotion had been kind to Gregori: he had gained weight and lost hair since Johnson met him last, but it looked well on him. Yet in his years in the backwater of research, Johnson's constant struggle for funding had made him hypersensitive to the moods of his superior officers, and behind Gregori's authority he sensed a profound—disquiet?—

discontent? "It looks as if we'll be in action in a few hours, so you'd better rest while you can."

"The Highlanders are still moving south, sir?"

"They are, Johnson. They stopped yesterday, but they were past Sheffield at first light today. Their mobility, I grieve to say, exceeds ours."

Johnson was shocked. Of course there had been rumours, dismissed as attempts of reactionaries to undermine the confidence of loyal soldiers, and he himself had never credited them. . . . "A ragged peasant army, outmaneuvering and outflanking the troops of the Soviet? Sir, I can't believe that!"

"Your pride in the armies of the Soviet does you credit," said Gregori. Was that—could it be—a hint of sarcasm? "Unfortunately, Captain, once they got through the Scottish lowlands there were relatively few of our glorious troops to oppose them. Most of our units in the north of England have been despatched to the continent, just as they were when the Young Pretender marched into England in 1745. As well as the trouble in Spain, which may do for the USSR what it did once for Napoleon, we are holding down both Hungary and Czechoslovakia yet again. As for Poland—you were going to say, Captain?"

Johnson had been through enough political education classes to think he knew a test when he saw one. "Surely, sir, on Marx's progressive view of history, the fluctuations of the dying monarchies have no relationship—"

Gregori cut him off with an impatient wave of his hand. "Much as we admire the progressive view of history, Captain, as practical military men we must consider the possibility that history may *appear* to repeat itself. It's apparent that there are two clear historical precedents for the situation facing us: the Jacobite rebellion, as I said, and before that—before that, Captain, are you a drinking man?"

To Johnson's astonishment, Gregori yanked open a filing cabinet drawer to reveal a bottle of vodka and two elegant glasses, which he transferred to the desk top with slightly too steady a hand. Had he been brought all this way overnight just to be put through elementary tests of character and political soundness by the commanding General of the People's Army? "Never, sir, while on duty," he answered woodenly.

"As you please," said Gregori, pouring himself a large measure. He half-turned to indicate the map of the British

Isles on the wall behind him. "Perhaps you have been too engrossed in your research to mark a disturbing trend in recent years. Increasingly the troops of other Soviet states have been withdrawn from Britain to suppress counter-revolutionary developments in Europe and Scandinavia. Now the British People's Army is taking over those security operations in Europe, while other Soviet troops are withdrawn to protect the Russian homeland from the barbarians in the ruins of Germany. Their attacks across the wastelands are becoming ever more serious. In short, Captain, our leaders in Moscow are calling the legions home." He waved at the bottle. "Still sure you won't join me?"

"No, thank you, sir." One of us has to keep a grip on reality, thought Johnson. He would have put the whole line of conversation down to the vodka, were Gregori's hands and voice not so steady. Nevertheless, as Gregori topped his own glass, the explanation was turning into a lecture.

"As I said before, Captain, we military men must take a pragmatic view of history. Rome had troubles remarkably similar to ours. They never mastered Scotland, 'Never conquered and not likely to be.' Though we've held Britain for a hundred and fifty years we've never been supreme beyond the Firths of Forth and Clyde. If we ever hoped to integrate that area with the USSR, the two bombs in the west of Scotland were a strategic mistake: if we had to do that we shouldn't have left Glasgow standing in between. The first two battalions of the brigade we sent in to occupy the Glasgow area disappeared in a manner unknown to military history since the Ninth Legion went north from the Wall."

He struck the map for emphasis. "When Castro looked at the map of Britain he cried, 'Ah, Scotland! The mountains!' Unfortunately the mountains remained in the hands of counter-revolutionaries. When the first punitive expedition went north from Edinburgh, after the eight months it took to clear the commandos out of the tunnels under the Castle there, it got precisely half-way across the Forth Road Bridge and then went crash to the sea-bed. It was rumoured at the time that they hadn't paid the toll. And so things continued in the Highlands to the present day, with the clan structure reforming as an underground movement, the old regiments regenerating as guerilla groups and arming themselves at our expense. Often they do better than we do with our own weapons: your 'dirty wee pict' is proving himself deadly at close quarters with a laser bayonet. You have Glaswegians treating it as a big brother to the photon flick-knife. It's my opinion, comparing this rising with Bonnie Prince Charlie's, that if the Scots get past Derby this time they'll never be stopped.''

This was too much for Johnson. "Oh, come now, sir. Reinforcements . . .''

"There will be no reinforcements,'' Gregori said grimly, staring into his glass. "Oh, some heavy machines are coming north from outside London. But there are no aircraft to lift them to us, and they won't reach us in time to do any good. The Scots will go 'round them, as they did the armour in the north of England, if they pass us here. All the troops we can spare from the south-east are already here, little more than a division, all told.''

So few! Johnson could scarcely believe it. But if it were true it would have been kept quiet . . . and it would explain why the budget for research was vanishingly small. "But sir? What about the troops from the West Country—there are two regiments almost on our doorstep. . . .''

"The West Country is in arms," said Gregori. "Drake's Drum, they say, is sounding again. Drake, the bourgeois adventurer, a pioneer of the capitalist era! They've a good marching song down there, I hear—whoever Trelawney was, we shouldn't have shot him.''

"What about the Welsh regiments—''

"Changing sides, I believe. Richard the Second had some trouble of the same kind, and as for Wales itself, they have the precedent of Owen Glendower—who outdid Ché himself, since Glendower was never caught. When the English claimed no invasions since 1066, we were already thinking of Britain as a unit. At the moment it seems that all the historical rebellions are recurring at once.''

Johnson was aghast. For all his skill in interpreting and exploiting the attitudes of senior officers—a survival skill, for the continuation of his research—he had remained a scientist, untouched by politics within the army or outside. What he saw in Gregori was an Englishman who had spent his life in the effort to become a Russian, and now suspected—incredibly, to Johnson—that he might have chosen the wrong side. Why had Gregori brought him here? Had the General perceived some way in which he, a humble captain in research, could save the revolution in England?

"Now you know how bad it is," said Gregori. "The battle

here in a few hours may stem the tide. If we lose, I think this
is the beginning of the end for the revolution, for the unity of
Europe and for the USSR as we know it. In our desire to
extend that revolution over all the globe, we've overstretched
our resources—technically, militarily and economically. It
would have been easier to colonize the moon than to reclaim
North America after the Last War, as we optimistically named
it. But we—Russia—panicked when we had a temporary
advantage, and Russia's guilt, Russia's attempted reparation,
has ruined us all. We're standing here today against the new
Dark Ages, Captain, and we're going to lose because we're
so few. Your discovery may serve to swing the balance, as a
last desperate chance. Can you do it?"

"I don't know, sir," Johnson stammered, caught unprepared in the middle of his analysis of Gregori. "It's only a
prototype . . . successful in a few controlled tests, untried in
battle conditions. . . . the paradoxes—"

"Courage, Captain! For the revolution, for the Soviet, for
the future of the world, today you stand in the breach!"
Outright sarcasm—not just the vodka. "Your field works.
You can project a shell backwards in time?"

"Regressive Ballistics, sir. We can fire a shell through the
field generated in front of the tank, and it will move backwards through time as its trajectory continues. At the maximum range of the gun we have, the shell is displaced only an
hour into the past."

"That hour may be enough, Captain," said Gregori. "We
shall fight ferociously, of course, but if we can last an hour
against the Scottish horde I shall be surprised. Over the
battle, however, Remotely Piloted Vehicles will record everything for transmission to my command post, and as we and
our computers analyse the battle we shall transmit the edited
highlights to you. An hour after battle is joined, you will
know which elements in the enemy advance were to prove
crucial; and on the empty battlefield, you will fire the shells
that are to change history."

"But sir, the firepower of our prototype rig—"

"If you recall, Captain, I asked for your shell specifica-
tions to be radioed ahead. Just an hour ago, an aircraft arrived
from Moscow with a consignment of the latest antimatter
shells, specially made for your puny gun." Gregori hefted the
vodka bottle. "This came with them, unrequested; intended
as a farewell gift, I suspect . . . but we shall see. It's just as

well the explosions will be an hour in the past, if your range is what you've reported! Was 120 mm the heaviest piece you could requisition?''

"We couldn't get any guns at all for research, sir. We . . . we dug this one out of the ground.''

"Out of the ground! What, a wreck from the Battle of Stonehenge?''

"Yes, sir. The radioactivity's almost gone now, of course, but it took quite a while to make it serviceable.''

"It must have done,'' said Gregori with respect. "My confidence in you is restored, Captain. I was beginning to put you down as a mere researcher, lacking in initiative. Perhaps if anyone can turn the tide of history. . . . But the field itself, the projector. You mentioned a tank. Not something that will take hours to set up, I trust—a tank of oil? Not liquid helium!''

"Not a tank *of* anything, sir,'' Johnson explained, still more embarrassed. "A tank in the historical sense: a manned armoured vehicle, with rotating turret for low-powered cannon.''

Gregori was fascinated. "Propulsion?''

"Caterpillar tracks only, sir. Diesel engine.''

"And I was lecturing you on military history. It's a real museum piece, the forerunner of today's military armour?''

"Yes indeed, sir. It's an FV 4030 Challenger, once the most advanced fighting machines of its day. Its type were entering service with the British Army in 1985 as successors to the Chieftain series—incorporating the same armament and Integrated Fire Control System, but with Chobham armour and a more powerful engine.'' Johnson could have warmed to his subject, but that was a prerogative for superior officers.

"This is excellent,'' said Gregori. "So you don't have just a temperamental prototype, you have a mobile combat unit, however antiquated. Its antiquity may even be an advantage—it may let you pass the advancing Scots without attracting attention. Lenin knows what they'll take it to be, but the idea that it's a threat will escape them—especially since it'll be crawling on to the field of their victory!''

"You realise, sir, that the tank doesn't have anything like its former turn of speed. Once it could exceed fifty-six kilometres per hour, but not now.''

"So much the better, to avoid attracting attention. We'll have you behind the lines, under deep camouflage. The High-landers will be able to storm right over the top of you by the time our experts have finished. But afterwards, when battle ends, we'll give you a sonic pulse from divisional HQ to move forward. If I can I'll join you myself to direct your fire—if not, Captain, you must assess the battle's course for yourself and destroy the key Scottish units.''

When shall we next meet again? thought Gregori, when Johnson had gone. When the battle's lost and won? The idea was fantastic; yet the chance was there to save the State and his own career, very probably his neck. The best of it was that he could make good his escape, in that Russian aircraft, when defeat became certain—and if Johnson reversed the outcome, the General would thereby be restored to his post, ready to claim the rewards of the otherwise unattainable victory. If Johnson achieved nothing, General Gregori would have escaped shellfire, firing squad or prison camp and be on his way to a new life. But where was he to go, he wondered, standing before the map with vodka glass in hand like an English Roman in his villa, nursing the last cup of wine from Italy when the galleys had gone. Where was his refuge to be?

Ireland?

> Now's the day and now's the hour;
> See the front of battle lour;
> See approach proud Edward's power,
> Chains and slaverie.
> —Robert Burns, ''Scots Wha Hae''

1500 hours (A): Sergeant Macdonald of the Cameron Highlanders Artillery, Blue Section, finished the deployment of his guns. They were Russian mobile cannon, captured in the Lowlands after the second battle of Prestonpans; relatively light, they could be shifted swiftly on air-cushions to come to bear on new targets. Against the armoured division barring the way to Derby their firepower would be well-nigh ineffective, but ostensibly their function was to provide covering fire for the Scots' commandos, to help to pin down whatever troops the English had mustered, while the teams moved in and the shaped charges were placed. Unless the massive fighting machines of the People's Army could be knocked out, with their superior range and firepower they could hold England from the Pennines to the Wash. The Scottish army had had to split up for the night dash that brought them close enough to do battle, or those juggernauts might have blown them apart at Sheffield, forty miles away.

Macdonald checked again, though their position was the best possible. On the right-hand tip of the Highland crescent, well forward but aside from the heaviest fighting, they could provide crossfire and also spot targets for the more substantial Highland artillery. That was their true function, though other such units spaced out along the line and providing covering fire would conceal the fact. Blue Section's true task was to spotlight, at the right time and not before, what the English were holding in reserve and when the outgunned Scots *must* take it out.

He lowered himself briefly from the slit to the controls of the command unit, to glance back at the youth at the impact predictor panel. "All set, Alastair?"

The lad swallowed hard. "It's shaping up nicely, Sergeant." The flickering colours of the computer display chased across his pale face.

"Fair enough." Macdonald picked up the hand mike. "Dheargh Mhatan to Claymore—activated and ready."

"Stand by, Dheargh Mhatan."

In the First, Second and Third World Wars, the Scots had been known to their enemies as "Demons in Skirts," "Ladies from Hell," and "Poison Dwarves." One of their demonic tricks had been to use Gaelic on the radio when they might be overheard. This army's mix of English-speaking Lowlanders meant that Gaelic was used only for code-words, but that would be enough to keep the English guessing. "Claymore" was Lochiel himself, commanding the Scottish push south as once his ancestor had advised Prince Charles Edward in the same desperate game. It was no accident that he had taken for his call-sign a word which had been *claidheamh mòr*, a great sword, and had been applied to more than three types of deadly weapon.

"Claymore to all units—Caber Feidh is sounded. Dheargh Mhatan, do you hear?"

Macdonald smiled. "Caber Feidh" was the old regimental march of the Seaforths: when it was sounded on the pipes in a situation like this, they would be advancing into battle. An Englishman listening would probably think it was a place which had been checked out. There was a check-out in progress, but of a very different kind; after another glance towards Alastair, Macdonald again raised the mike.

"We hear, Claymore—Caber Feidh is quite clear." If anyone out there knows pipe music, Macdonald told himself, let them think we're having a concert. They'll dance to our tune soon enough.

"Claymore to Hielan' Laddie: Bundle and Go. March, March, Ettrick and Teviotdale!"

That was the Black Watch committed; and now, the King's Own Scottish Borderers. The Black Watch should have been in Macdonald's direct field of view, and as he stood up to the slit his movement-sensitive scope picked out the infantry moving through the trees on their jet-packs, their suits dialled to winter camouflage tartan.

"Alert for Hielan' Laddie," said Alastair. Guided by the screen display, Alastair was now locked on to the advancing troops with strange powers of his own, tracking them and projecting their track forward into the future. His trance lasted only seconds. "Two machine-gun posts, automated, concealed half-a-mile ahead of them. They'll open fire in sixty-five seconds. I'm laying-in the target now."

"We can take care of those ourselves, it doesn't need heavy bombardment. We'll do it now and clear your view for the next hazard." As Macdonald spoke, the guns of Blue Section were swinging towards the target Alastair had pinpointed. "Two rounds each, fire at will!"

Sergeant Macdonald was a reliable NCO picked by Lochiel for his lack of imagination. He accepted Alastair's gift of the Second Sight as he might accept that another man could paint, or play the fiddle. Told by the young Adept of the threats the near future held, he would act to counter them without questioning the information; without raising an atmosphere of doubt that might blur Alastair's predictions. The boy was Lochiel's secret weapon, trained in the Western Isles by agents brought by submarine from the unknown base of the American government in exile. Personally, Sergeant Macdonald had no time for the new jargon of "Adepts" and "Psionics"; privately he doubted the value of the training, which had sharpened Alastair's erratic gift into a practical tool of warfare but had unnerved the lad, particularly in combat. To Macdonald, who had known him since childhood, it was a good soldier spoiled. But he wouldn't question what Alastair told him, and he would act on it as a trained soldier, and that made him an ideal anchor for the Adept.

*   *   *

1525 hrs. (A): It had fallen to Macdonald's unit to open the battle, despite their orders to keep a low profile. But with troops already committed across so much of the battlefield, it could have happened anywhere, and fire-fights swiftly broke out all along the front. The enemy's fighting vehicles, huge Russian machines which in another age would have been big enough to carry moon-rockets to their pads, ground slowly forward from cover to meet the Highlanders with firepower nothing on Earth could resist. They had been developed after the Last War, when the armoured divisions of both sides were annihilated in the tactical holocaust of Germany. Only a direct nuclear hit would destroy them. But the Black Watch had been working their way up, making use of smokescreens and barrages laid down for other parts of the battle. Given their timing by Alastair, they rushed a nearby hill and plastered the war machines with old-fashioned anti-tank missiles, while the commandos made their suicide runs to plant the shaped nuclear charges. The troops took heavy losses, despite the covering fire from Blue Section and its counterparts; but the land dreadnoughts were stopped or even disabled, with their fields of fire consequently restricted, and one by one the commandos took them out.

1545 hrs. (A): Such was the firepower of modern armies, an engagement that might once have lasted hours was already over. Casualties had been fearsome: it might be said that the Scots had won only in the sense that they still had some men and guns left when the People's Army was annihilated. But there would be reinforcements within hours, now that the North was up and taking arms; and prompted perhaps by the Scottish success, Welsh forces were leaving the mountains against Wolverhampton, Worcester and Gloucester. The heavy Soviet armour coming from London was in trouble with guerillas at St. Albans. All Lochiel's army had to do was occupy Derby and hold it.

"Dheargh Mhatan from Claymore, Dheargh Mhatan from Claymore, clear us a path into the town. We'll be mopping up behind you."

"Dheargh Mhatan, aye. Leader to all Blue Section units, prepare to move off!"

They breasted the rise ahead, swung 'round the burning wreck of a war machine in the field beyond, and roared down to the main road. Taking up line astern, they put down their heavy drive wheels, shutting off ground effect. They met no trouble on the way in; surviving units of the People's Army, hands raised, were left to surrender to the main force. The news of their coming spread like wildfire from the outskirts of Derby: by the time they neared the town centre cheering crowds were lining the route. Macdonald saw in the rear scanner that Fraser in No.2, defying snipers, was up in the hatch with the pipes. The external microphone picked up "The March of the Cameron Men."

As said before, Macdonald was not imaginative, but the historical significance of the moment wasn't lost on him. Turning over the controls to his co-driver, he too stood up at the observation slit and threw open the top hatch. Out among the cheering, with the Cameron pennants fluttering before him on the whip aerials, tradition really got to him. As they entered the centre of Derby he took off his tin hat and flourished it in triumph, shouting "The Prince is coming! The Prince is coming!"

1550 hrs. (A): Though the Highland army was passing on both sides, regrouping as they went for the march into Derby, a dreadful quiet occupied the battlefield. Johnson had never seen active service, not even skirmishes with the small forces China could still miraculously generate after all this time. There hadn't been as devastating an engagement as this within living memory.

Though the sonic pulse hadn't come, and neither had Gregori, he couldn't wait in hiding any longer. His shells could go back only an hour in time, and to hit the Black Watch (unfamiliar with the tartans, he had classified them "X group") before they got too close to the front line of the People's Army, his little team would have to move. He pushed a button, and the heavier parts of their camouflage parted explosively above them. Among the ruins of the armoured division, that little bang would never be noticed. Their treads bit into the earth ramp, and the tank heaved up towards the winter sky.

The rearguard of the Highland army, passing at speed to left and right, took no notice of the Challenger as it rumbled down a clear alley between the flaming war machines to the fields beyond. Why should they? The least of the weapon-carriers, lesser, captured units though they were, dwarfed it. If it weren't for the gun it might almost pass as some kind of a lifeboat or tender for the stricken giants nearby; and the gun was no threat, pointing to where the Highlanders had come from, not where they were now. If any of the infantry swooping along on their jet-packs swerved to check it out, they were reassured by the saltires which Gregori had suggested be flown from the turret aerials.

Though it had been convenient to have the gun and projector mobile for the trials on Salisbury Plain, Johnson had never ridden in the tank himself. The noise and vibration appalled him. How people had managed to fight these machines at speed, with what precision the crude instruments of 1985 afforded, he couldn't see. He wasn't even able to follow the RPV record when he tried to re-check his interpretation of the battle.

1610 hrs. (A): They were in position. The time projector was on, its antennae extended to engage the shell at the focus of the field, as it left the barrel. Johnson was at the contra-rotating cupola periscope, his left-eye to the roll-ball, split field monocular sighting in real-time. The overhead film of the battle, now synchronised to exactly one hour in the past, was presented to his right eye by a modern holographic head-up display, from whose reference grid he could read off the range. He adjusted the antique tank helmet, checked position of throat mike and ear muffs, and cleared his throat.

"Target range 800 metres. Antimatter, one round. Come to bear."

The old gun swung in traverse and elevation, locking (as accurately as its guidance system would allow) on to the Black Watch advance an hour before. With these blockbuster shells, any lack of precision there would be quite academic. The field had better work, Johnson told himself, or we'll blow ourselves right off the hillside at this range.

"Fixed," said the gunner. Two tracers flashed from the ranging machine gun, off into the empty fields. The electronics of the tank's laser ranging system had been knocked out by electromagnetic pulse 150 years before, and there was no chance of replacements from Barr & Stroud in Glasgow—but in this case, the older method was what was needed. There was no target for laser and infrared sensors out there, only the images on the synchronised record, about to become ghosts in every sense.

"On target," said Johnson. The old command sequence

gave him a feeling of continuity with the traditions of the British Army. Marlborough, Wellington—no, perhaps not. At 1611 (A) precisely, he ordered, "Fire!"

1512 hrs. (B) (the projector wasn't quite at maximum range): Sgt. Macdonald had just received confirmation from Observer Ewan Cameron that the machine-gun posts were destroyed, when there was a colossal flash of light about a mile to the east. By sheer luck he happened not to be looking directly into it, but half his vision was filled with after images. Though the command unit's shock absorbers coped, the sway relative to the ground outside was plainly visible. Beyond the Black Watch advance, which must have been wiped out, the bare winter trees had come down: those nearest to ground zero were still standing, but furiously ablaze.

"Dheargh Mhatan to Claymore, Dheargh Mhatan to Claymore—nuclear strike on Hielan' Laddie. Hielan' Laddie is taken out. They must have read Lochiel's mind!" he added after switching off. Macdonald's soft Highland accent, subdued by years of shouted orders, was brought out by his anger.

"That can only have been antimatter," his co-driver said from the instrument panel. "They must have stunned their own front line, using it at that range."

"Aye." Macdonald dropped from the slit, twisting out of the seat to face Alastair. In the cramped interior of the Command Unit, that put him only a foot from the Adept.

"I didn't see it, Sergeant!" Alastair was distraught at his failure. "I didn't even see the shell coming!"

"Never mind, lad," said Macdonald, boiling. "Where did it come from?"

Alastair looked desperate, but said his piece. "That hillside there, Sergeant—right in front of us. I can *feel* it. But the detectors show nothing there. . . ."

"Our own eyes show nothing there!" Macdonald twisted himself viciously left, then right, back up to the slit. "There's *bugger-all* there," he hissed. "Nevertheless, lay it in. . . ."

Blue Section's guns roared together. At that range it was almost a flat trajectory. The hillside facing them split open, again and again.

1613 hrs. (B): Johnson had been watching the synchronised record eagerly, expecting to see the flash of the shell interrupt the sequence he had followed earlier. But no, the advance went on as before. For a terrible moment he feared failure; but looking up, he found the battlefield had changed, though the record paradoxically remained the same. The ruined formation of war machines had overtaken him, though they had been destroyed in the end: their burning wreckage lay along the top of the slope, one or two further forward on his right where the ground levelled out. And the Highland rearguard had been pushed back; though still victorious, the units now passing him were fewer and slower. Casualties were heavier, damage more severe. He had changed the course of the battle, though his records of it were unaltered. After a moment he realised that his recording of the last hour must remain unchanged, or memory too would have gone. This was the first of the paradoxes he had feared when transferring his half-completed research project to the front.

He would have to act fast if the new course of recent events, of which he had no record, was not to diverge too far from the previous track still running on the synchronised display. He had the Challenger's gun fixed on the next target when suddenly his situation changed. Though he felt nothing, there was a discontinuity in his perceptions: the tank was nose-down and there was less light coming in. The periscope showed that now they were lying at the bottom of a deep crater, the gun almost in the earth. For another dreadful moment he thought that the time-projector antennae had been smashed, but they were just clear of the fresh-turned soil.

So the Highlanders had "spotted" him! It would do them no good. An hour in their future, nothing they did could touch him. A sense of real power possessed Johnson. He alone would save the Soviet State of Britain. But he must move fast, or his next shell might light on the advancing English front line in the new past he had created. The driver restarted the engine, engaged the caterpillar tracks, and began to reverse up the steep slope of the crater.

1515 hrs. (B): The smoke had cleared on the hillside blasted by Blue Section's bombardment. Macdonald was scanning the pattern of craters. "We've dug nothing up there," he said, but without scepticism.

"Sergeant . . ." Alastair began uncertainly. He was sitting back from the computer display, eyes glazed again.

Macdonald continued scanning. "What, lad?"

"Sergeant, I can see that shell now."

"Yes?"

"I don't . . . you'll not . . ."

Macdonald dropped and swung out of the chair again. Whatever "the Sight" revealed, by God he had to know it. Very gently, he took hold of the tranced Adept by the lapels of his battledress. The Highland accent still more noticeable, he said slowly and forcefully, with even a hint of menace, "Alastair, tell me what you see!"

"Just the shell, Sergeant. As if it were going backwards from its target to the hillside. I can still only see the nearest part of its trajectory. It's up there, right now, with us in time!"

Sergeant Macdonald was not imaginative. He accepted that Alastair could see what he himself could not, and was not plagued by the kind of doubt which could argue or interfere with that source of information. His technical education told him that matter going backwards in time could look like antimatter coming forwards, and vice versa—the words "Feynman diagram" were at the back of his mind somewhere, but if Alastair described it, Macdonald took his word for it.

"Oh, the bastards," he said quietly. That the English could send shells backwards through time, came as no great surprise to him. The English were capable of anything. "You can see into the future, lad," he went on as quietly as before. "You can see that launcher. When will it be there?"

"I can't see it," said Alastair, turning his head from side to side in mental anguish. "It's as if the future that shell came from has been wiped away. . . ."

"The shell itself gives you a link," Macdonald said, soothing, directing the Adept's attention. "Just tell me, lad, when will it 'return' to that hillside?"

Alastair said nothing. He began to tremble in his seat.

"Switch everything off," snapped Macdonald. "No talking, no distractions." The shifting patterns of the computer display died. Alastair's powers alone linked him to the battle.

"An hour from now, nearly," he gasped, and snapped out of the trance, weeping from the strain.

"That's all we need to know. . . ." The satisfaction in Macdonald's voice was filled with menace now, as he swung back to the control position. "Switches on! . . . Lachlan, we want a barrage fused to explode in one hour. Make it fast."

"But Sergeant, our delay fuses only run in seconds," the armourer protested over the intercom from No. 3 gun.

"So fix me some for thirty-six hundred seconds," said Macdonald, some of the menace transferred from the enemy. "One round at a time if need be. Let me know when you're ready, Lachie. . . ." He switched off, turning to the recovering Adept. "Don't you worry, laddie. To make an explosion an hour before you in time may be the work of the devil, but to plant one an hour in time behind you is an old, established art."

1555 hrs. (B): Lachlan's old, established art seemed to have won the contest. Correcting the fuse settings to get an approximately simultaneous detonation, No. 3 gun had sown the mangled hillside with a broad pattern of shells. No more disabling fire had come back from the future, and the battle had raged on. Alastair's warnings didn't completely forestall the war machines' contribution, but one by one they had been immobilised by suicide squads and hammered out of the action. The Highland army had survived, though drastically weakened; and Lochiel ordered Macdonald to enter Derby at once, to consolidate the victory.

"Prepare to move off," said Macdonald. "No. 4: In about twenty-three minutes our charges should go off in that hillside. Get you into the cover of those trees and watch. If by any chance we failed to catch the devilish contrivance that will appear there, don't you make any mistake with it." Blue Section started up on their air cushions, moving down into the valley. Only No. 4 gun separated from them, moving along the top of the rise into the trees.

1600 hrs. (B): Ewan Cameron saw the ancient challenger trundling up the field to the hillside opposite. He could scarcely believe his eyes, and one by one his crew snatched quick looks to confirm it. Only the knowledge that the shambling tank with its false saltires could have turned the battle gave strain to their laughter. The tank nosed over the brow of the hill, then came to rest apparently poised over one of the craters. It seemed as if there had to be solid ground below it, yet to Ewan it seemed at the same time that the tank hung over empty air. After some delay, two silvery antennae were extended parallel to the old-fashioned gun barrel, and twisted to focus on the space just before the muzzle. The gun swung, then slowly began to track the movements of the Black Watch an hour before. Though he watched carefully, Ewan was certain afterwards that he didn't see the first shell fired—a paradox that would have interested Johnson. At 1614, however, for no apparent reason, the Challenger's invisible support was no longer there and the tank itself was suddenly almost out of sight, nose down in the crater. When it came out No. 4 gun was laid in, in case there should be any mistake. But at 1622, just when the tank gun was locked on its next target and Ewan himself was about to fire, the hillside erupted once more. Two charges went off directly below the Challenger: it was blown high into the air, its treads disintegrating as it turned over. The gun flailed and the turret flew off. The tank fell, burning, and after the impact came three brilliant explosions, each bigger than the last.

No. 4 gun was overturned by the blast and hammered into the hillside; and though only the first flash had pierced Ewan's polaroid goggles, it would be days before his eyes were unbandaged. Still it was with great cheer that the crew extricated themselves from the wreckage and set off on foot, following the Highland army's advance into Derby.

EDITOR'S INTRODUCTION TO:

HOUSE OF WEAPONS
by Gordon R. Dickson

Gordon Dickson is deservedly well known for his *Dorsai* novels. (His name for the series is *The Childe Cycle*.) "House of Weapons" is part of his *other* series: stories of the invasion of Earth by the Aalaag.

The Aalaag are a warrior race. Frighteningly competent, they reduced the Earth's defenses to powder within days of their arrival, and soon installed themselves as the new rulers of humanity—whom they think of as cattle.

Their weapons are as superior to the best on Earth as the Red Army's weapons are superior to the Enfields of the *mujahadeen*. Moreover, long accustomed to military power, the Aalaag are also experienced in government. They rule an empire of many stars and races and their history teaches them that eventually the conquered cattle learn to love their conquerors.

So has it always been, and on the surface so it is on Earth. A few hardy souls hide in the hills; a few guerrillas resist, to their peril. The Aalaag have expected that. What they have not expected is that even the most servile may become warriors, that there may be resistance within the House of Weapons itself.

HOUSE OF WEAPONS
by Gordon R. Dickson

The dumbbell shape of the two-place Aalaag courier ship in which Shane Everts was being transported dropped like a meteorite slung from the altitude of its extra-orbital journey.

Shane felt his body temporarily weightless, held in place only by the restraining arms of the seat in which he sat. A meter and a half before his nose, his November view of the Twin Cities of Minneapolis and St. Paul, below, was all but hidden by the massive, white-uniformed shoulders of the eight-foot Aalaag female, who was his pilot.

In summer these cities, chief population centers of what had once been Minnesota, one of the former United States of America, would have been only partly visible from this angle above them. Thick-treed avenues and streets would then have given the illusion of nothing more than two small, separate downtown business centers surrounded by heavy forest. But now, in the final months of the dying year, the full extent of both cities and their suburbs lay revealed among the leaves stripped from tree limbs by the winds of early winter.

No snow was yet on the ground to soften what the fallen leaves had uncovered. Shane looked around the pilot and down into the empty-seeming thoroughfares. Under Aalaag rule they would be as clean as those of Milan in northern Italy. He had just left that city to be carried here to the headquarters of all the alien power on Earth. Its building was placed about the headwaters of navigation on the Mississippi River. To this place Shane now, his nerves on edge, returned.

The body odor of his pilot forced itself once more on his attention. It was inescapable in the close confines of the small vessel—as no doubt his human smell was to her. Though as an Aalaag she would never have lowered herself to admit noticing such a fact. The scent of her in his nostrils was hardly agreeable, but not specifically disagreeable, either.

It was the smell of a different animal, only. Something like the reek of a horse or cow barn, only with that slightly acid tinge which identifies a meat-eater. For the Aalaag (though they required that Earthly foodstuffs be reconstituted for their different digestive systems) were like humanity, omnivores who made a certain portion of their diet out of flesh—though of earthly creatures other than human.

That exception of human flesh from the Aalaag diet might be merely policy on the part of the aliens. Or it might not, thought Shane. Even after two years of living here at the very heart and center of the Aalaag Command on Earth, in many cases like this he had no way of knowing what their real reasons were, or whether what he believed might be merely an assumption on his part. . . .

He forced his mind to stop playing with the question of the aliens' diet. It was unimportant, as unimportant as the differences in appearance of the Twin Cities between June and November. Both thoughts were only straw men thrown up by his subconscious as excuses to avoid thinking of the situation which would be facing him momentarily.

In only a few minutes he would be once more in the House of his master, reporting to him—to Lyt Ahn, First Captain and Commander of all the Aalaag on this captive and subject Earth. And this time, for the first time, he would face that ruler, knowing himself guilty of what to these Aalaag were two capital crimes, for themselves, or any one of their servants. Chief of these was not merely the violation of an order, but the violation of it while he was on duty, as a translator and courier for the First Captain.

It was ironic. He had clung to the thought of himself as someone well able to endure existence under the domination of the alien rulers. This belief had persisted in him until just a few hours ago. But now he had to face the fact that even though he had been among the most favored of humans, there was one vital area in which he was no less vulnerable than any of the rest of his race.

As a courier-translator for Lyt Ahn, he was well fed, well housed, well paid—tremendously so in comparison with the overwhelming mass of his fellow humans. He had therefore believed in his own ability to avoid trouble with the overlords. But in spite of all this, twice now, the insanity which the Aalaag

called *yowaragh*—a sudden overwhelming urge to revolt against
the conquerors, regardless of personal consequences—had
overtaken him, just as if he had been one of the ordinary,
starving mass of Earth's population.

The first explosion of that suicidal emotion had come on
him two years ago in a square of the City of Aalborg, in
Denmark, when he had been an involuntary witness to a man
being executed by the Aalaag; and—to his own later shock—in
a half-drunken reaction of defiance, had secretly drawn on the
wall under the executed man the stick figure of a pilgrim with
a staff. The act had had unexpected consequences. To his
astonishment, that figure had since been picked up by other
humans and spread over the world as the particular symbol of
covert opposition to the alien rulers. Its authorship had never
been traced back to him, even by those humans who had
come to use it. Nonetheless, for a moment there, he had
blindly courted execution, himself. Even though neither alien
nor human knew it, he had defied the all-powerful masters.

Then, once again in the grip of *yowaragh*, in the hours just
past in Milan, he had risked himself to rescue a woman called
only Maria, whom he had never seen before; and this had
revealed his existence, if not his identity, to the human
Resistance group there, of which she was one.

It was only now, on the return trip to his master's headquarters, aboard an Aalaag special courier ship, that he had
finally admitted to himself that he, like all the rest of his race,
walked a razor's edge between the absolute power of his
rulers—and a possibility, which he now recognized starkly,
that at any moment an uncontrollable inner explosion might
drive him to do something that would bring his hatred of the
Aalaag to their attention.

It was strange, he thought now, that this should only be
striking home to him at this time, three years after the aliens
had landed and taken over Earth in one swift and effortless
moment. Squarely, he faced the fact that he was terrified of
the consequences of another such bout of madness in him. He
had seen Aalaag interrogation and discipline at work. He
knew, as the underground Resistance people did not, that
there was literally no hope of a successful revolt against the
overwhelming military power of their alien masters. Anyone
attempting to act against the Aalaag was courting not only
certain eventual discovery, but equally certain, and painful,

death—as an object lesson to other humans who might also be tempted to revolt.

And this would be as true for him as for any other human, in spite of the value of his work to the aliens and the kindness with which his own master had always seemed to regard him.

At the same time the logical front of his mind was reading him this lesson, the back of it was playing with the notion of finding ways around his situation and avoiding any such future risks of triggering off the *yowaragh* reaction in him. He remembered how simple it would be to contact the Resistance people again. All he had to do was buy himself a used pilgrim's gown of two different colors, one inside and one outside—and pay for the purchase with the gold that only an alien-employed human like himself would be carrying. The dream of revolt was an unbelievably seductive one—in the years before the coming of the Aalaag, he could never have imagined how seductive—but at the same time he must never forget how hopeless and false it was. He must always remember to hold himself under tight control and continue to chart his way cool-headedly in the Aalaag Headquarters and under the Aalaag eyes that were always upon him.

His problem was twofold, he reminded himself as he flew toward his destination. He must cover up any dangerous results that might come from his previous attacks of *yowaragh;* and he must make sure that he never, never, fell into the grasp of that dangerous emotional explosion again.

To begin with, as soon as he got the ear of Lyt Ahn, he must set up excuses against the two crimes he had just committed in Milan. The lie to Laa Ehon must be covered; and there was still deep danger in the fact that he had helped to rescue Maria. The Aalaag, if they should ever actually come to suspect him, had devices which, like bloodhounds, could sniff out his having slipped away from the Milanese Headquarters without orders, to confront and confuse the alien guard who had originally arrested Maria—all this while he had supposedly been given time off to rest in a human dormitory in the building.

That was the most dangerous of the two crimes he had just committed in Aalaag terms—crimes, as they would be seen by Aalaag eyes. The lesser crime, but one sufficient enough for his execution, was that he had lied to Laa Ehon, the Commander of the Milanese District, when that Aalaag had asked him what the price was that Lyt Ahn had placed upon him—obviously with an eye to buying Shane from the First Captain. Shane had claimed a price that Lyt Ahn had never mentioned, gambling that his master would not remember never having set such a price and that the price, was one that Lyt Ahn would have set, if he had indeed ever gotten around to doing so.

A lying beast, in Aalaag eyes, was an untrustworthy beast; and should therefore be destroyed. Somehow, this statement of his to Laa Ehon must be handled—but at the moment he had no idea how to do it. Perhaps, if he simply relaxed and put it deliberately out of his mind once more, a solution would come to him naturally. . . .

He made a conscious effort to relax; and instinctively his released mind drifted off into its favorite fantasy—of an individual called The Pilgrim, who was at the same time himself, under the cover of being a translator-courier for Lyt Ahn; and who was also superior to all Aalaag, as they were superior to all ordinary humans. It was this familiar daydream that had caused him to choose the pilgrim image for the stick-figure he had drawn under the executed man.

The Pilgrim, he luxuriated in his dream, would wear the same anonymous garb in which Shane himself came and went among his fellow humans who, otherwise, catching him alone and away from Aalaags or the Interior Guard who policed them, would have torn him apart if they had known that he was one of those favored and employed by their masters.

The Pilgrim would be uncatchable and uncontrollable by the Aalaag. He would set their laws and their might at defiance. He would succor humans who had fallen afoul of those same alien rules and laws—as Shane had, by sheer luck more than anything else, managed to get Maria out of the clutches of the Milanese garrison.

Above all, The Pilgrim would bring home to the aliens the fact that they were not the masters of Earth that they thought themselves to be. . . .

For a little while, as the courier ship dipped down toward its destination he let himself indulge in that fantasy, seeing himself as The Pilgrim with a power that put him above even Lyt Ahn, and all those other alien masters who made his insides go hollow every time they so much as looked at him.

Then he roused himself and shook it off. It was all right as a means to keep him sane; but it was dangerous, indulged in when he was actually under alien observation, as he was about to be within seconds. Besides, he could afford to put it aside for the moment. Five minutes from now he would be in the small cubicle that was his living quarters and he could think what he liked, including how to protect himself against Lyt Ahn's discovery of either of his recent crimes.

The courier ship was now right over its destination. The landing spot to which it dropped was only a couple of hundred meters below, the rooftop of an enormous construction with only some twenty stories or so above ground but as many below, and covering several acres in area. Like all structures now taken over or built by the Aalaag, it gleamed; in this chill, thin November sunlight looking as if liquid mercury had been poured over it. That shining surface was a defensive screen or coating—Shane had never been able to discover which, since the Aalaag took it so for granted that they never spoke of it. Once in place, apparently, it needed neither renewal or maintenance.

Just as it seemed their ship must crash into the rooftop, a space of the silver surface vanished. Revealed were a flat landing area and a platoon of the oversized humans recruited as Ordinary Guards to the aliens. These stood, fully armed, under the command of an Aalaag officer who towered in full, white armor above the tallest of them. The officer was a male, Shane saw, the fact betrayed by the narrowness of his lower-body armor.

As the ship touched down, its port opened and Shane's pilot stepped out. The Ordinary Guards at once fell back, leaving the Aalaag to come forward alone and meet the pilot. Shane, lost behind her powerful shape, had followed her out.

"Am Mehon, twenty-eighth rank," the pilot introduced herself. "I return one of the First Captain's cattle, at his orders—"

She half-turned to indicate, with the massive thumb of her left hand, Shane, who was standing a respectful two paces behind her and to her left.

"Aral Te Kinn," the Aalaag on guard introduced himself. "Thirty-second rank. . . ."

His armored head bent slightly, acknowledging the fact that the courier pilot outranked him by four degrees. But it would have bent no further for the First Captain, himself.

Theoretically all Aalaag were equal; and the lowest of them, when on duty, could give orders to the highest, if the other was not. Here, on the roof landing space of the House of Weapons, as the First Captain's residence and headquarters were always called, the officer on guard, being in control ot the area, was therefore in authority. Only courtesy dictated the slight inclination of his head.

"This beast is to report itself to the First Captain immediately," he went on now. His helmet turned slightly, bringing its viewing slit to focus on Shane. "You heard me, beast?"

Shane felt a sudden, sickening emptiness in his stomach. Surely it was impossible that what he had done in Milan could have been found out and reported to his master this quickly? He shook off the sudden weakness. Of course it was impossible. But even with the sudden fear gone, he felt robbed of the anticipated peace and quiet of his cubicle, the chance to think and plan, he had been looking forward to. But there was no gainsaying the order.

"I heard and I obey, untarnished sir," answered Shane in Aalaag, bending his own head in a considerably deeper bow.

He walked past the pilot and Aral Te Kinn toward the shed-like structure containing the drop pad that would lower him to his meeting with the alien overlord of all Earth. The tall humans who were the Ordinary Guards gazed down at him with faint contempt as their ranks parted to let him through. But Shane was by now so used to their attitudes to such as himself that he hardly noticed.

". . . I had heard there were a rare few among these cattle who could speak the actual language as a real person does," he could hear the pilot saying to Aral Te Kinn behind him, "but I'd never believed it until now. If it were not for the squeakiness of its high voice—"

Shane shut the door to the shed on the rest of her words and on the scene behind him, as he entered the structure. He stepped onto the round green disk of the drop pad.

"Subfloor twenty," he told it, and the alien-built elevator obeyed, dropping him swiftly toward his destination, twenty floors beneath the surface of the surrounding city.

Its fall stopped with equal suddenness, and his knees bent under a deceleration that would not have been noticed by an Aalaag. He stepped forward into a wide corridor with black and white tiles on its polished floor, with walls and ceiling of a hard, uniformly gray material.

A male Aalaag officer sat at the duty desk opposite the elevator, engaged in conversation with someone in the communication screen set in the surface of the desk before him.

Shane had halted at once after his first step out of the dropshoot and stood motionless, until the talk was ended and the Aalaag cut the connection, looking up at him.

"I am Shane Evert, translator-courier for the First Captain, untarnished sir," said Shane as the pale, heavy-boned and expressionless, human-like face, under its mane of pure white hair, considered him. This particular alien had seen him at least a couple of hundred times previously; but most Aalaag were not good at distinguishing one human from another, even if the two were of opposite sexes.

The Aalaag continued to stare, waiting.

"I have returned from a courier run," Shane went on, "and the untarnished sir on duty at the roof parking area said I was ordered to report myself immediately to the First Captain." The desk officer looked down and spoke again into his communications screen—checking, of course, on what Shane had said. Ordinarily, the movements of a single human would be of little concern to any Aalaag, but entrance to the apartments of the First Captain, along the corridor to Shane's right, was a matter of unique security. Shane glanced briefly and longingly along the corridor in the opposite direction, toward his left, and his own distant quarters with those of the other translators, and such other private servants of Lyt Ahn, or his mate-consort, the female Adtha Or Ain.

Shane had been continuously on duty and in the presence of Aalaag for three days, culminating in that disastrous, if still secret, act of insanity he had given way to in Milan. His desire to return to his own quarters, to be alone, was like a living hunger in him, a desperate hunger to lock himself away in a place that for a moment would be closed off, away from all the daily terrors and orders; a place where he could at last put aside his constant fears and lick his wounds in peace.

"You may report as instructed."

The voice of the Aalaag on duty behind the desk cut across his thoughts.

"I obey, untarnished sir," he answered.

He turned to his right and went away down the long hall, hearing the clicking of his heels on the hard tiles underfoot echoing back from the unyielding walls. Along those walls at intervals of what would be not more than half a dozen strides for an Aalaag, hung long-weapons—equivalents of human rifles—armed and ready for use. But for all their real deadliness, they were there for show only; a part of the militaristic

Aalaag culture pattern that justified the name of House of Weapons for this abode of Lyt Ahn.

A house of weapons it was indeed; but its military potency lay not in the awesomely destructive, by human standards, devices on its walls. Behind the silver protective screen that covered the building were larger mounted devices capable of leveling to slagged ruin the earth surrounding, to and beyond the horizon in all directions. For a moment Shane was reminded of what he had not thought of for years, of those human military units that in the first few days of the Aalaag landing on Earth had been foolish enough to try resisting the alien invasion. They had been destroyed almost without thought on the invaders' part, like tiny hills of ants trodden underfoot by giants.

To any engine of destruction known to human science and technology, including the nuclear ones, even a single Aalaag in full battle armor was invulnerable. Against the least weapon carried by an individual Aalaag, no human army could, in the end, survive. Nor would an Aalaag weapon work in the hands of any but one of the aliens. It was not merely a matter of humans understanding how to activate it. There was also some built-in recognition by the weapon itself that it was not in alien hands, which in others turned it into no more than a dead piece of heavy material; at most, a weighty club.

Walking down the wide, high-ceilinged, solitary corridor where no other figures, human or alien, were to be seen, Shane felt coming over him once again a sensation he hated, but which he never seemed to be able to escape from here, the sense of shrinking that always took him over in this place.

It was a feeling like that which Swift's hero, Lemuel Gulliver, had described in *Gulliver's Travels*, as happening when he had found himself in the land of the giant Brobdingnagians. Like Gulliver, then, each time Shane found himself in this place, a time would come when he would begin to feel that it was the Aalaag and all their artifacts which were normal in size; while he, like all other humans and human creations, was shrunken to the scale of a pygmy. Shrunken, not only in a physical sense but in all other senses as well; in mind and spirit and courage and wisdom, in all those things that could make one race into something more than mere "cattle" to another.

He checked abruptly, passing a door that was uncharacteristically human-sized in one wall of that overlarge hall, and turned in through it to one of the few rooms on this corridor equipped to dispose of human waste. There would be no telling how long he might be in the presence of Lyt Ahn, and there would be no excusing himself then for physical or personal needs. No Aalaag would have dreamed of so excusing himself while on duty, and therefore no human servant might.

He stood before a urinal, emptying his bladder with a momentary sense of stolen freedom, only secondary to that which he yearned for in his own quarters. Here, too, for the moment, in theory he was free of Aalaag observation and rules, and the Gulliver-like sensation lifted, briefly.

But the moment passed. A minute later he was toy-sized again, back outside in the corridor, walking ever nearer to the entrance of Lyt Ahn's private office.

He stopped at last before great double doors of bronze-colored material. With the tip of the index figure of his right hand, he lightly touched the smooth surface of the panel closest to him.

There was a pause. He could not hear, but he knew that within the office a sensor had recorded his touch as being that of a human and a mechanical voice was announcing that "a beast desires admittance."

"Who?" came an Aalaag voice from the ceiling. Unusually, it was not that of an Aalaag secretary or aide but of Lyt Ahn himself.

"One of your cattle, most immaculate sir," answered Shane. "Shane Evert, reporting as ordered, following a courier run to the immaculate sir in command at Milan, Italy."

The right hand door swung open and Shane walked through it, into the office. Under a white ceiling as lofty as that of the hall, and large enough for a small ballroom by human standards, the gray-colored desk, the chairs, the couches standing on the rugless floor wearing the same black and white tiles, were all almost human in their design. Only the fact that they were all built to the scale of the eight-foot aliens made them different. That, and the fact that there was no padding or upholstery on any of them.

Lyt Ahn was indeed alone, seated, looming behind his desk; which held in its surface a screen like that in the desk of the officer in the corridor, plus a scattering of some small artifacts, each tiny enough to be encompassed in Shane's merely human hand, but showing no recognizable shapes or purposes. In a like situation, on a human desk, they might have been miniature sculptures. But the Aalaag owned no art, nor showed interest in any. What they really were, and their purpose in being there, still puzzled him. On the wall to his right was a larger screen, now unlit, some three by two meters in area. In the left wall was an Aalaag-sized single door that led to Lyt Ahn's private apartments.

Lyt Ahn raised his head to look at Shane as the human stepped through the doorway, taking one pace and then halting.

"Come here," the alien commander said; and, both permitted and ordered—the words were one word in Aalaag— Shane came up to the far side of the desk.

The First Captain of all Earth gazed at him. Just as Aalaag had difficulty distinguishing between individual humans, so most humans, aside from the fact that they saw their overlords most commonly in armor and therefore faceless, were not adept at telling one Aalaag from another. Shane gazed back. He had been in close contact with the alien commander since Lyt Ahn had formed his corps of human interpreters, nearly three years before. Shane not only recognized the First Captain, he had become expert at studying the other for small clues to his master's momentary mood. Like all subjects he was dependent, in this case dependent upon the First Captain not only for food and shelter, but for a continuance of life itself. He studied the First Captain daily, as a lamb might study the lion with which it was required to lie down each night; and just at the moment, he thought now that he read fatigue and a deep-seated worry, plus something else he could not identify, in the visage of the towering individual before him.

"Laa Ehon, of the fifth rank and Commander of the Milan garrison has received your sending, most immaculate sir, and sends his courtesies to the First Captain," said Shane. "He returned no message by me."

"Did he not, little Shane-beast?" said Lyt Ahn. Shane's name was uttered in as close to an affectionate diminutive as the alien language allowed; but the words were obviously spoken more to himself than to the human.

Shane's heart took an upward leap. Lyt Ahn was clearly in as warm and confidential a mood as it was possible for an Aalaag to be—and more so than Shane had ever seen any other alien permit himself. Nonetheless, there was also that impression of worry and some concern for an unknown source that he had noted on first entering the room; and he continued covertly to study the heavy-boned face opposite. There was a greater impression of age about his master than he had ever seen before, although the face was barely lined, as always; and there was no way that age could have made the hair of the Earth's supreme commander any whiter than that of any other adult Aalaag—it would have been yellowish at birth, but purely snow-colored by puberty, which in the aliens seemed to come about the age of eighteen to twenty-five Earthly years.

Nor was there anything else different about the grayish eyes, in the pale Aalaag skin that never appeared to tan. With its great, sharp bones and pale color it gave the impression of being carved out of a soft, gray-white stone. But still, somehow it also managed to give Shane not only the impression of great age, but of that same weariness and emotion that currently seemed to be at work in the First Captain.

As Shane watched, the massive figure got slowly to its feet, walked around from behind its desk and sat down on one of the couches. The change of position was a signal that the meeting had now become informal. Lyt Ahn was dressed in black boots and a white, single-piece suit, like any other alien on duty. Shane turned as the other moved, in order to keep facing his master; and, after a moment, saw the eyes that had been more looking through him than otherwise focus once more directly upon him.

"Come here, Shane-beast," said Lyt Ahn.

Shane moved forward until he stood one step from the seated alien. Lyt Ahn studied him for a long moment. Their heads were on a level. Then, reaching out, he cupped an enormous hand gently, for a moment, over Shane's head.

Shane checked his body from tensing just in time. Physical contact was almost unknown amongst the Aalaag themselves, and unheard of between Aalaag and human; but Shane had learned over the last two years that Lyt Ahn permitted himself freedoms beyond those generally used by those lesser in rank than himself. The large hand that could easily have crushed the bones of Shane's skull rested lightly for a moment on Shane's head and then was withdrawn.

"Little Shane-beast," said Lyt Ahn—and unless it was his imagination it seemed to Shane that he heard in the Aalaag voice the same tiredness he had suspected in the First Captain's face—"are you contented?"

There was no word in the Aalaag language for "happy." "Contented" was the closest possible expression to it. Shane felt a sudden fear of an unknown trap in the question; and for a second he debated telling Lyt Ahn that he was, indeed, contented. But the Aalaag could accept nothing but truth; and the First Captain had always allowed his human interpreters a freedom of opinion no other Aalaag permitted.

"No, most immaculate sir," Shane answered. "I would be contented only if this world was as it was before the untarnished race came among us."

Lyt Ahn did not sigh. But Shane, used to the First Captain, and having studied him as only children, animals and slaves have always studied those who hold their life and every freedom in their hands, received the clear impression that the other would have sighed if he had only been physiologically and psychologically capable of doing so.

"Yes," said the First Captain, absently looking through him once more, "your race makes unhappy cattle, true enough."

Fear came back to Shane and chilled him to the bone. He told himself that Lyt Ahn could by no means have discovered this soon what he had done illegally in Milan; but the words the alien supreme commander had just now used came too close to his knowledge of guilt not to cause him to stiffen internally.

For a second he debated trying to entice Lyt Ahn to be more explicit about whatever had caused him to make such a remark. Ordinarily, a human did not speak unless ordered to do so. But the First Captain had always allowed Shane and the other translators unusual freedom in that respect. Shane checked, however, at the thought for two reasons. One, his uncertainty of how such a question could be phrased without offense; and two, a fear that if Lyt Ahn did indeed suspect him of some violation of proper conduct, any such asking would only confirm the suspicion.

He stood silent, therefore, and simply waited, in the helplessness of the totally dependent. Either Lyt Ahn would speak further, or the First Captain would dismiss him; and neither of these things could Shane control.

"Do you find your fellow cattle in any way different these days, Shane-beast?" asked Lyt Ahn.

Shane thought involuntarily of the small tenement room in Milan to which he had been kidnapped; and in which he had been held and questioned by those human revolutionaries who had innocently adopted as their symbol the rude sketch he had himself conceived of a year earlier, in a moment of drunken desperation—though that was not something they or any other, human or alien, could have known.

"No, most immaculate sir," he answered; and felt the danger of his lie like a heavy weight in his chest.

There was another pause that could have been a sigh from Lyt Ahn.

"No," said the alien commander, "perhaps . . . perhaps even if they were, it would not be such as you they would admit their feelings to. Your fellow cattle do not love those who work for us, do they, little Shane-beast?"

"No," said Shane, truthfully and bitterly.

It was that very fact that required him to wear the pilgrim's cloak and carry the pilgrim's staff when he moved about the Earth on Lyt Ahn's business. Among so many true wearers of that costume, it became a cloak of protective anonymity, particularly with the hood of the cloak pulled up over his head and shadowing his features. If he had betrayed the fact that he was actually a servant of the aliens, his life would literally have been in danger from his fellow humans, from the moment he was out of sight of an Aalaag, or one of the armed, human Interior Guards—who themselves did not dare go among the mass of ordinary humans without their uniforms and unarmed. Lyt Ahn was in a strange mood, with his mind off on some problem which at this moment was still unclear to Shane; but which had plainly directed his attention elsewhere than at Shane himself. It occurred to Shane suddenly that now might be an opportunity to cover his tracks in regard to the lesser matter of his having lied to Laa Ehon, the Aalaag commanding the Milan area, when that alien had asked him what price Lyt Ahn might put upon him.

"If the most immaculate sir pleases," Shane said, "this beast was asked a question by the sir who is called Laa Ehon. The question was what price my master might put upon me."

"So," replied Lyt Ahn, his thoughts clearly still occupied with that primary concern Shane had noted in him. The First Captain's response was in fact no response at all, merely an acknowledgment of the fact that he had heard what Shane had said. Shane allowed himself to hope.

"I answered," said Shane, "that to the best of my knowledge, the most immaculate sir had valued all of his translator-beasts at half a possession of land"—Shane tried to keep his voice unchanged but for a fraction of a second his breath caught in his throat—"and the favor of my master."

"So," said Lyt Ahn, still in the same tone of voice.

He had heard, but clearly he had not heard. Internally, Shane felt the weakness of relief. The truth was that Lyt Ahn had never, to Shane's knowledge, put any kind of price on Shane or any of the other humans in the translator section. Shane had gambled in answering Laa Ehon that the First Captain would not remember whether he had or not—and the gamble had now paid off. The half a possession of land, in what it represented in terms of Earthly territory according to Aalaag measurements, was a princely enough price for any single human beast. But the favor which Shane had mentioned meant far more. Effectively, its meaning was that in addition to any other price, the buyer could be called upon at any time in the future to return an as-yet unnamed favor to the seller, with a worth in direct proportion as the buyer envisaged its value. In theory, at least, the cost of buying Shane might include Lyt Ahn's calling upon Laa Ehon sometime in the future for anything the other owned, up to and including his life.

A single musical note from the door leading to the private apartments of the First Captain interrupted the thoughts of both Shane and Lyt Ahn.

The door swung open to let in a second Aalaag. But this one was a female—and Shane recognized her with something close to panic. She was Adtha Or Ain, the consort of Lyt Ahn; and the panic arose from the fact that Shane was, for the first time in a long time, encountering a situation involving Aalaag mores with which he was not familiar. When, on rare occasions before this, he had to do with the consort of the First Captain, it had been with her alone; when he had been sent about the planet with one of her private messages.

His encounters with her had been purely formal and entirely conducted within the known code of behavior between Aalaag and human beast. On the other hand his private meetings with Lyt Ahn had largely come to be informal. There was no way of telling now how she would react to the informality he was used to being permitted by Lyt Ahn. On the other hand, it would raise the question of his disobeying Lyt Ahn's authority if he suddenly reverted to the formal mode, after Lyt Ahn, by sitting down on the couch, had, in effect, ordered him to abandon it. There was no way for him to tell whether, if either should address him, he should respond in the formal or the informal mode. Either mode could be a response that would offend either Lyt Ahn or Adtha Or Ain.

Shane stood motionless and silent, praying that he would be ignored by both aliens. He studied Adtha Or Ain as he had studied Lyt Ahn earlier—and for the same reasons. There was something like a bitterness that he had always noted in her, but it had always seemed to be hard held under control. In this moment, however, that control seemed to have loosened.

For the moment, his luck seemed to be holding. Lyt Ahn had risen from the couch and gone to meet Adtha Or Ain. They stopped, facing each other, an Aalaag arm's length apart, looking into each other's faces.

Adtha Or Ain was slightly the taller of the two; but, aside from that, if Shane had not come to recognize the sexual differences in Aalaag bodies, it would have been hard to tell the two apart. Their dress was identical. Only the slight individuality of their features, that individuality which Shane had finally taught himself to look for over these past years, and the difference in their voices, marked them apart. Adult Aalaag females, like human ones, tended to speak in somewhat higher voices than the males of their race—although the difference was nowhere near as marked as in humans—particularly in the case of an older Aalaag female like Adtha Or Ain, whose voice had deepened with age.

Now, the two stood facing each other. There was a tension between them that Shane sensed strongly, and with that sensing came another wave of relief. If these two would just stay completely concerned with each other, he would in effect be invisible—of no more importance to them than the furniture in the room; and the chances of either requiring an answer from him were almost nil. For the first time, Shane dared to look on them as an observer might, rather than as a potential victim of their meeting.

They did not touch. Nonetheless, Shane's experience with the Aalaag, and elsewhere, let him read into their confrontation a closeness—"love" was a word that did not exist in the Aalaag language—which implied that, had they been humans, they might have touched. At the same time, however, Shane felt a sadness and an anger in Adtha Or Ain and a sort of helpless pity in Lyt Ahn.

The two ignored him.

"Perhaps," said Lyt Ahn, "you should rest."

"No," said Adtha Or Ain. "Rest is no rest to me, at times like this."

"You make yourself suffer unnecessarily."

She turned aside and walked around the First Captain. He turned also to look after her. She went to the wall bearing the large screen; and although Shane could not see her make any motion to turn it on, it woke to light and image before her, the starkness of what it showed dominating the room.

The three-dimensional shape on it was the last that Shane could have imagined. It was of an adult male Aalaag, without armor, but carrying all personal weapons and encased in a block of something brownishly transparent, like a fly in amber.

It was only after he got past his first shock of seeing it and began to examine it in detail that he noticed two unusual things. One was that there was a faintish yellow tinge to the roots of the white hair on the head of the encased Aalaag, and the second—it was unbelievable, but the Aalaag shown was alive, if completely helpless.

He could see the pupils of gray eyes move minutely, as he watched. They were focused on something that seemed to be outside the scene imaged on the screen. Other expression there was none—nor could there be any, since the face, like all the rest of the body, was imprisoned and held immobile by the enclosing material.

"No," said Lyt Ahn behind him.

Shane's ears, sharpened by over two years of servitude, heard that rare thing, a note of emotion in an Aalaag voice; and, faint as it was, he read it clearly as a note of pain. Those years of attuning himself to the moods of the First Captain had finally created a bond that was all but empathic between them; and his own emotions felt Lyt Ahn's in this moment without uncertainty.

"I must look at it," said Adtha Or Ain, standing before the screen.

Lyt Ahn took three steps forward, moving up behind her. His two great hands reached out part way toward her shoulders and then fell back to his sides.

"It's only a conception," he said. "A mock-up. You've no reason for assuming it represents reality. Almost certainly no such thing has happened. Undoubtedly he and his team are dead, destroyed utterly."

"But perhaps he is like this," said Adtha Or Ain, without turning her head from the screen. "Maybe they have him so, and will keep him so for thousands of lifetimes. I will have no more children. I had only this one, and perhaps this is how he is now."

Lyt Ahn stood, saying nothing. She turned to face him.

"You let him go," she said.

"You know—as I know," he answered. "Some of us must keep watch on the Inner Race who stole our homes, in case they move again and the movement is in this direction. He was my son—my son as well as yours—and he wanted to be one of those to go and check."

"You could have denied him. I asked you to order him to stay. You did not."

"How could I?"

"By speaking."

Shane had never before seen emotion at this level between two of the normally expressionless Aalaagi and he felt like someone tossed about in a hurricane. He could not leave; but to stay and listen was all but unbearable. Against his will, the empathic response he had so painstakingly developed to the feelings of Lyt Ahn was at him now with a pain he felt at second hand, pain he could not understand or do anything about.

"In a thousand lifetimes," she said, "a thousand lifetimes and more, they made no sign of moving again. They only wanted our worlds, our homes; and once they had them they were content enough. We all know that. Why send our children back to what's theirs now—so that they can catch them and make toys for themselves of our flesh and blood—make a toy and a thing of my son?"

"There was no choice," said Lyt Ahn. "Could I protect my son before others—when he'd asked to go?"

"He was a child. He didn't know."

"It was his duty. It was my duty—and your duty—to let him go. So the Aalaag survive. You know your duty. And I tell you again, you've no way of knowing he's not at peace, safely dead and destroyed. You make yourself a nightmare of the one most unlikely thing that could happen."

"Prove it to me," Adtha Or Ain said. "Send an expedition to find out."

"You know I can't. Not yet. We've only held this world

three of its years. It's not properly tamed, yet. The crew, the needs for the expedition you want aren't to spare.''

"You promised me.''

"I promised to send an expedition as soon as team and materials were to spare.''

"And it's been three years, and still you say there're none.''

"None for only a possibility—none for what may be nothing more than a nightmare grown in your own mind. As soon as I can in duty and honor spare people for something of that level, the expedition will go. I promise you. It will bring back the truth of what happened to our son. But not yet.''

She turned from him.

"Three years,'' she said.

"These beasts are not like some on other worlds we've taken. I've done with this planet as much as I might, given the force I had to work with. No one could do more. You are unfair, Adtha Or Ain.''

Silently, she turned, crossed the room once more and passed back through the doorway by which she had entered. Its doors closed behind her.

Lyt Ahn stood for a moment, then looked at the screen. It went blank and gray once more. He turned and went to sit down again at his desk, touching the smaller screen inset in it and apparently returning to the work he had been doing when Shane had come in.

Shane continued to stand, unmoving. He stood, and the minutes went by. It was not unusual that a human should have to hold his place indefinitely, waiting for the attention of an Aalaag; and Shane was trained to it. But this time his mind was a seething, bewildered mass. He longed for the First Captain to remember he was there and do something about him.

A very long time later, it seemed, Lyt Ahn did lift his head from his screen and his eyes look notice of Shane's presence.

"You may go,'' he said. His gaze was back on the desk screen before the words had left his lips.

Shane turned and left.

He went back down the long corridor, past the Aalaag officer still on duty at the desk and, after some distance, to the door of his own cubicle. Opening that door at last, he saw, seated in the room's single armchair by the narrow bed, a human figure. It was one of the other translators, a brown-haired young woman named Sylvia Onjin.

"I heard you were back," she told him.

He made himself smile at her. How she had heard did not matter. There was an informational grapevine, among all humans in the House of Weapons, that operated entirely without reference to whether the giver and receiver of information were personally on good terms. It was to the benefit of all humans in the House that as much as possible be known about the activities of both Aalaag and humans there.

Probably, word of his return had been passed through the ranks of the Interior Guards, either directly to the corps of translators, or by way of one of the other groups of human specialists personally owned and used by the First Captain.

What did matter was that now, of all times, was not a moment in which he wanted to see her—or anyone. The need for privacy was so strong in him that he felt ready to break down emotionally and mentally if he did not have it. But he could not easily tell her to go.

The humans owned by Lyt Ahn, being picked beasts and therefore of good quality, were encouraged to intermingle; and even to mate and have young if they wished, although Aalaag mores stood in the way of the aliens making any specific command or order that they do so. Only the Interior Guard welcomed the idea of being parents under these conditions. None of those in the translator ranks had any desire to perpetuate their kind as slaves of the aliens. But still, sheer physical and emotional hungers drew individuals together.

Sylvia Onjin and Shane had been two so drawn. They had no real lust or love for each other in the ordinary senses of those words. Only, they found each other slightly more compatible than either found others of the human opposite sex in the House of Weapons. In the world as it had been before the Aalaag came, Shane thought now, if they two had met they would almost undoubtedly have parted again immediately with no great desire to see more of each other. But in this place they clung instinctively together.

But the thought of Sylvia's company, now, when his mind was in turmoil and his emotions had just been stretched to a breaking-point, was more than Shane could face. At best, it was only an act he and she played together, a pretense that erected a small, flimsy and temporary private existence for them both; away from the alien-dominated world that held their lives and daily actions in its indifferent hand. Also, now, after Shane's encounter with the other young woman, the one called Maria, whom he had saved from questioning by the Aalaag, and who had later been a member of the Milanese resistance group that had later kidnapped him, there was something about Sylvia that almost repelled him, the way a tamed animal might suffer in comparison with one still wild and free.

But the narrow face of Sylvia smiled confidently back up at him. Her smile was her best feature; and in the days before the Aalaag she might have emphasized her other good features with makeup to the point where she could have been considered attractive, if not seductive. But the aliens classed lipstick and all such other beauty aids with that uncleanliness they were so adamant in erasing from any world they owned. To an Aalaag, a woman with makeup on had merely dirtied her face. Ordinary humans, in private, might indulge in such actions, but not those human servants which the Aalaag saw daily.

So Sylvia's face was starkly clean, pale-looking under her close-cropped, ordinary brown hair. It was a small-boned face. She was a woman of one hundred and thirty-four centimeters in height—barely over five feet, a corner of Shane's western mind automatically calculated—and narrow-bodied even for that height. Her figure was unremarkable, but not bad for a woman in her early twenties. Like Shane himself she had been a graduate student when the Aalaag landed.

She sat now with her legs crossed, the skirt of the black taffeta cocktail dress she had put on lifted by the action to reveal her knees. In her lap was a heavy-looking, cylindrical object about ten inches long wrapped in white documentary paper, held in place by a narrow strip of such paper wrapped around its neck, formed into a bow and colored red, apparently by some homemade substance, since such a thing as red tape—let alone the red ribbon the paper strip was evidently intended to mimic—was not something which the Aalaag would find any reason for allowing.

"Happy homecoming!" She held it out to him.

He stepped forward automatically and took it, making himself smile back at her. He could feel through the paper, that it was obviously a full bottle of something. He hardly drank, as she knew—there was too much danger of making some mistake in front of their owners if some unexpected call to duty should come—but it was about the only gift available for any of them to give each other. He held it, feeling how obvious the falseness of his smile must be. The image of Maria was still between them—but then suddenly it cleared and it was as if he saw Sylvia unexpectedly wiped clean of all artifice, naked in her hopes and fears as in the pretensions with which she strove to battle those fears.

His heart turned suddenly within him. It was a physical feeling like a palpable lurch in his chest. He saw Sylvia clearly for the first time and understood that he could never betray her, could never deny help to her in this or any like moment. For all that, there was not even the shadow of real love between them. He felt his smile become genuine and tender as he looked down at her; and he felt—not the actual love for which she yearned, or even the pretense of it, for which she was willing to settle—but a literal affection that was based in the fact that they were simply two humans together in this alien house.

Not understanding the reasons for it, but instinctively recognizing the emotion that had come into him, she rose suddenly and came into his arms; and he felt a strong gush of tenderness, such as he had never felt before in his long months in this place of weapons, that made him hold her tightly to him.

Later, lying on his back in the darkness, the slight body of Sylvia sleeping contentedly beside him, he was assaulted by an unexpected tidal wave of self-pity that washed over him and threatened to drown him. He fought it off; and after a while he, too, slept.

He was roused from deep slumber by the burring of his bedside phone. He reached out toward it and the action triggered to life the light over the nightstand where the square screen of the phone sat. He touched the screen and the face of an Aalaag above the collar of a duty officer appeared on it.

"You are ordered to attend the First Captain, beast," said the officer's deep remote voice. "Report to him in the Council Conference Room."

"I hear and obey, untarnished sir," Shane heard his own voice, still thick with sleep, answering.

The screen went blank, leaving a silvery gray, opaque surface. Shane rose and dressed. Sylvia was already gone and the chronometer by his bed showed that the hour was barely past dawn.

Twenty minutes later, shaven, clean and dressed, he touched the bronze surface of the door to the Council Conference Room.

"Come," said the voice of Lyt Ahn.

The door opened itself and he entered to find twelve Aalaag, five males and seven females, seated around the floating, shimmering surface that served them as a conference table. Lyt Ahn sat at the far end. On his right was Laa Ehon, the Commander for the area capitaled in Milan, Italy; and for a second a dryness tightened Shane's throat as he remembered his secret crimes against that officer and his Command. But then common sense reasserted itself. No such august assemblage would be convened only to deal with the criminal acts of a simple beast; and his tension slackened. He looked down the table surface toward the First Captain and waited for orders. He had halted instinctively, from custom, two paces inside the opened door; and the twelve powerful alien faces were studying him as just-fed lions might study some small animal that had wandered into the midst of their pride.

"This is the one you spoke of?" asked the female Aalaag closest on Lyt Ahn's left and second down the table from him.

Her voice had the depth of age and it came to Shane that she—in fact, all the aliens here—would be officers of no lower than the fifth rank. Otherwise they would not have been called into a Council such as this. He wondered what District the speaker commanded. She was no alien he recognized.

"It is one of the cattle I call Shane-beast," said Lyt Ahn. "It is the one I sent only the day before yesterday to Laa Ehon with communications."

He turned to look at the Commander of the Milanese area.

"I'm still uncertain as to how you think his presence here can contribute to the discussion," he went on to Laa Ehon.

"Order it to speak," replied Laa Ehon.

"Identify yourself and your work," Lyt Ahn said to Shane.

"By your command, immaculate sir," said Shane clearly: "I am a translator and courier of your staff and have been so for nearly three of our planet's years."

There was a moment's silence around the table.

"Remarkable," said the female Aalaag on Lyt Ahn's right, who had spoken earlier.

"Exactly," put in Laa Ehon. "Notice how perfectly it speaks the true language—all of you who are so used to the

limited mouthings of your beasts, when they can be brought
to attempt to communicate in real speech at all.''

"It's one of a special, limited corps of the creatures, all of
whom have been selected for special ability in this regard,"
said Lyt Ahn. "I'm still waiting to hear how you think, Laa
Ehon, that its presence here can contribute to our discussion.''

" 'Special,' " echoed Laa Ehon. The single sound of the
word in the Aalaag tongue was completely without emphasis.

"As I said," replied Lyt Ahn.

Laa Ehon turned his head to the First Captain, inclined it in
a brief gesture of respect, and then turned back to look around
the table at the others there.

"Let's return to the matter in hand, then," Laa Ehon said.
"I asked for this meeting because it's been three local years
approximately since our Expedition to this world first set
down upon it. That length of time has now passed and certain
signs of adjustments to our presence here, in the attitudes of
the local dominant race, that should by now be showing
themselves have not done so—"

"The incidence of *yowaragh* among the beasts," interrupted the female who had spoken before, "isn't that much
above the norm for such a period. Granted, no two situations
on any two acquired worlds are ever the same —"

"Granted exactly that," Laa Ehon reinterrupted in his turn,
"it is not *yowaragh* with which I am primarily concerned, but
a general failure on the part of the cattle to keep production
levels as expected. Past Expeditions on other worlds have
found such a slump in production in their early years, but
always it's turned out in the end to be caused by depression in
the beasts at finding themselves governed—even though that
governing has resulted for them in a safer, cleaner world—as
it has here. On this world, however, it is something much
more like silent defiance than depression with which we seem
to be dealing. I repeat, it is this, not incidents of *yowaragh*,
with which I am concerned.''

A cold shiver threatened to emerge from its hiding place in
the center of Shane's body and betray itself as a visible
tremor. With a great effort, he held it under control, reminding himself that the aliens here were not watching him. For
the moment, once more, he had become invisible, in the same
sense that the furniture and the walls of the room about them
were invisible.

". . . It is," Laa Ehon's voice drew his attention back to

what the Milanese Commander was saying to the rest of the
table, "a matter of hard statistics. May I remind the untarnished and immaculate officers here assembled that the preliminary survey of this world, carried on over several decades
of the planet's time, gave no intimation of such an attitude or
such a potential falling off of production. The projection gave
us instead every reason to believe that the local dominant race
should be tameable and useful in a high degree; especially
when faced with the alternative of giving up the level of
civilization they had so far achieved; and on which, in so
many ways, they had become dependent. Remember, they
were given a free choice and they chose the merciful
alternative."

"I've never been quite sure, Laa Ehon," put in Lyt Ahn
from the head of the table, "about the accuracy of that
adjective for the alternative. It doesn't seem to me that I can
bring to mind a single incident in which a race of conquered
cattle believed the alternative they had chosen to be one
deserving of the word 'merciful.' "

"It was clear they understood at the time of takeover, First
Captain," said Laa Ehon, "even if your corps of translators
had not yet been established. I remember there was no doubt
that they understood that their choice was between accepting
the true race as their masters, or having all their cities and
technology reduced to rubble, leaving them at their original
level of stone-chipping savages. How can that alternative not
have been merciful when they also clearly understood that we
also had the power to eradicate each and every one of them
from the face of their planet, but chose not to use it?"

"Well, well," said Lyt Ahn, "perhaps you're right. In any
case, let's avoid side issues. Please get to whatever point you
were going to make."

"Of course, First Captain," said Laa Ehon.

The words were said mildly enough; but for the first time it
exploded in Shane's mind what he suddenly realized he should
have sensed from the first: and that was that there was a
power struggle going on in this room, at this table.

And the antagonists were Laa Ehon and Lyt Ahn.

Immediately the realization was born in him, his mind was
ready with excuses for its not being obvious to him minutes
before. Even six weeks ago, he told himself, he would not
have recognized the subtle signals of such a conflict, blinded
by an unquestioning assumption that his master's supreme

position among the Aalaag was unquestioned and unassailable. But now those same signals leaped out at him. They were everywhere, in the tone of the voices of those speaking, in the attitudes with which the various officers sat in their places about the table—in the very fact Laa Ehon could request that Lyt Ahn have Shane himself brought here; and then delay this long in giving his full reasons why he had requested it.

Shane had not read those signals more swiftly because he had been too secure in his belief in Lyt Ahn's authority. Only now, the curious small freedoms allowed him by the First Captain, as well as the momentary Aalaag-uncharacteristic confidences and transient betrayals of emotion on the part of the ruling officer should have prepared him for this moment of understanding, but had not.

Lyt Ahn, he suddenly realized, was vulnerable. The First Captain had to be vulnerable in this sense. Shane had come to understand how the Aalaag lived by tradition and the mores developed by that tradition. Tradition and those mores could not have failed to provide means for removing a supreme commander who became incapable or proved himself inept. Just how such a procedure would work, Shane as yet had no idea. But of this he was suddenly, utterly convinced. Lyt Ahn was under attack here and now; and Laa Ehon was either the attacker or the spearhead of that attack.

As for the others present . . . Shane was reminded of the social patterns of a wolf pack. All those there would follow unquestioningly the Alpha leader—who was Lyt Ahn—right up until the moment when his leadership was seriously brought into question. Then, if that question was not effectively answered, they would turn to follow the questioner and aid him in rending their former leader. But, if it was effectively answered, then the questioner would lose all support from them—until the next time of questioning. It was that moment of doubt in which the majority would swing behind the questioner that Lyt Ahn must foresee and avoid.

". . . I have requested this meeting," Laa Ehon was saying, "primarily because of my own difficulties in meeting production estimates with the cattle of my area; and hoping that my fellow senior officers could suggest ways by which I might improve the situation. I must admit, however, that it begins to appear to me lately that the problems I notice are not restricted to my district alone, but reflect a general problem of attitude which is worldwide—and may even be growing—among the subject beasts.''

"It seems to me," broke in a thick-chested male Aalaag halfway down the table on Lyt Ahn's right, "that what you say almost approaches insult to the rest of us. Laa Ehon, are you saying we others have failed to notice something that you've clearly seen?"

"I did not say, or imply, that I had seen anything with particular clearness," said Laa Ehon. "I'm only attempting to point to the importance of something you must all have already noticed—the discrepancy between the original estimates of beast-adjustment to our presence in the time since our landing, and the actuality of that adjustment. I believe there's cause for concern in that discrepancy."

"We've been following the patterns established by successful subjugations on other worlds in the past," said another of the female Aalaag, one whose face showed the hollowness of age beneath her cheekbones. "It is true, as Maa Alyn just said, that each world is different, each race of beasts different—"

"And some, a rare few such races, have even turned out to be failures," said Laa Ehon.

A feeling of shock permeated the conference, perceptible to Shane where it might not have been to any other human, even another one of the special handful of humans employed by Lyt Ahn; the expressions of the Aalaag officers there had not changed at Laa Ehon's last words. There had been only an unnaturally prolonged moment of unnatural silence; but Shane was sure he had read it correctly.

"It seems to me, Laa Ehon," said Lyt Ahn, finally breaking that silence, his heavy voice sounding strangely loud in the room, "that you're holding back something it's in your mind to tell us. Did you ask for this conference merely to air a concern, or have you some special suggestion for us?"

"I have a suggestion," said Laa Ehon.

He turned to look again at Shane, and the eyes of the others at the table followed the changed angle of his gaze.

"I suggest that the situation here—insofar as it reflects a delay in beast-adjustment to our presence—calls for some actions which must necessarily break to some small extent with the patterns of successful subjugation mentioned by Maa Alyn—"

He glanced toward and inclined his head slightly toward the elderly Aalaag female who had recently spoken.

"I suggest," he went on, "that we vary that pattern—oh, in no large way, but experimentally, by attempting to counter this marking on walls we've all been seeing in our districts, this evidence of some rebellious feeling among a few of these beasts—"

—A chill passed through Shane. Clearly now, Laa Ehon was talking of the activities of foolish and doomed underground groups like Maria's in Milan; and the marking was equally clearly his sketch of the pilgrim figure.

"Such things," said the thick-chested Aalaag, "are familiar, even expected, during the early years of the subjugation of any race of beasts. Such defacements cease as succeeding generations adapt to serving our purposes, and forget the resentments of their forebearers. This is far too soon to see a problem in a few rogue creatures."

"I beg to disagree," said Laa Ehon. "We know that, of course, the beasts communicate among themselves. This one standing before us now may be aware of more discontent among its race than we suspect—"

"You suggest we put it to the question?" inquired the female Aalaag called Maa Alyn, who had been the first to reply to Laa Ehon; and the chill within Shane became a solid iciness of fear.

"If I may interrupt," said the heavy voice of Lyt Ahn, almost sardonically, "the beast in question is my property. Moreover, it is an extremely valuable beast, as are all the talented small handful like it that I keep and use. I would not agree to its being questioned to destruction, without adequate proof of need."

"Of course I don't suggest the damaging of such a valuable beast, particularly one which is the property of the First Captain, and which I myself have seen to be so useful." Laa Ehon turned back to face Lyt Ahn. "In fact, quite the contrary. I only asked the beast be produced in order to illustrate a point I think is important to us all. With all due respect, First Captain, I've yet to be convinced that what this beast does can't also be done by at least a large number of its fellow beasts, if not most of them. Certainly, if they have the physical vocal apparatus which can correctly approximate the sounds of the true speech—or even approach those sounds understandably—and their minds have the ability to organize that speech in coherent and usable fashion, one almost has to assume this to be a property common to their species as a whole.''

"I can only assure you," said Lyt Ahn, with a touch of formality in his voice, "that this isn't the case. There seems to be something more necessary—a conceptual ability, rare among them. At my orders many such cattle were tested and only the few I use here were found capable on a level with this one you see before you. In fact, this particular beast is the most capable of all those I own. None speaks as accentlessly as this one.''

"Far be it from me to differ with you, First Captain and immaculate sir," said Laa Ehon. "You are informed on this subject and I'm not. Nevertheless, as I have pointed out, faced as we are with a problem of adjustment on the part of this species—"

"—As you have continued to point out to us, untarnished sir," said the thick-chested Aalaag, "almost to the point of weariness since we first sat down together here.''

"If I have overemphasized the point," said Laa Ehon, "I apologize for that to the immaculate and untarnished persons here assembled. It merely seemed to me that enunciating the point is necessary as a preamble to stating my personal belief; and that is that under the circumstances it's worth exploring even some unorthodox solutions to the problem, since it threatens to diminish world-wide production by these beasts. A production, which I don't need remind any of us, that is important, not merely to us on this planet, but to all our true people on all the worlds we have taken over; not only for our present survival, but for the protection of the immaculate people as a whole in case the inner race that stole our home worlds originally should make another move, this time in this direction.''

"As you say," murmured the voice of Lyt Ahn, "you don't need to remind us of that. What exactly is this suggestion of yours, then?''

"Simply," said Laa Ehon, "I propose we depart from standard procedure and set up specific beasts as governors in our respective districts, holding them responsible for the production of the cattle in their districts; and allowing them to use other cattle as subsidiary officers to set up their own structures of authority to guarantee such production.''

"Absolutely against standard procedure," said the thick-chested officer, promptly.

"Indeed," said Maa Alyn, leaning her body slightly forward to stare down the tabletop directly at Laa Ehon, "those who've gone before us have found by hard experience that the best way to handle native cattle is to give them all possible freedoms of custom and society according to what they have been used to, but never to allow individuals among them power as intermediaries between ourselves and the rest of the beasts. Whenever we've set up intermediaries of their own race like that, between us and them, corruption on the part of their officials has almost invariably occurred. Moreover, resentment is born among the general mass of the cattle, and this, in the end, costs us more than the original gains achieved by using intermediaries."

"I seem to remember something just said, however," answered Laa Ehon, "about each world and each race upon it being a different and unique problem. The recalcitrance shown by the local cattle as a whole on this particular world of ours, as shown by the statistics, are of an order above those shown on any previous world we have taken over. It's true there's been no show of overt antagonism on the part of the general mass of cattle—yet, at least. But on the other hand, it would be hard to show any except our directly used beasts, such as those in the Interior Guard, or this translator-courier corps of the First Captain, who can be said sincerely to have made a full and proper adaptation to us, as their owners and rulers."

"That doesn't mean your proposal is the correct solution to the problem," put in a male Aalaag who had not spoken before. He sat little more than a meter from Shane's right hand, at the extreme far end of the table from Lyt Ahn.

"Of course," answered Laa Ehon. "I recognize the danger of making any large changes—let alone ones that go against established procedure—without having adequate data first. Therefore, what I'm actually suggesting is that certain measures be put into effect on a trial basis."

He tapped the tabletop before him and screens alit with data in the Aalaag script appeared in it before each alien there.

"I've had surveys made," he went on, "and you see the results of them on the screens before you. I've also had hard copies delivered to your offices by available underofficers of mine. You'll note my survey turned up three districts best

suited to the putting into effect of temporary test procedures
to see if my estimations are correct. Two were island areas;
one being what the cattle formerly called the Japanese Islands, the other called the British Islands. There are advantages of homogeneity and diversity in each case. Of these
two, the British Islands seems the better prospect—''

''These islands, of course, are within my district,'' said
Maa Alyn, stiffly. ''But you also mentioned, I think, three—
not two—areas as being possibly suitable as testing areas?''

''I did,'' said Laa Ehon. ''However, the third area, according to my surveys, would be this one surrounding the House
of Weapons; and I didn't think we'd want to make any
experiments that close to our prime seat of authority, even if
the First Captain would give permission . . . as, of course, I
would expect to wait upon your permission, Maa Alyn, before proposing to experiment in the area of the British Islands.''

There was a murmur around the table that seemed to Shane
to express diverse opinions.

''So,'' went on Laa Ehon, ignoring the sound, ''what I
would like to suggest, with the concurrence of this Council
and everyone concerned, is to set up a temporary governing
structure such as I described earlier; monitored directly by us,
with an officer of the true race supervising and working in
parallel with each individual beast who is in a position of
intermediate authority as governor.''

There was a moment's silence.

''I see a great many difficulties . . .'' began Maa Alyn.

''Frankly, I do myself,'' said Laa Ehon. ''This is unknown
territory to all of us. For one thing, as has been pointed out,
any tendencies for the beast-governor and his staff to take
advantage of their positions over their fellow cattle would be
difficult for us to see and check promptly. This, however—it
has recently occurred to me and this was why I asked our
First Captain to send for the beast who stands before us
now—could be greatly helped by requiring all beast-governor
staff to have contact with their supervisory numbers of the
true race in the real language.''

''But such a condition would need that the beast-governor,
to say nothing of his staff, be not merely adequate, but fluent,
in the true language—'' the thick-chested Aalaag broke off
suddenly. ''Are you proposing that the First Captain lend his
corps of translators to this task? If so, that immaculate sir

would of course have to volunteer them for the duty. There is no way in honor this Council could suggest—"

"Not at all—not at all," said Laa Ehon. "I was merely about to suggest that the beasts chosen to be governor and staff be put first through an intensive course of teaching, to make them fluent in the true language, using as teachers—if the First Captain agrees—some of his translators such as the beast before us—and, of course, provided that my overall suggestion meets with the approval of the Council. The intent would be to produce cattle who'd be able to explain themselves clearly to their own kind while still being clear and understandable in their reports to ourselves, thereby making for a strong, plain link of understanding between us and the mass of cattle in general."

"I have already said," put in Lyt Ahn, "that it is only the rare beast that can be taught to speak with such adequate clearness. The evidence for this is in the efforts I mentioned, to which I was put in staffing this particular corps of beast-translators and couriers, to which you refer and of which the beast now present is an example."

"It seems to me we lose nothing by trying," said Laa Ehon.

"We stand to lose something by trying," said Lyt Ahn, "if what we are trying is foredoomed to a failure that may make us look ridiculous in the eyes of our beasts."

"Of course," said Laa Ehon, "but at the same time I find it hard to believe that what this handful you use as translators can do, others of their kind can't also be brought to do. The idea flies in the face of logic and reason. What is hypothesized to be missing from those who, according to your experience, are incapable of being taught to use the true language clearly?"

"Exactly what the blocking factor is, we've never been able to discover," answered Lyt Ahn. "Would you care to question the beast we have present?"

"Ask a beast?" said Laa Ehon; and experience made Shane perceptive enough to catch the evidence of shock and surprise, not only in Laa Ehon, but in the others about the table.

"As you have said," replied Lyt Ahn, "it'll do no harm to explore any and all possibilities; and this beast might, indeed, be able to provide you with some information or insight."

"The suggestion is a—" Laa Ehon hesitated, obviously searching for a way of putting what he wanted to say in words that would not fall into the category of insult to his First Captain, but would still express his reaction to such a suggestion, ''—far-fetched idea.''

''What have you to lose?'' said Lyt Ahn; and a murmur of agreement ran around the table. Laa Ehon's expression showed no change, but Shane guessed that the Milanese Commander was seething with anger, within. He turned and his eyes met Shane's.

''Beast,'' he said, ''can you offer any information as to why a majority of your species cannot be taught to speak the true language as well as you, yourself, have come to?''

''Immaculate sirs and dames—'' Shane's voice sounded high-pitched and strange in his own ears after the deep tones of those around the table, ''it is a characteristic of our species that during our first few years of life at a time when our pups are learning how to speak that their capability for so learning is very great. In the years just before the untarnished race came among us, it had been established that our young could learn as many as four or five different variants of our tongue, simultaneously; but that this facility was lost for most beasts by the time these young were five to eight years of age. Only a fortunate few of us keep that ability; and it's been from such fortunate few that the First Captain's corps of translator-couriers has been drawn.''

There was a moment of silence—a long moment.

''I don't think I'm completely ready to believe this without independent substantiation,'' said Laa Ehon. ''It's well known that, unlike ourselves, these subject races use the lie quite commonly. Moreover, even when they do not consciously lie, they can be ignorant or subject to superstitions. The point this beast has just made, that the language learning ability of his race is largely lost after the first five to eight years of their life, may be a lie, the result of ignorance, or simply belief in a superstition that has no real basis in fact.''

''I,'' said Lyt Ahn from the far end of the table, heavily, ''am inclined to believe this Shane-beast—such being its name. I've had much contact with it over the last two years and always found it truthful, as well as remarkably lacking in ignorance for one of its species, and not superstitious . . . even in the meaning of that term as understood by our own race.''

''If what the beast says is true, however,'' put in Maa

Alyn, "there'd be no point in trying your experiment, Laa Ehon."

Laa Ehon turned toward her.

"When were the plans of the untarnished race ever made or changed upon the basis of input from one of the subject species?" he said. "I mean no disrespect to the First Captain; but the fact remains the beast here may be mistaken, or may not know what we or it are talking about. We should hardly make any decision here on an unsupported faith in its possible correctness."

"True enough," murmured another female, who had not spoken before. "True enough."

"What's been said here does suggest one thing, however," said Laa Ehon, "and that's that we should begin immediately, on the chance that the beast is correct, to put some of the young beasts to exposure to the true language. Then, if this one is correct, we may breed up a generation which takes advantage of this early language ability of theirs, if such actually exists. Certainly, nothing can be lost by trying."

A mutter of agreement sounded around the table, interrupted once more by the heavy voice of Lyt Ahn.

"Am I correct then?" the First Captain said, looking around the table. "At least a number of you are agreeable to taking young beasts into your households and keeping them more or less continuously with you?"

There was a silence.

"A nurse-beast, of course," said Laa Ehon, "could be detailed to take care of each young creature. The young one would no more be in the way, then, under such circumstances, than the adult beasts are when we use them for various duties. The only requirement would be that the nurse-beast keep the infant creature in position to overhear as much of our speech as possible."

"I think Laa Ehon may have the answer," Maa Alyn said. "I can't see any flaws in his reasoning."

"Nor can I—but I am a member of the true race," said Lyt Ahn. "However, perhaps it would be wise for the untarnished and immaculate individuals here assembled to check first with the representative of the beasts we have with us at the moment—in case there might be some unseen flaw in this course? It's always possible that there are pitfalls in it perceptible to one of the species, but which none of us have observed."

Once more, Shane found the eyes of all the Aalaag there turned upon him.

"Beast," said Maa Alyn, "we have been discussing the possibilities of raising some of your young with early exposure to true language, assuming this theory of yours for early aptitude for the learning of it is a fact—"

"You need not recap, Maa Alyn," interrupted Lyt Ahn. "I can assure you that this Shane-beast has overheard and understood all we've been saying."

There was a strange, almost startled silence around the table. Almost as if it had been suggested that there was a spy in their midst. Shane realized that, with the exception of Lyt Ahn, all those there had until that moment not really made the connection between his knowledge of their language and the fact he would be able not only to follow but to understand all that they had been saying to each other. Comprehension of that fact clashed violently with their habit of ignoring the underraces.

"Well then, Shane-beast, since the First Captain assures us that's your name," said Laa Ehon after a second. "Have you any comment on our plan to raise some young of your species where they can overhear the true language being spoken, during their receptive years of growth?"

"Only," answered Shane, "if the immaculate sir pleases, that I believe if you follow the plan as you have outlined it, the result will be that these young of my species will understand Aalaag, but not necesarily be able to speak it."

He hesitated. He had been given no order to volunteer information. To do so would be greatly daring. But that lack was almost immediately remedied.

"Go on, Shane-beast," said Lyt Ahn from the head of the table. "If you have any suggestions to make, make them."

"Yes, make them," said Laa Ehon, his black eyes glittering on Shane. "The most immaculate First Captain seems to feel there may be a flaw in our reasoning which you might have discerned."

"I might merely suggest," said Shane, picking his way as carefully through the alien vocabulary as through a mine field, in search of words which would at once be absolutely truthful but at the same time carry his meaning without implying any pretense to equality, or possible offense, "a danger could lie in the fact that you have the young of my species merely listening to the true language as it's correctly spoken. As I say, there might be a danger that the young referred to might only learn to understand, but not to speak, the true language; since they are given no opportunity to speak it.''

He hesitated. There was a dangerous silence around the table.

"What I am trying to say," he said, "is that perhaps the untarnished or immaculate individuals dealing with these young beasts should consider speaking to and allowing themselves to be answered by these young ones in the true tongue. It would have to be understood that, being so young still, the small beasts would not yet have acquired a knowledge of polite response; and might inadvertently fail to show the proper respect. . . .''

The shock around the table this time was a palpable thing; and the pause was longer than at any time since Shane had entered the room.

"You are suggesting," said Maa Alyn, "almost that we treat these young of your species as if they were young of the true race.''

"I am afraid that is my meaning, immaculate dame," said Shane.

There was a further silence, broken at last by Maa Alyn.

"The suggestion is disgusting," she said. "Moreover, even more than any other suggestion put forward here today, this flies in the face of all the rules evolved from the experience of the true race with their underspecies over many worlds and many centuries. There must be some other way. . . .''

There was a general noise of concurrence from those gathered around the table. For a moment, Shane was sure that while Laa Ehon had lost his point about introducing humans into Aalaag inner households, he had come dangerously close to gathering the leadership of the Council to him. He saw that all eyes had now turned sharply to Lyt Ahn, as if awaiting some magical alternate solution from him. Then the First Captain spoke; and with the first words, Shane realized his master had seized the most propitious moment for forestalling Laa Ehon's bid for power and regaining his own position of Alpha leader in the Council. To the clear surprise of those around the table, he not only overrode Maa Alyn by endorsing the Milanese Commander's suggestion; but went beyond it, in part assuming authorship and control of the plan.

"I fully realize the distastefulness of the suggestion. Nonetheless," said Lyt Ahn, "I'm going to ask all those around this table to take this matter of bringing human young into their households into consideration, and think about it seriously between now and our next meeting. It is true that we're at variance with the prognosis and the estimates originally made for our settling of this particular world; and recently there has been an outbreak of what can only be regarded as an attitude inimical to the true race in these drawings that appear in the cities from time to time—and, I believe, more frequently lately."

"Clearly they are of a human wearing what they call 'pilgrim' clothing," said Maa Alyn. "Has the First Captain considered ordering that no such clothing be worn in the future?"

"It's hard to see what that would accomplish at this date, untarnished dame," answered Lyt Ahn. "The symbol has already been established. In fact, we would be dignifying it by paying that much attention to it. The beasts might consider that we actually saw the drawing as a threat—which is what those who put them up undoubtedly want."

"True enough," Maa Alyn nodded.

"On the other hand, something undoubtedly must be done; and the untarnished sir who is our Commander in Milan has at least come up with a proposal, which is more than anyone else has done. I suggest in addition to considering the taking of beast children into our households, we put Laa Ehon's other suggestion to trial. I therefore authorize him—hopefully, Maa Alyn will not object—to set up a trial beast as governor in the British Islands area, with whatever staff is necessary; and I will temporarily lend the project one of my translators to ensure communication between governor and the true race to commence with."

"I do not object." It was very nearly a growl from Maa Alyn.

"If I might have this Shane beast as translator, then—" Laa Ehon was beginning, and Shane chilled. But Lyt Ahn interrupted the other.

"The Shane-beast I have special uses of my own for," said the First Captain. "I will, however, provide you with a beast adequate to your needs. I will permit this much—that Shane-beast be available to you as liaison on this project to keep me informed of its progress and such special advice as you wish to pass on to me by courier.''

"If you wish, and as you wish, of course, First Captain,'' said Laa Ehon, smoothly; but his eyes flashed for a moment on Shane with something of cold calculation in them. Shane chilled again.

"That being settled,'' said Lyt Ahn, "shall we close this meeting?''

There were sounds of agreement in which the Milanese Commander joined. A moment later, Shane found himself outside the room, in the corridor, hurrying to match Lyt Ahn's long-legged strides back toward the First Captain's private offices. Shane had been given no orders to follow. On the other hand he had not been dismissed, so he hurried along, half a pace behind his master, waiting for orders.

These were not forthcoming even after they had reached and passed into the office. Perhaps they would have been, but when they stepped inside the heavy doors, they found Adtha Or Ain. She was standing once more before the large screen, which was again showing the figure of their son in whatever it was that encased him. She turned as they entered; and spoke to Lyt Ahn.

"It went well—the meeting?''

The First Captain looked at her soberly.

"Not well,'' he said, "I have broken slightly with custom to allow Laa Ehon to make a trial of interposing native governors between ourselves and the cattle, using the British Islands as an experimental area.''

He turned to Shane.

"I will lend him a translator to help. Shane-beast here, however, will act as my liaison with the project, and as my own private eyes and ears upon its progress.''

His eyes were steady on Shane.

"You understand, Shane-beast?'' he said. "You will observe everything carefully, and I will question you equally carefully each time you return from there.''

"So, it did not go well,'' repeated Adtha Or Ain, as much to herself as to the First Captain.

"No, how could you expect it to?'' said Lyt Ahn. He seemed to become suddenly conscious of the image in the large screen. "Put that away.''

"I need to look at it,'' responded Adtha Or Ain.

"You mean you need it to use as a club against me,'' said

Lyt Ahn. He made no visible gesture that Shane could see, except a small jerk of the head; but the image disappeared from the screen, leaving it pearly gray and blank.

"It doesn't matter if you take it from me," said Adtha Or Ain. "I can see it just as well with the screen off. I see it night and day. Now, more than ever."

"Why, now more than ever?"

"Because I can't avoid seeing what's coming."

Adtha Or Ain turned from the empty screen to face Lyt Ahn.

"What do you mean?" There was a note of demand in Lyt Ahn's voice.

"No expedition will go to look for my son."

"Why do you say that? I've promised you—" began Lyt Ahn.

"Your promise is only as good as your authority," said Adtha Or Ain, "and your authority. . . ."

She did not finish.

"I was elected by the senior officers of this Expedition. I hold my rank by that authority, which remains with me," answered Lyt Ahn in a steady voice, "and the rank can only be taken from me by popular vote of these same officers—which will never happen."

"No," said Adtha Or Ain. "But you could resign it on your own decision, as other First Captains on other New World Expeditions have occasionally done before you."

"I have no intention of resigning."

"What does that matter? You will resign," said Adtha Or Ain. "It's as much a certainty as that screen on the wall before us—the screen you do not want me to use; and once you are no longer First Captain, whoever holds that rank will have no interest in sending an expedition to find out what happened to my son."

"You talk in impossibilities," said Lyt Ahn. "Even if I could spare the officers and material for such an expedition now, who would lead it?"

"I would, of course," said Adtha Or Ain. "I'm of fourth rank—or had you forgotten that?"

"I can't spare you," retorted Lyt Ahn. "The Consort of the First Captain belongs with the First Captain."

"Particularly when the position of that First Captain may become questionable," said Adtha Or Ain.

"There is no 'may.' My position is not questionable; and it is not going to become questionable."

The attitude of Adtha Or Ain changed subtly, although the signs of that change were so slight that only Shane's long experience with her allowed him to note them. But some of the tension went out of her. She seemed to soften and went to Lyt Ahn, close enough to touch him, standing to one side of him and looking very slightly down into his eyes.

"In all things I am your Consort," she said, in a lower voice. "Also, in all things I am the mother of the son you had. I must see clearly, even if you refuse to. Laa Ehon intends to replace you as First Captain. Let that, at least, be out in the open between us."

"I have no intention," said Lyt Ahn, "of abandoning the First Captaincy to Laa Ehon, or anyone else."

"Consider the situation honestly," said Adtha Or Ain. "The possibility is there. The possibility means that no expedition would ever be sent to find my son; and not only that, it means I would lose you as well, since I think you would not merely accept duties under another's command."

"That much is true," said Lyt Ahn. "If it was shown to me that I was no longer worthy of the post of First Captain, I would consider myself excess of our effort here and make sure that the expedition was no longer burdened by my presence."

Shane felt a new sense of shock. This was the first intimation he had had that some sort of honorable suicide was practiced among the Aalaag. But the fact that there was such a practice made sense. It made very good sense for this race of male and female warriors. He thought of Laa Ehon in the post of First Captain of Earth and, if anything, his inner fears increased.

His own life was just barely endurable now under Lyt Ahn. It could become literally unbearable under Laa Ehon; and if it became literally unbearable, sooner rather than later a fit of *yowaragh* would take him again and he would do something that would lead to his own end. The best he could hope for under those circumstances would be that it would lead him to a quick and relatively painless end.

"You may go, Shane-beast," said Lyt Ahn.

Shane went. The next two days were a blur of duties in attendance on Lyt Ahn, during one of the periodic twice-yearly internal inspections of all services housed within the

House of Weapons. On the third day, however, he was summoned back to Lyt Ahn's office, where an assistant Aalaag officer handed him a hard copy message to be hand-delivered to Laa Ehon. Laa Ehon, he was told by Lyt Ahn, had already set himself up in London with the staff of the Project he had described to the Council.

". . . I deduce from this, small Shane-beast," said Lyt Ahn, once the underofficer had left and they two were alone in the office together, "that the immaculate Commander of Milan had already picked and trained the individuals he would need for his Project before mentioning his plan to the Council. You will find his offices already in place and staffed. I would desire you to take particular notice of what kind of humans he uses. You will be in a better position to judge this than myself or any of the true race. Also, report to me anything else you think I might find of interest. I'll want to know, of course, about the general arrangement. I have the plans on record, of course, but that's not the same thing as receiving a direct observation report from a trustworthy pair of eyes."

"I will do as the First Captain orders," said Shane.

"You may go."

"I thank the immaculate sir."

Two hours later, once more in a courier ship and headed toward London, Shane watched from the window beside his seat as the vessel lifted, until the world's horizon was a perceptible curve and the sky overhead was black with the airlessness of space. Curiously, now that he was on his way, for the first time he had a moment in which to think, and to his surprise, he found himself strangely clearheaded.

It was remarkable—remarkable almost to the point of being funny. After the episode in Milan, when he had first seen and saved Maria, then later when he had been kidnapped, he had yearned for the sanctuary of his small cubicle in the House of Weapons, as a retreat where he could sit down and take stock of what had happened, and was happening, to him. Then that imagined oasis of peace had ceased to be an oasis, when he found Sylvia Onjin waiting there for him.

In the end, in the House of Weapons, he had found no time—no moment of personal freedom at all in which to try and think of some way of avoiding what seemed to be a greased slide to inevitable self-destruction. Now, here, in the last place he would have looked for it, he had found it. He was on duty. Therefore the eyes of the Aalaag were momentarily off him, and he was free at last to stand back and consider his position, to think his own thoughts for a small while before they touched down in the British Isles.

It was freedom-on-duty. There was no human word for it, but there was an Aalaag one, *alleinen*. It meant the supreme authority and freedom of being under orders—one's own master or mistress within strictly specified limits.

He pronounced it now, silently in his mind—*alleinen*—and smiled slightly to himself. For of course he did not pronounce it correctly, in the strict sense. The truth was he did not speak Aalaag as well as even his masters gave him credit for doing. Certain sounds were physical impossibilities to his human throat and tongue.

The truth, in fact, was that he cheated in all his Aalaag-speaking. The alien word that had just come to his mind should properly be pronounced with something like a deep bass cough in the middle syllable; and that deep bass cough, which was so much a part of many Aalaag words, was simply beyond his capabilities. He had always got away with pronouncing it without the cough, however, because he was able to hide behind the fact that his voice was too high-pitched to manage the sound. He had learned to pronounce words containing such a sound as the equally high voice of a very young Aalaag child would say them; and while the ears of such as Lyt Ahn and even of Laa Ehon and others consciously noted the lack, they unconsciously excused him for not making it, because of the otherwise excellence of his pronunciation and because the word as heard resembled what they had heard so many times from the high voices of their own children.

So, in just such a manner, had humans always excused (and with familiarity, become deaf to) the accents of their own children and foreign-born friends. The Aalaag, he thought now, were indeed humanoid (or humans were Aalaagoid?). Similar physical environments on similar worlds during the emergence of both races had shaped them, not only physically, but psychologically and emotionally, in similar ways. Yet they were not really like humans in the fine points—any more than, for example, the average human was eight feet tall. In the fine points, they differed. They had to differ. One race could not catch the other race's diseases, for example.

There had been a time when he had dreamed of a plague on

Earth that would decimate the aliens but leave the humans untouched—a sudden plague that would wipe out the conquerors before those conquerors had time to pass, to their own kind on other worlds, the word that they were dying. Of course, such a plague had never come; and probably, long ago, the Aalaag had devised medical protections against any such happening. He pulled his mind away from such wool-gathering. The important problem was a solution to his own situation. In the silence of the hurtling courier ship, caught between the green of Earth below and the black of space above, he forced himself to face that question squarely, now, while there was a chance.

Leaving Milan, several days earlier, headed back to the House of Weapons, he had faced the fact that *yowaragh* had twice driven him to do foolishly desperate things against the Aalaag regime; and that, therefore, it was only a matter of time until he would be drawn back—for powerful emotional reasons with which the last words of Maria had been connected—into contact with this human Resistance, this Resistance that he knew, if those in it did not, was doomed to certain discovery and destruction at Aalaag hands.

He had faced the fact then that, given sufficient provocation, he would not be able to help himself; as he had not been able to help himself the year before, when an uncontrollable burst of rage had driven him to draw the first pilgrim-symbol on the wall under the executed man in Aalborg, Denmark—as he had not been able to stop himself from acting, a week since, when he had seen through the one-way glass the captive woman who was Maria awaiting questioning by the Aalaag.

Human cattle, according to the way the Aalaag thought, were not supposed to have such reactions as *yowaragh*. It was not their deliberate fault, only a weakness in them. But those who showed it were obviously untrustworthy and sick, and must be disposed of.

Even when they were as valuable as Shane-beast.

Therefore, leaving Milan, he had finally faced the fact that what had happened twice must happen again. Eventually, a third attack of *yowaragh* would catch him in a visible situation where either he had no choice but to appear openly as one of the Resistance people and share their fate, or else he would simply make some wild, personal attack upon one of the aliens which would result in his death. He did not want either of those fates. But there had seemed no way of avoiding one or the other; and it was this dilemma he had carried back with him to the House of Weapons, with a desperate desire to study the situation for some kind of solution.

But now, out of nowhere, events pushed by Laa Ehon's ambition seemed to have offered him a possible way out. The basic situation had not changed; but just now, sitting here in his first moment of *alleinen* peace, for the first time, unexpectedly, he saw the glimmer of a hope he might have something with which he could bargain for his own life and possibly that of Maria as well. It was a wild hope, a crazy hope, but it was nonetheless a hope where before there had been none.

As he considered it, the small glimmer suddenly expanded into a glare like that from a doorway suddenly opened to outer sunlight. It would be a matter of setting two dragons to destroy each other, of using one evil to eat the other up—like the Gingham Dog and the Calico Cat of the children's poem.

The operative factor behind it all was the fact that even after three years together the two races did not understand each other. Humans did not understand Aalaag, and the Aalaag did not understand humans.

Basically, the solution to his problem was no less than the fact that he should destroy Laa Ehon. It was a far-fetched thought, like that of a mouse deciding to destroy a giant. On the face of it the notion seemed ridiculous; but he had one advantage which even Lyt Ahn—who was even larger as a giant than Laa Ehon—did not have. He, Shane, was not restricted by the Aalaag mores. In fact, he was restricted by no mores at all, alien or human; but only by his own need to survive and, if possible, save Maria.

The operative factor was that the two races did not really understand each other. He repeated that to himself. Humans did not understand the Aalaag, with whom they had never had any real chance to have contact on what might be called a person-to-person basis; and the Aalaag could not understand humans, walled in as they were by the armor of their own alien attitudes and traditions.

It was because of this that what had been planned at the Council table would not work. The theory of bringing up the children in the Aalaag households would never turn out as Laa Ehon and the others hoped. Shane thought of the human

babies to be used this way and shuddered—out of his knowledge of the difference in human and alien responses.

The bitter part of it would be that the scheme would
actually seem to work at first as the human youngsters began
to pick up the Aalaag tongue and get responses that would
seem at least friendly, if not loving, from these large creatures looming over them. The children would respond automatically with affection, which would last up until that
devastating moment when they were reminded clearly by the
large figures that they were only humans—only beasts. In that
discovery, as the children matured and began to have minds
of their own, was more fertile ground for *yowaragh* than in
anything else the aliens had done on Earth since their arrival;
and it would be *yowaragh* by humans who knew their overlords, better than these had ever been known before by any of
the underraces.

For the same reason of racial misunderstanding, Laa Ehon's
plan to set up human governors would not work. The Aalaag
who lived under unquestioned authority among themselves
could not really appreciate that a human governor would be
no more palatable to most other humans than an alien would—
perhaps even less so. The governor would simply be included
in the detestation in which the mass of humanity already held
all servants of the Aalaag, such as the Interior Guards and the
translators like Shane, himself. Noncooperation would be the
order of the day, automatically. Unless. . . .

It was in exactly this area that his own scheme might work.
He owed nothing to the Resistance groups, he told himself,
once more. They had no hope of success—no hope at all,
though it would be impossible to tell them that. Inevitably
they would be caught, found out and executed by the Aalaag.
He shuddered again, thinking of what would happen to them.
But he reminded himself that that happening was unavoidable, no matter what he might do or not do. Meanwhile, they
could be the instrument which would save him; and, possibly
even more important, aid him in destroying Laa Ehon at one
and the same time.

He looked more closely at the plan that had just been born
in him.

It would be risky. He would have to appear to lend his aid
to the Resistance groups; and without letting Lyt Ahn know.
For Lyt Ahn would never countenance what Shane was planning, although he might well concur with what Shane had

done once Laa Ehon had been destroyed as a result of the translator's efforts.

It would be necessary for Shane to keep his identity as secret as possible from the Resistance people themselves. Those few who had captured him in Milan already had some idea of who he was—but if it could be done, they should remain the only ones. That would be difficult because he would have to do more than just join them; he would have to effectively take charge of their movement.

This was possible, since he knew more about their enemy than they did themselves. His scheme itself was simple in the extreme. It would merely be a matter of coordinating the Resistance groups and there must be some in at least every large city and they must know each other, already, even if they were not already part of one overall organization. With their help he could cause an apparent cooperation to take place with the governorship organizations Laa Ehon had in mind; so that these seemed to be an unqualified success. While, at the same time, the organization of the Resistances into a single coordinating unit could make possible a plan for a world-wide uprising against the aliens everywhere. That would attract the revolutionaries.

Only he would know that such a revolt would stand no chance of success. In fact, it would almost certainly never reach the point of taking place. Long before it was ready to explode, he would have pulled the plug of the cooperation that had been given the governors; and Laa Ehon's plan—in which by this time the Aalaag would have invested deeply—would reveal itself as a total failure. For which Laa Ehon could only take the blame.

And, if some sort of honorable suicide was indeed part of the Aalaag tradition, Laa Ehon might thereupon remove himself. Even if he did not, his power within the Council and his presence as a threat to succeed Lyt Ahn would be destroyed.

Meanwhile, of course, the Resistance members, who by this time would have exposed themselves, or become easily identifiable, would be rounded up and disposed of by the aliens. Shane set his teeth against the mental picture of what that would mean, reminding himself fiercely that he had a right to think of his own survival first; and again, that there had never been any hope for them in any case.

It was a cruel and bitter plan. It had no justification beyond the fact that its fall-out would save him—and possibly Maria as well. He might be able to rescue her in the process. Just at the moment he was not sure how he might do that; but the beginnings of some ideas were tickling at the back of his mind, all of them dependent upon the claim he would have on Lyt Ahn's good graces after Laa Ehon was taken care of.

One necessary matter would be to get the Resistance's agreement to Maria's helping him personally. Later on, therefore, to Lyt Ahn, he could credit part of his success to her association with him, which he would make appear to be a willing and informed one.

The strange thing, he found himself thinking, was that he should be contemplating doing what he had earlier been deathly afraid of doing—associating with those who were subversive to the aliens. The equation of life and death for him in any association like that had not changed; and yet he found himself now feeling good, almost buoyant, about the plans he had just considered. He felt in fact more alive than he had felt since word had first come of the Aalaag landings on Earth.

A sense of something almost like triumph possessed him. So engrossed was he in his thoughts that he hardly noticed when the courier ship set down at last with a slight jolt in the main terminal area which had been blasted out of the center of London. As a member of Lyt Ahn's special corps, he was allowed a special consideration in choosing where he might be let off. He preferred that this be at terminals where he could mingle with the ordinary human traffic and be lost to the sight of anyone who might otherwise identify him as one who worked for the aliens.

He took the subway into the city and registered at a small, middle-class hotel. His destination was Laa Ehon's Project, but they were not expecting him there at any particular time. He was beneath contempt and therefore, happily, beneath suspicion; and meanwhile, there was time for the things he had to do.

He sought out a shop selling second hand clothing, and bought himself a two-color robe—blue on its outer side, brown when turned inside out. It was a common enough purchase, but the gold oblongs he threw down in payment were not. He saw the eyes of the lean but pot-bellied, middle-aged shopkeeper flash as the man picked them up and ducked into a back room to make change in the ordinary base-metal currency of ordinary human commerce. Such gold tabs, in which Shane and the other translators were ordinarily paid, saw their way into ordinary human monetary channels only through the hands of those who worked for the aliens or those who dealt in the black market that sold special luxuries to those who so worked. The word of his purchase would reach local Resistance headquarters quickly.

"Deliver this robe to room 421, the Sheldon Arms Hotel," Shane said to the proprietor. "Can you do that for me?"

"Of course sir, of course," said the proprietor, making a note on a piece of unbleached wrapping paper.

Scooping up his change, Shane returned to his room in the hotel. He ordered up a meal, ate, and then lay on the bed, thinking and waiting.

It was only a little over two hours before there was a knock at the door of his room.

"Delivery for you, sir," said a voice beyond the door.

He was on his feet instantly and as silently as he was able to move. He stepped across to the darkest corner of the room and stood there with his back to the window. He pulled up his pilgrim's hood over his head, drawing the sides of the hood in, so that his face was hidden in deep shadow. He said nothing.

He had expected at least one more knock at the door; but there was a sudden splintering crash as the lock gave and two very large men erupted into the room. They stared at the empty bed and around them, for a moment plainly not identifying him as a human figure in his stillness and the shadow of the corner. In that moment a third man moved into the room from behind them. It was the man called Peter who spoke Italian with an English accent and had been in charge of the group that had kidnapped Shane in Milan.

"I thought this was your home ground," Shane said to him.

At the sound of Shane's voice they saw him. Before they could move, he went on. "I am the Pilgrim. I'll talk to you, Peter, and you only. Get the others out."

There was a moment in which it seemed anything might happen. The two large men glanced back at Peter.

"All right," said Peter, after a moment's hesitation. "Outside, both of you, and put the door back in place. But wait right outside it, there."

He looked directly at Shane.

"But what you've got to say better be worthwhile," he added.

"It is," said Shane. "I'm going to help you. I know the Aalaag and what their weaknesses are. I can tell you how to fight them." Having said this much, the rest came easily to his lips. "I may even be able to tell you how to get rid of them, altogether. But you're the only one who ought to hear what I've got to say, or know who I am."

Peter stared at him for a long, blank-faced moment. Then he turned to the two men, who were lifting the door back into place in its opening.

"On second thought, wait down the hall," he said. "That's an order."

He turned back and smiled at Shane. It was a smile of pure relief.

"It's good to have you with us," he said. "You don't know how good it is."